To Be the *Daughter* of Two Worlds

To Be the *Daughter* of Two Worlds

Gita Bhattacharji

TO BE THE DAUGHTER OF TWO WORLDS

iUniverse books may be ordered through booksellers or by contacting:

iUniverse
1663 Liberty Drive
Bloomington, IN 47403
www.iuniverse.com
1-800-Authors (1-800-288-4677)

ISBN: 978-1-4917-3756-9 (sc)
ISBN: 978-1-4917-3757-6 (e)

Library of Congress Control Number: 2014910693

Printed in the United States of America.

iUniverse rev. date: 10/14/2014

Chapter One

On a warm summer day in June 2001, Sita Rampal stood by the window of her fourteenth floor office on Madison Avenue and looked down at the world below. Yellow taxi cabs crawled along Madison Avenue, competing with crosstown buses and jaywalking pedestrians for space. Every now and again, the taxis picked up speed, surging forward to fill a gap in the traffic. Then a bigger car, bus, or truck would lumber alongside the tiny car and cut it off. Other times, people crossing the streets either alone, or in groups for safety, would cause the traffic to stop and start, and that pattern would repeat itself throughout the day.

From Sita's vantage point, people scurrying in and out of her building looked like lines of miniature robots, mechanically driven to work more, earn more, and spend more. Many of them carried shopping bags filled with things they had hurriedly bought or exchanged during lunch hour from the numerous designer clothing stores and shoe stores nearby. Others scurried in after buying lunch at the many small catering establishments that sold Chinese food, pizza, or some other ethnic delicacy. The frantic speed of life down on the avenue was broken by the amble of a slouching dog walker trying to juggle five pooches that wanted to walk in different directions.

Across from Madison Avenue was Madison Park—the only patch of green in a concrete landscape made up of tall buildings, shops and busy streets. The big trees in the park seemed to reach up to the skies and join together in a huge umbrella protecting the tranquility within the park. Here children played on the swings, people sat on benches to snatch a brief respite from the activity around. Tourists walked around taking pictures, stopping by the statues to see what was written about H. W. Seward and Konklin. Older people came here to relax, to enjoy the well-kept garden, to feed the birds, and giggle at the splatter of bird poop on the imposing statues.

The quiet calm of Madison Park reminded her of India. Sita closed her eyes, imagining she was back-home in India. In place of the yellow cabs she saw three-wheel scooter rickshaws spluttering down the street making more noise than movement. No one was scurrying. Obese women swayed about in billowing saris as they shopped at the vegetable market; cows ambled along, and occasionally paused in the middle of the street to decide if that was a good place for a nap.

Every middle class home in India could boast of servants. Mona came every morning to dust and sweep. Squatting on the floor, she pushed the dust around with a broom, moving quickly on her dirt encrusted bare feet. Silver chains glistened against her ebony skin, calling attention to her cracked and calloused heels ripped apart by years of neglect and sheer hard work. After she had finished sweeping, she would mop the floor with a rag, dipping it into a pail of grimy water that got darker with each dip. After squeezing out the murky brew, she would waddle across the floor moving quickly in squatting position, working the mop this way and that way, until she felt the floor looked clean, even if was mostly wet and slippery with moistened dirt. It was also Mona's job to empty the trash cans every day. The trash can was really a blue plastic bucket where all the garbage from the kitchen was deposited. There were no garbage bags, and the plastic bucket was stained and soiled with stale residue that left a lingering stench even after it was emptied.

Sona was another maid. She had been a servant in the family for over thirty years, serving three generations. She had stayed on with the family, first working for Sita's grandma, her Aunt, and now her mother. She could make the choicest fish curries and the best fried chicken, but for herself she liked to eat only lentil and *roti*. She could have found herself another job but she had grown attached to the family. Sona had accepted her lot in life, attributing it all to karma. She believed she was born to serve, and she bent and touched Sita's mom's feet every month when she got her wages. She would fold the crisp rupee notes into the corner of her sari and tuck it away safely. She had no bank account and lived hand-to-mouth on the wages paid in cash every month. She lived in a makeshift house with a tarpaulin roof held up by four poles. Inside, there was room for a rope bed and a few bundles of clothes. The lavatory was any nook or cranny that could be used to dispose of waste. The kitchen was just an oil stove in front of the tent on which Sona cooked nice hot homemade bread called *roti,* and lentils, sitting cross-legged outside her house and placing the fruits of her labor on a plantain leaf. Then she would sit with her family enjoying the roti and lentil salted with street dust, licking her lips as though she had just eaten the finest foods—looking thoroughly pleased with herself as though she knew something others did not—that money could never buy contentment.

The shrill ring of the phone shook Sita out of her walk down memory lane.

"Hullo, this is Sita Rampal in Editorial. How can I help you?" she asked in her clipped English accent that had been learned from the Irish nuns at the Convent School in India.

It was the typesetter. They had received a file that did not have the primary tagging necessary for disk conversion. *Oh dear,* Sita thought, *so much emphasis on creating a viable web product took away from the editorial pleasure of reading, enjoying, and critiquing a well written article. It was hard to analyze the nuances of a phrase and to edit, if the pressure was on to code accurately. A forgotten code or an extra punctuation mark boomeranged into a monstrous error making it difficult to format the file for the electronic version.*

"Send the article back to me," she said with resignation. "I'll look over the coding again." *Thank heavens it was Friday and the weekend was finally here!* She stepped out of her Nine West shoes and tossed them into the bottom drawer of her desk.

Yes! She could say she had done it. She had a decent job as a senior editor. She liked her work and had a nice office with a view.

She had a good boss, and her work was appreciated. The money could be better, but these days' computer programmers and stock brokers made all the money. Still, she had come a long way. She remembered coming to America many years ago with big dreams, but no plans. Every day almost, she went to employment agencies. Their interest always peaked when she said she had an MA degree.

"No kidding! What university did you go to?"

"St Stephens in India," she would say proudly.

"Then can you type?" was always their next question.

That was history. America was a land of opportunity and she had found opportunity trapped in an elevator with the managing editor of a major publishing company. After the moment of sheer panic she felt when the elevator lights went off, and the elevator stopped, Sita realized she was not alone and there was no need to be so frightened. Someone with a big booming voice whom she had barely noticed before was in the same predicament as she. Glad not to be alone, and happy that the stranger with her knew how to get help, Sita had nothing to do but talk. She struck up a conversation with the owner of the big booming voice. The darkness gave her an anonymity, and she found herself telling this stranger all about herself, how she wanted to find a job as an editor, why she thought she would be good, but didn't know where to begin, and how everyone asked her if she could type, and how she found that terribly frustrating because she knew she could be a good editor. "I would be good, you know," she told the stranger with conviction in her voice. "I use to write for the local newspapers, I have a degree in Literature." She then proceeded to tell him that no one in the family wanted her to work, but she wanted to do something for herself—something that would give her a sense of contributing, of having an identity of her own. She wanted to be more than someone's daughter or niece. She went on and on, rambling along to this total stranger.

Almost twenty minutes later the lights came on, and she found herself looking into the piercing blue eyes set in a kind face. He introduced himself as Mr. Smith and handed her his card. "Give me a call," he said. She looked at the card. She had been spilling her guts to the Managing Editor of a major publishing company!

"I think I have the right spot for you."

"You're asking me to come for an interview," she said breathless, thinking how hard it had been to get her foot in the door.

"Well, I think we just did an interview, don't you? The longest one I can remember," he chuckled. "You're hired if you can find two references."

The following day, Sita went out and invested in a pinstriped business suit. It looked great in the store, and made the mannequin wearing it look so professional. But when Sita wore the skirt it was different. It was the first time she had worn a short skirt since her school days. She looked down critically at her legs. They were too thin. The beige of her panty hose was too light, and made her legs look several shades lighter than her face. She had forgotten to shave, and she saw a few stray strands poke their way through the hosiery like a hedgehog's bristles. The low heeled pumps did nothing for her ankles, and her feet looked like two big boats. She looked so self-conscious, as though the whole world was staring at her legs. *Best to keep them covered* she thought—*like she always had. She would just wear the pant suit with a crisp white blouse, and shiny patent leather pumps, and go see Mr. Smith.*

She was there bright and early the following morning. She stood outside the Met Life building on Madison Avenue and stared upward at the skyscraper that seemed to disappear into the sky. She saw people entering through the revolving door and followed. She hurriedly got into the same section of the revolving door with another person. *Why did her companion seem irritable and push the door so hard?* She winced when the rotating piece behind her, clipped her heels.

She made it to Mr. Smith's office in one piece. He was there. His kindly face and shrewd eyes had not been a figment of her imagination. He motioned for her to sit down. Mr. Smith told her that she would be starting out as junior editor and would have to work her way up. He saw her worried frown and said, "I'm sure you can handle it, Sita."

"I can't type fast enough....What if my computer skills are not up to par?"

"Are you willing to learn?"

"Oh yes! I'll do whatever it takes."

"Then I don't see a problem," Mr. Smith said. "We'll see you here next week."

From the first day, Sita worked hard. She stayed late, came in early, and did her utmost to learn everything. She endeared herself to the support staff by trying to do her own filing and Xeroxing to help out. Of course the machine didn't work right. She put in an article of twenty pages and ten came out; the others were in limbo in the interior spaces of the darn machine, crumpled somewhere in its depths. Everything worked out when she made friends. She learned how to extricate the jammed paper, went on to learn the details of Excel and the magic of Power Point computer applications. She worked hard, to say the least. She was determined to live up to the confidence placed in her by Mr. Smith.

Within a short time she was promoted. *She had done well* she thought, running her fingers over the cherry finish of her desk. She had moved up quickly, and now she had her own office with a window view. She looked at the framed photos of Mom, Dad, and Aunt Priya on her desk. *Why couldn't they be happy for her? Wish they could appreciate how far she had come.* She wished with a pang in her heart that *just for once they would say they were proud of her.* But all they could think about was how to arrange her marriage and make her forget about a career.

The clock in her office said 5-o'clock. It was time to call it a day. She pulled off her headphones, and made her last stop at the Ladies Room. She looked at herself in the mirror. An oval face with a nutmeg complexion and kohl-lined brown eyes stared back at her. Her hair was swept back in an elegant chignon that showed off her long neck and high cheekbones to advantage, and her lips were stained a translucent rusty orange. She had finally started feeling comfortable in skirts, and today she wore a beige skirt topped by a cream blouse. A navy and cream scarf knotted around her neck peeked from a navy Ann Taylor jacket, and completed the ensemble.

You are so pretty. We must find you a good man she could imagine Aunt Priya saying. *I wonder when your parents will begin looking for a good man for you.*

She fixed her lipstick and decided to remove her contacts. Her eyes were starting to tear a bit, and she wanted to give them a rest. All done, she went off to get her headphones and got lost in Madonna's, "My, My, My Miss American Pie…." There was a spring in her step as she got off the elevator. She paused for a moment to applaud an Elvis impersonator in the lobby who was dressed in enormous white flares and a flashy belt.

"Love me tender…" he crooned, gyrating to the beat of the song.

Not half bad, Sita thought. *She knew even grandma in India liked Elvis. But then grandma, whom they called nani, always had love and marriage on her mind, so any love song sounded good to her.*

Sita slapped her headphones back on, and hurried to the Union Square station to ride the "F" train that would take her to her home in Jackson Heights. On the way there, she noticed a tractor trailer, and about a dozen tents that had mushroomed overnight.

"Come to the Farmer's Market," was written in bright orange letters. "Try fresh homemade bread, 2 for $1," the sign said.

Sita was tempted to buy some. The only bread they ever ate was '*roti*'. Made from whole wheat flour, the dough was mashed and squished to beat the staleness out of it every single day. Mom's small fingers moved fast, and her dimpled wrists got covered with flour as she molded it into small round balls and flattened it into large pancakes, and cooked it on a griddle until it ballooned to the size of a small ball. *Maybe another day*, she thought. She moved on to the flower stall. *Rose bushes were what she wanted, but how was she going to carry them on the train sandwiched between stinky bodies during rush hour? Perhaps she could buy a couple of pots of dahlias. She couldn't leave them behind!* She also bought some petunias—the wild purple kind that tumbled out of containers or flower beds in brilliant waves of purple. She imagined them falling over themselves to greet her as she came up the driveway.

The driveway was a narrow strip of fractured tarmac that separated her two-family brownstone in Queens, New York, from the apartment complex next door. It was a fun place for the neighborhood kids, James, Patrick and Edwin, the three musketeers from the apartment complex who had chosen it as their private ball field. It was a clean, safe place for them to ride their bikes, play with water balloons and water guns, and occasionally some baseball. The cracks and craters in the driveway told a story of fast-break pitches and hurtling skateboards. The three human missiles could come exploding out of the driveway onto the avenue at any time. Pedestrians on 32nd Avenue knew not to pass the gates of house number 11 without checking for the three boys who could come whizzing down the driveway at any given moment. Even the "Wa Wa" man, shuffling down the sidewalk beneath the weight of his ninety-four years, never said a word; he simply knotted his brow in pretend reproof that belied the twinkle in his eyes and said, "Wa, wa, wa, go slowly. Don't knock me down. I'm your friend!"

Sita's mom did not mind the rattle of skateboards and the swish of bikes. On the contrary, she was always leaning out of the kitchen window and saying, "Here's a bag of chips. Want a drink too?"

"Oh yeah," they would nod vigorously, rushing toward the window, their faces flushed with exercise and excitement.

"Thanks," they said. "You're nice."

"Get those brats out of my driveway," Papa would bellow.

"Hush, Rohit must have someone to play with too."

"Why do you worry about that brat downstairs? Let his mother worry about him."

"Now dear, hush," Mom would repeat in the quiet firm voice that was more effective than all the arguing in the world. It never failed to give her what she wanted, and allowed laughter and fun to continue in the driveway.

The driveway led to the side entrance that had a flight of green linoleum-lined stairs. There was always a lingering smell of

Pine Sol because Mom liked to clean. She cleaned so much that she had scrubbed the green linoleum right off the stairs, and the broken edges curled upward at the corners. It looked like someone had tried to scrub the walls clean, also. It was probably Rohit, her four-year old cousin who lived downstairs. She could hear him tell Mom, "Let me help, oh please, please, please." He must have then taken a sponge and scrubbed an area about four feet above the ground vigorously, getting all red in the face, and sticking his tongue out the way he did when he was concentrating. The fruits of his labor were seen in a circular patch, four feet above the ground where the coating of egg-shell-white was washed away to reveal a hideous green that had been the original color of the stairwell.

Papa had no interest in fixing the stairs on the side entrance. "Don't fix what's not broken," he bellowed, oblivious to the chipping paint and the worn linoleum. "Besides no one important comes up those stairs."

The front stairs were beautifully carpeted in pearl gray DuPont Stainmaster carpeting that blended perfectly with the marble-tiled hallway. The walls were egg-shell off-white, and tastefully decorated with wall plaques from India. There were two, that Sita liked the most. The one with the Taj Mahal inlaid in brown sandstone, and another, a marble plate inlaid with semi-precious stones in an intricate pattern, a replica of the inlay work inside the Taj Mahal.

As Papa put it, all important people came up these stairs. These included Rita Aunty who lived a block away, and came every Sunday dressed in a crisply starched sari, matching blouse and handbag, and big dark glasses that were in the height of fashion at the time. Up the stairs also came Uncle Vijay wearing Calvin Klein jeans and T-shirt. Ramu dada, another uncle, and Priya Aunty and her son Rohit also walked up these stairs. All these people had one worry in common. They all had to make sure that Sita was suitably married by arrangement.

Chapter Two

Priya Aunty had come to live in Sita's brownstone almost two years earlier, but Sita could never forget the day it happened. She had been curled up in the recliner with her feet tucked under her, absorbed in Charlotte Bronte's Jane Eyre. Mr. Rochester had just proposed to Jane Eyre, and though she had read the book many times before, she waited for the answer with the same excitement as the day she had read it for the first time. She hadn't heard the doorbell at first, but its persistent ring had brought her to her feet. Uncoiling her long legs that were clad in hip-hugging jeans, she hurried to the front door.

A lady dressed in a brightly colored sari with every color of the rainbow stood at the door, with a toddler straddled across her hip. Bright red lipstick slashed across her face, clashing brilliantly with the fuchsia and yellow flowers on her sari.

"Can I help you?" Sita asked.

"Why didn't anyone come to the airport to pick me up?" Without waiting for an answer, she picked up her suitcase that was held together by a frayed leather belt, and was trying to push her way in. The shoulder bag she carried had a broken zipper and was held together with safety pins. Prominently stuck on the suitcase with orange duct tape was Sita's home address.

"You're looking at the orange tape? Nice color eh? Makes it so easy to find my luggage at the airport," the stranger said following Sita's gaze. "I wonder why nobody uses bright cheery colors anymore."

At a loss for words Sita said, "Actually, I was looking at the tape too, but the address...that's our address...should we be expecting you...?" Her voice trailed away because the lady had begun to push her way into the hallway. At first she set the child down, and the cute fellow toddled in, as though this was where he belonged.

"If you wait here, I'll go and get Papa," Sita began, but the lady, who looked about fifty years old, was already urging the toddler up the stairs to the second floor.

"O...ne, two...oo, thr...ee," the woman counted, stretching out the words as the toddler took his time to go up the stairs. "Count Rohit, count, one....see how well he can count," she said, turning back to see if Sita was listening.

She paused in the middle of the stairs, "Where is your father? I know he said you all lived on the second floor. I need him to bring up my suitcase. A little slip of a girl like you won't be able to." She looked at Sita up and down, seeing her for the first time as it were. "We have to put some meat on your bones while I'm here."

"I'm fine and quite happy with how I look," Sita snapped. *Who was she anyway? Some distant, far removed third or fourth cousin Papa had forgotten about perhaps...It didn't look like she carried a whole lot in the crappy suitcase, so perhaps she would leave in a week or so.*

"Come here you," the woman said. Her right arm reached for Sita, and she held onto the toddler with the other. "Now you're angry at me. I forget how you young girls want to fit into these tight clothes." She eyed Sita's form fitting jeans, "Come and give your Aunt Priya a hug."

So that's who she was. Then Sita was enveloped in a bear hug that felt clammy with sweat. She had heard the name before, but as far as she could remember she was Papa's sister. *How could that be? They were nothing alike. Papa and her blood sisters!* She extricated herself in a hurry anxious to get away from this strange person. "Let me go and get Papa."

Papa appeared at the top of the stairs dressed in his well-starched pinstriped shirt and his gray pants with the perfect crease that ran down the middle. That was how he dressed every day, even though he had retired from his position as Professor of Law at Columbia University.

"What's going on?" he asked. Then he saw Aunt Priya in her sari with the colors of a clown suit holding onto a toddler.

"Priya?" And Sita could tell from his face he had no clue she was coming. "How did you get here?"

"What! No hug, no welcome, no apology that you didn't come to the airport. Nothing of the sort from you! Not even, *I know you must be tired after a twenty-two hour flight from India.* Still the same tall, cranky brother," Aunt Priya said. Her breath came in gasps as she pulled the toddler up the stairs to the top. "You never thought I would come here, did you? Thought I was a girl—couldn't do anything for myself. Didn't think I could get to America by myself, did you? Well, surprise! This is not the first time I have been to New York." The words just tumbled out of her like the bubbles floating out of an overheated pot of soup. She stood side by side with her brother. At 4'8" she was just a few inches above his waist, and had to tilt her head back to look up at him. That annoyed her even more. "Do you remember when we were little, I was almost two feet shorter than you, but that didn't stop me from jumping up and pulling your hair when you aggravated me." Aunt Priya stood on her tiptoes in a jerky movement, and punched the air as though she was grabbing a fistful of hair. "Remember when you took my share of the candy. I got it back from you in my own way. You lost some hair. And ...and then, you never took my food again."

Papa stooped down to kiss his sister. "I had no idea you were coming. Do you believe that?" he asked. Aunt Priya looked at him doubtfully. *Sita could tell she wanted to believe him.* Then Papa said, "Let me go and get your bags." He came back upstairs with the scrappy bits of luggage and took a long look at her. "You're exactly the same after all these years. Look the same. Act the same. You are still stubborn and overbearing. Fierce too." He touched the bald spot behind his ear. "I haven't forgotten how angry you can get. But you were *the* kindest person in the neighborhood. I can't forget the number of birds with broken wings you rescued, how many stray dogs you fed, and the kittens you snuck into the house without anyone knowing. You were clever too....Mom and dad never knew where you kept the strays, and how you fed them."

"And who is this?" Papa asked as the toddler walked past him into the living room where Nicky, the family dog lay asleep on the carpet. Nicky got up to greet his young visitor, and after a perfunctory wag of her tail sat down at his feet waiting for a back rub.

"Doggy likes me," the child squealed, stroking the animal gently. Nicky knew she had a succor here. She arched her back and wanted another back rub. The little boy obliged and squealed every time the dog licked him. Finally, exhausted from his long trip he curled up beside the dog and fell fast asleep. That's how Sita's Mom found them, with the young boy's head between Nicky's paws, and a chubby little arm slung over the dog's back.

"That's my son Rohit," Sita heard Aunt Priya say.

"*Your* son Rohit?"

"Yes, I adopted him."

"What madness is this?"

"No madness. Why will you deny me a son? No one thought to arrange my marriage. I was the short plain one, no one thought much of. Well, I got myself a son who thinks the world of me."

"A son?" Papa repeated, still shocked by the news.

"Yes, a son—someone who will remember me when I am old. I know for sure you won't." She paused. Her face was turned up to her brother's, "You have forgotten our culture. An older brother is supposed to take care of his sister. Do you remember anything about "Raakhi"? The tinsel bracelet I use to tie around your wrist that was a symbolic bond between brother and sister. It didn't mean anything to you, did it? You never thought to do anything for me, did you? Well, now I don't need you to."

Papa shuffled uncomfortably, still carrying the scrappy luggage that threatened to fall apart any moment. "Well, what matters is that you are here now, and there is no reason why you can't live here. The first floor is vacant and from now on, it can be your home for as long as you like."

"And Rohit's home too," Aunt Priya replied. "I won't live here forever you know. I have my pride."

That was said more than two years earlier, Sita remembered. Since then, Aunt Priya had done her utmost to introduce Sita's family to all the people they had lost touch with.

"When can Ramu dada come?" Sita heard her ask Papa one day.

"Why would I want that grease monkey here?"

Drawing herself up to her full height of 4'8" Aunt Priya yelled, "Ramu dada has been most helpful to me. He's a better brother to me than you could ever be."

"Now look here...."

"No, you listen to me for once. He is a successful businessman, he bought three Jiffy Lube franchises and a car wash, and he's doing well." She tucked her sari out of the way, put her hands on her hips, and spoke fast and loud. "He's come up by working very hard. No Harvard, no big degrees after his name, but just a lot of ambition and hard work. He is the best, the nicest man in the whole world." She adjusted her sari again, "He put up his car wash as collateral and bought me a partnership in an Indian restaurant. Would you have done that? What can you do to top that?"

"Hold it just a moment. You own an Indian restaurant? Why did he put up the collateral for you?"

"Perhaps because unlike you, he knew I was not a good-for-nothing sort of person. You thought we were both rejects because we didn't have a good education like you. You know what...life dealt us a different deck of cards to what you got. You got the opportunities. We were told to wait until you helped us. Why should I wait and wait all the time?"

"You didn't even call."

"Why should I? Ramu dada did everything for me."

"What did he do?"

"I just told you, but you like to act stupid when you talk to me. But, let me tell you everything anyway." She paused for a moment, changed her tone and started explaining as one would to someone who did not understand quickly. "When I first came to this country two years ago, yes, I have been in New Jersey for two years. I had no idea what to do. People did not understand my English. I could not understand their English. But still, I spoke."

"I can believe that," Papa said, his eyes twinkling.

"I spoke to everybody. I spoke to the supermarket man, to the pizza man, to the ice cream man, to the mail man...and now, I can talk American."

"American?"

"Yes. I speak good American. I say, "Have a nice day" to everyone. Everyone says that back to me. I am friends with everyone."

Papa looked amused. "Where did all this friendship get you?"

"Get me?" Aunt Priya tossed the phrase around in her mind making sure she understood correctly. Then she said, "The pizza man told me about a nice Indian family who owned restaurants. Ramu dada helped me again with money so I could become a partner and now, "Little India" is part mine." She rubbed her small hands together with a satisfied smile. "Then I wanted to do as the Americans do. I wanted to sell American food too. I got my wish. I have an Arby franchise. Now, I make more money than you!"

Sita thought Papa would get mad and say something, but he kept his thoughts to himself and Aunt Priya continued talking. "That's the beauty of America. There's opportunity here for everyone. Even if your English is no good, you still have a chance to make good money. Do you know that people who're good with their hands like mechanics, plumbers, and electricians make as much money as professors and editors. They have cars and nice houses too. You never hear about that in India," she said. "You have to push papers around on a desk to get respect. A mechanic is a "grease monkey," a cook, unless he works in a 5-star hotel is the same as a servant. Not so in America. Here there is dignity of labor."

"I can't believe you own a restaurant," Papa said more to himself than to her.

"Two." She stuck two fingers up. "Not one, but two. One Indian, and one American."

"You didn't tell me you were in the country for two years. I can't believe you never visited us earlier."

"I called and I wrote. I said I wanted to help you to find a good husband for Sita. You never replied. So I've come. Now I've proved I'm not useless."

"You were never useless…."

"Oh I knew that. You didn't. Neither you, nor anyone else believed in me."

"It's just that our parents were traditional," Papa said, trying his best to explain and calm her down. "I was the eldest boy, and since they could only afford to send one child to Harvard, I was chosen."

"Of course, and I was told to be a good woman. I must learn to serve. I must learn how to cook and clean, and keep house." Aunt Priya punctuated each word by shaking her fist at her brother. "Well, you thought I wouldn't be able to do anything…..I was so mad. But everything worked well. I am a business woman now." Then just as soon as she looked all calmed down and content, she remembered Papa had still not agreed to meet the others whom he referred to as "as those uncouth relatives."

"You haven't answered my question. When can Ramu dada, and Vijay, and Rita come here?"

"Oh Rita can come anytime."

"Is it because she dresses fashionably and speaks good English? Or because she teaches, what is the word …when you teach people how to pronounce correctly—Elocution?"

"Elocution is correct."

"I must tell you something funny." Aunt Priya's eyes gleamed with excitement. "When she taught in a Convent school in India, she gave each girl a little mirror so the student could see where to put the tongue to say the sounds correctly. For instance, she wanted them to say "how now brown cow" with the correct "ow" sound. Except that no child was looking at her tongue in the mirror. They were all checking their hair and makeup." Aunt Priya moved her head this way, and that way, in the exaggerated movement of a pantomime performer. "The nuns at the convent didn't like that at all. And she had to quit. Do you know, she still thinks it's so important to have the right accent? She was telling

Rohit to say, "Moses supposes his toeses are roses," with the right "o" sound. Even *I know* there is no word likes *toeses*." She laughed uncontrollably. "Do you know, people in India use to send their children to Catholic schools because they were run by Irish nuns, and were more westernized, and taught better English? They think English is so necessary for girls to mix in society, sort of like a finishing school people go to in England."

"Well, Catholic Schools have an excellent educational system." Papa had gone to an all-boys St. Xavier's school in India and was quick to defend the system.

"Never said they didn't," Aunt Priya retorted. "But when the English left, they left behind the brown Englishman."

"What's that for heaven's sake?"

"Papa, I think she means those people who think they are superior because they speak good English," Sita said. "Those people are so confused when people with superior math and science backgrounds get high paying jobs."

"There's nothing wrong with speaking good English."

"No, there is nothing wrong with it. Nothing wrong at all, and nor is there anything wrong with being good with your hands, being able to cook, or fix cars either."

"Point well taken," Papa said.

"Good, then you won't object if Ramu dada, Vijay, and Rita all come over," Aunt Priya said with a determined gleam in her eyes.

Sita suppressed an amused smile because Papa looked so exasperated. "Why do you keep asking the same thing?" he muttered. "Why is it so important they come here?"

"Because they are family, and we should keep in touch with family and, who knows when we might need their help. What am I to do with you!" Aunt Priya lapsed into her native tongue and began to hiss and splutter in Hindi like an overheated tea kettle with a broken spout.

"You know, you think like the English did when they ruled India," Aunt Priya said. "They never expected Gandhi, the person they made fun of all the time because he would not wear western clothes—the man with the loin cloth, *he can't do anything* they thought." She paused, opened her arms wide, "Well he did so-o much. He sent the British out of India and made India free."

"You are so melodramatic! You're equating an educated barrister like Gandhi with Ramu and Vijay. What next!"

"I am telling you not to judge a book by its cover. Not to think that Ramu and Vijay can't help. Maybe they cannot, but then again, maybe they will. And we will never know unless they come here," she said stubbornly. "Actually Sita's Mom has already agreed to invite them. She and I have a lot in common, you know."

"You must be joking," Papa said. "You have nothing in common with Sita's Mom."

"We have plenty in common."

"You're as different as apples and oranges."

"So, at least we are both fruit!" Aunt Priya replied quoting straight out of the movie called *Big Fat Greek Wedding.*

"Ah, you see English movies now," Papa murmured.

"There are many things I have in common with my sister-in-law."

"Name one."

"She loves Rohit, and as far as I care that is all the sameness I need."

Well, she was right. Sita remembered Mom had been quite taken with Rohit from the time she had seen him sleeping with the dog in her living room. She had scooped him up from the floor, cradling him in her arms and sniffed up the sweet smell of Johnsons baby shampoo mixed in with a doggy smell. It had been so long since she had carried a young child, and he had looked so vulnerable sleeping with the dog, that she wanted so much to be able to care for him. She had encouraged Priya Aunty to stay on in the apartment downstairs so she could be a part of Rohit's life.

"Do you want to call me Aunty?" she had asked Rohit.

"Okay, if you play Playstation with me."

"I don't know how."

"No problem. I'll show you. Here you hold this control, and I'll take the other one. Let's play the Nascar racing game. You are the red car, and I'll be the blue one. See, you have to push this button to go forward, press the pedal to go faster. Go Aunty go," he would say, "I'll push the pedal down for you."

Without warning he pushed the game pedal down, and the little red car whizzed across the television screen at 200 miles per hour, swerving along the curves in the road, and dodging past other cars on the track. One time when she didn't press the right button, the car veered onto the curb, smashing into the sidewalk.

"Oh—h-h," Sita's mom sighed. She hadn't realized she had been holding her breath until now. Game over, the screen said. Mom ran her hands over the leather couch to be reassured that she was still in the living room, and not on the autobahn across the Atlantic.

"That was so much fun," Rohit said. "I'm so glad I have a new Aunty."

"And I'm so glad we are all family," Sita's mom said, ruffling his hair.

Chapter Three

Sita awoke to the resounding clap of thunder, and the sound of the wind slapping against the house. She pulled the covers over her ears and curled into a ball, glad it was Saturday, and she had the day off. She would have hated to walk ten blocks to the Roosevelt Avenue subway station in pouring rain. She would have to hold an umbrella that the wind wanted to pull away from her, get splattered with slush as she hurried along the avenue, and then get on to a rush hour train sandwiched between people in wet raincoats and, most likely be poked by a wet umbrella as she moved to fit into an opening in the crowd. She lay back in bed feeling lucky. The storm had subsided into a constant drizzle. Sita slid deeper under the covers, enjoying the soothing patter of rain against the windows. She stayed in bed until she heard the tea kettle whistle, and the rattle of pots and pans in the sink. It sounded like Mom and Priya Aunty were cooking up a storm. Then she heard Priya Aunty's voice, "When I was younger no one arranged my marriage. Otherwise I could have had a handsome husband too, you know. My mom and dad thought it should just happen. Nothing happens by itself." The lids of the pots clattered as she set them down quickly, without watching. They slid to the side, and rolled away into the sink, with a sound that could not drown out Aunt Priya's loud voice. "I am fifty years old and still single. For Sita that won't happen. I will make sure." She looked accusingly at the runaway pan cover. "You must make sure a good man doesn't get away," she said to Mom without taking her eyes away from the pots and pans. "You have to get the word out, and it takes a lot of planning. You must act fast." She looked up. "If you don't do anything, I will." Still Mom said nothing. "Look at her, already twenty-two and no one is doing anything for her," Aunt Priya said. "Do you know Sheela?"

"Is that Anita's daughter?"

"Yes, the very same girl. Do you know from the time Sheela was born, her mother started collecting jewelry. At every birthday when Sita got dolls and toys, Sheela got at least one piece of jewelry. Do you know how many sets she has?"

"I really don't care," Mom said. "My daughter doesn't wear a whole lot of jewelry. In America, where does one get to wear all these Indian things.... She has couple of sets, and that's enough."

"Then when she turned thirteen, she knew how to cook and keep house," Priya Aunty continued as though Mom had not spoken. "She didn't waste time at the mall, looking for Madonna CDs," she said, and Sita could imagine Aunt Priya moving her big behind up and down in an attempt to mimic Madonna's gyrations. She smiled at the thought, and lifted her head to catch more of the conversation.

"She did practical stuff."

"Like what?"

"She took cooking classes and learned interior decorating. No wonder she snapped up Dr. Vikram."

"Sort of like the nationally televised *Who wants to marry a millionaire* show," Mom said. "Those marriages do not last."

As usual Priya Aunty did not listen. "Do you know he is a neurosurgeon at Mount Sinai Medical School? They have a luxurious house with a swimming pool, and all her hopes and dreams have come true."

"Is she happy?"

"What kind of question is that? Of course she is! Just like Sita is going to be. Bring me a slip of paper and I'll write an advertisement for the newspaper. *India Abroad*—have you heard of it? It has a big circulation—and that is where Sita's advertisement will appear." She lowered the flame on the stove and made her way to the kitchen table. "I want everyone to know about my beautiful niece."

Sita got out of bed and peeked into the kitchen. She saw Priya Aunty sitting at the kitchen table with her chin resting on her hands, chewing a pencil, and gazing intently at the ceiling, lost in deep thought. Finally, she shifted her gaze back to the paper and stopped chewing on the pencil. "Okay we'll say, *Wanted an educated Christian, professionally qualified boy, 25-30 years old, from a cultured family, for a slim, attractive, educated girl, well versed in domestic responsibilities.*

"What domestic responsibilities, Priya Aunty?" Sita asked, stepping into the kitchen.

That was enough to get Priya Aunty started. "Sita you know, you really must be more homely."

"Wear comfortable clothes—nothing too tight fitting?" Sita said, deliberately misunderstanding her.

Aunt Priya immediately took the bait and began her lecture. "You must be able to keep a nice house. I must tell your mother to order some *House and Garden* magazines. They have some great decorating tips. If you can't decorate a home you will end up with an uncouth, uncultured bumpkin." She shook her head as though she could already see Sita married to one.

"But I have a good job. Doesn't that count for anything?"

Aunt Priya rolled her eyes. "Shush. We must not harp so much about this job of yours. People may think we are poor, and that's why we put you to work. Besides, what use is a good job if you can't feed yourself and your man, Missy?"

"Won't peanut butter sandwiches do?" Sita asked provokingly.

Of course Priya Aunty fell right into the trap, and started off, "You must be able to make *roti* at least." She marched toward the kitchen table and pointed to the small mound of flour she had been kneading. "Come, let me show you. First you take flour, add some water, and then knead it real well. If you don't do a good job, your *roti* bread won't rise," she said getting breathless as she punched the dough with small pudgy fingers and dimpled wrists. "For special occasions you must learn to make *paratha*. You can stuff them with whatever you want. Use potatoes, or cauliflower, or even chopped meat." Sita backed away from the stove. "Today,

I am making plain *parathas*. You can help me," Aunt Priya said. "I'll roll and you fry." She took a chunk of dough, rolled it out into a pancake, and smeared it generously with butter.

"People will get a heart attack with so much grease," Sita grumbled. *Why did she have to be tied to the stove on her day off?*

"You can use *Olivo* or what is that packet that calls itself, *I can't believe it is not butter?* You can use that. But I know for a fact, there is no taste like butter. We don't eat *paratha* every day. No harm in using butter." She turned to look at Sita, "Now look, sprinkle some dry flour on the butter to make sure you get nice layers of bread when you roll out the dough." She tucked her sari out of the way, "Well, first you have to fold the pancake in a square. Then you add more butter." She ignored Sita's disapproving look, "Sprinkle more flour, fold it again, and then keep going until you are sure to get a nice flaky *paratha*. Here, this one is done." She tossed it to Sita. "Now put some butter on the griddle, and let the paratha fry. Be careful not to let the edges burn, and then you can flip it over, and do the other side. I will tell everyone you made the parathas." She stood by Sita watching as she flipped the paratha. *Oops!* Sita almost dropped it, but caught it before it hit the floor. She looked up nervously. Aunt Priya said, "Good job. You need more practice. Try again."

"What are we eating besides *roti* and *paratha?*" Sita picked up the covers of the four pots simmering on Mom's new Kenmore oven, one by one. She was sorry she asked because now, Aunt Priya decided to explain how the *panir* curry was made.

"You know what *panir* is right? I will explain. *Panir* is homemade cheese. Some people buy their cheese in the store. I like to make it," Aunt Priya announced.

"But of course," Sita muttered under her breath. "You would do anything to make life harder for women."

"It is not hard. It is fun." Aunt Priya gave Sita a quelling look. "First, you take a gallon of milk. Then you boil it. You must watch it doesn't stick or boil over. Then you keep three or four lemons cut in half, ready on the side. As soon as you see the milk beginning to rise, you squeeze the lemon juice into it. Sita reached for the stove knob as the milk threatened to spill over. "Don't turn off the stove," Aunt Priya said. "You want the milk to keep rising so you can push it down with lemon juice. Here, you take one lemon, and I'll take the other. See, can you see how the milk is separating?" She pointed to the white curd that had separated from the whey. "Now go get me a sieve."

This is completely nuts! "I don't think we have one that is big enough."

"I don't know how your mother runs this kitchen."

"Wouldn't it be simpler to have just bought the cheese," Sita whined.

"Taste this," Aunt Priya said, pushing some cheese crumbs under Sita's unsuspecting lips. "No store bought cheese is as good as mine. Now, I will show you how to make the gravy. First you cut two onions really fine. I don't like to use the blender or the chopper because I think it takes out too much of the juice, and the onions don't have the same flavor."

"What else is new," Sita said.

Aunt Priya knotted her eyebrows, "What do you mean by that question?"

"Nothing," Sita said quickly. She watched Aunt Priya deftly cut onions, slice the ginger, and peel garlic. "We will sauté these three things together. Now watch," she said, "when the onions get a little bit brown, you can add the spice. I like to use cumin, cardamom, and cinnamon, along with the regular curry powder. If you want a stronger taste, it is a good idea to roast the spice quickly in a pan, and then grind it."

"What's wrong with ground spices that come in a packet?" Sita said before she could stop herself.

"This tastes much better."

"Well mother doesn't have a spice mill."

"I saw a coffee grinder in the kitchen. That will do just fine," Aunt Priya said. "You must learn to improvise in the kitchen. Not always be saying I can't do this, or that I can't do that. Make do with what you have, and make it into something special."

"Well, now that you have all the spices ready, you pour them into the pan and then, we can slice some green chilies." Aunt Priya slit two green chilies deftly down the middle and extracted the seeds, cut them finely, and poured them in the mix. "Now we will let this cook until the spices separate from the onions. Once that is ready, we will add the tomatoes. Before you use the tomatoes, it is a good idea to soak them in warm water and take off the skin. That way they will cook quicker, and make nice thick gravy. Some people like to use a little bit of tomato paste. I suppose you could, if you want to, but sometimes store bought tomato paste changes the Indian flavor of the curry. Well, I don't know everything. If you are in a hurry, you can use it."

"If I were in a hurry I would just go and buy the food," Sita quipped.

"I don't know what to do with you," Aunt Priya said. "I don't want to talk about this problem with you today. Come look at everything I have made. There's lamb curry cooked with spinach, and tandoori chicken." She paused and tried to remember how Sita had described it the last time. "It is… how they say in America, *tender and succulent.* It's made with homemade spices, and there is cheese curry, also." Aunt Priya pointed to the gravy that was simmering on the stove, and slurped down a spoonful. "Just right," she grunted in satisfaction. "I think Ramu dada will like it."

"He's coming today?" Sita asked.

"Yes, with Rita Aunty, and Vijay Uncle," Priya Aunty said.

"Why?"

"Well child, we have to do something about your marriage," Mom said.

Sita had forgotten she was even there. She had been so quiet drafting and editing the matrimonial advertisement that would run in the *India Abroad* newspaper. Sita turned really quiet. *It was one thing for Priya Aunty to harp on her wedding, but now, Mom too.* "Mom, am I a burden that you want to marry me away to get rid of me?" she asked.

Mom looked up then, "How can you think that? We only want what is best for you." A stray tear escaped Mom's penciled eyelids, and she turned away to hide her moment of weakness.

"So why rush?" Sita asked. "You don't look happy arranging this marriage."

Mom turned around. "It has to be done. You have been sheltered and are too inexperienced to choose your own husband. Papa and I have been married a long time, and so have Ramu Uncle, Rita Aunty, and Vijay Uncle. We know what makes for a long and happy marriage, and it is not the good looks."

"So you'll marry me to an ugly fool, three inches shorter than me?"

"Not if I can help it, but we will examine the goods, not just the packaging."

"What packaging? What are you talking about now?"

"It's easy to be dazzled by appearances and taken in by flattery," Mom said.

"So I can't hope for red roses and a box of chocolates, and someone to tell me he likes me for myself, and not my family?"

"What's all this about red roses," Papa grunted from behind his newspaper. "If you want red roses so badly, there are plenty of wild ones growing in the backyard. Go and pick some."

"Papa, you don't understand."

"Damn right I don't. I'm certainly not going to give my daughter away to some fool because he brings her red roses."

So typical of Papa Sita thought, *only wanting to be practical and never showing any emotion.* She hadn't even known he was there. He was sitting in the high-backed recliner that hid him so well. Sita could imagine his face if she said she wanted to find her own man. Once she had tentatively asked, "Papa why can't I find my own man? Why does the family want to find me one?"

"For the same reason we took Nicky to the vet to be mated with a suitable thoroughbred Golden Retriever," he retorted.

"But I'm not a dog!"

"Exactly, so how much more careful must I be in finding a suitable and very lucky boy for my only daughter," Papa said. He patted the top of her head as if she were still two years old. "Don't worry. I'll find a good one," he said in the same tone he had used fifteen years ago when he had promised to buy her a good dog.

Mother too, was no different. She told Sita, "A woman's life is not complete without marriage and family. All we want is your happiness...." She looked so sad, as though she knew that she would lose her daughter. "In India, once the girl was married, the boy's family becomes *her* family. But the husband—he can do what he wants. If he wants to be nice, that's great, but if not, no one will think the worse of him. There are still different rules for men and women."

Not so in America. Sita thought. *Here they say, "A son is your son till he takes a wife, but a daughter is your daughter for the rest of your life." Mom did not know that.*

What if they screwed up? What if they found someone with weird habits—like picking his nose perhaps, or maybe someone who wouldn't use silverware but preferred to use his hands to shovel food into his mouth. Someone who never thought to say "excuse me," when he burped? She shuddered. She wished she had known a Mr. Right but there had been very little opportunity to find one. She had gone to an all girls' school, and then an all girls' college. No boys were invited to the house, or encouraged to call.

Now, she was a working woman, but had to be home right after work. The family was quite unhappy that she was working in the first place. Perhaps she should just trust her family and not worry so much. Mom and Papa had been married for almost twenty-five years. Dad was the strong silent type, who provided for the family. Mom was the sociable one, and loved going to parties. She was always active in one club or another, whenever she was tied up with her PTA work at the Jackson Heights Elementary school that Rohit attended. Papa never joined her at the parties, but never discouraged her from going. Mom never went, until she was sure Papa's food was cooked just so, the house was clean, and all his creature comforts were taken care of. "You have to find your own method to make marriage work," she said. For Mom, the way to a man's heart was through his stomach! Papa was always sure of a delicious home-cooked meal, topped by dessert that he loved so much. Mom always said, "Always put the family first. Never try to compete with your man. Make him feel like the king of his castle and he will treat you as his queen."

Sita had said, "But I won't even know the man, what if I don't want to cook for, nurture, and treat this stranger like a king? What if I can't love him?"

Mom had replied, "Love comes slowly, my dear. I did not know your father when I married him. Like good wine, love becomes better, more fulfilling, with the passage of years." Mom had then looked her straight in the eye and said, "Passion ignites fast, and dies faster. But the fire of true love and caring grows brighter as the years roll by."

Mom's voice interrupted her thoughts. "Go and get dressed dear, everyone will be here soon."

"Can I wear jeans?"

"No," Mom said, in a voice that brooked no argument. "If you don't want to wear the sari, put on a decent *salwar kameez*."

Sita loved the *salwar kameez*, a graceful outfit with a knee length tunic, and pleated pants, topped by a matching scarf. Today though, she was being petulant. "Oh, you mean the long dress slit thigh high, and the parachute pants," she quipped.

"Whatever," Mom retorted, refusing to be drawn into an argument. She hurried away to finish cooking, cleaning, and preparing for the visitors who were going to come today.

"This is all Aunt Priya's fault." Sita said out loud. "She is the one who is so obsessed with arranging my marriage. I wish I knew why."

Chapter Four

The front stairs had been freshly vacuumed leaving a lingering aroma of potpourri. Sita had watched Aunt Priya's little frame doubled over on the stairs as she tried to vacuum every particle of dirt that should dare to be visible on the pearl gray carpet. She had taken down each one of the brass wall plaques in the stairwell, and scrubbed them with fresh lemon juice. "Nothing like good old lemon," she had told Sita. Sita saw her scrub the brass plaques vigorously, and the flesh on her arms jiggled uncontrollably, "I don't believe any of your new-fangled cleaners can replace lemon juice," she said.

All the scrubbing had taken place at the kitchen sink, and Sita noticed that Aunt Priya was never too far from the four well-worn pots simmering on Mom's new Kenmore oven. Sita watched mesmerized, as Priya Aunty managed to scrub the plaques down, and to stir the lamb curry simultaneously. Beads of sweat had collected on her brow, and one drop chased down her glasses. She had to take them off, and her glasses, suspended by a cord, now rested on the shelf of her bosom. "Sita, go and hang these in place," she said, squinting at the wall plaques that now dazzled and winked in the daylight.

Under her breath Sita heard her say, "I wish Sita would learn to do this." Sita bit back a retort. *What's so great about shiny plaques? It would have taken two minutes to get some brass cleaner out of a bottle, and a whole lot less messy than playing around with lemons and a scrub pad.* Aloud she said, "Sure Aunty, they look wonderful."

Aunt Priya had put on her glasses and was gazing admiringly at the fruits of her labor. "You must learn to do this," she said. Sita was about to say something back, but Rohit was yelling downstairs.

"Ma, are you almost done? I can smell the curry down here. Can you stop now?" Sita heard the side door slam shut and Rohit came in from the driveway where he had been playing. He climbed the stairs two at a time, not stopping even to catch his breath. He had taken off his tee-shirt, and his skin was damp with sweat. He raced upstairs dragging his tee-shirt on the floor. His hair was messed up, and the spikes gelled into place only that morning, had flattened into place. A brightly colored school bag containing all his action figures and toys bounced on his back and he almost tripped on the untied shoelaces of his Reebok sneakers. He made it to the top. He paused for a second, grimaced at the dust streaks on the tee-shirt, picked it up, then pushed the door ajar, and peered at everyone with his flushed face and shiny eyes.

"Come in," Aunt Priya said. "Ooph you took off your tee-shirt again! So many times I have told you not to take off your tee-shirt outside. Insects will bite you. Besides what will people think?"

"But Ma, James and the others did."

"Did you bring all your toys in?" Aunt Priya asked looking at the school bag he had discarded on the floor. "Come, you must have a glass of cold milk to give you energy."

"I want chocolate milk," he said eagerly. He grabbed the glass with both hands and proceeded to drain it empty. Aunt Priya smiled and reached for a napkin to wipe away the chocolate moustache on his upper lip.

"People will be coming soon," she told him. "I want you to be a good boy and get cleaned up."

"Everything is done," Sita heard Aunt Priya say as she took a last look at the kitchen. All the dishes had been washed and put away. The splatter of curry on the oven had been wiped down, and the sink shone brightly under the renewed onslaught of *Brillo* and lemon juice. Four pots stood on the stove holding the curries. "See Sita, I have put the *parathas* you made on the top." She pointed to the foil covered stack of *paratha*s on the kitchen counter. "I am going to tell everybody that you made them, and that you also made the *panir* curry."

"That's not completely true," Sita said. She tried to make a quick exit before Aunt Priya could think of another chore for her. It was too late.

"Come and help me cut the salad," Aunt Priya said before Sita could escape.

"You know, we could have just bought the salad shooter at Macy's. They were having a sale."

"What's wrong with our hands?" Aunt Priya snapped. "Here," she said passing her a knife, "you slice the tomatoes really fine, and I'll chop up the cucumber. I should also slice up some onions."

"Everyone's breath will smell," Sita warned. She remembered the early days at work when she used to take packed lunch to the office. Even though the curries were discretely wrapped in *roti* and disguised as rolls, there was no mistaking the strong curry flavor the instant they were warmed in the microwave. "Something smells good," people would say, but she always had a nagging feeling that what they meant was, *that something smelt very different. Not necessarily good.* Later she had stopped taking packed lunches, opting instead for cheese sandwiches. But she always added fresh onions. Then she noticed that after lunch people would back away from her, until one day someone actually told her that her breath smelled! She never ate raw onions at the office again.

"Don't serve raw onions." Sita said again.

"I like raw onions dripping with lemon juice—tastes good with the tandoori chicken. Here, I'll cut them if you think cutting onions is going to make your eyes tear." She cut two purple onions, separating the pieces into circular rings which she placed over the finely chopped tomatoes and cucumber. "We can add a few green chilies on the side," she said, "just in case some people like their food hot."

Sita stepped away, ready to make a quick exit. "Okay. We're all done now."

"Yes we are," Aunt Priya agreed, admiring her freshly cut salad. Sita had just left the room and heard her name being called. "Sita, where did you go? Let me see what you decided to wear today."

"Coming," Sita said in resignation. Five minutes later, she was back in the kitchen where she knew Aunt Priya would still be busy with one thing or another. She was holding a turquoise *salwar kameeze* with matching dupatta (scarf) draped around the hanger. "This meets with your approval, Aunt Priya?" She asked meekly. She hadn't meant to be so agreeable, but that's how the words came out. That's how they always came out when she was with Aunt Priya.

"Put it on. Let me see how it fits," Aunt Priya said taking the fabric in her hands and studying the embroidery detail at the neckline. There was something in Aunt Priya's eyes that let Sita know that her Aunt would not take 'no' for an answer.

Sita grumbled under her breath. Sometimes Aunt Priya thought she was her mother. *Where was Mom anyway?* Then she looked closely at this woman who was not her mother, who slaved over a hot stove all morning, cleaned the stairs, scrubbed the plaques, and put together a matrimonial advertisement that had attracted the attention of so many bachelors—all because she loved her, and thought she knew best. After slight hesitation, Sita got changed. Obediently she put on the blue outfit she had been holding, and modeled it for Aunt Priya, strutting up and down the kitchen floor as though it were a ramp in a fashion show, pausing in front of Aunt Priya with hands on her hips. She twirled away with a swirl of her scarf, just when she thought Aunt Priya was getting ready to say something.

"Pull the dupatta lower," Aunt Priya said, eyeing the fabric stretched tight over her breast and tucked at the waist. "Don't know why they make clothes so tight these days, they want to leave nothing to the imagination. Bah! That's better," she said when Sita did as she was told and pulled down the scarf to hide her natural endowments. Aunt Priya struggled with words as she eyed the outfit that clung to Sita's slim Barbie doll shape. "We all know you're well err…err….have a good figure. There is no need to show it so much."

Sita couldn't resist a smile. *What would Aunt Priya say if she saw her in shorts and a tank top?* She made a mental note to wear shorts next weekend, if only to see her Aunt's reaction.

"Go and get dressed Aunt Priya," Sita smiled indulgently at this petite lady who had become so much a part of her life. "Mom and Papa are dressed already. The guests will be coming soon."

Sita saw Mom appear all dressed up in a patterned gray chiffon sari, which looked refreshingly cool on a hot June day. She smelled good too, and Sita thought she recognized the scent of Elizabeth Taylor's "White Diamonds," perfume. A string of pearls hung around her neck, and her well-coiffed hair gave her an air of distinction. Papa looked debonair in his gray slacks and pinstriped shirt. He had grayed at the temples this past year, but to Sita, that had only served to make him look more distinguished.

While Priya Aunty had been busy in the kitchen, Mom had outdone herself sprucing up the living room. The parquet floors had been mopped to a gloss that reflected everything placed on the floor. The white leather couch and love-seat felt nice and cool on a hot summer day, and showed off the white and navy Indian handmade rugs to advantage. The matching end tables, of Italian white lacquer, had an exotic Ikebana arrangement of fresh flowers that Mom had created painstakingly. She had used dried flowers in the back, interspersed with a cascade of fresh flowers, especially pale pink petunias that tumbled out of the vase and hung just above the table surface. On the mantel just above the fireplace, were family pictures of Sita—when she was a baby, later a little tomboy trying to climb a tree in shorts, then a gawky teenager in round horn-rimmed glasses that she had to wear since she was twelve because as Nani said, "You like to read way too much." She had gone on to say, "I don't know the point of that. But never mind when you get older we will have to get you contacts. Very hard to find a good man if you don't look your best."

The older pictures were in black and white and looked good beside their more recent counterparts. The picture of Sita in glasses was somehow always hidden behind a new picture of her dressed in a sari, looking very quiet and demure. "That is a nice picture," Aunt Priya said whenever she had the chance. "Makes you look like a good girl."

The wall unit with its freshly cleaned glass showed off the choicest curios. There were wood carvings, a copper jar, and a brass peacock whose iridescent blue feathers gleamed brilliantly in the well-lit wall unit. Many other knick-knacks, bought each time the family went back to India, were displayed, adding to the décor of the room.

The dining room sparkled under the soft glow of the chandelier lights. The maple wood table with eight chairs, had plastic covered seats to safeguard against curry spills. That was the only concession Mom had made to being practical today. Everything else was different and special. Instead of the usual flannel-backed vinyl tablecloth, Mom had used her damask table cloth and cloth napkins, and instead of the everyday plates, she had taken out her favorite bone china with a lacy pattern of floral pastels.

Aunt Rita in her crisp cotton sari that had remained clean and crisp in the downpour, was the first to arrive. Sita heard her exclaim, "My you've got new wall plaques, how beautiful," in carefully enunciated words, just like the good elocution teacher she was so proud of being. She took off her shoes so as not to stain the good carpeting. Picking her sari pleats with one hand, she climbed up the stairs in her bare feet, showing off the silver anklet and her brightly polished red toe nails. As always, she was dressed to the hilt. She wore a pale pink cotton sari, and a well-fitting matching pale pink blouse. A string of smoky topaz beads and matching earrings completed the ensemble. She spoke little, and her sense of quiet dignity was in striking contrast to Aunt Priya. It was so hard for Sita to imagine that they were all related.

Aunt Rita was followed by Rohit, who had run up the side stairs—the ones with worn linoleum. He had cleaned up. His hair was neatly parted on the side and slicked back with coconut oil the way his mother liked him to wear it. He wore jeans with a tee-shirt of his favorite cartoon character. It was hard to see what it was, because he moved around so much. That was a good thing. Sita knew she could always count on his bouncy happy-go-lucky presence to relieve any tension she felt.

"Hi Sita," he yelled, "Can we play Playstation? Shall I bring my Playstation upstairs?"

"Not now Rohit," Aunt Priya said, and Sita could hear her also coming up the side stairs, panting with the exertion of keeping up with her son. She had spruced up too, and looked nice in pale green chiffon. A roll of flesh hung out from the space between the blouse and sari. She used talcum powder liberally on her face, and the whiteness stopped abruptly just below the chin. Her face could have looked like a white mask if her hyperactive sweat glands hadn't ensured that the white powder washed down to her neck, and beyond.

"Did you put the air conditioner on? It's hotter upstairs than in my apartment," Aunt Priya said, releasing a wad of papers and letters from her pudgy palms. "Keep these safely," she told Sita. "We'll discuss them after lunch. No peeking."

"All these came in from the *India Abroad* advertisement!" Sita said in astonishment.

"Yes, and new ones come every day," Aunt Priya said happily. She turned to look at Rohit who was tugging at her sari.

"What's for dinner," Rohit asked. "Not just curry right? You have macaroni and cheese? Oh, not that hot chicken again!" he exclaimed, rolling his eyes when he saw the plate of tandoori chicken piled high in the dish.

He was just four, and was already beginning to be torn between wanting to be American, and having to be Indian. He went to nursery school. All his friends were American. James, Edwin, and Patrick, from the apartment complex, who practically lived in his driveway, riding their bikes and skateboards down the slope, were American. He loved *Sesame Street* and had just outgrown *Barney,* and everybody he knew, and loved, in those television series were American. Once he had turned four, he had become conscious of his complexion, and Sita had remembered him asking, "Sita I'm not white, and I'm not black, so am I beige? Am I more American or am I more Indian?"

"No we don't have macaroni and cheese," Priya Aunty clicked her tongue impatiently. By now Ramu dada had arrived along with Vijay. As usual, Ramu dada was dressed in his polyester pants and shiny shoes. The pants belted high on his waist to conceal his pot belly made his pants look short—as though he were expecting a flood. He spoke in a heavily accented tone, tried hard to be social, and greeted everyone by name. "Hello Priya," he said, giving her quick hug. He hesitated for a moment, then greeted Papa and Mom cordially.

Aunt Priya waddled around the room introducing everybody. "This is Sita," she said. Ramu dada looked up and smiled approvingly at Sita in her blue *salwar kameeze*. He then circulated around the room looking visibly uncomfortable in the company of Aunt Rita and her perfect accent, but to his credit, he did not ignore her. Instead, he stretched out his clammy hands in a hesitant hand shake. She responded, and then withdrew her hand quickly. Uncle Vijay had also come. He had donned a pair of past season Calvin Klein jeans in his last ditch effort to look young. He was also wearing a Calvin Klein tee-shirt, several sizes too small for him. Sita couldn't help wondering if he had picked it up in a thrift store, or had bought it at a regular store and then shrunk it in the washing machine, because he thought he looked cool to have all his chest hair hanging out. Not that he was lacking money. He said he had it all invested in this, and that, and had no cash to spare. But he spent an awful lot on his jewelry. A flashy gold chain gleamed over his hairy chest, and the rings he wore on every finger, glimmered crudely under the chandelier lights.

Papa in his somber gray outfit looked strangely out of place in his own home. Sita knew Mom was trying to put on her society voice though her heart wasn't in this party. "Come along, how nice to see you," Sita heard her say in a high pitch unnatural tone. She was going to lose her daughter, and tied as she was to tradition, she had to arrange to make that happen.

"The tandoori chicken is great," Mom crooned, "have some more." She got up to pass the plate around.

"You must try the *panir* curry with *paratha*," Aunt Priya interrupted. "Sita made it."

"Oh ho, then I must try those items. *Paratha* is of course best enjoyed eaten with one's fingers," Ramu dada announced. "What do you say, we eat the Indian way?"

"Go ahead," Aunt Priya smiled, and without further ado, Ramu dada was tearing at the *parathas* and shoveling the food into his mouth with his hands.

"Pass me the rice," Uncle Vijay said. Then he too discarded the silverware, and proceeded to mix the curry into the rice, making little round balls which he then shoved into his mouth, licking his fingertips clean of the last rice grain.

"Food was delicious," Ramu dada said rubbing his belly.

"Oh yes," Uncle Vijay said, letting out a loud belch followed by a series of hiccups and burps that sent Rohit into a fit of laughter.

"Come now, let us have some fruit," Aunt Priya announced bringing out the fruit salad and whipped cream.

"Uncle Vijay is *so-o* funny," Rohit giggled. He stood on the chair to reach for some tasty looking water melon. "No!" He knocked over a glass of orange juice.

"Watch it!" Aunt Priya yelled, but it was too late. The glass lay sideward. Orange juice spilled over Mom's fine tablecloth, and dripped down to the floor in an orange puddle. Sita heard Aunt Priya say, "I think we should all go to the other room if everyone has finished, I'll clean up later."

Chapter Five

"Sita," Aunt Priya called. "Bring me the letters." She took them from Sita and ambled over to Sita's father.

"That's quite a bundle you have there," Sita heard Papa say. Envelopes of all sizes and colors had been tightly tied together with a frayed and greasy orange ribbon—most likely used the night before to confine Aunt Priya's coconut oil saturated hair in place. She pulled the ribbon off with a gentle tug, and spread the letters in her lap, separating a few from the rest.

"Some of them are excellent prospects for my niece." She settled herself comfortably next to Papa, and put her feet up, hiding her calloused heels under the folds of her sari. She ignored Papa's glare, and sat cross-legged on the sofa to sift through the pile of letters in her lap.

Papa moved his chair closer. "You know, all these people who have written, are they from here, or are they writing about boys in India?"

"Well, *India Abroad* has a local circulation so they should be from here. Why?"

"No reason. I just don't want my daughter marrying somebody from India who is simply using her to get a Green Card and get to America."

"So you want Sita to go back and live in India?"

"No," Papa answered quickly.

"Then let us at least read through the letters before we start arguing," Aunt Priya reasoned. "Here, you take the first few and start reading, and then we can talk about them."

"I still think we could have done this by ourselves. There was no need to call Ramu, and Vijay, and everybody else."

Aunt Priya gave Papa an annoyed look and said, "You will see I was right to call everybody. Where are they? *Oiy* Ramu," she yelled, "Vijay—come on. Tell Rita to come too. Don't you want to help me here?"

"They must be talking about some other business. Maybe they want to buy a car shop, or a *7 Eleven* store," Papa said sarcastically.

"They didn't ask me. What do they think? I'll frighten the customers away?" Then she marched back into the dining room and stood there, until everybody got up from the dining table and followed her into the living room.

Aunt Priya waddled back to the chair beside Papa and eased her weight into it. Mom hovered behind them both, anxious to see what kind of prospective grooms Aunt Priya had rounded up for her daughter. Slowly the others followed, and took their place around Aunt Priya and Papa. Sita noted that her father, brows knotted in concentration, scanned through the first letter then exclaimed, "Good! The boy has an MBA degree."

Mom peered over his shoulder, and Sita heard her comment, "But he has eight brothers and sisters. I don't want my daughter to deal with so many in-laws. Small families are much better. There is less expense, less meddling, less interference, less problems if the family is small."

Aunt Rita nodded in agreement, "Who knows what kind of people they are. And even if they are really nice people, there are just too many of them. Once they know you live in America, they think the streets are paved with gold and it's no big deal to ask for this, that, and the other. Once in a while it's okay, but Sita will have her own household expenses and no time to be buying a camcorder for this one, and a DVD player for someone else, and a laptop for one cousin, and a digital camera for another cousin, and so on."

"Well, these days there is free trade in India, and so you can get everything in India. No one needs to ask so much," Aunt Priya snapped.

"Aha, but that's where you are wrong. Everyone likes "phoren" things made in the USA. They think it is so cheap to buy in America."

"Yes, that will not work," Ramu dada said. "Then there will be birthdays, and sweet sixteens, and graduations, and weddings, and our Sita will always be giving and giving. She has no sisters or brothers so she will not be getting anything."

"Priya," Ramu said suddenly. "In the advertisement I hope you did not say Sita is an only daughter. Because then we will get all these hungry people looking for her money. See this letter... It says here the boy is a doctor, and because his parents spent so much money for his education, they feel it is reasonable to expect that the girl's family would buy the newlyweds their first home."

"Let me take a look at that!" Papa roared. "Do they not know dowry has been outlawed? It is illegal to ask for anything."

"Well, you know the dowry system still continues secretly," Aunt Priya mumbled. "Just yesterday, there was a news report about the wife dying mysteriously after a few weeks of being married. It was made to look like an accident, but it turned out the mother-in-law had set fire to the poor girl because she did not bring in enough money. Then once she was out of the picture, there were plans to marry off the son again to someone who came from a richer or more generous family."

"Lord knows what these people will do if they don't get what they expect," Ramu dada said waving the letter.

"You know, the more I read these letters, the more I think advertising was not the best idea."

"Here's another," Aunt Rita exclaimed. "This one swears his undying love for Sita. Promises to love, honor, and cherish, her forever," she said. "He hasn't even seen the girl's picture. How can he make such an affirmation?"

"What do you people want?" Aunt Priya said irritably. "You're annoyed if someone promises to be good to Sita. And you're also mad if one sees this as a business transaction—what is so bad about that, I don't know. At least they are being honest about the expectations. If you only want to criticize, it is not going to help."

"Let's see what else there is," Papa said. "Let's all calm down." He grabbed a letter from the top of the pile. "This one is a captain of a cargo ship."

"Oh, that sounds nice. Sita will get to see so many countries," Aunt Priya said.

"Who knows if the wives can travel with the husbands? Most of these sailors have a wife in every port," Papa grumbled.

"You know the old-fashioned way was the best—when people matched horoscopes and decided who got along with whom. You know, like they say certain zodiac signs are more compatible with others."

"Well, we don't believe in that," Aunt Rita said disdainfully. "What about this one? He says he is a computer engineer. He lives with his parents and runs the family business." In a lower voice she said, "He is 38 years old. Why does he still live with his parents?"

Uncle Vijay leaned over, popping a shirt button around his middle, "Oooph!" he said, "Ate too much. Food was very good. Here, give me a few of the letters and I'll sort through them." His pudgy hands, the backs of which were covered with curly, springy, hair closed on a small pile of letters. "Oh look! This is a good one!" Sita saw the gleam in his eye as he read, "This one is a doctor! Oh, but he is not even five and a half feet tall," he said in a lower voice. "That would never do. Sita is so tall," he said wistfully. He turned and looked at Sita again, as though mentally trying to shrink her down so she could marry the doctor, and live happily ever after.

Ramu dada who had been quiet for a long time said, "This one looks good, has a good job." Then Sita heard him comment, "but he comes from a conservative, vegetarian family. Sita will not fit in."

They kept the conversation going, and kept talking about Sita as though she weren't there. *How come everyone was so sad just because she did not have a husband? Why were they so preoccupied with the boy's background? What did it matter who his parents were, and what his grandparents had done for a living. After all, wasn't this supposed to be the land of opportunity, and if you worked hard, wasn't the sky the limit?*

"Why Mom, why do we have to care about the ancestry so much?" she had asked.

"You won't understand now, but people act a certain way because of who they are, but also because of what their family is like."

"How?"

"Look at you," Mom exclaimed. "You're an educated girl, exposed to new and different ideas at work, but you know your father and everyone in your family, have expectations of you. You won't forget that. Will you now?"

"What expectations does my family have?"

"Well, you're not going to run off and marry a guy that we don't like."

Sita fell silent. *What if she did? Suppose she met a guy at work, fell in love and wanted to marry him. She had no special person in mind, and this was just a hypothetical question. Was that possible? She had been raised to understand that she would be married by arrangement. So why was she getting confused now?*

"I know you couldn't hurt Papa like that," Mom said. "Papa would probably say nothing, but his silence would be more potent than words."

Mom would probably be the vocal one. And she would most likely beat up on herself, thinking that she had made a gross error in raising her daughter. Perhaps she had not treated her well, trusted her enough, been too strict with her, or not been strict enough, she would think. She would lay awake tormenting herself with what she had done wrong, and why their daughter had not trusted them enough to find her a suitable man. She would never blame Sita, only herself. That's what made it so hard to understand, but even harder to displease them.

"And what would family and friends say?" Sita heard Mom's voice breaking into her thoughts. "They have been preoccupied with your marriage ever since you turned twenty-one. Names of eligible bachelors had been given to Papa scrawled on scraps of paper, backs of envelopes, visiting cards—all with clippings of matrimonial advertisements."

That was true. How could Sita offend all these people? But then, could she give up her right to decide her future. Well, if it was any comfort, Mom had not chosen her own life partner, and neither had Grandma, whom they affectionately called Nani. And, it had worked well, for both of them.

"Family is very important," Nani had said when she had last seen her in India. "Believe me dear," she looked up from the big pot of curry she had been stirring, "an educated man from a cultured family will be less macho toward you. He will appreciate the arts, be open to new ideas, and so more receptive to your ideas as well."

"What do you mean by 'cultured,' Nani?" Sita asked.

"I mean just what I said. We want to find you a young man who likes reading, writing, and the fine arts."

"So you're looking to hook me up with an English professor?"

"No. Someone with brains and initiative, like a doctor or a businessman, but with the sensitivity of an artist," Nani said.

"You won't find that in any one person."

"You have so little faith in us child? We will surprise you then."

Sita hadn't seen Nani in three years. She loved the dear old lady. Barely 5' tall, she always wore freshly starched saris, stapled at the left shoulder with her favorite opal and ruby brooch. Her hair was poofed up in the front and rested at the nape of her neck in a small bun. Nani only wore white after Grandpa died, but to Sita, she looked beautiful. She wondered when she would see her again.

Sita caught a glimpse of herself in the wall unit mirror. Fleeting expressions of curiosity and exasperation chased each other in her kohl lined eyes. Here she was, all dressed up, and no one seemed to know that she was there. They continued talking about her as though she wasn't in the room. She felt a growing sense of frustration as she saw letter after letter being discarded. She wanted to say something, to express an opinion, but she stayed quiet. To show an interest in her marriage so openly would seem inappropriate, and very forward by the elders. After all, she wasn't desperate.

A little later, Aunt Priya fished out another letter from the pile. "Here is something good," she said with the air of someone who had haggled and won a bargain.

"This boy, just listen to this, he is:

-A computer engineer

-Good looking

-Tall, almost 6 ft.

-Comes from a small family

-Has no dependents"

Aunt Priya reeled off his credentials one by one, with the air of a magician drawing treasures from a hat. "What do you think of that? After a short pause she murmured, "Such a good catch, he is."

"Great!" Mom said, "Where does he live? Let's invite his family for tea." Mom still liked her afternoon teas. This was a tradition that had been left to us by the British, and something she would not let go off. On any normal day, tea was served with cookies, and occasionally, savory snacks like *pakoras* or knishes. But on a special occasion it became a lavish event, with four or five different kinds of sweets, and an assortment of mouth-watering snacks.

"That could be difficult," Aunt Priya said. "He lives in India. But that's no problem," she said in a rush of eagerness—like a used car salesman trying to downplay a defect in the car. "Why can't you all visit him over summer vacation?" She spoke as though she wanted everyone to step outside for a minute and go next door for a visit.

"I'm not sure I want to send my daughter so far away," Mom said.

"Who said anything about sending Sita anywhere?" She snapped her fingers. "Once they are married we'll bring the boy here, in a flash."

"We'll have to think about this," Papa said. "My daughter doesn't need to go chasing after a man. And then who knows, he may be just after a Green Card to get to the US. Why doesn't he come here for a visit?"

Sita smiled discretely at the way Aunt Priya contorted her brows probably thinking what to say next. *Aunt Priya would probably have to build another elaborate scheme, and go through the same ritual of consulting everyone in the family, and it would take time. She was safe!*

Aunt Priya had stopped talking. Her brows were still pushed together as she thought of a new plan. *Just like a spider trying to build its web without a thread in sight, Aunt Priya was not to be deterred in her desperate desire to find a suitable match for Sita.* After just a slight hesitation, Sita noticed her brows relaxed, and a new scheme was formed. She braced herself as Aunt Priya said, "Sita is so fond of Nani, why doesn't she just take a trip to India and visit some old family and friends, and maybe the boy can be seen too. What do you think Sita, would you like to see your grandma, and catch up with some of your old friends?"

For the first time, everyone turned around to look at her. "I'm not sure I have enough vacation," Sita stuttered. She had never expected Aunt Priya to put her on the spot like that.

"Well dear you can find out on Monday, can't you?" Aunt Priya said. Sita could tell she was beginning to lose her patience.

"And if they don't give you vacation, just quit. After all, what can be more important for a girl than her marriage?"

"Sita won't want to quit her job," Mom said. Aunt Priya looked angry and clicked her tongue in exasperation. She began putting the letters away, "You people don't know what is good for you."

Aunt Rita had been quiet for a while, and Sita could picture the wheels in her head turning. She too, was probably looking for a diplomatic way to tell her to go to India so she could meet more Indian boys. Sita looked at her suspiciously.

"Didn't you get an invitation for Renu's wedding? Maybe you all can go for that. That should be fun. Sita, what do you think? There's no pressure in that, is there?"

Hmm, Sita thought. *Aunt Rita probably knew that the boy's family would be there. She must have everything planned in her head already. Weddings were the time when so many young people came together, a God sent opportunity for a match maker.*

"There is no pressure in going for a friend's wedding," Ramu dada said jumping on the bandwagon. "We all know how Sita gets when we talk about her marriage. But why should she object to go to her best friend's wedding."

"So it is decided then. You all will go for Renu's wedding in July," Priya Aunty said.

"It's not a bad idea," Papa murmured. "We have known Renu's family for so long. Then if something good comes out of it, well and good, otherwise it will be just be nice to meet old friends and make new ones. I must find out more about this boy's family and research this fellow's background."

Sita saw Aunt Priya looked happy again. "Oh I know it is a good idea," she said. "I'll get to go to India too. See, I knew this was a great idea, getting everyone together to discuss things. After all there is nothing more important than family."

Chapter Six

Monday morning dawned bright and clear, and Sita dressed hurriedly, looking forward to going back to work. The haven of an impersonal office was just what she needed to get away from the chaos of nosy relatives. They meant well she was sure, but today, she didn't have to deal with them. She would forget about her personal life in the mound of papers that overflowed from her inbox, and the never-ending stream of e-mails that invaded her computer every day. She would answer them all today quite gladly. There would be questions about the print run of an issue, when would a particular issue be published, when would the author get galley proofs, why was the charge for printing in color so high, what was the cost for reprints. Then there would be other questions from authors who wanted to make last minute changes, there would be requests to see final proofs before the issue went to press, and so on and so forth. Hopefully there would be no complaints; no disaster such as the one there was last week when "Clinical Trials on the Breast" printed as "Clinical Trials on the Beast." The Editorial office went into a rampage and an irate managing editor had screamed, "What the heck goes on at the typesetters! Are you people blind or brain dead?"

There were other e-mails that would also be there—mostly those giving instructions, or making announcements. A computer training class had been scheduled for next week, a new feature had been added to the production tracking system, a new code must be learned, and new hot keys must be memorized to enhance speed and accuracy of routine coding features.

Coding manuscripts could be quite tedious, but today was a good day to get involved in the details of SGML codes and to get her mind off marriage. She quickened her steps as she entered the office building. The impersonal gray floors, people dressed in business suits who smiled their fake smiles and said, "Have a nice day," walked briskly, smiled falsely, did not know, or want to know the personal life of their co-workers, were a welcome distraction, and she found comfort in her workplace.

Enroute to her fourteenth floor office, Sita made her routine stop at the *Ladies Room*. Roz was there, looking three shades darker than she had on Friday.

"Had fun at the beach? That's some serious sunburn," Sita said.

Roz winced uncomfortably. She wore a black mini skirt that showed long slender legs that seemed to go on forever, until they ended in big clumpy shoes with 4-inch heels.

"Are you okay?" Sita asked.

"Yes, except for my back."

"Hurt it?"

"Well, I sort of did—got a tattoo. Want to see?" Roz lifted her white shirt from the waistband of her skirt. A bright yellow sun tattooed on her back stared back at Sita, with the name *Sonny* scrawled below it."

"That's nice," Sita said averting her eyes so Roz would not know she was lying.

"Yeah, isn't it?" Roz's pearly white teeth showed from beneath her maroon, almost black lipstick when she smiled.

"They didn't quite get the sun to a bright yellow. I'm going to go back again and tell them to put more color. And look, do you like this?" Roz pointed to the hoop that embellished her belly button. "I got that this weekend too. Isn't it cute?"

Sita did not know what to say. The only kind of tattoos that she was familiar with were the peel and stick ones that Rohit bought for a quarter at the supermarket. Roz had two other real tattoos aside from the sun that emblazoned her back. There was one at the nape of her neck with something that looked like

Chinese writing, and a dark red rose on her ankle. As for the ring on her navel, Sita could never figure out why people endured so much pain for it.

Actually, the two, Roz and Sita were nothing alike. Sita wore knee length business suits and small pearl earrings. Roz wore short skirts, and rings on fingers, toes, and everywhere else. But they say opposites attract, and the two girls had formed a strong friendship.

"You look kind of down today," Roz said with the perceptiveness of a good friend. "Is everything okay?"

"Yes."

"It's not about my tattoos. I can tell you don't like them, but I know that's not it. So are you going to tell me?"

Sita hesitated for a moment, and then it all come out. How Aunt Priya and every other relative had been hell-bent on finding her a man, and how they had talked about the same thing all weekend long, and how she was now so terribly confused and didn't know what to do anymore. She wanted to forget about it all, but every now and again she had the nagging sense that she would have to deal with it sooner or later.

"And do you know how many possibilities Aunt Priya has lined up, it is so confusing," Sita said.

"They want to find you a man and you are grumbling! You are a lucky girl to have a host of people looking out for you. You don't have guys' names tattooed on your back, or go on strange dates."

"You don't either," Sita said in a low voice.

"You don't know what weird people I deal with. I went out with this really nice looking clean-cut guy who was well-dressed. He took me to this really nice lounge, with this really nice décor, and do you know what he did?"

"Bought you a really nice drink?"

"No. Uh, you're laughing at me now, aren't you?"

"Not at all," Sita lied. "What happened next?"

"He disappeared for what seemed like ages. I sat there nibbling at the bread, looking at my French manicure, looking at the run in my stockings, wishing I had some nail polish left over to use on the tear in my stocking, wishing he would come back, wishing I could get something to eat. Well, he eventually came back but he was totally out of it. His eyes were bloodshot, his speech was slurred, and he could barely walk.

"No! What did you do?" Sita asked.

"Told him I had received an urgent call and had to leave right away, and that I would take myself home." She paused, sighed deeply. "You are actually the lucky one. You have so many people looking out for you, and there's no chance of something like that happening to you. Wouldn't I just love to meet your Aunt Priya!"

Well, that certainly was an idea. It would be fun to see Roz and Aunt Priya together. They couldn't possibly get along. Or could they? That was something to consider, Sita thought as she hurried toward the conference room for the staff meeting.

Ms. Valentine sat at the head of the table dressed in a pinstriped skirt suit, a prim polka-dotted bow of her Victorian blouse rested just below her chin. No matter how hot it got, Ms. Valentine always wore the bow-tie blouse with its long sleeves buttoned at the wrist. Not a hair was out of place, and her finger nails were a bright white under the translucent nail polish she wore. You could see she gave a lot of attention to detail. The same attention she gave to every punctuation mark, to every html code, and to every editorial concern. She was the head of the editorial department. At the weekly editorial meetings she wanted to ensure that copyeditors and production managers were giving as much attention to the manuscript as she would like, and it was hard to forget the way she glared at her staff over horn-rimmed glasses.

"Today I want to talk about style guides, why we need them, and why some are better than others." She peered over the rim of her reading glasses and frowned at the crew of production editors who stared back, bleary-eyed over their morning cup of coffee. They had all asked for the meeting to start at 9:30 to give them a few minutes to settle in, but Ms. Valentine had been unrelenting.

"Punctuality is the key to success," she said, enjoying the cat and mouse game she got to play, pouncing on unsuspecting employees if they were a few minutes late. "If you can't get here on time, then how can we expect anything else from you?" She always made it a point to stand behind the side door to confront any late newcomer who thought they could manage to sneak past her.

"A book or a monthly journal needs to be consistent in its usage of terms, punctuation, capitalization, hyphenation, spelling, and editorial preferences. So we must have a good style-guide. The more specific the guide, the more examples it includes about how to handle all of the above, the less chance for errors."

Her staccato delivery of this monologue was like drops of water being splattered on overheated oil that made the copyeditors hiss and sizzle in indignation at the way they were addressed. Some tolerated her out of respect for her level of expertise. Others had simply learned to tune her out.

"Style guides are important to everything," Roz interjected. She made a sweeping gesture with her hands. "They are important to editing, important to living, important to dressing. I could never wear black shoes with a navy blue skirt. There's no style in that." Everyone smiled except for Ms. Valentine.

Ms. Valentine took off her glasses, that now hung over her flat chest by what looked like a steel cord. The cord served the dual purpose of holding her glasses, as well as holding every emotion, all feelings, particularly feelings of happiness, in check. On the rare occasions that she smiled, her thin lips seemed to disappear into her face giving her an even more grotesque appearance. Today she was not smiling. She said, "Just as Roz can't wear black shoes with a blue dress, we cannot have a series comma, or hyphenate particular words, if that is not the style. We have to establish what Roz would call a "dress code" for our journal. That is not to say another journal will not have a completely different set of rules, just as another person would see nothing wrong with wearing black shoes with a navy skirt. Therefore, we need to establish what categories to use when developing this style guide. Your point of reference should of course be the *American Medical Association* guide, or *Words into Type*." She spoke without stopping as though she knew that if she paused, the crew would probably tune her out. Her staccato voice was the only one heard in the conference room. She spoke like an express-train, and her speedy delivery was already a blur to her half-awake colleagues.

Ms. Valentines started talking about the categories in a style guide and Sita's mind started drifting.... Involuntarily, Sita's thoughts turned to Aunt Priya and the categories she used in her husband hunt. *The boy had to be from a similar background, with similar interest in food and lifestyle, have a good job, make enough money, come from a small family, have an appreciation for the fine arts....*As hard as Sita tried to keep her personal problems out of her work, thoughts of Aunt Priya and her relatives invaded her mind and called for attention. Random ideas, and random categories competed for attention. Like kindergarten children in Rohit's class, all demanded attention at the same time. *What attributes in a husband were important to her? What categories did Roz use,* she wondered. *Why was this pretty, outgoing girl having a hard time finding a nice man? It would be neat to sit her down with Aunt Priya,* Sita thought. She smiled at the thought of the two women together. Then she started thinking about all the shopping she had to do before she went to India and tuned out Ms. Valentine completely.

Sita had to put together her shopping list. She wanted to be able to buy things for everyone. What about a camera? What about a television? Free trade had been established so the import duty would not be too high on televisions, video recorders and the like. Their next door neighbor had asked for a camcorder. "It must be SONY," they said. "No other brand."

"Okay," Papa had said, thinking perhaps that the older models had become a lot cheaper recently, and it would be possible to get a good one for less than five hundred dollars. He remembered the time when camcorders had first come out—they cost almost a thousand dollars. But the neighbors were well-versed about the latest models in America. "We want a digital camcorder," they announced. "If you can get it for the equivalent of twenty-two thousand rupees, or about five hundred dollars at that time, we will give you the money in Indian currency here," they said. Papa had looked surprised. Even *he* had not thought to buy a digital one, and was quite content to use one of the older models. "I'm not sure the newer ones would be as cheap," he said. "Then what about a laptop?" they asked. *That would have the same problems,* Sita thought. *Now everything was available in India at a price. Perhaps we should buy some little gadgets? How about a vegetable chopper for Nani? Perhaps she would like a blender better? But then, would Nani say the vegetables taste different when cut with a knife? The last time she had taken a microwave, she had said the food tasted better when it was warmed on the stove, and not to bring anything. She said it in a nice way, not critically, but Nani was the dearest, sweetest person in the whole wide world.* A light bulb went off in her head. *Bingo! She knew what she what she would buy. She would buy her electric heaters. Nani was always cold, and so was Reema Aunty. The temperature never fell below 40 degrees in the winter, but because the houses were not heated, and it was often rainy and damp, it felt a lot colder.*

Reema Aunty always sat in the living room with a hot water bottle on her lap. *A heater would be so much more sophisticated. It would be a lot cheaper too than other electronic items.* She could see her sitting by it, resting her knitting on the enormous shelf of her bosom as she warmed her hands. *So she would buy a few heaters, perhaps a few watches, and maybe some cosmetics. Everybody was still crazy over "foreign" things—anything made overseas, even if "foreign" was not always better.*

The meeting was coming to an end. It was almost 10:00 AM and people were getting more involved. They asked questions about the Cap Coding manual which listed all the coding rules for the web product. Sita's mind drifted again, and she thought the first thing she needed to do when the meeting ended was to put in her application for a two-week vacation. She would tell Ms. Valentine that she was going to India to attend a wedding. *If only Ms. Valentine knew Sita was going husband hunting!*

Chapter Seven

Aunt Priya was coming up the worn linoleum stairs. Sita could tell from the split-splat sound of her flip-flops. Sita saw she was clutching something in pastel colors under her armpits.

"Look what I bought today?" She pulled out the pink pastels from her armpits and waved them in front of her. She paused at the top of the stairs to catch her breath and waited for Sita's reaction, "Nice eh?" she asked.

"Yes, but aren't saris cheaper in India, why not wait and buy them there next month?"

"These are synthetic, can't you see? No need to iron. Just wash and wear. You won't want to spend your time ironing 6 yards of cloth when you want to be going about having fun."

You can get synthetics in India too, Sita thought. Rather than argue with Aunt Priya she asked, "What about the servants? Can't they help with ironing? Labor is cheap in India. Everyone has servants. What happened to Durga who use to sit under the mango tree down the block and charged a buck a piece for everything she ironed?"

"Oh ho," Priya Aunty said disdainfully, "you think Durga is still there? Well, she's not. Her son went to Dubai and started earning in foreign exchange. Now he sends money to his mother. Durga doesn't have to sit outside in 100 degree hot weather to iron people's clothes. You haven't been to India in so long, you don't know that times have changed, and you understand nothing. C'mon let's go shopping today. I think you should buy a couple of these saris, but if you don't want to, let's see what else we can find to take to India. And then you promised to drive me to Rohit's baseball game."

"Well actually, Roz is coming over today," Sita said gently.

"Who's that?" Aunt Priya knotted her brows and rolled the name around in her mind to try and match a face with the name. "What sort of name is Roz? Is it South Indian?"

A different name could be explained away as South Indian. This way of rationalizing was not unusual. India was a large country with so many different dialects and differences in food so that sometimes one part of India felt like its own different country. There were times when the Sikhs in India thought they were so different from everybody else in the country and wanted their own state called Sikhistan; and the Nagas, a tribal group in Eastern India were so distinct from everybody else, that they called their area Nagaland. South Indians too, saw themselves as very different from the North. Sometimes they said they were the authentic Indians, undefiled by Aryan invasion. North Indians thought they were better because they were lighter skinned. South Indians said that was because they had intermarried with the foreign Aryans who invaded North India."

"So, is she South Indian?" Aunt Priya asked again.

"No she's American." Aunt Priya's eyebrows shot up squishing her lined forehead against her hair.

"She's real nice," Sita said.

"And you would rather go out with a white girl than go shopping with me, or go to Rohit's game? Oh well, have your way." Aunt Priya grabbed the diaphanous pastel saris and got ready to waddle back downstairs.

"Aunt Priya don't go! Roz will come with us to the game. She likes kids. She loves baseball...." Her voice trailed away, interrupted by the insistent ring of the doorbell. "She's here now...."

Sita hurried downstairs, hoping against hope, Roz had the sense not to wear a mini skirt or the belly-button ring.

"Hi" Sita said brightly. Her eyes scanned Roz's attire. There was no exposed skin, and Sita heaved an inward sigh of relief. Roz was adequately covered up in hip-hugging jeans and a denim jacket. *Thank heavens! she looked okay to introduce to family. Aunt Priya was probably waiting upstairs to scrutinize her.*

Sita was right. Aunt Priya had made herself comfortable in the living room. The saris were in a heap by her side, and she sat with her chin in her hands, pretending to watch television. Even when both girls walked in, she kept her face firmly planted in her hands as though to prove she was not the least bit curious. She turned her head briefly to acknowledge Roz's greeting, and then returned her gaze to the television. Sita noticed that all the time she was pretending to watch television, she was following Roz from the corner of her eye, no doubt taking in the tight jeans stretched across the well-endowed figure, the four inch high platform shoes, and the black nail polish.

Completely unaware of the scrutiny, Roz flopped down on the couch next to Aunt Priya, and stretched her long legs in front of her. Her jacket parted from the waistband of her jeans to show the belly-button ring that glinted seductively in the morning light. At first all Aunt Priya could do, was to sink her head deeper into her hands to keep from staring long and hard. Then as though this was just a prelude to the opening act, Roz decided to take off her jacket so that the big bright sun tattooed on her back seemed to jump out and demand attention. Aunt Priya could no longer confine her chin in her hands. Abruptly she released her face and stared unabashedly at the yellow sun. *Clearly,* Sita thought *Roz had gone back to the tattoo parlor to have the color brightened.* It was a brighter yellow than Sita remembered, and had been fiercely outlined in red.

"Sita," Priya Aunty looked her straight in the eye, "I need to talk to you." She took her time easing herself out of the chair and gathering up the saris. She glared at her niece making it clear she wasn't happy with the company Sita kept. Sita could sense the words rumbling in her throat, longing to burst out, telling Sita what she thought of Roz. *You will get strange ideas in your head if you mix with people like this. Better have friends of your own kind....* But Sita was spared this lecture because of the sound of thumping feet. Rohit was charging up the stairs, probably taking them two at a time. His shoelaces were untied, and he almost tripped over them.

"Guess what," Rohit said, "I'm going to Peter's house after the baseball game." He flung his school bag on the floor. "Peter said if I went to his house we could go swimming together. I already packed my things in the school bag." He pushed the blue *Thomas the Tank Engine* school bag on the floor with his toe, and flung his *Scooby Doo* jacket on top of it.

"Now wait just a minute," Aunt Priya exploded. "You can't do that. You are going shopping with me. Who is this Peter boy? You can't go there. I've told you so many times I cannot take you to people's houses."

"You don't have to take me. Peter's mom will pick me up after the game."

Aunt Priya slapped the table. "You cannot go." Rohit's face puckered and his lower lip curled downward as one big tear slid down his face. Aunt Priya sat down. She put the saris down on the kitchen table after wiping it quickly with the palm of her hand. "Come, come," she said feeling at a loss for words. "Don't cry." But once Rohit started crying, there was no stopping him. The first tear was followed by a steady stream of tears that washed down his face. Hearing the commotion Roz walked into the room.

"What's up sport?" Roz crouched down to be eye level with Rohit.

"Who're you?"

"I'm Sita's friend. Give me five." She raised her palms in high-five.

Rohit wiped his eyes with the back of his hand, and slapped down a hard high-five.

"Wow! You've got some real power there. I hear you're quite a slugger on the baseball field. Can I come watch your game today?"

"Sure, how do you know I have a game? Wow! that's a neat tattoo you have on your back. I want a big one too. But I don't want the sun. Maybe I could get Taz, the Tasmanian Devil?"

"Well if your Mom lets me, we could go to the supermarket and get you one," Roz said, "but you must listen to what Mom says about everything."

"I'll buy him one later," Aunt Priya said quickly, clearly not wanting hippie looking Roz around her son too much.

"Why don't you and Sita, how you say it, "hang out" today? You won't have any fun at a kiddy baseball game. No handsome guys there." She forced a laugh and tried to make a joke. "All of them are married men with little kids."

"Well, then maybe *you* could find Roz a guy, Aunt Priya," Roz said.

Aunt Priya's eyes bulged bigger. "Are you mad? Roz is probably not even looking for a husband."

"Oh, but I am. And I'll take all the help I can get," Roz said, looking her straight in the eye.

Aunt Priya clutched her saris and stared back. The response that began as a growl in the back of her throat turned to a bewildered croak, and she tried to cover it up by coughing loudly. "I don't know that I could find anyone that would suit you..."

Rohit broke the silence. "C'mon people," he yelled. "It's time to go. We'll be late for the game. I've got to show Roz that I can play."

When they got to the field, Rohit saw his team was already there. A small blonde kid wearing round glasses raced up to meet him. Aunt Priya being her usual over-protective self, waddled closer to see who her son was talking to.

"Hi Peter," Rohit said. "I can't come to your house today. I have to go shopping with Mom. Roz says I must always listen to Mom, and I can't make plans without checking with her first. I'll come some other time. Okay?"

Sita saw Aunt Priya staring hard at Roz. She squinted in an effort to decide whether she should like her, or not.

"What's up Aunt Priya," Sita couldn't resist asking. "You always told us not to judge a book by its cover. Now can I ask you to do the same?"

"What are you talking about?" Aunt Priya said.

"Remember when we did not want to meet Ramu dada, and you said we were judging people by their looks, and we had no right to do that. Well, aren't you doing the same? You are judging

Roz by how she looks. Get to know her, before you judge her. Your son likes her. Maybe you will too."

Aunt Priya shifted uncomfortably from one foot to the other. Instead of responding to Sita, she changed the subject quickly, hoping Sita would focus attention on Rohit. "Oh look, how handsome he looks in his uniform." Rohit had taken his batting stance, one foot in front of the other, adjusted the grip on his bat, and waited for the pitcher. His bat was poised over his left shoulder. He saw the ball coming, and took a gigantic swing at it, but did not connect. The ball sped past him, and traveled harmlessly into the catcher's glove.

"C'mon Rohit, you can do it," Roz yelled and Aunt Priya turned around to stare at her. Not to be outdone, she yelled louder. "Rohit, Rohit, Rohit, come oo…n." She clapped her pudgy little hands till they turned red. *If Rohit had been a bit older he would have been incredibly embarrassed,* Sita thought. Today, he was so immersed in his game that he probably didn't notice that everyone had stopped to stare at his mom.

Rohit got ready to bat again, but again there was no luck. The chanting which had risen to a crescendo stopped. "Strike two," the umpire yelled. The score was tied at three all. Rohit settled into his batting stance for the third time. He saw the ball leave the pitcher's glove, and hurtle toward him. He aimed, and swung at it. The ball popped up, and away. Rohit ran for all he was worth, pausing at third base because he saw the other team scrambling for the ball. He stood his ground.

"Way to go Rohit," Roz yelled.

"That's my boy," Aunt Priya shrieked.

"Yes, and isn't he something!" Roz said oblivious to the long look Aunt Priya gave her.

Peter was up to bat. He was a good batter, and now it was up to him to score the winning run.

"Too bad Rohit won't have the chance to score the winning run," Roz said to Aunt Priya. Aunt Priya smiled back politely. A moment later, a missed throw caught the back of Peter's helmet. He wasn't hurt, but his glasses were whipped off and lay broken at his feet. *Oh goodness,* Sita remembered, Rohit use to say *Peter was blind without his glasses.* She turned to look at the coach, but saw the other team was continuing to pitch. And before she could protest, she heard the thud of ball and bat connecting, and realized that Peter must have swung valiantly and got a lucky hit. He ran hard and heard the crowd cheer. He made it to home plate safely, and they won 4-3.

"You guys played real well," Roz said.

"My boy was so brilliant," Aunt Priya said, rushing over to Rohit to make sure she was not outdone by this new white girl.

"How about I treat everyone for pizza and ice cream?" Roz said."

"We were going to have the tandoori chicken special at my restaurant."

"Can we do both, please, please, pretty please, Mom?" Rohit begged.

"If that's what you want," Aunt Priya muttered.

"Cheer up Aunt Priya, we can do some shopping before we go down to the restaurant. It should be fun," Sita said. "Roz would love to try your tandoori chicken, and you two will get a chance to get to know one another."

"I really wanted to go swimming. It's so hot. Peter is going. Why can't I?" Rohit asked.

"You don't know how to swim." Aunt Priya said abruptly.

"I could learn…."

"Rohit's chicken. He's scared of water," Peter said coming up from behind. "And he's a crybaby too. Last summer he always stood by the edge of the pool. If anyone tried to get him to swim, he yelled like crazy."

"Rohit could race you, want to bet?" Roz said out of the blue.

"You got to be kidding. Rohit is never going to be allowed to go swimming."

All eyes were on Aunt Priya.

"What do you think?" Roz asked. "If you agree, we can go the Garden School pool for a few minutes. It's a private school, but in the evenings they open the facilities to the public for a five dollar per hour charge. It's right here. So maybe," Roz said, looking at Sita, "if you can get your Aunt to agree we can cool off for a bit, and then go for dinner."

"We will have to go back to the house to pick up Rohit's trunks." Aunt Priya said grudgingly. "Is Peter going to the same place to do his swimming?"

Peter nodded vigorously.

Soon Rohit was in the pool. Although he had jumped in bravely, now he looked scared and seemed to be in trouble. He disappeared under the surface and then came up gasping. He clung to the side rail, wiping his eyes.

"The water tastes yucky and my nose feels itchy. I can't breathe down there. It feels weird keeping my eyes open under water."

"He's a scaredy cat—told you, told you."

"Come Rohit, I'll help you," Roz said. Without further ado, she had stripped off her clothes and stood on the side of the pool clad in the skimpiest of bikinis.

Aunt Priya looked like she would faint.

Rohit listened as Roz said, "First let's wade across the pool, just to get the feel of being in water."

It was fun to push one's way in the water on a hot summer's day. When they reached the other side of the shallow end, Roz asked Rohit to hold the side rail and kick. This was a bit trickier. Oops! His back arched and he started sinking, the harder he tried to pull himself up, the lower he sank.

Sita heard Peter snicker, "He can't swim, he'll never learn."

Roz was telling him to put his face in the water. This took some getting use to, but it wasn't too bad. He found he couldn't take a deep breath under water. He tried it once, and water rushed in through his nose and mouth choking him. Breathing out was easy. He loved to watch the bubbles he made when he exhaled. Roz told him to float across the pool. He took a deep breath, put his face in the water, stretched his arms out, and kicked in scissor-like movement. Hey Presto! He was off.

"My boy learned to swim in one lesson," Aunt Priya said proudly.

"Peter you know, I could race you now," Rohit said.

"You must be joking!"

"I don't see why not," Roz said, "but because today is your first day, let's just put swimming floaties on you."

"That's not fair," Peter wailed.

"So then, how about both of you wear floaties?" Roz asked getting out of the water, quite oblivious of the people who had turned round to stare appreciatively at her. She wore a tiny pendent that glinted seductively between her breasts. Roz seemed completely unaware of the effect she was having. "Come I'll put on the floats for both of you," she said to Peter and Rohit. "That way if you get tired, you will stay afloat."

"Put some clothes on," Aunt Priya snapped.

Roz smiled sheepishly. She saw the lifeguard staring her down and blushed. Then she quickly pulled on her t-shirt, uncaring of the two wet splotches on her chest where the wetness of her bikini came through. She toweled herself hurriedly, pulled on her jeans, and sat down close to Aunt Priya.

"Thank you for teaching my boy to swim," Aunt Priya said brusquely. "I was too scared to let him try before today."

As Sita expected, Roz said "No worries—it was fun! This was a good idea, don't you think? Now we have built up quite an appetite for some good Indian food."

Chapter Eight

Rohit skipped along happily beside Roz, holding on to his new friend. Aunt Priya tried to waddle quicker, swinging her arms to keep up with Roz's effortless strides. She found her place alongside her son, so that all three took up the width of the narrow sidewalk in Jackson Heights. The three of them made heads turn—Aunt Priya, her four-foot frame wrapped around in a multi-colored floral sari, tugged at a four-year old who scampered along tall, denim-clad, model-like Roz. Sita walked behind the three of them and deliberately tried to maintain a distance so that she would not be included in the curious scrutiny of passersby. *Little India* as this area was called was a medley of Indian clothing stores, restaurants and electronic stores.

Rohit stared at the mannequins in the window wearing flashy Indian saris and plenty of gold jewelry. "People here dress funny," he said.

"They are statues, not people, and there is nothing funny about them. Let's go in," Aunt Priya said. She entered a tiny hole-in-the-wall establishment. The salesman gave a wide beetle-nut stained toothy grin, and proceeded to pull out one sari after another. "That one is nice," Aunt Priya would say, and the salesman would unravel the six yards, stand up, and with an expert twist of fabric, drape it on himself, and stand unashamed before the four of them. Rohit giggled outright and Roz smiled hesitantly. The salesman said "You have to see how the fabric drapes *baba* before you can pick something."

"He is quite right," Aunt Priya said. After she had made the poor salesman wear four or five saris, she picked one, haggled over the price, and tried to get out of paying sales tax. "Forty dollars!" she exclaimed when she learned the price. "I'll give you twenty-five."

"Madam twenty-five dollars won't even cover my cost."

"Very well, I will give you thirty-five dollars," Aunt Priya announced magnanimously. The shopkeeper refused. Aunt Priya argued. The shopkeeper said they were worth a lot more. Aunt Priya said he was trying to cheat her. Back and forth they argued like the pendulum of a grandfather clock that goes tick-tock with no intent to stop. But when the shopkeeper would not budge, Aunt Priya pretended she didn't care for the sari anyway, and got ready to walk away. She stood up, tucked her sari out of the way in a huff, grabbed her sari pleats and got ready to leave the small confines of the sari shop. The salesman called her back. "Madam I give you good price. Tell me how many you will buy."

"Let us talk about this," Aunt Priya said. She motioned to the others to sit down. "What about some coffee?" she asked Roz. Then without waiting for a response she lambasted the salesman for not showing any hospitality. "Not even a glass of water," she lamented. She motioned toward Roz, "Look, we have a foreigner with us. She is going to think we Indians are such inhospitable people."

"Oh I'm fine," Roz looked embarrassed. "I wasn't expecting anything."

Suitably chastened the shopkeeper yelled to his *Help* "*Oiy*, bring some Coca Cola for these people." Four bottles of coke on a brightly patterned, dented metal tray arrived. Rohit grabbed one quickly, and so did Roz and Sita. They sat there for another thirty minutes, watching Aunt Priya's haggling antics. Finally, she bought three saris.

"Got good deals," she murmured in satisfaction.

They walked down the sidewalk to look at more shops.

"My, isn't it dangerous to put so much gold in the windows?" Roz asked looking at all the jewelry. Made of yellow gold, the necklaces and bangles boasted of intricate designs, and each one was different from the other because they were all hand carved.

Some of the gold necklaces were encrusted with precious stones. Rubies seem to be the favorite.

"How do you like our jewelry?" Aunt Priya asked Roz. "This is real gold. It is twenty-four carat gold. What you get elsewhere, doesn't look this good."

"It's very nice." Roz said politely.

Sita pointed to a classy necklace with a tiny pearl and sapphire pendant. "I prefer the white gold. I think that would look good on me. It would cover the collar bones that seem to bother you so much, Aunt Priya."

"No Indian wears white gold. And if you ate right, you wouldn't have this problem of collar bones showing."

"I think the jewelry here is too expensive any way. Let us look at the electronic store," Sita said.

"I want to buy a heater for Nani" Aunt Priya announced. "Let's go there."

"I was thinking about that too, but it will be summer when we go, Aunt Priya," Sita said.

"It will be winter eventually," Aunt Priya retorted, "That is so typical of you. You are always thinking about the moment. You never think about the future. Ooof! What am I going to do with you? Not only do I have to find you a man, but I must teach you how to think, and do everything else for you too." She walked faster toward R&R Electronics, her arms swinging once again. Roz raised her eyebrows, unused to the sudden outbursts.

The sight of the diminutive multi-colored person striding down the street brought a smile to Sita's lips. *Why was it that no matter what she said, Aunt Priya could never make her angry for too long.* The three of them had to walk quicker to get caught up with Aunt Priya.

"Can you give me a quarter? Roz will take me on the horse," Rohit asked.

"What horse?" Aunt Priya clicked her tongue.

"The rocking horse. You put the quarter in. The music goes on. You get to sit on it and pretend you are a cowboy galloping down the street," Rohit said.

"It's a rocking horse. It goes nowhere."

She's putting her foot in her mouth again, thought Sita and sure enough Rohit had begun screaming.

"Oh I know it does. Yes it does." He grabbed on to an imaginary rein and charged around everyone in circles.

"You come with me," yelled Aunt Priya. Sita looked on. Aunt Priya had grabbed him by the arm and brought him to an abrupt halt. Rohit looked up at her with big black eyes. His lower lip curled down suppressing the yowl that Sita knew was welling up within him.

"Oh let's go and see if we can find some stick-on tattoos there, shall we?" Roz said to divert his attention. "I see all kinds of stuff in the store." She squatted down beside him. "There's the electrical stuff your Mom wants, but look there are vending machines. One with bubble gum, one with candy, and I see one with tattoos. Come on, let's hurry."

Rohit was happily occupied with Roz, and Aunt Priya was able to buy a heater for Nani, a cordless phone for Uncle, a portable television that worked with batteries, and four watches.

"Let us walk around some more," Aunt Priya said.

"What about me?" Rohit whined, "Aren't I going to get something more?"

"Oh. Over there on the pavement, I think they sell *Nike* shirts for three dollars. See that man sitting there," Aunt Priya pointed to a street vendor who had set up a make-shift table on the sidewalk and was selling his wares.

"What do you think of this Rohit—Three shirts for nine ninety-nine? I can buy you three. Not one, but three."

"Aunt Priya," Roz interjected, "those look fake. I don't think they will wash well. Look," she examined the shirt closely, "the *Nike* check is peeling off right here. It's not going to last."

"Hush! Let us pick one where the check is not peeling. Nine ninety-nine for three is a very good price. I am not going to leave these." She waddled over to the shoe store. "Look here," she announced excitedly. "They have *Nike* shoes in Rohit's size on sale for fifteen dollars. You know I paid almost forty dollars for them last year."

"Oh, but look it has a purple check," Roz said. "Everyone will make fun of Rohit and say he's wearing girl's shoes."

This time Aunt Priya kept quiet. "I don't want them to make fun of my boy," she agreed glumly. "I don't know why they are so particular about girl's things and boys things. Those were nice shoes. Do you know in New Jersey where I used to live before, I had all Indian neighbors."

"No kidding," Roz said.

"First they had a baby girl and then, a baby boy. And the boy wore pink for such a long time. People in the apartment building would tell her, "What a pretty baby girl," and she would smile and say, *thank you*. Why you have to care what other people think as long as you can conserve your money," Aunt Priya grumbled.

"But Aunt Priya," Sita said, "you can't do that to Rohit. He's not a baby any more. The kids in school will make fun of him."

"Why you have to keep saying that?" Aunt Priya looked annoyed. "I told you I won't buy the shoes." She walked away. "There are just so many hurdles you people put. Why can't small boys wear girls' shoes? What's the harm?"

"Listen to yourself!" Sita exclaimed, but Aunt Priya kept talking.

"I can't buy perfectly good cheap t-shirts which he only needs to play ball in, I can't put oil in his hair, or part it neatly on the side, I can't do this, and I can't do the other." She walked away quickly, looking annoyed and Sita knew better than to argue with her.

Roz and Sita stopped at a store window to check out an aqua *kurti*. It was like a long-sleeved tunic with white embroidery at the neck,

"That's pretty," Roz said. "Blue is my favorite color."

"You like that, really? I'll buy it for you," Aunt Priya said.

Sita knew her Aunt well. She knew Aunt Priya was irked by the strip of belly visible beneath Roz's denim jacket even though she never had the chance to voice her feelings. The aqua *kurti* would cover it nicely, and hide the nasty tattoo that had been so visible when Roz had squatted down to talk to Rohit a moment ago. She had seen Aunt Priya's eyes bulge at the renewed sight of the garish sun on this white girl's back. Now she was willing to spend money to hide it.

"This will look good on you," Aunt Priya said. "It is the same color as your eyes."

"That's not my real color," Roz said. She popped out the blue contact lens and laid it in the palm of her hand.

"See, that is why my eyes look blue."

Aunt Priya's gaze shifted from the pale blue circle in Roz's palm, back to Roz's face.

"Oh baba," she gasped, lapsing into Hindi. She stared at Roz, who now returned her stare with one brown eye and one blue one.

"Arrey baba, what you youngsters will do these days. Is all this to catch a man?" she said before she could stop herself.

"What do you mean?" Sita asked.

"Well, you know the American saying, "*Gentlemen prefer blondes*. Maybe there is one that says *Gentlemen prefer blue eyes*, too. I don't know everything about western sayings. But I know something," she said with her hands on her hips. "I wouldn't want to be in a man's shoes today."

"Why not, Aunt Priya?" Roz asked addressing her as "Aunt" for the first time. Sita saw that Aunt Priya noticed, but did not seem to mind.

"Everything is so false these days. Fake hair, fake eyelashes, now you are showing me fake eyes," she said.

"Even nails are fake, and they fall off."

"Nails fall off?"

Sita said, "She must have seen nail tips come off."

"You can call it a *tip*. To me it was a nail. One minute this girl was eating a savory snack at my restaurant and I was admiring her long red nails and thinking why my nails didn't grow, and when I looked back again, one nail had fallen off and she was fishing it out of her coke! And do you know something—my natural nails were much better than hers. Hers were dirty and had chipped nail polish." Aunt Priya spread out her pudgy fingers, "At least what I have is real."

"What's your point Aunt Priya, why are you telling us this?" Sita asked.

"I'm not a man, you see—"

"We know," Roz said grinning.

"But I still think men would like someone who was more real. They might run after glamour girls, like our dog runs after the ball that is thrown, and is moving, and ignores the one right next to him. Or like your friend's kitty that likes to chase after the ball of yarn that is unraveling, but ignores the one right next to it. Men will chase after what looks glamorous, but once they have it...."

"It becomes a whole different ball game, eh Aunt Priya?" Roz commented.

"Uh huh. But you must not give up hope," Aunt Priya looked at Roz pointedly. "No need to go all crazy trying to attract attention either. Balance is the key to everything."

"You promised me pizza," Rohit whined. "Aren't you going to get me some? You promised. Liar, liar, pants on fire."

"Aunt Priya is one allowed to eat other food at your restaurant?" Roz asked.

"You don't have to come to my restaurant Roz," Aunt Priya snapped. "Eat what you want anywhere. You owe me no favors."

"All I was trying to find out was whether I should go buy Rohit his pizza, and he could eat it at the restaurant while the rest of us eat Indian food."

Roz and Rohit went off to buy pizza. Aunt Priya stared hard and clicked her tongue, "Why does she wear such high heels?"

"What's wrong, Aunt Priya?" Sita asked.

"She's reducing her selection of husbands by four inches wearing those things."

"You mean because she towers over most men and won't settle for someone shorter?"

"You got it!" Aunt Priya said, snapping her fingers in a rare use of an American expression.

"So tell her," Sita said.

"I will. Over a tasty dish of tandoori chicken, I'll tell her everything she's doing wrong. And you'd better listen up missy. You should be able to pick up some tips too."

Roz returned soon, balancing on the four-inch heel stilts. Rohit, grinning from ear to ear followed close behind. Roz had bought him an Italian ice, and the little boy had decided to eat his ice before the pizza. The rainbow colors of the ice stained his lips, and dripped down his chin. Unconcerned he wiped the drip with the back of his hand, and then wiped the stickiness on his pants.

"*Arrey baba*," Aunt Priya gave him a crumpled tea-stained handkerchief, "Here wipe your face and let's go inside."

Aunt Priya was visibly proud of her little enterprise *Little India,* and boasted about it being the best in the area. The smell of spices hung in the air, and the gentle strum of Ravi Shankar's Sitar played in the background. There were quite a few people there, and no shortage of white faces, Sita noted.

"See how my food makes everyone happy. You can order things *mild*, *medium*, or *hot*. For $9.99, you can partake of the lunch buffet, and see what a wide variety there is to choose from," she said with a sweep of her hands. "Come let us sit down and eat. Rohit can miss the feast and eat crumbs of his pizza."

"Look," Aunt Priya said to Roz. "See that man with the curly hair. Isn't he handsome? Blue eyes, blonde hair, match so well with your brown eyes and brown hair."

"Aunt Priya!" Sita said, shocked at this blatant matchmaking.

Roz blushed crimson and choked on a piece of tandoori chicken.

"He's short," she spluttered.

"Aha, so you noticed him too. And if you took off those shoes, he'd be taller than you."

"I like my shoes," Roz said indignantly. "I can't wear flats. My feet hurt. Besides I like how these look, and I am not changing that for any man."

Aunt Priya picked the chicken bone clean of the last bit of meat. "Why are you so stuck on shoes?"

"Uh."

"To find yourself a man, you have to get out of the little square box. You must not restrict yourself in this way. You must clear your head of too many details about looks," she said. She attacked her chicken with a fork, jabbed at it as it slid across her plate. "I will use my hands," she said. "Only two things are required to make a match."

"Good appetite and great food?" Roz quipped.

"You must have some similarity in interest, and where you have differences, you must agree to disagree. Never look for a soul mate, or another person to complete your life. Look within yourself to see how to make life more complete with another person. Now, Sita is a different matter. I'm choosing her husband because she knows nothing," Aunt Priya said between mouthfuls of tandoori chicken.

"What?" Sita exclaimed. "I will make the final decision. You always said I could."

"Okay, okay...why do you get worked up over everything?" She looked at Roz and said, "For Roz I'll keep a look-out when we get back from India."

"So Aunt Priya you think I will never find a soul mate?" Roz asked.

Sita noted that Aunt Priya did not miss a beat.

"Never say *never*, but don't throw away what life brings you, dreaming of one."

Chapter Nine

"Tomorrow we are going to India?"

"That's right, Rohit." Aunt Priya replied, trying to pull her bulging suitcase together. "Rohit can you sit on it, and then maybe I will be able to close it." Aunt Priya pushed down with her elbows and added her weight to his, so she could fasten it. "There you go," she said. "We did it."

"Careful the hinges don't break," Sita said, when she saw them struggling with the suitcase.

"Everything is good," Aunt Priya grinned in satisfaction. "Give me the tickets. I'm so glad I made friends with the Indian travel agent. He got us a good price. Much better than what you can get if you buy direct from the Airlines. You see, these travel agents buy tickets in bulk, and they get a good deal from the Airline so they can pass the savings on to us."

"Only eight-hundred dollars for a round trip ticket to India is really good," Roz agreed. "Last month the company paid more than a thousand bucks for a round trip ticket to California."

"Don't talk so much about business trips when you go to India. People won't like that a young girl like you travels alone."

"But I…." Sita began, when Rohit interrupted and said, "Shall I get you the orange tape you like to decorate your suitcase with when we travel? What about you, Sita? Want some?"

"I think I'll pass," Sita said quickly, remembering Aunt Priya's colorful clumsy-looking suitcase.

"Do what you want, I'll just find my suitcase quicker than you will."

"Let's go," Sita said, anxious not to get into an argument.

The three of them took a cab to LaGuardia airport from where the Air Canada Flight to India would leave. Mom and Papa had decided to come a few days later, so it was left to Sita to manage Aunt Priya's bulging suitcases, plus miscellaneous pieces of hand baggage slung over her shoulder in plastic bags.

"Let's put everything in my carry-on luggage," she told Aunt Priya, relieving her of the numerous colored bags. "Let's get that trolley."

"Move," Aunt Priya said. "Thin girl like you will not be able to carry anything." Tucking her sari out of the way, she hauled the pieces on to the trolley, and barreled her way through the crowd. Her breath came in gasps as she struggled with the cart that squeaked along with its rusty wheel. She stopped suddenly, and winced when someone bumped into her. "Do you know," she said, "I did not bring my camera."

"Well, I have one in my suitcase," Sita said. "Let's go."

"No. Just let's buy a disposable one. We may need it soon." So they stopped at one of the airport shops.

"Give me one that will take pictures in the dark and comes with a flash," Aunt Priya said to the clerk who also happened to be Indian.

She picked one up, put it in a plastic bag, and rang it up. "That will be fifteen dollars," she said.

"What?" Aunt Priya barked. "I buy them for nine ninety-nine, everywhere else. I am not paying fifteen dollars."

"Sorry ma'am," the clerk said removing the camera from the plastic bag.

"How does an Indian girl like you, try and rob another Indian person?"

The clerk shook her head so that her long braid writhed down her back "Everything at the airport costs a lot more money than things outside," she said.

"Call the owner."

"He's not here."

Rohit tugged at her hand, and Sita too was anxious to move on. For the first time in her life, Aunt Priya had to accept defeat.

Angrily, she slapped down the fifteen dollars, "I'm not paying tax," she said, in her last ditch attempt to have final say. She snatched the camera from the store clerk and put it away. She didn't know that Sita took out the one dollar and change to cover the tax amount, so that the poor clerk would not be short at the cash register at the end of the day.

They moved along, attracting curious glances as they walked along with their odd-looking luggage. Sita was so grateful when they could finally get it x-rayed and tagged, and sent away on the conveyor belt to the airplane, so she was no longer embarrassed by it. Of course, Aunt Priya's bags were over the allowed limit, and she had to pay extra—but not before she haggled her way with the airline agent who, very gently but firmly told her, "Madam, I can't do that. I will lose my job." Always a supporter of the underdog, Aunt Priya said, "I don't want that to happen to a young girl like you." Without further ado, she emptied her purse of fifty dollars in singles. She took her time to count each bill before handing over the money reluctantly.

After the luggage was gone, the three of them had to go through the security check. Their jackets and handbags were emptied into a tray that took them through a screening device. They had to walk through a metal detector, and be searched by security personnel. "Spread your arms sideways," the woman told Aunt Priya running the detector around her arms and over her chest. Aunt Priya relented, but when the woman ran her fingers over her chest feathering her bra, Aunt Priya jerked away, "Why? Does your metal detector not work that you have to go digging in my blouse?"

"Just doing my job," the security guard said releasing her. Sita tried hard to distance herself from Aunt Priya. Once they were in the waiting lounge, she offered to go buy cold drinks and pretzels for the three of them, just so she did not have to sit next to her. Their Flight Boeing 732 would first go to Toronto. They would change there for a direct sixteen hour flight to New Delhi. She lingered near the coffee shop as long as she could, and was about to go in and look for souvenirs, but from the corner of her eye she saw both Aunt Priya and Rohit making their way toward her.

"What is taking so long? My boy is thirsty." Aunt Priya snatched up the cold drinks. Fortunately they didn't have long to wait after that. Their Flight was called and rows *M* onward were asked to get into line and keep their boarding pass and passports handy.

"What row are we in?" Rohit whined.

"We're in *F*," Aunt Priya said. "They want to fill up the back rows of the aircraft first so those people don't trip over us on the way to the rear."

"I wish they would hurry up."

The flight attendant in a dark green uniform, a crisp white blouse with a red maple leaf, the Air Canada insignia, welcomed them into the aircraft. Rohit wanted a window seat, so that's where he sat. He quickly fastened his seat belt and got ready for take-off. It took about an hour to get to Toronto, and soon they were hurrying through Canadian customs. Aunt Priya was the only one with an Indian passport, so she was stopped.

"Do you have a visa?" the ticket agent asked.

"Why you don't ask anybody else that?" Aunt Priya looked at Sita and Rohit who flashed their American passports and sailed through. "I am only passing through. I have not come here to live in your country, so I do not need a visa. Wait a minute," Aunt Priya said, "Is my luggage going straight through to India? I booked it straight through. Now some people are saying we have to get the baggage and check it in again."

Oh no, Sita thought, remembering the bulging bags with orange duct tape that she had tried so hard to distance herself from.

"No, it will go straight through. Just follow the signs to *Terminal Two* and ask the Air Canada personnel if you have further questions." Aunt Priya was starting to ask more questions and Sita quickly urged her to move along. She guided them to the right escalator that took them to *Terminal Two.* They got in line. This time the passengers were almost all Indian. There were young children, toddlers, and babies. Old people were being pushed around in wheelchairs. The old people did not speak a word of English, but were easily understood because there were so many co-passengers who spoke Hindi. The aircraft was really crowded. Sita sat next to a woman with a baby and a toddler.

"I need milk for the baby," the woman said to Sita. She spoke broken English so Sita asked the flight attendant on her behalf.

"I'll get it to you once we're in the air," the air hostess said. She was busy checking the carry-ons, and making sure everyone's luggage was stowed properly in the overhead cabinets, or neatly under the seat in front of them.

"Sure." Sita said quickly. She did not want to bother the woman who was struggling with some really heavy carry-on luggage.

"I need the milk now," the Indian woman said in Hindi. "When the aircraft takes off the baby's ears will hurt, and I want her to be sucking something."

Once again Sita called the air hostess. "She really needs the milk before take-off."

The woman sighed, but kept her professional smile in place. "Will be right back," she said. And she was. She handed the woman a bottle of milk.

The woman put a drop of milk in the palm of her hand and said, "This is too hot."

"There's no way I can make this cooler," The air hostess said calmly. "Just hold on to it until it gets cooler."

"Tell her to add some cold milk," Sita's persistent neighbor said. Sita wished she could change places with Aunt Priya and not have to deal with her annoying neighbor. Once again she asked the flight attendant for milk. Without a word the woman took the bottle, and came back with the milk at the right temperature. "We aim to please," she said, but her voice had an edge, as though she had meant to say something quite different.

The problem was resolved. Sita fastened her seatbelt and got ready for take-off. All through take-off, the baby was guzzling down milk, and was quite happy. She was quite a pleasant child and was gurgling happily. Sita even offered to hold her while the mother took the older one to the bathroom. The baby tugged at

Sita's hair and smiled up at her as though she had known her all her life. Then she found the light switch on the arm rest, and got quite a kick watching the light go on, and off. Rohit suddenly saw the baby and Sita getting along well together, and deposited himself in the empty seat next to her. Every time the baby turned the light on, he turned it off. She would turn it on and he would turn it off—*on and off, on and off,* over and over again. The little girl's lip curled down and she burst into tears. Once she got started, there was no stopping. Sita looked down the aisle anxiously and hoped the mother would come back.

"What's the matter, what happened?" the mother barked accusingly as soon as she was close enough. Even though Sita had not done anything wrong, she felt bad. She handed the baby back to her mother. Rohit pouted when he had to move. He found himself a place on the floor to play instead. "Get up from there," Aunt Priya commanded. "The floor is dirty, and you are in everybody's way. Come here."

"Are we there yet?" Rohit whined as the Boeing continued its 16-hour flight to the subcontinent.

"Look… see …look down there," Aunt Priya said, pointing to the cottony puffs of clouds below. "See your plane is high above the clouds."

"This doesn't feel like a plane. It's just a roomful of chairs. And I'm tired of sitting," Rohit said glumly. "Those clouds are dumb. They are like beat up pillows in a pillow fight, and there is no pillow fight to watch. Besides those clouds they stick together, and cover up everything, and you can't even see what is happening below. This is boring, boring, very, very, boring. I want to go home."

"Want to play something?" Sita asked in response to Aunt Priya's imploring look. Whenever Aunt Priya didn't know what to do about something, her black eyes would get bigger until they bulged out of their sockets, to reach out and implore.

"Play with him," she begged.

"Want to play scrabble?" Sita asked. Her literary instincts got the better of her common sense. A four year-old who had barely learned to write the alphabet could have no interest in spelling games. And so, as one would expect Rohit said, "Boring. Everything is boring. I thought the plane ride would be fun, but most of the time you can't even feel you are moving. There's nothing to see outside the window except those dumb clouds."

"In another hour everything will change," Sita said. "Your plane is going to start the descent and your ears are going to pop. You're going to start seeing trees—first they will be patches of green, then they will look like little shrubs. And then the houses….do you know what they will look like?" she asked. Rohit shook his head, "They will look like little matchboxes. What do you think the people will look like?"

"I don't know," Rohit said opening his eyes wide, just like his mother.

"They'll look like miniature dolls."

"Smaller than me?" Rohit asked, drawing his legs up under his chin to make himself even smaller.

"Grownups are going to look much smaller than you."

"Wow! Do you have any gum? Roz said I must chew gum when the plane starts to land, otherwise my ears will hurt."

"Sure, what flavor do you want?"

"I want grape, apple and double mint"

"Aye, aye, Sir," Sita said with a mock salute. She rummaged for the three different packs of gum as the plane began its descent. They landed, and Rohit began bouncing up and down in his seat, restless to get out.

"Rohit, Rohit, we have to wait till the plane stops. If you keep jumping it's not going to stop."

Rohit stopped bouncing, looked at her doubtfully, but decided to stay quiet until it was finally time to make his way out from the narrow aisles. He ran out, glad to be able to stretch his little legs.

"Wait!" Aunt Priya shouted. But Rohit had already stopped. He cringed at the wave of hot July air that slapped everyone as they walked off the air-conditioned confines of the plane.

"Why is it so hot?" Rohit asked.

"It will get cooler soon," Aunt Priya said. "The monsoons will come soon. Monsoons are rainy weather," she said in response to his unspoken question.

"Oh dear Sita," Aunt Priya said, "Your *salwar kameez* looks so crumpled. Did you bring a change of clothes in the carry-on?"

"You're not serious. You want me to change at the airport! Don't tell me I'm going to be under scrutiny even here. Who's coming to pick us up anyway?"

Sita had wanted to travel in jeans, but Aunt Priya looked like she might cry if Sita wore jeans. So she had given in, and put on the *salwar kameez*. The voluminous folds of the pants were in fact cooler than tight jeans would have been, and the modest *kurti* that hinted at the curves had been freshly starched at the start of the journey, but was now patterned with cris-crossing creases at her rear and her belly.

"No, I don't have a change of clothes," she said abruptly. "Who is coming to pick us up?" She felt like a beetle under a microscope. She walked faster, and tried to get away from Aunt Priya.

The luggage was slow in coming, and looking back over her shoulder, Sita saw Aunt Priya cannon ball her way past everyone. Her diminutive figure a blur of color, she made her way toward Sita dodging the throngs of sari clad women, and men wearing polyester pants.

"Look Rohit, look," she said, pulling the four-year old in front of her. "Let's see if you can be the first to find mummy's luggage. Look for the orange tape. Okay? Let's see how quickly we do this. Then if Ajay is not here, we'll take a taxi and go to his house."

"We're going to Ajay's house?" Sita asked.

"Huh, I thought you would like to live in the house you grew up in," she said kindly. "Your Papa gave it to his brother when he moved away, but Ajay knows that little house will always be home to every relative who comes to India."

"And Rohit you're going to love it." She tugged his arm to get attention. "They have a big golden retriever. He is so friendly—too friendly." She tried to liven up her little boy who stood quietly twisting her sari round and round in his bony fingers. Rohit looked completely fed up with all this standing, waiting, and watching.

Finally, the rounder filled with luggage from their Air Canada flight. Aunt Priya's eyes lit up when she saw her bright orange taped suitcase. "See mine got here first," she exclaimed, heaving it off the belt.

Sita closed her eyes imagining the frayed leather belt break, and the suitcases erupt in a tangled pile of clothing, and perfume. She could imagine the attention that would attract, especially the heaters clattering out of the suitcase in close to 100 degree summer weather.

Sita's luggage, sans any orange tape was close behind. The next stop was customs. Customs was a breeze. After the open trade agreement came into effect, customs regulations were a lot less strict, and they sailed through the green channel toward the exit.

Ajay was at the airport, a shorter version of his more illustrious brother, but just as handsome. "Hullo, young man," he said to Rohit. "Want some chocolate?" He fished out a partially melted slab from his pocket. Rohit smiled. "I am your uncle Ajay." He pointed to his wife, a short fat lady, wearing bright red lipstick, and bright red nail polish on her talon nails. "That is your Aunt Sonia."

"Oh, nice little boy with cheeks like apples," the wife said, digging her red talons into his cheeks. "Come give me a hug," she pleaded. Rohit squirmed to be free from the loud, fat lady. He dropped his chocolate in the scuffle.

"Go away!" he screamed. "You're a mean person." He reached for his chocolate, but it was now squished under someone's foot. "I want to go home. I don't like it here."

"Hush sweetie, hush," Sita said picking him up. "There, there, now. You're very tired. Aunt Sonia wasn't trying to hurt you, she was just being friendly."

Rohit quietened down, but continued to sniffle and Sita carried him, grateful for the diversion. At least, now she would not have to make small talk with all the people who had come with Ajay. Ramu dada was there in his polyester pants, and Vijay was there with his shirt unbuttoned to his waist. Aunt Rita hadn't come, and neither had Nani. There were many other people Sita didn't know. She used Rohit as her excuse, and was able to get away from them all.

Sita struggled to carry all of his seventy pounds. She straddled him across her hip, and hurried toward the waiting Ambassador car.

Chapter Ten

"Why is it so hot?" Rohit wailed. Sita wanted to put him down and make him walk, but then she felt his warm, moist, tears and hugged him closer. His tears dripped onto her shirt. He wiped them off with the back of his hand, and dragged his grubby fingers stained with melted chocolate across his nose. He frowned at the sticky feel of snot, and hurriedly wiped them on his pants.

"Don't do that," Sita said, and his tears came down harder and faster. He squirmed to come down and Sita put him down gladly. They finally got to the white Ambassador car but there was no air conditioning and it was hotter inside the car, than outside. She hurriedly rolled down the windows, hoping for a breeze while they waited for Aunt Priya and Ajay to come. They looked around them. So many people lay stretched out on the sidewalk. Bodies snuggled close together, or simply grouped together, in a tangle of arms and legs. The hard stone pavement cooled by the night, was their only mattress and the countless stars on this clear night, their only cover. They slept peacefully, with no sleeping pills, or sleep aids, until their cover of night lifted, and it was time to wake up.

While Sita and Rohit waited, they saw some of the people get up and line up near a water tap. One man was already performing his morning ablutions. Clad only in a loin cloth, he crouched beneath the tap, letting the water wash away the sleep from his eyes, and then hurriedly moved away to make room for the next person. As the time went by, more and more people lined up near the tap, and Rohit wished they could move on.

It felt better once the car started moving. The dry, warm air was cooling to Sita's sweaty skin. The car moved slowly, crawling along buses, cyclists, and animals all sharing the same dusty road. "What's that?" Rohit asked pointing to a three-wheeler with a hood and no doors that spluttered alongside the other vehicles on the road.

"That's an auto rickshaw." Sita put her hands to her ears. "It's open on both sides so you can feel the breeze, but it does make an awful lot of noise."

"Look there's a cow," Rohit said. Sure enough, there was one ambling along the middle of the road, unmindful of the traffic snarl it created. It stopped smack in the middle of the street. Horns blared and tempers flared, as drivers tried to skirt around the cow, who had now decided to sit down in the middle of the street. Rohit grinned happily, loving every minute of the chaos. Perhaps one day, the volume of traffic would force the cows off the road. For now, everything about New Delhi traffic was chaotic. For one, the steering wheel was on the right side, and everyone drove on the wrong side of the road. If one wanted to cross an intersection and looked first to the left, then right, then quickly to the left again before moving, as one did in America, one was certain to crash headlong into oncoming traffic. Cars of every shape and size were on the road. Suzukis, Fiats, Hyundais, Ambassadors all competed for space. Vehicles came in all directions. Cars showed no hesitation in honking—their horns drowning the ring of the cycle rickshaw bell, the yells of the scooter driver, and the splutter of the moped. It was as if a giant's hand had collected all types of vehicles and tossed them helter skelter on the road, so that big and small, had to compete for space. The bicyclist carrying long steel poles wedged his way between a construction truck and a belligerent moped driver, who in turn, was trying to dodge past larger vehicles and worm his way out of the standstill traffic. Construction work was in full swing, so makeshift barricades diverted the traffic and squeezed it into even narrower roads, until one felt that it would be quicker to walk than to drive.

The air was heavy with dust and pollution, and a heavy layer coated all plants and trees, giving them a gray-green look. People seemed to be accustomed to dust storms. Street children ran around with dusty faces and matted hair, looking pleased as punch. They were completely unmindful of their tattered clothes that parted to show their private parts. Ajay was able to make some headway, and all was quiet. They passed row after row of houses, washed in what was once a light pink or light yellow paint. But now, last year's rain had washed the houses, sending smears of brown and black streaking down their sides.

"I want to stop at my sister's house," Ajay's wife said. "Just drop me off, and I will come back later."

"Sure." Ajay stopped at an apartment complex on Mall road. A series of speed bumps slowed their progress until they halted at a badminton court where some kids were having an early morning game. *They must do that every day because they were appropriately dressed in white shorts and sneakers, and were different from the street children,* Sita thought. Sita and Rohit got out of the car to cool off, and stood there until Ajay's wife waved for them to go away. Rohit still cowered behind Sita, worried the fat lady would reappear to pinch his cheeks in farewell.

"Let's go get a drink," Sita said. They crossed the narrow street outside the apartment complex and walked over to *Khanna's Grocery*—a makeshift store with a tarpaulin roof. A fan whirred ineffectively in the corner. People stood around to buy toothpaste, or soap, or other essential products like bread, butter, and cheese. There was one woman who was trying to make a call to America. Apparently, one couldn't just pick up the phone and dial, but had to come down to this little grocery store, and the owner would dial the number for you. At the end of the conversation—which everyone crowded around to hear, the shopkeeper would tell you how much you had to pay. This little store also sold bug spray, cold drinks, snacks, and chocolate.

"May I have two cokes please?" Sita asked in Hindi to the store clerk.

"*Chotoo*," the man yelled, calling his *Help*. A boy came down from his perch at the back of the store. He dived into a huge garbage can filled with ice and pulled out two ice-cold cokes.

Rohit's eyes lit up. "Can I have a piece of chocolate?" he asked Sita tentatively. Sita nodded, and *Chotoo* dived into the icy garbage can once again, tossing the butter and cheese out of the way until he found the pile of chocolate that was all jumbled together in the same garbage can.

"Let's just finish the coke here, so we can give the bottles back and get the deposit," Sita said. So they stood there, and Rohit thirstily guzzled down the coke. Sita stood nearby and tried to shoo away the flies with a rolled up newspaper. There was an open drain nearby teeming with flies, but no one except Sita and Rohit, seemed to care.

"Why isn't *Chottoo* in school?" Rohit asked suddenly. "Does he have vacation?"

"He doesn't go to school," the owner said. "Who will help me in the shop if he goes to school? He can learn all the arithmetic and counting he needs to know by working for me. I have no money to hire a person to work. Maybe when you're a big sahib you can call my boy over, and he will work for you."

"He's so lucky he doesn't have to go to school."

"You lucky," *Chottoo* said in broken English. "You are from America." Then lapsing into Hindi he told Sita, "I want to go to school and learn English so I can go to America too. Then I could help Papa even more."

All of a sudden Rohit was screaming, and yelling so loud that Aunt Priya came waddling out of the car.

"What happened?"

"I see a monkey," he screamed. "I see two. No there are more. See the baby hanging onto its mommy's stomach."

"Yes, yes, we see," Aunt Priya said sounding bored. "Let's go back to the car. I want to try and take a nap."

"There'll be more monkeys along the way?" Rohit asked his eyes shining. "Let's hurry." They drove for about forty miles, but the traffic was so slow it felt like a hundred. Finally, they were within sight of the house she had grown up in. The familiar yellow walls were now streaked with black where dirty rain water had smeared them. The grass was parched by the hot summer sun, and the burnt spots were the color of hay. The backyard still had the chicken pen, and in the early morning hours, the rooster crowed loudly as they rounded the red dirt driveway. The backyard wall still had the muddy circular imprint of tennis balls, where it had been punished by Sita's incessant practice before tennis tournaments, more than five years ago. The swings were still there, and so was the slide her father had built for her when she was a little girl.

"Look Rohit, you see the slide? I use to have so much fun with Nicky there." Sita said.

"Who was Nicky? The same dog we have now?"

"Yes. Ajay has Nicky's daughter Brandi, so you'll get to play with her."

"We often played *catch me if you can*.

"What's that," Rohit asked, his eyes gleaming in anticipation.

"Just what I said. I was about 8 or 9 years old and I would run up the slide steps. Nicky would follow behind me in hot pursuit."

"What's hot pursuit?"

"Oh, it just means to chase after someone real fast," Sita explained. "Then we would reach the top of the slide and Nicky thought she had got me, and I would slide down real fast. She would wait at the top and bark, and keep barking and barking, until dad came out to see what all the barking was for, and then she would slide down too. Then when she got the hang of it, we would keep doing it. When I got tired I would get on the swing to cool off. Nicky couldn't join, and she would stay down and bark and bark, getting more and more mad when I swung higher and higher, until my toes touched the leaves of the bamboo tree a short distance away."

"Wow," Rohit said. "Can I go on the slide?"

"Sure can," Priya Aunty said in a rare burst of American lingo. "And we are going to have your birthday party here too. Come, let's all go and meet Nani now."

"Yes let's." Sita scanned the doorway, looking for the familiar gray-haired lady she adored so much. She saw Nani's diminutive four foot frame. Dressed in an embroidered cotton sari, she looked as fresh as a daisy in the sweltering summer heat. Sita rushed toward her, outstretched arms dropped to touch her feet at first, in the customary sign of respect before she was swept into a tight embrace. She had to stoop quite a bit to be eye level with Nani. The little old lady with snowy white hair as soft as cotton balls, and arms as cushiony as a down pillow, held her close, and then at arm's length, to soak in the image of her favorite granddaughter.

"You look wonderful," she said before hugging and kissing her all over again. The maid who helped in the kitchen stopped chopping onions for the morning omelet and grinned from ear to ear, and her little brown face showed a display of pearly white teeth that gleamed bright against the brown skin.

"Namaste baby ji," she said, using Sita's nickname. It had been years and years since anyone had called her *baby ji* and it made Sita feel even more at home.

"Come let's go out to the verandah. It's cooler outside," Nani said. She shuffled out ahead of Sita. "I haven't seen Rohit yet. His birthday is coming up. I hope the monsoons come, and it gets cooler. We have invited a lot of people. They all want to meet you, Sita."

Oh no Sita groaned. "You're not going to try and match-make at this party too, are you? I thought I was going to be under scrutiny one time only, when Aunt Priya took me to see somebody's parents."

"*Beta*, marriage is an inevitable part of a girl's life, my child. When a young lady turns 21, all friends and well-wishers are going to try and help find a 'good boy.' What's the harm in that? Don't think about it so much. Just remember your Grandma will never allow anyone to harm her precious child. Come let's sit outside for a while before it gets too hot. The servants will put the luggage away, and the maid will bring us some lime juice. Then we can have breakfast."

Roma soon walked in with four tall glasses of lime juice. "Delicious," Sita said, savoring the tangy sweetness of juice as it slid down her throat, soaking away the dryness.

"Rohit, want to try lime juice?" Nani asked as the little boy walked in with the family dog Brandi in tow. "Come and give me a hug. I have not seen you for such a long time. Remember me?"

"No.... But I like Brandi," Rohit said, stroking the retriever who was almost shoulder high for Rohit. Brandi wagged her tail, and almost knocked down the lime juice on the low coffee table.

"Watch it, bad dog," Nani yelled. "Out! Get out of here—putting your nose in everything, and shedding hair all over the place. Bad dog." It was clear there was no love lost between them, and Brandi retreated under the chair with her tail between her legs. Rohit was close to tears, and hugged the dog close.

"Don't worry Brandi, you're not bad. Sometimes you do bad things, the *things* you do are bad, but *you're* not bad," Rohit said repeating what Roz had said to him a couple of times when he got yelled at for being a bad boy. "Get the difference, Brandi?" He held the dog's big face in his small hands and stayed down with the dog, talking in low tones. Brandi stared back at him with big brown eyes, as though she understood every word.

"Come Rohit, come out of there, and let's plan your birthday," Nani said anxious to make amends. "It looks like it might get cooler in time for your birthday." She looked up at the darkening sky, "Hope the rains come. Do you have a list of things you want for your birthday?" There was a clap of thunder, and lightning streaked across the sky. Were the monsoons finally here? Another clap of thunder was a joyful reminder that the sweltering heat of summer was over. The darkened sky was welcome relief from the blazing fury of the summer sun. The cement floor of the verandah no longer scorched one's bare feet. It was comfortable to stand in the verandah and watch the rain come down in sheets, and feel the refreshingly cool spray.

The servants' children ran out in the yard laughing, and yelping with joy. The damp ground was soon covered with small footprints; some foot impressions deeper than others. Soon there were little holes and puddles in the ground, filled with muddy, chocolate water. The children splashed merrily, their wet clothes covered with chocolate splotches of mud. Sita, Nani and Rohit stayed in the verandah until the maid came to take away the lime juice glasses and to ask how everyone would like their eggs—scrambled, fried, or hard boiled. "What is good?" she asked. She smiled proudly, saying perhaps the only three words of English she knew.

"Come let's go inside for breakfast," Nani said, and everyone followed.

The rain lessened momentarily. Birds with damp, ruffled feathers came out of their hiding places for a drink of rain water. Others flew around in search of earthworms and other food. The pedestal fan in the verandah whirred persistently. The breeze was cool, different from the dry, hot air it spewed out in summer. The sweet smell of damp earth assailed one's nostrils. The parched grass was coming back to life, and tips of green were now visible in the dry lawn. The wilting plants stood up a little straighter, a little taller, and were refreshed by the rain. The aroma of freshly roasted corn wafted in the breeze. Corn on the cob was a favorite during the monsoons. It's dry, spicy flavor, a perfect foil for the cool, damp atmosphere. Sita remembered women anxious to make a quick buck, who squatted on the sidewalk to sell roasted corn rubbed down with indigenous spices and lemon. They must be there today.

"Tomorrow is your birthday," Aunt Priya told Rohit.

"I know," Rohit said. His eyes shone, and he stood with both hands stuffed in his pockets like a little man. He was thinking about the presents he would get.

"I want to play in the rain," Rohit said, pointing to the youngsters outside.

"Those are servants' children. You must stay nice and clean inside." Aunt Priya said.

"I want to be a servant's child," Rohit said.

"Servants' children don't get presents," Aunt Priya said crossly. "Why don't you take Brandi and play with her for a little while? When it stops raining you can go out on the swings."

It rained most of the day, and Sita was content to stay indoors, catch up on all the news, and relax. The after effects of jet lag had just begun to set in, and she was content to sit down and have the servants serve her breakfast, lunch, and dinner, without having to lift a finger. She could see Aunt Priya was also enjoying this new found luxury.

Within a couple of hours, the long grey fingers of dusk enveloped the house. A single outdoor light illuminated the verandah. A variety of moths and bees buzzed and hummed, as they chased each other around the light. Mosquitoes breeding in the puddles of rain water buzzed around. The stars had hidden themselves behind the grey clouds that blanketed the sky. It was time to sleep.

"Rohit, Nani has made your bed in the verandah, go to sleep now," Aunt Priya said.

"In the verandah," Rohit echoed.

"The verandah is everyone's favorite place to sleep."

It was a lot cooler in the verandah than inside the house. The steady rhythm of falling rain was soothing to young and old alike. The persistent whirring of the fan, and the occasional croak of a frog, were the only other sounds to be heard.

The beds used here were quaint, made of a wooden frame, covered with rope, especially woven to comfortably accommodate the weight of a person without sagging. A hand made cotton mattress covered the rope base. Mosquito netting made of fine white mesh, covered the bed, tied to the four bamboo poles attached to the corners of the bed.

Sita heard Rohit say, "Sleeping in the verandah is just like camping out. C'mon Brandi, let's go. In a few hours it will be my birthday."

Chapter Eleven

Sita turned over on her back, wondering what had woken her up. It was still dark, and all one could hear was the drip-drop of falling rain. It seemed as though it was about to stop raining. *Just in time for Rohit's birthday,* Sita thought. She rolled over and pulled the sheet up to her chin. There was a slight nip in the damp dawn air, and she burrowed deeper into the thin cotton mattress to curl up prawn-like, to keep cozy and warm. It was hard to sleep anymore. Thoughts of tomorrow kept intruding and waking her up. She tossed and turned. It was almost as hard to shut out her fears as it was to ignore the strident call of the rooster in the early morning, or the crows as they cawed their morning greeting to the world.

"Early to bed, early to rise makes a man healthy, wealthy, and wise," Nani use to say. Well, she was awake early, but it was because she couldn't sleep. *What was she afraid of? Meeting someone a couple of times, maybe even just once, and then promising to love, cherish, and honor them for the rest of her life? Grandma had said she didn't have to settle for a man she didn't like. That was good. But she would still have to go through the meeting, and be inspected by so many strangers. She would have to pretend to be coy and demure, pretend she was having a good time, and put on her plastic smile at this birthday party.*

Sita stretched her lips sideward to practice her fake smile.

"Oh! This sucks," Sita said out loud. She put the pillow over her head to shut out the world. Even as a child, she had hated to get up early. Monday mornings were especially hard, and when the family rooster began his morning wake-up call, she told herself it was too early and kept sleeping well after the rooster had given up calling, and the crows had stopped cawing. She slept until the servants began cooking, dusting, and sweeping. Then she had no choice but to get up when Mom pulled off the covers so she would not be late for school. She lay in bed thinking of her life in this same house, years ago. She heard Rohit moving around in the bed. He must be impatient for his presents. *Just a little while more, and then I will get up,* she thought, snuggling against the cotton sheet.

Looking out though the mosquito netting, she saw Brandi had taken her place under Rohit's bed and was chewing on a ball. Later, she saw Rohit's bony little arm snake out of the mosquito net, pick up the ball and fling it. There was a scraping sound of claws and cement as Brandi hurried to scramble out from under the low bed. Sita saw Brandi sprinting down the lawn. She was back in a flash with her prize in her mouth. She set it down, and waited for the game to begin. She barked plaintively and then, longer and louder. When Rohit did not stir, Brandi picked up the ball, tossed it in the air then spun around in circles, barking all the time. Actually, that must have been exactly what Rohit wanted—for everyone to wake up and give him presents. Yet, when his plan worked he got scared, "Hush Brandi" he said, but to no avail. The dog kept barking until Rohit had no choice but to pick up the ball and throw it again.

"Has the dog gone mad?" she heard Aunt Priya say. "Why is she running in the rain like a lunatic?" She heard the bed creak when Aunt Priya got up. It was time for Sita to get up too.

Sita walked past Rohit's bed to go inside, and saw he had closed his eyes and was pretending to be asleep. The mosquito netting was untucked, and that was the only tell-tale sign that he had been wide awake and playing ball with Brandi.

Nani had been up bright and early, and Sita joined Aunt Priya and Nani to sing "happy birthday." Aunt Priya sang the loudest, not caring that she was completely off key. Rohit still had his eyes closed, and was pretending to sleep. Sita saw him smile involuntarily, and a smile tugged at the corners of his mouth.

Then he could pretend no more, and his eyes flew open. His eyes widened to feast at the sight of carefully wrapped presents, lying in a heap on his bed. Brandi knew something happy was going on. She barked excitedly, licked Rohit on the nose and then, tumbled on his bed in a muddy heap of wet golden hair.

"Down dog, down," Aunt Priya yelled, forgetting Brandi's name in her frustration with the 'dirty dog'.

Rohit, overwhelmed, jumped up and gave Aunt Priya a hug. His legs swung in the air as she scooped him up in a bear hug and kissed him on both cheeks. Mercifully she didn't have any of her brilliant lipstick on yet. Next, it was Nani's turn to get hugged. Rohit was nice and gentle with the dear old lady, who even this early in the morning, was already bathed and dressed, and her hair was puffed up just so. Brandi got hugged by Rohit more than everybody because he was right there—smiling with his tongue hanging low, and slapping everyone with his wet bushy tail.

"What about me?" Sita asked, and Rohit wrapped his arms around her too. Then bounced back on the bed with a groan as his butt hit the thin cotton mattress instead of the spring one he was accustomed to. Without a word he began opening the presents. He opened the red paper, and saw another box inside wrapped in green paper. His curiosity was sparked, his fingers worked faster. He ripped open the green box, and found another box wrapped in yellow paper. He hurried to open it, and finally found the present. In a flash, Sita remembered how her dad used to do the same for her when she was a little girl. "It makes suspense," Aunt Priya said in broken English. Now she was copying him. Inside the last box was a portable Nintendo game and five game cartridges—something Rohit had wanted for a long time, and something Roz had helped Aunt Priya pick out.

"Cool," Rohit yelled. "This is *perfect*. This is cool."

"Cool?" Nani repeated, "He is feeling cold?"

"No," Sita explained, "Cool means he likes it."

"I sure do," Rohit said. "When there's not much to do, I can keep playing by myself. I'll show you how, okay Nani." He opened his other presents exclaiming over each one of them. He had got a skate board, a pogo stick, roller blades, a new baseball glove, and now Sita was sure that Roz had been involved in picking them all out. *But when*?

"Oh dear, don't fall down and break something," Nani shook her head. "I didn't buy you anything, but I will give you money."

"My boy is very athletic." Aunt Priya boasted. "Do you know he plays baseball, and basketball, and so many games. He is not going to fall down." She turned and noticed Sita for the first time that morning, and looked at her critically. "Rohit is busy with his presents. We have to do something about you. Look at that hair. I'm going to make an appointment for you at the Sheraton Hotel. They had better do a good job."

"Why can't I wear my hair up, the way I usually do?" Sita asked.

"Because you look too professional, how shall I say....too much in control. I want you to have something soft and ladylike," Aunt Priya said.

"I'm not going to cut my hair." Sita said. She swung her long braid forward and grabbed it protectively.

"We'll ask Habib," Aunt Priya barked. "Right now, all you have is length. No style. Bah girl! Anyone else would be happy about a trip to the Sheraton for a haircut."

"Oh it doesn't mean I don't appreciate...."

"Stop babbling and come to my room, and see what I want you to wear today."

On her bed Aunt Priya had laid out Sita's outfit for the birthday bash. It was a *salwar kameez* in the palest pink. More white than pink, but with the slightest hint of blush. Made of a stretch synthetic fabric, it fitted snugly around her bosom showing off her slender waist before billowing into a knee length tunic, worn over matching pleated pants. There was a pretty pink scarf to go with it, because as Aunt Priya said, "the shirt was too tight around the chest."

All dressed up in time for the party, Sita twirled in front of the mirror the way she had when she was seven years old, and Mom bought her a new dress. Her cheeks flushed from excitement over her new look, she twirled again. Her hair swung around her before settling in a shiny sheath on her back. The ends freshly cut, lay in symmetry across the small of her back. The front had been angled in layers to frame her face. Expertly cut to curve just under her chin, it shimmered and tantalized in the afternoon sun.

"You look nice," Aunt Priya said. She had worn one of those diaphanous pastel chiffon saris she had bought in New York. Wrapped in a strawberry pink sari, her brown face lightened with white talcum powder, and her jelly arms hanging in loose folds by her sides, she reminded Sita of strawberry ice cream. The trademark red lipstick that slashed across her face reminded her of a cherry atop the ice cream cone. Sita smiled, and Aunt Priya pounced on the slight smile, "What's the matter?" she asked suspiciously.

"Nothing—I was just thinking of strawberry ice cream."

"Oh, I bought an ice cream cake for Rohit. Come and see."

She opened the box to show a huge cake decorated with bright pink flowers and toothpaste green leaves.

"You didn't find anything sporty?"

Aunt Priya snapped the box shut. "You got nothing good to say, then don't say anything."

"Where is Rohit anyway? Must be playing with the dog and getting his clothes all dirty. I must lock up the dog. We can't have him shedding hair, and knocking over drinks with that big tail."

Rohit entered the room just in time to hear Aunt Priya. "I don't want Brandi locked up," he said. He was dressed like a little man in pinstriped pants, and a white shirt and a bow tie. He hugged Brandi close, setting the ridiculous little red bow-tie askew, and getting golden hair on his freshly starched stiff shirt. "I don't like this birthday anymore. I want to play."

"Come, let's go and meet people." Aunt Priya took him by the hand, and nodded to Sita to tie up Brandi.

Guests had begun arriving. There were many families with young children. The little boys dressed neatly, their well-oiled hair parted on the side. They sat next to their parents and were quiet—too quiet. Almost as if someone had told them that children must be seen, and not heard.

Rohit was the only child walking around. His white shirt had come untucked from the waistband of his pants. He plucked at the red tie that was now dangling from his shirt, and looked disheveled. Clearly unhappy that Brandi had been tied up he said, "I am going back to sit with Brandi in the kitchen. You know where to find me," and then he walked out of the room. Sita and Aunt Priya exchanged glances. Sita was about to go after Rohit but Aunt Priya said, "Leave him alone. Go say hello to Ramu dada, and Uncle Vijay, and make sure they have everything they need."

"Namaste," Sita said in the traditional Indian greeting. "How are you, would you like some more tea?" she enquired politely. "Can I get you any of those sweets or anything else?" She made small talk, skirting around the marriage issue, though she desperately wanted to know who the cluster of young men in the corner were. They would surely know, but to ask would be inappropriate. She could imagine Ramu dada's eyebrows shoot up, and he would say something like, "You'll find out in no time, be patient." *Darn him, why couldn't she get an honest answer! Well to be honest, she hadn't actually asked. A couple of the guys weren't half bad looking, but some of them were weird, especially the one with oily hair slicked back looked like a bum who thought he was the king of the castle.* "They call me Raja," she heard him introduce himself, and then he continued talking loudly. It looked like the man was giving a speech to a not so rapt audience, or he was telling some jokes that no one was laughing at. Sita, feeling the way she did about men today, enjoyed his discomfort as the people who had circled around him started to walk away.

She continued to stand near Ramu dada even though she was running out of small talk. She knew no one else there. She heard Aunt Priya say, "So nice that you could come. I wanted you to meet my niece." She was talking to two obese ladies. From the corner of her eye, she saw Aunt Priya make her way toward her. "Sita must come now," she told Ramu dada and without further ado, took Sita by the hand and led her away to where the ladies were standing.

"This is my niece Sita," she said. "You all get to know each other and I'll be right back. I just want to see where Rohit went." She abandoned Sita to the fat ladies and waddled away.

The two women were laughing about something while they slurped tea and gorged down the sweets Nani had prepared. The fat one said something to the less fat one, and she laughed so much that the tea spilled onto the saucer and after a quick look to see that no one was watching she drained the liquid right off the saucer, spilling some on her chest. They giggled like school girls. But they didn't look anything like girls. The fatter one was dressed in a chiffon sari that stuck to her like second skin, undulating over the twin peaks on her chest and cascaded down her large posterior, except where the free flow of fabric was stopped by the wedge between her cheeks. Her friend was dressed in a canary yellow chiffon sari, tied precariously below the belly button, and held there by her stomach that overlapped over it. The tiniest sari blouse, cut low in the front to show the cleft of bosom through the diaphanous sari just barely covered her torso, and rolls of flesh spilled out of the constricting confines of this sari blouse. As Sita came nearer, she smelt the stench of sweat mixed in with a strong perfume.

"Hullo dear, how pretty you look," they gushed, just as Sita had expected they would. *Who knew what they were really thinking. That she was too tall, too short, too dark, too fair, or too thin. Why should she care?* She put on her practiced smile, and flashed them a row of pearly white teeth. Her freshly cut hair writhed down her back when she moved her head, and glinted in the afternoon sun. Unknown to her, she had caught the interest of a tall, dark, gentleman.

"Hullo Sita. That's your name, right?" The fatter lady said. "So tell us, what did you cook for this party?" She waved her hand toward the feast spread out on the table. She pointed to a white sweet, the size of a ping-pong ball that she had just popped in her mouth. "Did you make the *rasgolla?*"

"Actually, no," Sita said. "Nani and Aunt Priya did everything."

"Such a modest child," the other one chuckled refusing to believe her. "So tell me, what does your father do in America?

Where are your parents, by the way? I'm sure I'll meet them soon," she said in answer to her own question. "Let me just get another one of these." She pointed to the savory snack called *pakora,* "So delicious they are."

She returned, taking up the questioning where she had left off. "So you were telling me what your Papa does in America, and what sort of business he has."

"Actually, he is retired. He was a professor at Columbia University."

"I'm sure he will be starting his business soon. America is a land of opportunity," she droned determined to have her way. "And you dear, what do you do to pass the time. You have a part-time job perhaps?"

"Actually, I work full time as a senior editor in Manhattan," Sita said belligerently. *Why did she have to pretend she was this dumb, pretty woman and give people the impression she was so rich?* She soon knew why.

"Oh that is no good—working in the city every day. A young girl who is as pretty as you, should not be going alone in subways and riding elevators in those tall buildings. One reads about all sorts of things that happen there. What is everyone thinking of, we must hurry up and find a good boy for you so you don't have to work."

"But I ...." Sita began indignantly.

"Sita, can you come now?" Aunt Priya appeared from somewhere, and took her by the elbow. "Can you see why Rohit is being this way?"

It was as if Sita's role in a rehearsed act had come to an end, and she must exit the scene before she spoke out of line.

"Come," Aunt Priya repeated "I need your help with Rohit."

"What's the matter with him?" Sita said shortly. She tossed her head the way she did when she felt suppressed and wasn't allowed to say what she thought—which was becoming more and more often these days. Once again the sheath of hair slapped her back in a slight wave before falling back in place against the small of her back. Unknown to her, the mysterious stranger watched again, taking in her flushed cheeks and eyes bright with intelligence.

"Hi Rohit, what's up pal?" Sita asked. She sat on her haunches on the kitchen floor. Rohit sat under the table, crouching beside Brandi and did not reply. The dog was fast asleep, and didn't seem to care if Rohit was there. "How about you let Brandi sleep for a while and come talk to people?" she asked.

"Don't want to."

"Why not?

"Excuse me," she heard a voice behind her. "May I leave my plate in the sink?"

"Sure," Sita said standing up quickly. She looked at the stranger feeling awkward. She took in the long length of fine toned muscle, the slender fingers that held the plate, and the incredibly husky voice.

"Hello," the stranger said.

"Hello," Sita replied. She took a deep breath, *I hope Nani finds someone this handsome.*

The stranger bent low to be eye level with Rohit, "What's up pal?" he said.

"Nothing."

"Come, it's time to cut your birthday cake."

"Don't want to," Rohit mumbled.

"Not even for your doggy?"

For the first time a smile tugged at his mouth. "Dogs can't eat sweets silly," he said.

"On your birthday, he can have some cake. I'm sure your dog—what's his name, Brandi? Brandi will like a piece."

"Okay, let's go. And then mister, will you come back with me and bring cake for Brandi? You know some grownups might not let me, so I want you to come."

Brandi heard her name, cocked her ears and thumped her tail.

"Oh the lady here will gladly help you out with that, right?" He turned to look at Sita with gentle brown eyes.

"Will you Sita?" Rohit asked.

"Your name is Sita?" the handsome stranger asked.

"Yes," she said. She realized he had not told her his name. She thought she saw a strange expression flit across his face and then, Rohit pulled her away to cut the cake.

Rohit took his place at the table. His eyes widened seeing all his favorite sweets and all the things Nani had cooked and he had stubbornly refused to eat. The two fat women that Sita had spoken to earlier were very much around, and posed alongside Rohit for pictures. Everyone wanted pictures. Ramu dada, Vijay uncle, and a host of people—Sita had no idea who they were, all stood around Rohit and sang *happy birthday,* and tried to make nice, and act happy, so they could be in a lot of photos. When the flash bulbs stopped, the smiles faded. Slowly people began to leave. Sita felt an overwhelming sense of relief. The first round was over. She sighed.

"Hard day?" the handsome young man said, startling her because she had no clue he had been there.

"You don't know the half of it," she said without thinking.

"Don't be so sure. See you later," he said enigmatically.

Then he was gone and Sita was staring at the empty doorway.

Chapter Twelve

Sita sat under the cool fan breeze. Her sari billowed up in front of her like a party dress of the nineteen fifties. She pushed it down between her knees to stop its free flight, and picked up a magazine from the coffee table and sat down to read.

Aunt Priya sat down next to her. "It's cool under the fan. What are you reading—your parents are coming today," she said all in one breath. She thought Sita read entirely too much, and could never understand why.

"I know," Sita said without lifting her eyes from the magazine, hoping that Aunt Priya would go away.

"And in the evening, Ms. Shah has invited us."

Sita looked up quickly. "Who's Ms. Shah?"

"Raja's Aunt."

"Who's Raja?" Sita asked. She remembered the grease monkey at Rohit's party who none of the other guys seemed to like. Not him, surely not *him. Why couldn't Aunt Priya just spill the beans* she thought, irritated. *Today, extracting a simple answer from her was like pulling teeth.*

"Raja is the boy you're here to meet," Aunt Priya said confirming her worst fears.

Sita put down the magazine. *What a weird name! Raja meant king. Who did he think he was king of? He would never be her prince! Why did she have to go?* She mimed the words shaking her head, and rolling her eyes. Out loud she said, "Aunt Priya, Mom and Papa will be tired after their long flight. Maybe you can make up an excuse for us not to go."

"You are mad," Aunt Priya said bluntly. "Don't know what's good for you."

"Leave her alone." Nani entered the room just in time to hear the last comment. "Leave the girl alone." Each word was punctuated by an involuntary fart. Sita rubbed her nose discreetly. The dear old lady was losing control over some physical capabilities, but her mind was crystal clear. "Sita is a grown girl now." She pointed at Priya with her walking stick. Then she released her weight on the stick and fell back into the chair nearby. In a lower voice she added, "If you insist she does something, she's going to want to do the opposite. So leave her alone."

"This is what I get for trying to help. No one helped me, and when I try to help, no one lets me."

"Life is full of *could have, should have*, and the path not taken is always greener than the chosen one. But we have to move on Priya," Nani said gently. "We all want to help Sita, but we must be tactful with young people. Especially educated ones," Nani whispered. Her raspy voice carried to the other end of the room, and her conspiratorial tone made Sita cranky. Nani realized Sita had heard and said, "Sita beta, your parents wanted to meet the Shahs so just go with them, and get acquainted with the family. Raja won't be there, so there is no pressure."

"So, why do I have to go?"

"It will make me happy. The Shahs are good people."

Well, it was hard to argue with that, and Nani had known.

When Mom and Papa arrived later that day, she barely got to talk to them. Aunt Priya whisked Mom away to show her what Sita would wear for the "tea party." Amazing how high-*teas were still fashionable so many years after the British had left India*, Sita mused. She thought she could get Papa to talk to her, but he interrupted what she was trying to say with a, "hullo dear, I really must find Nani and talk to her now."

Left alone, Sita was bored. She picked up a magazine and sat down. The words on the pages danced before her until they made no sense. She flipped the pages till the pictures were a blur. She discarded the magazine and picked up another. Nothing made sense. She was starting to get angry again. *Why was her hard earned vacation being spent on checking out someone who called himself Raja?* The image of the egoistical grease monkey who told jokes at Rohit's party flashed across her mind and she shuddered.

"Come Sita, what are you reading?" Nani said. "Come and sit closer to us. I was just telling your Papa about Mrs. Shah. Do you know Mr. Shah's mother had arranged your parent's marriage?"

Sita perked up. "Really? Tell me more."

"Yes, I was from the south, your Mom from the north. It is unlikely we would have met, had it not been for senior Ms. Shah. I've always told people how I came all the way to the foothills of the Himalayas to pick the prettiest flower," Papa remembered with a sideways glance at Mom. She blushed and looked away.

"Look at your Mama blush—after all these years," Nani teased.

"Do you know they had their engagement party at *Gaylord* restaurant?

"What a name!"

"Well, it was one of the best in those days," Nani said. "Very expensive too, I remember. In those days 'gay' meant happy, nothing else." She snorted, and then she giggled like a school girl. "You should have seen your father's face when he saw the bill. His eyebrows shot up, but without a word he took out his wallet and said, 'What the good Lord gives, the good Lord takes!'"

Nani giggled at her own joke, and Papa shifted uncomfortably in his chair and turned red.

"Well, let's all go and get dressed," Nani said. "It will be time to go soon."

As if on cue, Aunt Priya appeared. "Should Sita wear blue, or should she wear pink again?"

"Why don't you ask her," Nani said.

She ignored Nani's comment. "Well, she wore pink for Rohit's birthday so maybe blue is better. Yes, she will look pretty in this aqua color. What do you think?" She looked at Mom. "I think it will go well with the gold jewelry."

"Let's see," Nani said. "Don't make her wear very flashy things in the daytime."

"No, it is not flashy." Aunt Priya said indignantly. She waved her small pudgy hands. "Just little gold with pearl and turquoise stones in it."

"Oh, that will be nice. I have metallic gold shoes that will go nicely. I use to wear them when I was young. She waddled away to get the shoes. "Come Sita, come and see."

Sita was finally dressed in the blue sari and matching gold jewelry. Her hair was piled up in a chignon, and a few tendrils escaped to frame her face in wispy curls.

"You look pretty," Aunt Priya stood back to look, and nodded approvingly.

"I'm not comfortable. The slippers hurt, the sari blouse is too tight, and I feel like a Christmas tree."

"Hush, you look fine. Come along now," Aunt Priya said, and then she lumbered along to the car. Sita followed. There was no point in fussing. She had been through this ritual before, and nothing had come of it. She had always had to get dolled up and present herself as a demure young woman. The elders always managed to find some flaw in the boy. He was either too short, too fat, or had crooked teeth; or he was cynical about religion, or his family showed an undue interest in her inheritance. "We can't have people marrying you for your money," Papa had said. "After all, you are our only child and will inherit everything." Sita remembered how everyone around him had agreed as well. No one thought to ask Sita's opinion, and she had just gone with the flow, doing whatever was expected of her, as she did now. She followed everyone to the car to go to Ms. Shah's house.

The Shah's lived in a bungalow cocooned behind tall metal gates from the everydayness of life in Delhi. Outside the gates, hawkers who pushed their vegetable and fruit carts sang out the names of the produce for sale. "Buy some potatoes or some mangoes. What about carrots and some coconuts?" they droned, competing with the sound of scooter rickshaws that spluttered their way around ambling cows, and right over the dung hills of cow poop on the street.

A dark short man stooped with age, opened the gates, and they drove up a rather long driveway. Papa's eyes brightened seeing a Benz in the driveway. A young man, who they later understood was the driver, was hosing down the car. His white cotton shirt flapped in the hot breeze and he was barefoot.

"Salaam." He raised his hand to his forehead in a quick greeting. "I will go and tell madam she has guests."

Everyone waited in the front. The man who had opened the metal gates was out in the garden and hard at work. The thick lawn, green from the roots up looked like it had been taken care of through the dry, hot, summer. The little old man, bent double over the little hand tool scooped and patted the soil into neat flower beds, muttering to himself as he pulled and pried weeds with his bare hands. His fingers were gnarled, and his hands were encrusted with dirt. Sweat dripped down his face, and he wiped his face on his well-worn shirt sleeve. Then he saw Sita and the others as though for the first time, standing in the shade watching him, and decided to take a break. He pulled out a "bide" or a local cigarette from behind his ear. Holding it between his thumb and forefinger, he lit it, and then leaned back against the tree trunk, blowing up clouds of smoke on this hot dusty day.

"Wish we could have servants in America," Mom sighed. "Imagine not having to cook or clean, wash cars, or pull weeds in the garden."

"Uh huh," Sita said, but all she could think of at the moment was how hot it was, and how she wished she could be wearing shorts!

"I wish your Ms. Shah would open the door." Sita shifted her weight from one foot to the other. "It's getting hot here." She felt her thighs stick together with sweat. A couple of drops trickled down her legs, and she rubbed her ankles to keep the little drops from appearing at her feet. Nani wiped her upper lip with her index finger and said, "Let me find out what is taking so long." She went back into the driveway to speak with the servants.

The door opened soon after, and there was a blast of cool air as they entered the air conditioned living room. It was dimly lit, and after the glare outside, it was a moment before Sita realized she was face to face with a fat lady, the very same one who had asked her all kinds of questions at Rohit's party while she downed one sweetmeat after another. This time she was wearing a crisp cotton sari, starched as sharp as a razor blade. The pleats down the middle moved like scissors as she made her way toward them. Her eyes remained beady, scrutinizing everyone, although her mouth was stretched in a fake smile.

"Come right in," she cooed. "Sorry you had to wait so long. Someone was on the phone from the Delhi Commonwealth Women's Meeting. They wanted me to be their chair person. As if I have nothing better to do! But I don't want to let them down….."

"Murderer-in-law" was the nickname that exploded in Sita's mind. She suppressed the thought, and chided herself for being so unkind especially to someone she barely knew. *Why was she thinking the worst in imagining this woman would be her mother-in-law?* Yet it was hard to ignore the steely glint in Ms. Shah's eyes. It was clear she could be a formidable opponent. One who would see no fault in her precious son, and woe to anyone, should they decide to point out the slightest imperfection in her precious Raja.

"Oh dear," she really must stop being so paranoid, Sita thought. *After all this was Nani's friend. How bad could she be?* She saw Ms. Shah's beady eyes soften as she saw Nani.

"Come, why you are standing so far away," she said. "I didn't even see you."

Nani smiled, "It's easy to be missed when one is small."

"And yet the best things come in small packages," Mrs. Shah said, and reached over to embrace her.

Mr. Shah, a thin gentleman with gray springy hair went over to welcome Nani to his home. He had gentle brown eyes, and was dressed in wrinkle-free khakis, and a down-to-earth heather blue shirt. He saw his wife and Nani together exchanging news and turned his attention to the others in the room.

"Come let's get comfortable in the living room," he said. There was just a hint of Indian accent which people nowadays refer to as "Indianese".

Sita saw how men and women instinctively parted company. The women made their way to a cozy nook in the living room done up with floral cushions and a Chinese rug in pastel colors, and the men gravitated toward the den with the entertainment center that held a bar. It was expected—this separation of the sexes. It was as instinctive as breathing, and as difficult to explain as the parting of the Red Sea. Sita stood her ground, wishing she didn't have to sit near Ms. Shah and be subjected to her beady eyed stare. Perhaps she could hang around Papa today.

"Oooh Papa, look here, there's an SLK roadster." She pointed to the model that was displayed in the entertainment center." Do you know, it first debuted as a concept car at the 1994 Turin Auto show and was an immediate hit?" Papa and Mr. Shah both turned to look at her.

"I didn't know you knew about SLKs" Papa said.

"This roadster is based on the classics 300SL and 190 SL of the 50s and 60s." Sita frowned trying to remember the details of the advertisement that had run in the journal's last issue. She knew it well, and remembered it because there had been an uproar about car advertising in a medical journal.

"Medical journals must restrict advertising to pharmaceutical products or medical issues. Not fancy cars and consumer products." The editor-in-chief exclaimed. "What next? Are we going to advertise a naked woman jumping out of a cake?"

"That's wishful thinking!" someone said.

Sita had read the advertisement often. She remembered it now. "A pushbutton retractable hardtop, which transforms it from coupe to roaster in less than 30 seconds," she said out loud.

"That is quite right," Mr. Shah said. He stroked his SLK in the entertainment center just like a little boy would. He pressed the little button on the side and watched the hood fall back. "Nice," he said, putting his toy back. "Do you know what SLK stands for my dear?"

"No, I doubt that she would," Papa said. "Let's go outside and take a look at the Benz you have outside.

Sita remembered the footnote in the advertisement, "SLK stands for Sportlich (sporty) Leicht (light) Kompakt (compact)," she said.

"That is quite a bright young lady you have there. Most unusual—I don't know of any other woman who shares quite the same level of interest in cars."

That was just the cue Sita needed to say, "Can I come outside and take a look at the Benz as well?"

She really had no clue about cars, but she wasn't going to let go of an opportunity to stay away from Priya Aunty today. And if Papa was going outside to the garage, it would be okay for her to follow him outside even though it might be slightly unusual. *Well, "highly unusual" would perhaps be more accurate,* Sita thought. She suppressed a smile. She could feel Aunt Priya's eyes boring into her back. The little lady was quite perplexed. She must have had this meeting so neatly choreographed in her mind, and the look on her face was worth a thousand words. *How was she going to bring this meeting back on schedule? How was she going to make Sita act more like a lady?* Aunt Priya sat there, not saying a word. Sita could tell she was desperately trying to make eye contact with her, and Sita was not about to give in and talk to her.

The lights went out, and the room was plunged into darkness. Every so often, especially in the summer months, power failure and the absence of electricity for a few hours every day was the norm in India—Too many people, and not enough power, was a problem.

"Here we go again," Ms. Shah said. "I thought power shedding was over for the day."

"I'll go and switch on the generator," Mr. Shah said. "I don't suppose you have this problem in America." He walked away to turn on the generator and did not wait for an answer.

A while later the generator restored light to the kitchen, and the formal living room. It was starting to get dark. All thoughts about going outside were forgotten. Trapped in the circle of light like the insects drawn toward the verandah light on a humid rainy evening, Sita felt upset. There was no way out of the inevitable question and answer session she had tried so hard to avoid. She dug her knuckles into the silk cushions. The velvet felt cool to her sweaty palms. She pressed her knuckles down, and looked at the indents imprinted on the fabric and wished she could make a dent in Aunt Priya's resolve to arrange her marriage during this short vacation. The harder Aunt Priya tried, the more Sita felt this might not be the best thing for her after all.

Mr. Shah returned to the living room. "You don't have this problem in the United States, do you?" he asked again.

"Huh, actually we do have power shortages. California especially, has suffered from load shedding during the hot summer," Sita said.

Nani leaned forward in her chair, "Sita is right, I didn't follow all the details in the paper, but there have been all kinds of talks about how to make more energy, and use what is there more effectively. There have been talks of off-shore drilling in Florida, and off the coast of Alaska to try and find more natural reserves of oil energy."

Papa joined in the conversation, "I don't know if that will solve the energy problem in California or impact oil prices in the country. At any rate, something needs to be done about both problems."

"California is a beautiful state," Aunt Priya said in an attempt to join this conversation.

"Have you been there?" Ms. Shah asked Sita with her usual fake smile.

"I went there to represent our publisher and to meet with the Editor-in-chief of the journal published by our company," Sita said. "It is a beautiful city. Actually, San Francisco is cleaner and picturesque, but one can't really complain about Los Angeles. I got to stay at the Omni, a 5-Star hotel, really quite a luxurious place. After business was concluded for the day, we got to go sight-seeing."

She thought she saw Aunt Priya look annoyed, and then she felt a stab of pain in her toe as Aunt Priya's big foot landed squarely on her foot. *She did it on purpose.* Sita was sure!

Ms. Shah's beady eyes bored in Sita, "And did you make this trip all by yourself?"

"Oh no, she was well chaperoned, weren't you Sita," Aunt Priya said, looking directly at her as if challenging her to dare contradict.

"Well, the Production Director and some other staff members were there. It was wonderful! After the meetings in the day, we went shopping in downtown Los Angeles. Not that we could afford anything, but window shopping was great. That is where the richest people shop."

"My word, you have certainly seen the world," Ms. Shah said. There was an edge to her voice.

"In the evening we went out to dinner, and had a company paid gourmet meal at a ritzy restaurant. I can never forget how the waiter filleted the fish, chopping off its head right there in front of us," Sita said.

"I like my cooking and cleaning done in the kitchen," Ms. Shah muttered under her breath.

Mr. Shah said, "I went to Los Angeles once. I visited the *Walk of Fame*. It was one of the few places that were free!"

"I liked the *Walk of Fame* too," Sita said, finding it easier to talk to him than to any of the women folk. "It has the handprints and footprints of the famous Hollywood people. I tried fitting my hand in Arnold Schwarzenegger's hand print and my word, it was so big!"

"So you are a Schwarzenegger fan?" Mr. Shah enquired.

"Well I like action movies," Sita said.

"Really, you don't like romantic comedies dripping with syrup, like most women I know do?"

Ms. Shah gave him a sharp look, and he subsided into his chair.

"You know what I mean," he said, grinning sheepishly.

"I like romantic comedy," Aunt Priya said, and Mr. Shah gave Sita a conspiratorial smile.

Aunt Priya went on, "You know a nice simple story, where the guy meets the girl, and they fall hopelessly in love."

Nani who had been so quiet laughed loudly and said with great gusto, "I like action movies too. Dushoom, dushoom, James Bond 007 to the rescue."

"See Nani likes action. *Great minds think alike*," Sita said.

A moment later she heard Aunt Priya say under her breath, "*And fools seldom, differ*."

Chapter Thirteen

Sita decided to go and visit her friend Renu in the morning. She got to Renu's apartment complex early. The vegetable man was still delivering vegetables on the push cart. The milk man too, was making his rounds with a big steel container delivering milk from house to house. Milk had to be boiled before it could be put in the refrigerator. Yes, everyone had refrigerators, but they were a lot smaller than the ones in America, and people tended to shop often. There were frequent power outages especially in the summer months so food did not stay fresh in the refrigerator. It was best to cook every day. So in most middle class households, the maid came every day and cooked, and another one came and mopped, and because most people had only one car, every household also had a driver.

Labor was cheap, but so many things that were common in America, were a luxury here. Although all houses had running water, in the summer months there was always a water shortage, and one had to wake up early in the morning, and store water in buckets for the day. Many houses did not have running hot water, and the geyser had to be switched on so that water in the metal tank was heated just warm enough for a bath. Often times though, the water pressure was so low that the showers wouldn't work and water was usually collected in buckets and poured with a mug to bathe. Renu had just come out of the bath, and was ready for the prenuptial henna application that would make pretty little tattoos all over her hands and feet.

When Sita walked in, she saw Renu sitting on a low stool, her arms outstretched. Someone was dexterously maneuvering the "pen" to make intricate designs.

"Hi Sita," Renu said, smiling brightly. She leaned over to give her pal a hug.

"Careful," the henna lady said, "this will smudge."

"Okay sorry," Renu muttered and gave Sita a quick peck on the cheek. Sita stood by her friend and watched the *mahendi* or henna paste being applied. The slimy goop was a mixture of henna, oil, lemon juice, and water tinted with tea.

"Come and sit," her friend said. "This takes about four hours to dry, and then I'm not allowed to wash my hands. I wonder if the design will be light orange or a deep red."

"Why" Sita asked, "do you prefer one over the other?"

"Don't you remember? *Mehendi* symbolizes the strength of love in marriage. The darker the *mehendi* the stronger the love," Renu said with conviction.

Sita was a loss for words. It had been so long since Sita had seen her friend. The last time she had seen Renu, they had both been in high school. They had kept in touch over the years and reminisced about those happy-go-lucky days when their biggest worries had been about keeping their grades up, and having a good time.

They had both gone to the local convent high school, which was the place all affluent people liked to send their children. Here real nuns roamed the hallways. They wore a habit that carefully concealed every inch of their bodies and enveloped them in a black shroud so that only their faces peeked out from under the wimple. They had names like *Mother Mary of Grace,* and one wondered about their *real* name. Was it simply *Mary* perhaps, or something totally different? The teachers there were mostly Catholic, many of them old and unmarried and very cranky most of the time. "Cleanliness is next to Godliness," they would murmur. It was an all-girls' school. They were all required to wear white skirts and blouses with three red buttons, a red belt, and knee high socks with white canvas shoes. A red hair band was a requirement if the hair was short. Red ribbons were mandatory for longer hair which had to be neatly confined in a ponytail, or imprisoned in two braids. No makeup was allowed in school, and heaven forbid if any of the nuns noticed that you wore it. The girls' school was adjacent to the boys' school, but no mixing was allowed.

When the teachers came in to teach they, made a great show of closing the windows. If anyone protested because it made the room stifling hot, they said, "What's the matter—want to look at boys today? Have you never seen pants walking?"

Sex education was out of the question. What everyone knew was learned from biology class. Boys were taboo, and "good girls" did not have boyfriends. You had to wait until the time was right, then your knight in shining armor would come and sweep you off your feet like the heroines in American movies. One knew from the start, that there was more than a strong possibility that marriage would be arranged, but there was always the hope that the guy would turn out to be prince charming. Sita wondered, *had Renu found her prince charming?*

Renu was awfully quiet today, and Sita struggled to reconcile this new image of a demure, traditional Renu with the spunky trouble shooter she knew in high school.

"Remember the time when we were kids…remember Miss Rondo?" Sita was sure Renu must surely recall all her girlhood spats with the "dragon lady," as she was known in school. The very same one who had sent her to the principal's office umpteen times—the one with salt and pepper hair, and drill sergeant demeanor.

"Do you remember how you found itching powder and spread it over Miss Rondo's desk?" Sita asked, trying to jog her friend's memory. "And do you remember when the Spanish teacher was trying to explain what a bangle was? She said 'a bangle is a round thing with a hollow inside.' That was such a dumb things to say! You were the only one with the nerve to say, 'Just like your head sir,' really loud and clear."

Renu smiled shyly. "That seems so long ago."

"What about the time you put Epsom salt in the ink—remember back then we used fountain pens and there was an ink stand on the desk? We had a South Indian teacher who always picked on you and said, "You yourself on the last bench, come to the front" in this heavy guttural accent. You couldn't stand her—remember? So while the rest of us sat and grumbled about her lectures that made no sense, you were the only one who did something about it. You put Epsom salt in the ink pots, and all the ink bottles in the classroom started fizzing and bubbling. Ink was splattered all over the place. Everyone ran to clean up. Needless to say that was the end of class. Remember?"

"Yes I remember," Renu said absently, "that was long ago." Sita could see she was wrapped up in her wedding plans and had no interest in memories of childhood pranks, no matter how daring they had seemed at the time.

Renu had always been the one to get into scrapes, and somehow was a real tomboy growing up. Sita remembered the last time the Hindi teacher had been pushed to the limit because Renu just would not listen. In a fit of rage she picked Renu up, and deposited her in the garbage can where she had to stand for the rest of the class. *They had so much to talk about then, why was today so different?*

"Let's go and see the rings," Sita said.

"Sure," Renu said brightening. "Do you remember why the ring is worn on the fourth finger?" Without waiting for a reply she went on, "Because, the vein from the fourth finger leads directly to the heart."

Gosh, was she smitten! She had barely seen this guy three times—unless this was a case of love at first sight.

"Oh, and did you know another custom?" Renu asked.

"What?"

"I'm supposed to sprinkle salt near the doorway of my new home. Remember why?"

"Go ahead, tell me."

"Just as salt blends in to enhance the taste of different food, so the bride blends into the family to enrich it."

"Oh no!" Sita said the words before she could stop herself.

"What's wrong with that?" Renu said defensively. "Isn't it nice to feel part of a family? American colleges have fraternities students would die to be part of, so what is wrong with this? You don't have to pass any initiation rite to be welcomed in. You just are."

"It's not the same thing, and you know it," Sita said. "You have to marry the man as well as the family."

"And your point is....."

"You have to lose your identity. Blend in, as you say. Gosh Renu, are you okay with that?"

"Well, what about you folks.... you have to cherish, honor and obey. Don't forget 'obey.'"

"I'll never do that," Sita said. "Obey like a dog."

Both girls looked at each other hard. Sita smiled stiffly at her friend. She got up from the low stool she had been sitting on and then walked over to the window trying to understand what her friend had just said. It wasn't easy. Renu use to be the rebel, Sita the peace-maker. Renu the leader, Sita listened to instruction. Now Renu was talking tradition and was happy with her arranged marriage, and Sita, who was on the brink of it, was wondering if it was the best thing for her.

"Why don't you stay over and we can catch up on some girl talk," Renu asked.

"Uh huh," Sita said.

"Raja seems like a nice guy," Renu said. "You're a lucky girl."

"What do you know about Raja?"

"Just that he's a nice guy," Renu repeated.

"You've actually met the grease monkey? How come you said nothing?"

"It never came up. Why is he a grease monkey?"

"Oh so now you like him, like all the others. And I thought you were my friend."

"Me thinks the lady doth protest too much" Renu said laughing.

"Very funny," Sita snapped.

"No. Honestly! They are a nice family. Mrs. Shah is a nice lady. She's coming this evening."

"Ms. Shah, did you say? She is going to be here?"

"Well, they are all going to be here for the *Sangeet* celebrations today. I thought you knew."

"No one told me of any music festivities today. In fact it looks like someone took every precaution to make sure I did not find out," Sita felt quite upset. "I think I need some fresh air."

Renu looked puzzled but did not stop her friend. "See you in a bit," she said trying to muster a polite smile.

Sita walked downstairs to the living room. *They had tricked her. How could they?* She had been so looking forward to time alone with Renu, and now she had to deal with the Shahs again! She knew her escape had been too easy the other night.

"Hullo there," a husky masculine voice interrupted her thoughts. She looked up to see the handsome stranger she had first met at Rohit's birthday—the very same one who had been successful in drawing Rohit out from under the table to cut his birthday cake.

"Hullo Sita," he smiled, and unlike all the others she had met here, his smile reached his eyes, making them crinkle at the corners till their warmth spilled out over his whole face.

He remembered her name. Sita thought. *That was nice. What was his name?* She realized with a start, she did not know it. He had never told her his name. "You have an unfair advantage. I don't know your name."

"Is that so," a gentle voice said behind her, and she turned around to see Mr. Shah. "Is that so, Sita?" he repeated. "We should remedy that at once."

"Hullo Mr. Shah. Nice to see you again," Sita said politely. "I didn't realize you were here. How are you?"

"I am well, and this is my son," he said putting both hands on the younger man in a sort of half-hug. "We call him Raja. I am so glad you two have met, but now I have to take him away. C'mon Raja, we need your help setting up for the party. See you later."

Sita's mind was reeling. *That was Raja? If that was his nickname what was his real name? How come no one told her?*

She stood there twisting her sari in her hands when Rohit came running toward her.

"Hi Sita," he shouted. "Guess what?"

"What?"

"Guess who I saw?"

"Who?" Sita repeated automatically.

"Raja uncle, Remember him? He helped me cut a slice of cake for Brandi."

"How do you know his name?" Sita asked, annoyed that a four -year old had learned it, and she had not known it until today.

Rohit looked confused, "I asked him. He said to call him Raja uncle. You always tell me all grownup men are "Uncles," and all grownup women are "Aunties." Why do you look so mad?"

"No reason. You run along and play."

"Actually, Raja uncle asked me to help set up for the party. Want to come and help too?"

"Did Raja uncle ask you to ask me?"

"Actually he did, I just didn't think of it myself," Rohit said innocently.

"That's quite okay," Sita said smiling at the innocent little face. *Why couldn't adults be as honest?* "Let me see what Renu is doing, and maybe I will come later."

"Okay, I'll go and tell Raja Uncle."

Sita made her way back upstairs. She hoped talking to Renu about the wedding would distract her from her own problems.

"Feeling better?" Renu asked. Sita nodded, not trusting herself to speak. She hoped Renu did not hear her heart pounding and know the many questions in her mind. Instead of asking about Raja, she talked about Renu's wedding.

"What's that?" She pointed at the platter on the table. Renu looked confused, "That," Sita repeated, pointing to the coconut, rice and other grains on the platter.

"Don't tell me you don't know," Renu said. "Looks like you've forgotten everything in the short time you've been away. Remember, coconut signifies fertility," she said, "rice, and other grains signify the food necessary to sustain life. Fresh flowers signify beauty."

"I remember the stuff about flowers," Sita muttered.

"Ghee is used to feed the sacred fire, and the red powder, also known as *kum kum* is used for marking the forehead to signify good luck and to say that your soul/husband is with you."

"I see," Sita said because she could think of nothing else to say.

"Let's go down now," Renu said "and see what's happening. I know Mom hired a live deejay and some other musicians. So let's go down and mingle, shall we?"

Downstairs the hallways were jammed with people. Women in thick silks saris with bright borders jostled one another. Their well-oiled hair gathered into buns, some slumped over their heads like melting ice cream, held there by crisp white jasmine blooms. Priya Aunty was there in her low cut sari blouse, stained at the sides with circles of sweat that were getting bigger.

"Let's all go outside into the *shamiana*," she heard a familiar voice say loud and clear.

Renu poked her in the ribs. "That's your Raja," she said.

"He's not my Raja," Sita said indignantly, "and how come he gets to order people around?" They went outside to a brightly patterned tent with a flat roof called a *shamiana*. It was made of symmetrical pieces of cloth in the brightest hues of red, yellow, and green, held together with poles dug deep into the ground, and by a "roof" that was equally bright. Sita was trapped in this colorful kaleidoscope with the Shahs and Raja, Priya Aunty, Ramu, and Vijay uncle, and all the others who said they had her best interests at heart. "Bah! Humbug," Sita said under her breath, in a phrase taken from *Scrooge* in the *Christmas Carol*. She should forget about them and enjoy the evening. She looked up to see if she could find Renu. *Usually pre wedding music celebrations were reserved for women. Why were these men here?*

"There you are Sita, I was looking for you," Rohit said. "Can you get me something to eat? I see a lot of stuff on the table but I'm not sure what's good, and I can't find Mom anywhere."

Sita grabbed his hand. "C'mon, let's find you something."

The music had changed. The slow devotional music had given way to bawdy film music, and then to rustic folk lore. People took to the floor to do the *bhangra*, a lively dance which required jump stepping, and waving, and exaggerated movements of the elbows and arms. Raja was on the floor too, jumping around looking ridiculous in a suit but feeling quite at home. The hair fell in his eyes and he tilted his head and brushed it away with long lean fingers. He saw Sita looking at him and smiled back.

"Care to join?" Raja asked.

"C'mon Sita, let's go," Rohit said.

"Maybe later."

"How come you never want to hang out with me and uncle Raja?"

"How come you like this uncle Raja so much?" Sita countered.

"That's easy," Rohit said. "I like you both. He and you are only ones who thought about giving Brandi some of my birthday cake. That makes the three of us buddies. So, if you don't want to hang out today, that's fine because we have all day tomorrow to be together at the wedding."

"And what makes you sure I would want to hang out with the two of you?" Sita asked.

"Because you don't know anyone else, and besides I thought you liked being around Uncle Raja. I saw you get all red and happy looking when he talks to you."

"What!" Sita yelled.

"Sort of like now. When you want to pretend you are angry, but I think you are happy about spending time with the two of us."

At a loss of words all Sita could do, was turn beetroot red.

Chapter Fourteen

The two-week visit to India was packed with things to do, and people to meet. The highlight of the visit was Renu's wedding.

Aunt Priya was on Sita's case, trying to make sure she looked her best. "So many people will be there, I want you to look so nice and pretty. Come," she said. She held out a container of yellow goop. "Come let me apply this on you, it will make your skin so fair and lovely."

Sita backed away from the yellow slime Aunt Priya was squelching between her fingers. "Renu is the bride—let her do all of these beauty treatments."

"Always you have some problem with whatever I do," Aunt Priya said. She continued to stir the yellow goop with her forefinger.

"Why doesn't this come in a jar like creams normal people use?" Sita muttered.

"Have you ever seen me make cake out of cake mix, or macaroni and cheese out of a box? Why should this be any different? This has all fresh ingredients and will make you glow like a princess."

"What's in it?"

"This is made of sandalwood powder, fresh from the sandalwood tree, and some turmeric which is an antiseptic. Some people only add water, but because you have such dry skin, I added some fresh cream. The servants just boiled the milk. I waited for it to cool, then took the cream."

"Come," she said. "Let's sit down." Because it was quicker to let Aunt Priya have her way than to argue, Sita changed into an old t-shirt and waited to be smeared with the turmeric paste. Aunt Priya looked at her closely. "Later you must go and get your eyebrows threaded," she said.

"You mean waxed?"

"I mean threaded," Aunt Priya said firmly. "That is the best way to shape them. That way they are shaped slowly, and you can adjust the shape as you go along."

"And extend the torture," Sita said under her breath. But though Sita grumbled, she invariably went along with Aunt Priya's wishes. Later that evening, Sita dressed in a rich pink and gold brocade sari that Aunt Priya picked, wore the jewelry chosen for her, and put on shoes with a very low heel to make sure she was shorter than all the eligible bachelors—just as Aunt Priya wanted. She had to admit she was glad she had listened to Aunt Priya. *She did look beautiful!*

Renu, she was sure would be a beautiful bride. An Indian bride can wear brilliant colored saris and plenty of jewelry on her wedding day. Depending on which part of India she comes from, she wears a different color. Punjabi brides wear red. An Indian bride is supposed to bring riches and prosperity to her husband's home and her clothing is, in a way, symbolic of this hope.

Renu's family was from Punjab in Northern India, so when Sita saw Renu the next day, she was dressed in a red and gold brocade sari. Gold bangles covered her arms from wrist to elbow. Her nails were painted a bright red and peeked out from under more gold that covered the back of her hand. Strips of gold reached out to the bangles above her wrists. Layers of dazzling gold chains covered her bosom. Huge gold earrings, too heavy to hang from the ear lobes were suspended from the top of her ears and hung down almost to her shoulders. The part in her hair was covered with a gold ornament. She sat on the bed, her feet up, head bowed. She looked gorgeous. Sita knew that it had taken days of effort to achieve this look. Visits to the intercontinental beauty salon for spa treatments, manicures, pedicures, waxing, facials, and the whole works had paid off. Not to mention the turmeric and sandalwood prenuptial body masks that softened and lightened the skin before the henna was applied.

Priya Aunty waddled into the room. "Renu you look so-o-nice," she said fervently as though her opinion was what everyone had been waiting for. "So rich she looks! Sita look at her. My! How many gold chains is she wearing? Your ma must have started collecting them when you were a baby."

The bridegroom's party was led by a band dressed in dazzling red, white, and gold. Loud filmy songs blasted from trumpets. Dusk was beginning to fall, so they carried lanterns to light the way. The groom rode a big white mare. The horse was decked in a ceremonial red and gold cover that hung half way down to the ground. The groom dressed in long pants, and a long jacket that came up to his knees. He had his face covered with strings of marigold. A little child was sitting astride the horse too, and she remembered this was to cast away any evil eye that might fall on the groom. Sita had not seen a Hindu wedding up close in a long time, and she hurried downstairs to catch a better look. As the groom got off his white horse, Sita's thoughts drifted again.... she thought about *her* knight in shining armor, who would one day sweep her off her feet? *Who would it be*?

"Hullo Sita," a deep masculine voice interrupted her thoughts. She looked up to see Raja smiling at her with his charming grin that began to tug at her heart strings. The dancing was over, and Raja walked over to her.

"Isn't that a cute child accompanying the groom? See him right there standing with family now," Raja said. Sita tried to stand on tip toes to get a better look over the heads of the crowd.

Renu was now in the "mandap," led to this canopy in her gorgeous red sari. She looked demure and content.

"Red looks quite striking at night," Sita commented.

Raja smiled at her. "Sure does, it stands for abundance and fertility." Sita smiled back.

The comfortable silence was broken by a little voice that said, "There you are! Both my favorite people are together." Worming his way to the space between them, Rohit grabbed Sita's hand first, and then Raja's, and looked up at them both. Then on a whim he picked up his legs, whistled, "Wee...eeee," and let the two adults support his full weight as he swung between them, whistling loudly. The whistling changed to a giggle as both grownups struggled with the sudden weight.

"What if we had let you go?" Sita asked indignantly.

"You wouldn't," he said, but then had second thoughts and quickly put his feet down on the ground.

Renu's parents were now doing the rituals to give away the bride.

"What's that white stuff?" Rohit asked, standing on tip toes.

"Milk," Raja answered. "Milk and water is what that looks like. It's used to purify the couple for a new life."

"Lucky, they don't have to drink it," Rohit commented. "I hate milk—unless it comes with chocolate. I love chocolate milk!"

Ever tried plain milk with chocolate biscuits," Raja asked.

"What's that?"

"Biscuits? Oh I forgot you call them *cookies* in America."

"Try it, it tastes good, and it will give you big muscles like Superman."

Rohit grabbed Sita's hand and was tugging at Raja's hand, "I can't see anything," he whined. "Can either of you pick me up?"

"Here we go," Raja scooped him up and hoisted him up on his shoulders. "There," he said, "much better, right? Now you can see everything."

Standing alongside Raja, Sita could smell the tantalizing aroma of his after shave lotion. Someone pushed past to get a better view, and she was pushed against the hard long length of his body. She turned quickly, drinking in the sight of the long lean fingers closed protectively around Rohit.

"What's happening now?" Rohit asked, interrupting Sita's thoughts.

"Well, this ceremony means 'joining of hands,'" Raja explained patiently. The bride's right hand is placed on the groom's while the priest chants holy verses."

"Hey, what's happening this time?" Rohit said. He had seen a loop of white cotton put around the couple's shoulders. "Are they going to tie them up?"

"No," Sita smiled. "The loop of white cloth binds the two together to fulfill their roles. Just as a single thread of cotton breaks easily, many strands in the white cloth form a strong bond between the new couple who will now work together to form a strong family unit."

"As Sita was saying," Raja said, and Sita felt a catch in her breath at the way he said her name. "As Sita said," he repeated, adjusting Rohit's position on his shoulder and holding on to his legs to make sure he did not fall off, "From now on, Renu and her husband will work together to make a happy family."

"Oh that's nice. I like it better when you explain," Rohit said with childlike candor.

"What's the fire for?" he asked. He had noticed a small fire in the center of the "mandap."

"Fire is supposed to purify everything, and is also a source of energy. All Hindu weddings take place around the fire. Only fire can separate the bond of unity between husband and wife who stay together until either dies and is cremated."

"Now *you're* using big words like Sita," Rohit said petulantly. "I don't know what the heck you said."

"Look, look" Sita said, "the bride and groom are joined by a piece of white cloth. One end is tied to the bride's sari and the other is thrown over the groom's shoulder, and the next ceremony is the..."

"The *mangal fera*," Raja said.

"Yes, that's when they walk round the fire seven times. The groom leads the wife the first four times and then, the wife leads the last three rounds."

"It's called "circumambulation," Raja said.

"Right. And it also signifies the four stages of life—childhood, youth, the third one is..."

"Middle age and then old age," Raja said.

Already he was finishing her sentences, saying what she would have said, as if they had known each other forever.

"Oh look, what are they pouring on those people's hands?"

"What people?" Sita asked automatically.

"The people who're getting married, silly—Oops! Sorry Sita." He covered his mouth after calling her *silly*. "But what is that? It doesn't look like candy."

"Because it's not," Sita said. "The bride's brother gives the couple grains of rice, oats and leaves."

"Which also stand for something bla bla bla," Rohit said. He bounced up and down on Raja's shoulder looking suddenly bored.

"Actually it stands for wealth, good health, and prosperity. They offer grains to the fire, signifying that all their worldly possessions they sacrifice to it, in the hope of invoking its blessings."

"This is too long," Rohit whined. "Can we do something else? Let's find a place to sit down." *He was assuming that the three of them would spend the rest of the evening together. Almost as if they were family,* Sita thought.

"So when can I see you again?" Raja asked.

Sita felt her breath catch in her throat. "I'm leaving to go back to the US next week. Give me your address, and I'll write if you promise to write back.

"Promise," he said solemnly.

Aunt Priya saw them and came running, "Hullo, hullo what are you two talking about? Raja you look so handsome in that suit! Doesn't he Sita?"

"Well aren't you going to answer your Aunt?" Raja asked, enjoying her discomfort.

Sita was at a complete loss of words. She couldn't possibly tell him he was drop dead gorgeous, and then neither could she lie. Thankfully Rohit saved the moment and said, "What about me? I've been dressed in this scratchy suit for three hours now, and no one has said a word of how good I look."

Here was one question Sita was not afraid to answer. "You look stunning," she said. "More handsome than any other 4-year-old I know."

"So how come you didn't say anything to me ma, you never even talked to me. And I did such a good job of keeping these two people together like you told me to."

"What?"

"It wasn't hard," Rohit stammered, scared at Sita's tone. "I like you and Raja so I stayed with the two of you, and we all hung out together." He paused, stared from one grown up to the other. "What's wrong?"

"I can't believe you used a child to manipulate me," Sita muttered.

"Don't be angry. Your Aunt meant well…." Raja's voice faded when he caught the angry look on Sita's face.

"All you want is a Green Card to get to America, and marrying me is the way to get it. To think I almost fell for your gimmick. You are one conniving fraud, and I'm happy I found out before it is too late." They were screaming at each other now.

"You think I am using you to get to America! I can manage all by myself, thank you very much!"

"Well don't knock yourself out on my account. I really don't care what you do, where you live, or anything else about you."

"That's for the best then, because I never want to see you again." Raja turned on his heel and walked away.

The ceremony was coming to an end. Renu was feeding her husband sweets to signify that she was his wife and it was her duty to cook for him and the family. Renu's husband did the same to signify it was his duty to provide for her and their family. Sita watched, and her eyes got misty as all the relatives including Raja were going up to wish the couple. *Well, in a couple of days she would go back to America and would never see him again. Why was she starting to feel bad?*

Chapter Fifteen

There was a letter from Roz the next morning. *How nice,* Sita's eyes lit up. For the first time in three weeks she thought of work, and the world she had left behind in the United States. Now, it was almost time to go back and she was glad—she found comfort in her work. Sita wondered how Ms. Valentine was holding up, how much work had piled up on her desk. She would have to dig through it and sift through all the e-mails. The more she thought about America, the more she yearned for things that had been so humdrum just two weeks ago. A McDonald's hamburger for instance, was something she craved out of the blue. Although there was a McDonalds down the block from Renu's house, the burgers tasted different. Made of goat meat and spiced up, they tasted more like kebabs than burgers. The pizza tasted a lot different too, smaller and spicier; she longed for the big triangular slice, fresh and greasy from the oven, served with garlic knots that were her favorite.

"I feel like having pizza or a burger," she had said one day to Aunt Priya.

"Who travels to India to eat burgers? You do everything wrong," Aunt Priya had retorted.

Sita tried to ignore her, but that was hard to do because Aunt Priya was close behind her. She picked up the letter on the table.

"Who's that from?"

Nosy as ever, Sita thought. Politely she said "It's from Roz."

"Ah nice girl," Aunt Priya said. "You must give me her address and telephone number."

"Why? I thought you felt white girls were bad and only Indian girls were good."

"I never meant that. I don't know enough white girls to make that decision. But now we are going back, I want to stay in touch with her. She is your friend after all. Also, I had promised to find her a husband—I must get busy," she said in the same tone one would use to say, *I must go to the market to buy vegetables.*

"You never give up on this husband hunting mission," Sita shook her head. "When will you let it go?"

"I will keep trying—don't *you* ever forget that," Aunt Priya said ominously.

Sita gave her a quick look wondering whether this was the beginning of a long lecture about how unforgivably rude she had been to Raja. Aunt Priya had not said a word so far. Maybe this was *it now.* She held her breath. After the fiasco with Raja she had expected to be berated, or at least told how disappointed they were that she had chosen to "act up." No one had said anything. Not Mom or Papa, Nani, not even Priya Aunty. *Far be it for her to bring up the matter.*

Finally, after Mom, Papa, and Nani—everyone had asked her who had written, she was able to curl up on her favorite white rocking chair by the window and read her letter in peace.

"I am in love," the first sentence read. "He's a real hunk. His name is Tom."

"He's so big and strong, and has the gentlest blue eyes," the letter continued. "He told me I was his princess. No one ever told me that. He's so different from any of the guys I've known, so caring and so giving. He is so different from the other jerk. Do you remember him? Well, this guy is not at all like him. I can't wait for you to meet him!"

"Guess what he does for a living? He's a fireman. I knew you wouldn't guess," Roz wrote, and Sita felt Roz was sitting right there talking to her. "I never thought I would fall in love with one either. I always thought my guy would be the three-piece-suit kind. I can't wait for you to meet him," she repeated. "Tell Priya Aunty I thought about what she said and she made a lot of sense."

The letter ended with, "...you're lucky to have someone like her looking out for you."

It was strange that Roz and Priya Aunty both thought of each other quite fondly. Sita folded the letter and uncurled herself from the rocking chair. *What was it that Aunt Priya had said to Roz that had made such a huge impact on her?* For the life of her she couldn't remember... Well, there was no time to write back. By the time her letter reached, she would be back in New York. If she could get to a computer, she might be able to email Roz and let her know when she was arriving. *Maybe Roz might even come to the airport—that would be fun.* She was leaving tomorrow, and she would finally be able to put thousands of miles between Raja and her life in the US. *What was his real name?* She realized with a start she only knew his nickname. *Just as well. She didn't want him invading her thoughts anymore after today. It was good Roz had got hooked up. They would have tons to talk about when she got home.*

"Do you have Roz's phone number? Ask her if she will come to the airport tomorrow and pick us up," Aunt Priya said breaking into her thoughts.

"She has a new boyfriend now. I don't want to bother her."

Aunt Priya perked up. "New boyfriend—she found one, eh?

"She said she took your advice. What did you say to her?"

"Never mind, missy. At least someone knows good advice when they hear it," she barked. "Give me her number, I'll call and ask her if she can come to the airport if you won't.

"I'll do it," Sita said quickly.

Early the next morning before the crack of dawn, they set off for the airport. Because of the heightened security, relatives were not allowed to come inside, so they said their hurried goodbyes at the gate to Uncle Vijay, Ramu dada, Uncle Ajay and his wife, who once again pinched Rohit's cheeks and gave him a loud kiss. Nani had not been able to come to the airport, and she was perhaps the only person Sita would miss.

Today, Sita was comfortably dressed in jeans and t-shirt. *Thank heavens,* she thought, no more people to impress, and no need for Aunt Priya to be all over her. In fact Aunt Priya was visibly relaxed and slept almost all the way home. Before they landed in New York they were each given immigration forms to fill out with the routine questions of what they had brought back to the United States.

"Look at this," Aunt Priya said, "they are asking me if I have brought back plants and animals, and all of sorts of funny questions. Why would I want to do that?"

"Well you know," Sita replied, "Once Ramu dada did bring back fruit. He brought back guavas because we don't get those back in America. And then he lied. He said he had no food and tried to hide the guavas, one in each corner of the suitcase. But the fruit rolled out of place, and when the officer opened the suitcase, it was clearly visible."

"So what's the harm?" Aunt Priya retorted.

"Well it's just immigration policy. They think food from overseas may carry germs and they don't want anything coming into the country. You don't have any food, so you don't have to worry."

"Well I did bring back some Indian sweets, but that is not food," Aunt Priya said emphatically. She quickly checked the "No" box on the form. Sita stared at her, but it was pointless to argue.

Once they picked up their baggage, they went to immigration. There were separate lines for US citizens, and separate ones for foreign nationals. Because Aunt Priya had an Indian passport she had to get on the longer line. Since they were all traveling together, Sita and Rohit also got in line with her. Sita went first, and customs was a breeze. She had nothing to declare, and it was so obvious that she was happy to be back that the officer just said, "Welcome home," and let them go.

Then it was Aunt Priya's turn. The officer asked to see her Green Card and ran it through his computer. Aunt Priya stood on tip toes and tried to see what was on the screen.

"Can you see the screen ma'am?" the officer asked.

"No," she said straining forward.

"Good," he said. "You're not supposed to." He looked at her form, looked at her diminutive frame wearing the multi-colored sari, and asked her if she had any plants and animals with her. She said "No" quickly. Then he asked if she had food, and Aunt Priya said she had brought back costume jewelry and beaded handbags. "What about food?" the man persisted. "I have sweets," Aunt Priya said sullenly. The man looked at her form, put a big red check next to the *Food* column and crossed off the part where she had written "No."

The customs agent directed her to go to another room, "Your suitcase must be examined."

"Why?" Aunt Priya demanded, but then had the sense not to argue.

Sita was not allowed in the room, but from Aunt Priya's sullen face she knew she was not happy. "They took away my sweets and threw them out. Why did they have to do that?"

"Rules are rules, Aunt Priya. We'll buy you Indian sweets from Jackson Heights tomorrow."

"They don't taste as good," she complained. She didn't say more because Roz was at the airport to meet them. There was a strapping blond man at her side. They made a striking couple—Roz in her leather pants and high heels barely reached Tom's shoulder. Tom had a tousled mop of blonde hair and looked as if he had just rolled out of bed and come to the airport.

"Hi Sita! Hullo Priya Aunty," Roz squealed.

"Hullo *beta*, so good you came. I heard all about your man. Nice. Very nice indeed." She took a step back so she could get a better look at Tom's face. "I am so happy you made a good catch," she whispered to Roz, and then in a louder voice she announced, "Your husband-to-be is a handsome man."

Tom tossed a mop of blonde hair from his eyes.

"Did you just say 'husband-to-be'? Does that mean your Aunt has just predicted the future and that you will marry me?" Tom asked and dropped to his knees.

"Tom! Not here. Not now!" Roz exclaimed.

"Why are you on your knees? Did you drop something?" Rohit asked. And the moment was lost.

"Rohit, you look even bigger than when you left New York! Come here, and give me a hug." Roz bent down to greet Rohit, and her skin-tight leather pants looked about ready to burst at the seams.

Rohit held back from hugging her. "If I am bigger, how come you didn't see me, and only said "hi" to the grown-ups?"

"Aren't you a bright kid," Tom said. "She does that to me sometimes kid—acts like she doesn't see me and doesn't know who I am."

"Who are you?" Rohit asked. He was eyeing the big man, raising an eyebrow at his particularly enormous Jordan sneakers in red and white. Sita couldn't help but remember how badly he had wanted those sneakers, and though they had been available in India, they cost a lot of money at the time, and his mom had said, "This free trade business only helps the rich people. I will not buy shoes for Rs. 6000 just because they are 'phoren' made. Your feet will grow in 6 months and then all my money will go to waste."

"Who are you?" Rohit asked Tom again.

"This is Tom, my boyfriend..." Roz began.

"....Roz's husband-to-be," Aunt Priya finished, visibly uncomfortable whenever Roz said the word 'boyfriend.'

"See what I mean," Tom said. "Sometimes she doesn't know me either, so we're both in the same boat."

"What boat?" Rohit asked.

"I meant the same team—you and I, give me five." Tom held up his big white hand, until Rohit tentatively slapped down a high five.

Tom grinned. "There you go! C'mon my man, let's go and find the luggage for the ladies." He scooped up Rohit in his arms, and took big strides toward the luggage wheel.

"Oh, it's good to see you," Sita said.

"Now, your fiancé has gone to bring our luggage. Such a nice man! We should have some—how you say in America...girl talk?" Aunt Priya said. "Where did you meet this fine man?"

"Oh you would never believe this," Roz waved her hands so everyone could see her scarlet red nail polish. "I was babysitting. Imagine me babysitting!"

"Go on!" Aunt Priya said impatiently.

"Well, I was upstairs watching this 10-month old at our house. From the window I saw the mailman and I couldn't wait to go downstairs. I put the baby in the walker and went downstairs." Roz said.

"You didn't leave the door open and the baby in the walker! You don't even have child safety gates in the house."

"Actually, no—that's the trouble. I was half way down the stairs and then I saw the baby in the hallway at the top of the stairs. I thought he would try and follow me, so I gently closed the door."

"Okay good. So then what happened?" Sita asked.

"I went and got the mail, and started looking at the sales brochures. I must have been gone less than two minutes but the little fellow was bawling his lungs out."

"So you rushed up the stairs and picked him up, I'm sure," Aunt Priya said. "You are making a very long story. Just tell me where you met your Tom."

"Wait, I wanted to run upstairs and pick up the baby, but when I turned the door knob, the door wouldn't open," Roz said opening her eyes very wide.

"But of course," Sita said. "It's a self-locking door."

"Why would you leave a child alone in the walker if you were going out of the room," Aunt Priya said. "It says right there on the box, 'DO NOT LEAVE CHILD UNATTENDED' in big red letters."

"I didn't think! Okay!"

"So what did you do?" Sita asked.

"I paced up and down the room and then I went to a pay phone," Roz said.

Sita, who had been pacing up and down in the room with a worried frown on her face, stopped walking in circles. "Did you call his parents?"

"No. I called the Fire department," Roz said.

"I always knew she had more sense than you," Aunt Priya said. "What the parents were going to do except to yell at the poor girl?"

"Let me guess," Sita said, ignoring Aunt Priya. "It was Tom who answered your call, broke open the door and walked straight into your heart."

"Well, sort of," Roz said. "He didn't want to damage the door."

"So what did he do?" Aunt Priya said.

"Well, he had this enormously long ladder on his truck that was able to reach the first floor. He pried open the window and was able to get into the house."

"Then what happened?"

"Then he opened the door from the inside, and that was the end of story. All's well that ends well." Roz grinned.

"You mean you charged into his arms in gratitude and the two of you have been an item ever since," Sita said her eyes gleaming.

Roz smiled shyly, I guess so," she said.

"Now don't tease her too much," Aunt Priya said. "I hope she can knock some sense into you and you will find a man you can get along with too."

"Well, Tom has some Indian friends, so maybe we can all hang out together," Roz said.

"What Indian friends? First, I got to see them before my niece—how you say," Aunt Priya said, as she searched for the right American phrase, "hangs out with any one. You all can hang out in Sita's house if you want."

"But not in Roz's house," Sita finished. "I knew it!"

"Why, Aunt Priya?" Roz asked.

"You won't understand, Roz. You're a nice girl. But a nice girl with different ways than what I know—who are these Indians anyway—the ones your fiancé knows?"

"He's not my fiancé," Roz repeated, "but I'll ask him about his friends, I can't seem to remember the names he mentioned just now."

"All right then," Aunt Priya said losing interest. "Come, let's go see what happened to the luggage. Let's go quickly." She walked so fast that rolls of flesh jiggled and bounced their way past the two girls. "Why are you so slow today?" she said.

Tom with Rohit in tow, had the luggage ready.

"You found everything so quickly," Aunt Priya enthused.

Tom eyed the fluorescent orange tape on Aunt Priya's scratched up suitcase, "Well, your tape helped enormously," he smiled.

"See great minds think alike," Aunt Priya said to Roz. "I like your fiancé."

"He is not my fiancé," Roz repeated gently.

"Oooph! This child likes to torture me," she said, and Sita saw Tom smile at them both.

Aunt Priya leaned back to look at Tom, "Tell me, Roz says you have Indian friends. Who are they?"

"Tom's eyebrows rose a bit," but he said "There's my buddy Ajay. He's a nice guy. Roz thinks he's a bit weird and withdrawn, but he is a computer specialist and works with Cantor Fitzgerald at the World Trade Center."

"He's your good friend?" Aunt Priya asked. "Okay good. Then we must all meet."

"Well Sita can come over any time," Tom said. "Maybe she and Ajay will hit it off."

"No." Aunt Priya said emphatically. Tom's eyebrows shot up so she softened her tone, "I would like to meet them too. There are so few educated Indian families that I know in New York."

"Well I could introduce you, but he has no family as far as I know. He just has a younger brother who is coming to America next month. He calls him Rajiv."

Aunt Priya perked up even more. "It is a small world," she gasped, "a very small world." She took Tom aside and whispered something and they were talking in hushed voices for quite some time.

Great! Sita thought. *Aunt Priya was at it again. Now she would try and hook her up with Ajay, or Rajiv, or someone else Tom knew.*

"I want to go home," Rohit whined. "Why is this taking so long? Everything always takes so long."

"You're tired aren't you sport," Tom said ruffling his hair.

"Boy! he must be tired if he let you touch his hair," Roz said. "I heard Rohit wants his hair gelled into place and spiked razor sharp."

Tom scooped him up and then carried him on his shoulders just the way Raja had, "C'mon big guy," Tom said, "let's get you home."

Darn it! Sita thought *why was she thinking of Raja? It was certain she would never see him again.*

Chapter Sixteen

It was good to be back at work and to see her friends once again. She had brought back souvenirs for some of them. Irene got a bag with mirror work, Mary an Indian bride doll, Lucy silver bangles with elephants carved on them, and a hand embroidered shirt for Sandra. Sadly, there was nothing for Ms. Valentine. There didn't seem to be anything she could find that would be good enough for someone so hard to please.

Ms. Valentine looked even more tight-lipped today—maybe because there was a ton of work. The company had acquired more journals and the editorial staff was hard pressed to get the work done on time so that the monthly journals could publish on schedule. Also, a number of editors had left the company and the workload had to be handled by those who remained, and that put a lot of added pressure on the employees. Sita found herself digging out from mounds of paper. One author wanted to know why his paper was late; another wanted an erratum published because of a typographical error. Another one wanted to know when Sita would be back even though her automated e-mail reply clearly said she would be gone until the middle of August. There was no end to things that needed to be done. It looked as though the backlog would never go away even though she had been chipping away at it day after day. There was one amusing email from an author in Greece who wrote about the copyeditor's queries in page proofs, "You ask very intelligent questions. Your name is Sita?" Then he went on to say he was unfamiliar with foreign names and wanted to know if she was a woman, and was she married!

"Hey maybe I got myself an admirer," Sita said out loud. This was an interesting tidbit to share with Roz. *Wonder how Roz was doing with Tom.* Her friend had never dated one guy for very long. It had been a while since she had a chance to talk to her friend although they passed each other in the corridors every day.

"Hi Roz, how've you been? Still seeing Tom?" she asked casually.

"Why shouldn't I be?" Roz said and Sita was struck by the hurt look in her eyes.

"No, no reason." It's just that…" Sita's voice trailed away.

"What?"

"Well, you always use to say variety was the spice of life and that seemed like your motto when you went out on dates."

"Oh well, things have changed, I'm just about ready to throw in the towel"

"Huh?"

"Abandon spinsterhood," Roz replied tersely.

"Okay." Sita slowly tried to digest this new piece of information. "So what's stopping you?"

"Well, Tom has to ask me first."

"But he did—at the airport—when he dropped to his knees. Don't you remember? You were acting like you didn't want him to be more than a boyfriend."

"He wasn't serious! I want him to ask me when we are alone, not in front of a bunch of people."

"So now, we are a bunch of people."

"You know what I mean. Besides he hasn't called in a week."

"Maybe he's on vacation."

"Well I called the firehouse and they said he was a volunteer fireman and doesn't work every day." Roz said.

"So he lied to you?"

"I don't know anything anymore. I thought I had it right this time." She sighed loudly. And then, like an overheated kettle letting off steam she hissed, "How can he do this to me? Give me a telephone number and then never be there. I thought he had the most honest eyes. He was so good with kids—so warm and caring. Even your Aunt Priya took an instant liking to him." She put her head in her hands. "I need a vacation."

"Roz, listen to me. You can't run away every time there is a problem."

"You're a fine one to talk about problems. You have a whole family trying to find you a husband."

"And that is a problem too."

"I wonder what it would take to know for sure that Tom is the guy for me," Roz said pensively.

Ms. Valentine walked in with a question for Roz, and looked at Sita pointedly, waiting for her to leave. Sita scurried away.

The work was endless. No sooner had one issue of the journal gone to press, then it was time to compile the next issue of her monthly journal. Sita decided that the only way she could catch up on the work was to get to the office an hour earlier. So for the past two weeks, she was at the office at 8:00 AM every day. On one such morning in early September, she had been immersed in her work when she heard the excited voice of a radio announcer on someone's radio. *It's probably John*, she thought *listening to what was surely a ball by ball commentary on a basketball game from the previous night. It was still early, and she was sure the volume would be turned down soon as people started coming in at 9:00A.M.* She stepped out of her office to Xerox some proofs and saw clusters of people around radios. Even Ms. Valentine who didn't have her own radio was listening. No one was attempting to turn down the volume, and no one was instructing them to.

"What's happening?" Sita asked, but everyone was so focused on the radio they didn't answer.

Sita moved closer, and heard that a plane had struck the World Trade Center tower.

An accident, she thought. *But on a bright sunny day with clear visibility—how could that happen?* She walked over to the Xerox machine to complete making a set of copies for the proofreader. *Have to get them out today,* she thought, *so I can get the corrections next week with enough time to incorporate them when the issue was compiled.*

"You look so calm," Lucy remarked as she passed Sita on the way back to her desk.

"Do I? Have to get this pile out today, and then there is a pile of manuscripts waiting to go out to the compositor. Don't really have the time to stop and listen about the accident on the radio. It's pretty sad though. Was there a lot of damage?"

"Well there might not be any mail picked up today," Lucy said. "So you don't have to rush like mad."

"What do you mean?"

"Haven't you heard?"

"What?"

"Subways are closed. All bridges and tunnels are closed. All traffic into the city stopped."

"Why?"

"A second plane hit the second tower. It was no accident."

"Who....What? Why?" Sita stuttered trying to make sense of what Lucy was saying.

"They think it was terrorists."

"Why would they drive a plane into a building? Didn't they understand they would die too?"

"That's what everyone is asking," Lucy said.

The pile of galley proofs was left forgotten on the Xerox as Sita joined the group clustered at the windows. Although the Met Life Building was almost twenty blocks away from the site, from the fourteenth floor they could see clouds of black smoke billowing into the sky. Sita tried to see through the cloud of smoke, to try and make sense of the enormity of what just happened. It looked almost like a scene from a movie, and she almost expected the black smoke to clear, and the World Trade towers to emerge from the darkness unharmed. But the incessant wail of sirens was the reality check that this was no movie. It appeared wave after wave of injured people were being taken to St. Vincent's Hospital, and other hospitals nearby.

"I saw the hit," Larry said. "I really did." Everyone turned to look at him. "I got off from the train at the 14th street station. It was a nice day and it was early, I decided to walk. I saw this plane fly real low, and then it looked as though it was aiming straight at the tower. *It couldn't be....* I couldn't take my eyes off. The plane struck the building and was embedded within it. First I thought it was a movie. I turned around to look for the camera crews, but there were none. I saw flames licking the walls of the tower and smoke billowing out."

Sita noticed that Ms. Valentine looked as white as a sheet and her thin lips quivered as she announced, "Everyone is free to leave for the day. However, please note there is no mass transit operating in or out of the city. Offices will remain closed tomorrow."

"What do they want us to do? Walk?" Sita muttered.

Ms. Valentine overheard her, and for once did not have a nasty comment. In a kind tone she said, "I hear some people are walking across the 59th bridge into Queens and then trying to find their way home. It might be best to stay on in the office and wait. I am too old to walk. I will stay right here. The company will provide free lunch and mats for those who want to hunker down for the night."

"I don't want to stay here the night," Sandra, another one of Sita's colleagues said. *Where was Roz*? Sita wondered. *She was probably still sleeping, with no clue that the city was coming apart. And Tom—If he was a fireman, he would surely be called into duty today regardless of what other job he might have.*

"You know what I am terrified of," Sandra said. "The long dark tunnel we have to go through on your way out of the city. Who knows who is hiding there, with what kind of bombs?"

"Let's not get paranoid now." Sita struggled to stay calm as she realized these terrorists would willingly sacrifice their lives for their mission, and their kamikaze outlook was their trump card.

"They're gone." Ms. Valentine wiped a stray tear that had escaped the barricade of her steely eyes, "I saw them go down."

She was staring out of her office window, and Sita followed her gaze to see a huge cloud of dust in the aftermath of the collapse. She stared in horror at the gaping hole in the skyline where the towers had once stood. There was a hush. Someone said, "Oh God!" and then everyone was talking at the same time.

"We have to get out of here," Sandra said. "Do you think they will open the subways soon? I mean this is ridiculous! They have to allow people to get out. It's one thing to stop traffic into the city, but you can't keep people caged up here."

Sita went back to her desk. There were around ten new messages on her voice mail in the short time she had been away. First there was Mom, "Are you okay?" she said. "Call me when you get to your desk." Then Dad called to say, "Did you get your Mom's message, why didn't you call back?" Aunt Priya said, "Child, call back we are worried. We saw the terrible things on the television. Hope you and Roz are okay. Have you heard from Tom?"

She called Papa back to say she was okay. "What about Roz, ask her," she heard Priya Aunty's voice in the background. "She took the day off and I haven't heard from her," Sita replied. *It was rather curious that Aunt Priya enquired about Roz so much.*

It was almost 3 o'clock and subways had begun functioning. Sandra pushed nervous fingers through her hair. "Hurry up, let's get out of here, while we can. Who knows what will happen next. Let's travel in groups."

"Coming, hold on," Sita yelled, slapping the proofs into a Fed Ex envelope for overnight delivery. Even though there was no mail going out today, at least it would be one less thing for her to do the next day.

"My, how can you think about work at a time like this?" Sandra asked. The four of them packed into the crowded elevator like sardines. Ms. Valentine stood by the door with a devastated look on her face.

"Take care, Ms. Valentine," Sita whispered to her boss. Her nephew worked on the 90th floor, Sita knew. Sita didn't know if she had heard from him. Ms. Valentine was far from her prickly self today, and Sita was tempted to get off the elevator to talk to her. But the door closed and they were on their way down.

The sidewalks that were normally deserted during office hours were jam-packed with pedestrians. Everyone had a drawn, tense look about them. People were stopping outside the local electronic stores to see if they could get a glimpse of the news on television. But soon the shutters were being pulled down, business was closed for the day, and people moved on. Those who were lucky to be driving, listened to car radios, and one man was kind enough to turn up the volume where he was parked so others could hear. The reports came in slowly as reporters and camera crew grappled with the unexpected enormity of what was happening. It was still too early to know for sure. By now people knew the Pentagon had been a target and another plane had crashed in the fields of Pennsylvania. *How many more planes were there? What would happen next? Were the subways safe?* The first impulse was to get away from the site, and away from the city. The subway platform was like a zoo. People pressed uncomfortably against one another in the subterranean jungle of human bodies.

Hold your handbag close to you," Sita told Sandra. "Someone slit my handbag last Christmas and took out my wallet, and I had no clue until I got home that everything was gone."

Sandra slung her handbag round her neck, and put her hand over it protectively. There were no benches to sit, barely enough room to stand on the platform. Every once in a while, the loudspeaker blared encouraging everyone to stay behind the yellow line and get away from the edge of the platform as the trains approached. Apparently, just one train at a time was being allowed through the tunnel and the going was real slow.

Finally, the four of them managed to get on, but in the shoving and pushing, they were separated from each other. *Well everything should be okay, at least we're in*, Sita thought. The train lurched. Sita tried to weave her hand around the pole and hold on. In front of her, was a short Indian woman dressed in black pants and a body-hugging sweater. She was giving someone a very animated description of the "hit" as she described it in heavily accented English. "I saw it," she said. "But you work at New York University. It's not even close to the site," someone said. The Indian lady opened her eyes wide, "By God, I saw it." With the pride of someone who was eyewitness to an event others would only read about, she said, "From our building the towers are clearly visible. I saw everything." She proceeded to describe the carnage in great detail. "Do you know," she said, "I saw people jump out of the building. They were like birds in the sky and they jumped out holding hands. First a man and a woman…."

"Shut up." someone yelled. "Shut up, right now," another person bellowed. The woman stopped. She looked confused. She had meant no harm. She made her way past the man to the other end of the car, and there continued her story in a lower voice. The man had a beer bottle in his hand. Someone asked him to calm down and he lunged and missed. Sita watched in horror as a fight erupted. Someone pulled the chain. The cops came. They wanted to get him off the train. He broke down.

"I only want to go home," he whined. "I meant no harm. I lost family in the World Trade Center. Please let me go home."

"Come sir, we'll get you on another train. There's one right behind this one. Come now," the cop said. The man did not move.

"You're holding everyone up," the cop continued. The man simply moaned. "I lost family man. I lost family."

"There are no charges on you just yet, but there might be, if you don't come now," the cop said. The man gave an angry look at the people in the car and got off.

The train moved for a bit and then the stress and discomfort of being in a congested car proved to be too much for someone and he fainted. Again the buzzer was pushed. The train stopped. Everyone stood and stewed, waiting over 20 minutes for the paramedics to come and take the person away. The doors closed. The train had barely begun moving again when a fight erupted and the buzzer was pushed again. This time the driver emerged. "Will y'all quit pushing the buzzer? I wanna go home. I've worked a 16 hour shift and I ain't taking this anymore." There were no trains coming into the city, and no railroad employees could get through to relieve their colleagues. The people who were in the city had no option but to work another shift. There was a hush, and the same question was on everyone's mind. *Was this driver competent and in control of the situation to get them home in one piece today?* The rest of the journey was uneventful. The train was slower than usual, but at least Sita got to her Jackson Heights station. She never liked to walk from the station to her home but today, more than ever she trusted her own two feet more than any other overcrowded mass transit.

The area wore a shuttered look. The darkened store windows urged people to go home to safety. Sita hurried. She wanted to go and watch the whole thing on television. To understand what had really happened. She had heard that there had been dancing in the streets in some Middle East Countries when the towers crumbled. Why did some people hate America so much?

Chapter Seventeen

It was a couple of days after the World Trade Center tragedy and there was still no word from Roz.

No news is usually good news, Sita thought. *Then again, that was not always true.*

"Definitely not for most of the thousands who didn't hear from their relatives in the World Trade Center," Sita said out loud. She was watching the nightmare unfold on the television screen. The same shot of the twin towers struck by an orange ball of fire, and framed in a cloud of smoke, was shown so many times, yet it was hard to look away. The orange ball of fire, grew bigger to devour more and more floors in its angry red death trap. Thousands tried to escape, screaming and running as fast as they could. The harrowing details were caught on television, and reported non-stop on all radio stations. The world watched America under attack. The mighty towers that had glittered imperiously in the morning summer sun had become vulnerable to the most unexpected enemy, an enemy that had used US aircraft as a bomb in the most unimaginable horror story of the decade.

"I don't like this," Rohit said. "It's scary. It never ends."

Aunt Priya put down the newspaper. "Just let me watch the evening news, then I will take you outside," she said.

"They keep talking about the same thing. I don't even get to watch any cartoons."

"Why you want to see cartoons all the time," Aunt Priya snapped. "Look how people are trying to help out. See people lining up outside hospitals to give blood. See the line," she said, "round and round it goes—so many people."

"Yes, and I heard that there was a tremendous response to an appeal for clothing. Just one appeal," Sita said, "and they got so much—they had to turn boxes away. But isn't it sad, that it takes a tragedy to bring out the goodness in people."

"I never thought that the World Trade Center would fall down flat, and just topple over," Aunt Priya said.

"Well it didn't actually topple," Sita said, "it just sort of folded down like a table whose legs gave away."

"What you mean? Still like to correct me always."

"Never meant to," Sita said quickly. "But I read somewhere that steel melts at temperature of 1000 degrees Celsius, so when the steel framework of the building melted, the floor just caved in, and fell on the floor below it, and that could not take the additional weight and caved in. So each story fell, one on top of the one below."

"Oh no," Aunt Priya exclaimed. "And there were people inside. All squished up."

"I hate all this sad talk. I wish it would stop," Rohit whined.

"Look at Mayor Giuliani," Sita said. "He is everywhere. He is a good man. It's got to be hard, trying to keep it together when so many city workers, so many firemen, so many people, have lost their lives trying to save other people. He must attend countless funerals, comfort hundreds of families, and try and be strong for all of them."

"Do we always have to talk about people dying?" Rohit moaned again.

"All right, let's go," Aunt Priya said. "Too much television is not good." She stood up, "Let's go out and find someone to play with."

Rohit burrowed his head in the cushions of the sofa, "I don't want to play."

"How come?"

"There's no one to play with. Edwin and Anthony went to their Aunt's house."

"How about we go to Peter's house?" Sita said. "Why don't you call him up and ask if you can come?"

"Peter's not my friend anymore."

"What you mean?" Aunt Priya said. She stood in the doorway, her brows knotted in a puzzled expression. Peter and Rohit had been baseball buddies as far back as she could remember.

"He's mean. That's all."

"What did he say?" Sita persisted.

"He asked if I was Muslim."

"Then?"

"I said I wasn't Muslim, and he said that was good."

"Go on," Aunt Priya said.

"I asked why that is good. And he said because if you were Muslim, you would grow up and then come and bomb my house, and kill us all."

Aunt Priya took a deep breath and asked "How you replied?"

"I said why would you say that? You know I wouldn't."

"And….?" Aunt Priya said impatiently.

"He said you're brown, and you look Muslim. That's what Muslims do when they grow up. Then he walked away."

"I am going to go and have a talk with his parents" Aunt Priya said. "I am going right now. Rohit you stay here with Sita until I get this settled." Aunt Priya was biting her lower lip, and she said to Sita, "Peter's mom should fix her son."

"It might be better to go in the morning," Sita said. *If her Aunt spoke to anyone in the mood she was in, she would stutter along in broken English and everyone would laugh at her.*

"I go now," Aunt Priya said adamantly.

"Aunt Priya, you know, all brown skin Asian looking people are under suspicion because of what happened. Peter is probably just repeating something he heard at home."

"It is not right. And I must fix it." Aunt Priya got ready to waddle down the stairs. "I will go and talk to Peter's mother."

"Aunt Priya wait." Sita sounded desperate because she thought her Aunt was going to make a scene. "The same thing happened at work, and I did not complain."

"What happened?" Aunt Priya said. Sita heaved a sigh of relief when she stopped in her tracks.

"Sit down," Sita said pressing her luck. "It's a long story."

Aunt Priya remained standing. "Go on," she said, "tell me what happened."

"Well they had a prayer meeting at work after the World Trade Center." Sita said.

"Glad to hear that," Aunt Priya said, "But sad that people only turn to prayer when things go wrong. So what this has to do with you?"

"Well, it wasn't really a prayer meeting. Everyone just stood in silence around the flag and sort of meditated in silence."

"So what's the problem? No one said anything. No one insulted anyone, so why are you telling me all this?" She stood in the doorway with hands on her hips ready to do battle.

"Well the boss did say something. He said it had been a horrible week. That we had done a phenomenal job in going about our daily work—by not getting scared and staying home, each one of us was fighting terrorists who wanted us to crumple up and quit."

Aunt Priya looked bored. There was nothing confrontational about this as far as she could see. "Okay. You can tell me the rest of this story when I come back from Peter's house." It was time to get her hands off her hips and go find Peter's mother. "It's beginning to get dark and I must talk to Peter's mother." She turned around to go downstairs.

"Well I wasn't invited to the meeting." Sita said.

"What you mean you weren't invited?" Aunt Priya took a few steps inside and stood by the dining table. "You just finished telling me how you all stood around the flag and meditated."

"Yes, but my name was not on the email that was sent around to the staff telling them to assemble in the conference room."

"Why not? Someone made a mistake. You went to your boss and reported the error and then you went to the meeting—Right?" Aunt Priya drummed her fingers on the back of the chair impatient to go downstairs.

"No I didn't say anything. I just went to the meeting. Some people looked at me strangely."

"Why?"

"I am brown skinned am I not? I could pass for Afghan or Muslim could I not? Well, some put two and two together and made five. They decided I didn't look American, so I couldn't possibly feel America's pain."

"How they can say that?" Aunt Priya said.

"No one said anything," Sita said. "I just thought they looked at me differently."

"Why you don't tell your boss how you feel. Why don't you wear the American flag brooch everyone is wearing? Why haven't you bought an American flag and put it up yet?" Aunt Priya said all in one breath. "You work in the city. You can buy a real big one for five dollars."

"Actually a real big one costs thirty dollars. The teeny tiny ones that go on cars and mail boxes go for five dollars these days. Even then, it's hard to find any. They sell out fast."

"How come other people in this neighborhood find flags and you can't," Aunt Priya said grumpily.

"So now you think I must wear a flag brooch and put a flag up, so people don't look at me funny."

"Now you don't twist the meaning of my words Miss Sita," Aunt Priya said, and Sita noted the way she hissed the words out, because she was mad.

"You're not even American," Sita said. "You're always talking about Indian culture, Indian food, and Indian husbands. Now, all of a sudden we must put up an American flag because people look at us differently if we don't?"

"Now you listen to me miss," Aunt Priya said, and Sita settled down to hear a long lecture. At least it was dark now, and the trip to Peter's house would certainly have to be postponed. "I am not American but America has been very good to me. I will not bite the hand that feeds me, or make a hole in the plate that has my food," Aunt Priya said, trying to translate an old Indian saying.

"I know. I know," Sita said soothingly.

"You know nothing. So listen up," she said. "America accepts me for who I am. Gives me opportunity the way it gives opportunity to the white man. Takes me with my limited English that you like to correct so much, and tells me it is okay. America has let me open not one restaurant but two. So when this country is in trouble, I will support her. I will go and find this flag myself and tomorrow, I will go and see Peter's mother and tell her, at this time I feel America's pain as much as she does, and if there is any other way I can help with fundraising for all the hurt people, I will."

"Yes, that's nice" Sita said to placate her. We'll go together tomorrow. How's that?"

"I will go when I please and with who I please, and alone if I want to," Aunt Priya thumped her small fists on the back of the dining room chair for emphasis. "I know you think people make fun of my English, my clothes, even how I decorate my restaurant. Let me tell you something missy, only my own people make fun of me. American people like the bright colors I wear. They call them happy colors. They like the red pepper lights I have hanging with the glass balls in my restaurant. They say it is like being right in the middle of a Christmas tree, and as for my sweaters with hand embroidery, they like those too. They say my sweaters have personality, that the feathers embroidered on them look carefree. Only *you* think everything I must wear has to be pastels. Look at you. Forever in those blue jeans that are brown in the bottom as though you sat in a heap of sand and were too lazy to wash your clothes. That's the look, you tell me." She took a deep breath and got ready to continue her tirade.

"Well it is the look, Aunt Priya," Sita said. "Most people my age wear jeans that look faded."

Aunt Priya waved a pudgy arm in the air, "Okay then. That's *your* look. And these bright colors are *my* look. And you know what? America has place for both kinds of looks. In fact she has place for all kinds of looks."

Fortunately, Sita didn't have to reply because the phone rang and Roz was on the other end. Aunt Priya who had been so anxious to go downstairs, promptly found something to do in the kitchen so she could be within earshot of the phone conversation.

"How have you been Roz?" Sita said. From the corner of her eye she noticed that Aunt Priya was trying to dry the same plate over, and over again.

"Oh is that so? Uh huh, uh huh," Sita said. "Oh my goodness, so you were stranded in Hoboken New Jersey, these past few days. What? Oh so you were coming into the city on the 11th and then the train wouldn't let the passengers off at Penn Station, huh," Sita said. She could hear perfectly well, but she thought if she repeated some of things Roz said, Aunt Priya would know Roz was okay, and leave her alone, so she could talk to her friend. "Then what did you do?" Sita asked. "Oh the train evacuated the people on the platform and then took you back to New Jersey. Goodness that must have been a really crowded ride. I'm glad you're okay," Sita said loudly. Still, Aunt Priya sat there, and busied herself with removing some flour that was caked on the rolling pin.

"Tell her Tom was worried about her, and that he asked about her," Aunt Priya said.

"How do you know?" Sita said surprised.

Aunt Priya wielded the rolling pin like a fencing sword, "Never mind. He cares for her very much. Just tell her. Go on, tell her. Don't just stare at me."

"Hello, Roz?" Sita said. There was silence at the other end. "Aunt Priya says she saw Tom and that he was worried about you….." she began. Roz squealed so loud, Sita had to pull the phone away from her. "Put her on, oh please put her on. When did she meet him? I have been worried sick. I knew if anything happened to him I would just die," Roz said.

Sita gave the phone to Aunt Priya and pulled up a chair to listen in. This was her friend after all, so she did not feel she was eavesdropping. Aunt Priya didn't seem to want Sita to have any part of this conversation. She took the cordless phone, walked into the living room, pulled her small feet under her bottom and settled herself in the recliner for a long conversation. "Roz dear," she began "so good to hear you…" Sita heard her say, and then her voice grew softer, and softer, and soon she was not audible. They kept talking, and Aunt Priya was giggling like a school girl. Her head was bent, and her chin rested in her hand. It was as if her mouth was full of words and her chin couldn't support itself until they were all said. They talked, and they talked, and they talked, until Sita could take it no more. "Can I have a word with Roz?" she said finally.

"She'll call you back," Aunt Priya said. Without further ado, she hung up the phone.

"What was all that about?" Sita said. "Why didn't Roz want to talk to me?"

Aunt Priya tried to pull herself up from the depths of the recliner and got her sari pleats caught in the process. "Someone was at the door. She had to go."

"So what was all that giggling about?"

Aunt Priya was still trying to straighten her sari, "Stop being so nosy," she snapped.

"Oh ho, so now the pot is calling the kettle black." Sita said.

"What you mean?" Aunt Priya said. "Always you like to talk in riddles. What you want to know? Where I met Tom? He came to my restaurant, that's where I met Tom."

"Why would he come to your restaurant?" Sita asked.

"I give free food to all the fire fighters from the neighborhood for three days after September 11th happened."

"What! I've never known you to give anything away for free."

"Like I said before, you think you know everything about me, but you don't."

"I suppose not too many firefighters like Indian food, so you knew you wouldn't go broke," Sita said.

"What you mean they don't like my food?" Aunt Priya banged the table with her small hands. "They like my food, they love my conversation. That Tom is a good boy. You know, he is just a volunteer firefighter. His real job is a bank manager somewhere. He is not a big manager but he is young, and he will go up, and up, and up. Very nice boy," she repeated. "Tom knew people in the World Trade Center—Friends who worked in the big financial firms there."

"You found out all this in one meeting? Did he tell you what it was like down there?" Sita asked. "Was he involved in some heroic rescues?"

"As a fireman it is part of his job to rescue people. I did not want him to keep talking about the same thing. I wanted him to enjoy my chicken. He looked so tired and dirty, but I respected him so much. To be there, risking his own life—I knew it must have been very hard to pull out people who were once his friends," Aunt Priya said. Sita felt her spine tingle, and then Aunt Priya said, "He did tell me one or two rescue stories…." She paused, probably debating whether to share them with Sita. She must have decided against it because she said, "I wanted to get his mind off work, when he was in my restaurant. I told him Roz loved him, and was waiting for him."

"Why did you do that? I mean how did you know?"

"Why? It does not take a brain surgeon to know what your friend is thinking. Besides if I don't tell him, who else will? Both you girls are one of a kind. Very stubborn," she said, and waddled away.

"Whew! Aunt Priya is something else," Sita muttered under her breath.

"I sure am, aren't I?" Aunt Priya shouted from the next room. *She had heard her! And she was using American lingo to boot*!

Chapter Eighteen

The office was open. They were not in the immediate vicinity of the disaster and there was no point in allowing the work to pile up. Sita slapped on her headphones, and began her 20-minute walk to the subway. It was a bright fall day, and the air felt crisp and clear, except when the wind carried the acrid smell of smoke and death. She was glad to be getting out of the house, glad to be going to work, glad to have not been hurt, and oh so glad to be alive. The radio gave her constant updates of the relief efforts at the disaster site. How high the death toll had reached, how many times the mayor had been there, and how many people were involved in the rescue efforts. Information about who was collecting donations, where to drop them off, where blood donations were being accepted and, so on. There were no commercials being aired—just a lot of religious music and patriotic songs, interrupted by the heart-rending first person accounts from survivors, and accounts of those who had not been so lucky. By the time she had neared the subway, her eyes were moist. She had been listening to recordings of 911 calls from cell phone users on the plane, minutes before it plunged into the towers.

What sort of madmen were these? How did they get in to the country—so many of them? She had never been able to get a visa for Nani. It had been denied twice. Immigration services had never said why, but Sita knew it was because they thought she wouldn't want to return to India and would become dependent on welfare. So thugs and murderers were allowed to slip through, but a gracious old lady was denied entry.

The train platform seemed a lot less crowded than usual. *Good!* She thought. Maybe she would be able to stand comfortably on her own two feet instead of being sandwiched by people in the train compartment, and pushed and poked whenever someone moved from their trapped position to find a more comfortable place. It was better than she could have hoped for. She found a small space between two buxom women, and squeezed herself in the seat. She slid her feet half way out of her shoes and wriggled her toes happily. "This is good!" she said out loud to one of the women. "Usually I never find a seat."

"Well, most wise folk stayed home today," the fat one said curtly. "The others are either dead, or tending to the families of those that died."

"Oh!" Sita immediately felt uncomfortable. She shoved her foot back in the shoe, feeling like perhaps she should not be sitting down so comfortably, today. Fortunately, the lady got off at the next stop. Sita did not dare try and initiate another conversation.

Sita put her headphones back on. Her eyes misted again. This really *is* overload she thought as she heard all the wonderful religious services, music, speeches, it was too much! To hear about Todd Beamer on the PA flight, who was so young, father of two children with another one on the way. He was a Sunday school teacher who always rallied his family to get in the car by saying, "Let's roll." He spoke with a 911 operator for 13 minutes, gave them the information they needed to make a decision, and decided to take over the plane. He left the phone on, so the operator could hear, and the last thing the operator heard was, "Let's roll."

It sounded like there was quite a scuffle from what could be heard over the static of the cell phone. A few minutes later, the plane plunged to a grizzly death in the fields of Pennsylvania. Sita stiffened and then shifted uncomfortably on the hard green subway chairs. *If only they could have saved themselves,* Sita thought desperately. *It was such a big price to pay to save other lives, and what a monumental price to pay to save another landmark!* The plane would almost certainly have hit either the White House, or some other building. *If only, someone there knew how to fly a plane—anyone else beside the mad men who were in charge.*

She pulled the headphones off. By turning off the narration, she felt she could shut out the reality of the gruesome event. The train pulled into the station. As she got off the train, Sita saw the walls of the station were plastered with pictures of people missing. "God Bless America," was scrawled below the pictures more than once. She paused before the pictures. She touched some of them as she said her goodbyes. They looked so vibrant, so alive in these pictures. She didn't know any of them, but that did not stop her from grieving. These were someone's mothers and fathers, brothers and sisters, sweethearts—all plucked in the prime of their lives. The posters said "missing," but Sita knew they were inevitably dead. Mayor Giuliani was still calling this a "rescue" rather than a "recovery operation," but as time wore on, he was making it clear that it was highly unlikely that any one else would be pulled out alive. How could they be? Hundreds of gallons of gasoline ignited by the crash reached record high temperatures, crumpling steel and concrete as easily as a paper cup. Every day, the newspapers carried pictures of twisted metal and destroyed hopes. Sita sighed loudly. She tried to put the events behind her, and walked on.

There was a significant police presence, and members of the National Guard were posted at every other corner. They stood around not doing much. *They were so young-looking,* Sita thought, what could they really *do* if disaster struck again? It didn't look like they expected anything more to happen. She overheard two of them talking. One was saying how interest rates would be cut, and how mortgage rates would fall.

"Yup," the other one said. "Great time to buy a house or refinance."

"Even a car," one of them said, "I'm sure car dealers are going to offer interest-free financing to lure in more buyers."

"Hey! I didn't think of that," the first one said eagerly. Sita walked on.

Sure enough, there were plenty of folks trying to see if there was anything in it for them. Walking down the street, Sita saw small rectangular bits of cloth lining the sidewalk in a patchwork quilt effect. As she came closer, she saw neatly arranged piles of postcards showing the World Trade Center. There were calendars and buttons, and all sorts of memorabilia. They sold quickly, and vendors competed with one another to attract customers. One guy was vigorously polishing a framed picture of the World Trade Center with a dirty rag. He stopped when he heard a siren to glance around furtively, unsure if that was a wail of an ambulance or the howl of a police car. He knew if the police were around, he would need to beat a hasty retreat. Sidewalk vendors were discouraged in the city.

Framed pictures of the World Trade Center sold for about fifteen bucks and the guy next to him was selling them for ten. Large flags, if one could find them, were going for 30 bucks a piece. Tee shirts imprinted with the World Trade Center photo were a hot item too, especially the one with the face of Osama Bin Laden that said "Wanted Dead or Alive." Someone had ingeniously come out with Bin Laden toilet paper. Sita bought a flag, and a pin, but cringed at the sight of the toilet paper. *Who would want a terrorist's face staring at you in the bathroom?* Sita walked slowly, trying to see everything that was being sold. There were firemen shields, and NYPD buttons being hawked. She picked one up to look. It did not look like the authentic product, and more than likely it was not. Profits from sales would not go to New York's finest or bravest, but to those who managed to produce the counterfeits the fastest.

It was almost 9:00 o'clock. *She had better hurry* Sita thought. Ms. Valentine would be having her meeting, and she didn't want to start the morning off on the wrong foot. It was good she had hurried! She got to work with 10 minutes to spare and Ms. Valentine was already in the conference room. She sat at the head of the table, presiding over a row of empty chairs, a captain with no crew. She looked out of the large glass windows of the conference room. There was a strange look on her face as she looked at the altered skyline. Her elbows were on the table, and the fingertips were touching. She had a pensive look about her, almost as if she were praying. The morning light softened the angles on her face.

Sita slipped in quietly, not wanting to interrupt Ms. Valentine's thoughts. Without turning her face Ms. Valentine said, "I was there when the towers were built. I remember it well. I had just started in publishing as a production assistant to three production managers."

Sita almost choked on her morning cup of coffee. "You were an assistant?" she asked. Somehow Ms. Valentine seemed like the person who had been Editor-in-Chief from day one.

"Yes, and a real good one I was too," Ms. Valentine said. She turned to look at Sita. "There was never a manuscript lost, a paper misfiled, or a schedule deadline missed. All letters that were to go out for the day were typed, copies filed, and packages mailed. Oh yes!" She looked at Sita's shocked face. "Why? You feel I would be incapable of that?"

"Oh, no! Not at all," Sita said fervently. She was struggling to come to grips with image of this neat little lady, who made sure her hands were well manicured, could have been filing and mailing packages in the pre-digital era. It was hard to picture her in the mailroom wrestling large packages of art and advertising film.

"I've learnt this business from the bottom up, which is why I am so darn proud of myself." She slapped the table with a return of her usual fierceness. "I was darn proud of those towers too," she said in a lower voice. She hunched her shoulders. "They were built by Minoru Yamasaki Associates and the firm of Emory Roth. Each one was over a thousand three hundred feet. Tower I was a few feet higher." She looked straight ahead, and reeled off facts and statistics from her encyclopedic brain. "I was there when this Frenchman Philippe Petit walked a tight rope between them. That was a feat worth watching," she said.

Slowly, and tentatively, the others filed into the conference room looking for the usual whiplash of sarcasm from Ms. Valentine. Usually she would say, "Almost on time," if they were even one minute past the hour. She wanted to make it known she hadn't missed anything.

"I am so emotionally and physically exhausted from the services and sad news," Lucy said. She put her coffee cup down.

Larry, who sat beside her, shook his head. "The heroic stories coming out of the Pennsylvania crash are so sad, and so amazing. Thank God for those brave people." Ms. Valentine did not comment. "My brother-in-law has been called up. He is a Ranger in the Special Forces reserve," Larry said. He was drawing circles on the writing pad. "He was on active duty for a long time before getting married. My sister is having a baby, a boy, any day." He added a smaller circle to the maze he had drawn. "We hope Tom doesn't have to go anywhere till the baby is here, and he gets time to spend time with him." He looked up and sighed. His pen stopped moving. He was looking for a way out of the maze drawn on the writing pad, and from all his problems.

Ms. Valentine did not attempt to stop him. She did not even say a word when Roz walked in a full 5 minutes late. Roz had caught the tail-end of Larry's account, and sensed it was okay to talk about her own experience.

"Has anyone been to Ground Zero? I went," she said. She stroked her coffee cup as though she was trying to massage the sadness away. It was hard to imagine Roz with her Gucci shoes and leather pants at Ground Zero. Her colleagues stared at her, and she answered their unasked question. "Well, Tom is a fireman, you know. I went to find him. I never get to see him these days. I wanted to see what he sees, what he deals with, why he has no time for me." She paused and in a lower voice said, "I couldn't stay. I tried, but I couldn't. It was such a mess there—a wasteland of melted steel, smoke, and death. Terrible!" She shuddered. Her fingers tightened around the coffee cup, and her red nails dug furrows into the half empty paper cup.

"It's okay," Ms. Valentine said kindly. "Be careful with the cup."

"I stayed for two hours," she said quietly. "I joined the crowd of supporters who cheered the workers on, as they went through the gates of hell to do their digging and retrieving."

"I don't know how they do it. I wish I could have seen Tom." She turned to Sita. "He seems to be more in touch with your Aunt Priya, than with me."

"I can't figure that out either. Tom is not even Indian, and you know how Aunt Priya is. I can't imagine how they have so much to talk about."

"Well Tom's taken. So she had better not try her matchmaking skill on my fiancé."

Ms. Valentine looked from one to the other, wondering if she should intervene, but Roz had quickly shifted gears. Now she was talking about the animals at Ground Zero.

"The dogs," Roz said. "Those poor innocent creatures sent out in that horrible place to look for life. Can you imagine how they must feel?"

"Who must feel?" Ms. Valentine asked.

"I mean the dogs of course—having to be there, pulled by a leash, their eyes tearing from the smoke and dust, their paws being ripped by splintered wood, steel, and debris."

"I thought the veterinarians were on-site flushing out their eyes with eye drops, and giving them those contraptions that could be fitted to their paws—sort of like shoes. I saw that on television. Some firm had donated them for the dogs with a mission. I can't remember the name now, but I am pretty sure," Larry said.

"Well," Ms. Valentine interjected. "I believe it is now time to move on to the business on hand." She peered over her glasses, and pulled out the agenda for the meeting. It was one thing to allow her crew to vent their anguish about September 11, but she wasn't about ready to give up meeting time for a discussion of animals. She was not a dog lover. Sita smiled quietly. She remembered the spaniel at the bus stop on a rainy afternoon. The little girl and her dog stood under an awning, away from the rain, while her mother shopped in the store. Ms. Valentine was nearby, waiting for a bus. Something made her turn around, and when she did, she was washed with slobbering licks, and muddy paw prints of the spaniel. "Down dog. Get down," she had yelled, backing away from the friendly animal. The dog was hastily pulled back by her young owner, away from the rain, under the awning, away from Ms. Valentine.

Sita too, was waiting at the same bus stop. "He only wants to be friends," Sita told Ms. Valentine.

The little girl looked at Sita gratefully. "Thanks, I don't want to get in trouble with my Mommy for not holding on to him tightly enough."

Ms. Valentine decided not to wait for the bus, and walked out in the rain as far as her spindly legs would carry her. Sita smiled at the memory.

"Well, Sita," Ms. Valentine said, "since you look so pleased with yourself this morning, maybe you can begin by telling us how you resolved the egregious copyediting error in the April issue of your journal."

Sita sighed. The bark was back in Ms. Valentine's tone. From now on, it would be business as usual.

Okay, everybody. Back to work. *Let's roll*, Sita thought, echoing the famous words of Todd Beamer.

Chapter Nineteen

"Be careful," Aunt Priya shouted as she had done every day since September 11th, when Sita went off to work in the morning.

"Don't worry, I will," she answered automatically. She looked at her watch to check if she was late. She couldn't spend the rest of her life looking over her shoulder, but it was simpler not to argue, and just say "okay." Days turned to weeks. Little by little, New York City was pulled up by its bootstraps to try and reach normalcy. Still numb from the attack, many of her colleagues still scoured the papers for hints of danger. A pile of box cutters, similar to the ones used by the hijackers, sent a ripple of fear that made everyone think other hijackers were still at large. Then there was the scare that the Sears building in Chicago would be the next target, and it was evacuated. What would happen next? Were nuclear plants going to be attacked next? Did we have a perfect evacuation plan?

All of a sudden, there were news reports of what one must do in the event of such an attack, followed by a laundry list of emergency essentials like bottled water and canned food, and duct tape and plastic to seal windows and vents in the house, in the event of nuclear terrorism. Suddenly these items were being sold off the shelves. People were standing in long lines at supermarkets, and the local home depot stores to buy them. The hijackers had been known to be checking out crop duster planes. Would crops be poisoned, the water contaminated, or would the mail transport the deadly anthrax? If one wanted to worry, there was no shortage of things to worry about. But with the first week under her belt, things were better. Lunch hour was again becoming a time of freedom, and hurried shopping sprees.

"I really want to show you this skirt at the Gap," Lucy said, "so bring a brown bag lunch so we can have more time at the mall during lunch hour."

"Nice skirt, huh?" Sita asked.

"Dynamite!" she said. Her fingers came alive as they described the skirt. "It's made of stretch denim that molds to you as you walk and. I've been waiting for it to go on sale." Her fingers glided, undulated, and stroked an imaginary dress, as she explained what it looked like.

"Wise girl!" Sita said. "I know the mayor's been telling everyone to go and shop. Help the economy," he says. "Spend money. But I am going to hold on to my bucks till the price is right."

"Talking about big bucks," Roma said in her accented English. "I paid the photographer four thousand dollars for my wedding pictures. Can you believe that? Want to see?" She tugged Sita's sleeve. "You've been asking to see them, but I never brought them in last week. Who knew what would happen to me on the way to work, and I didn't want anything to happen to the pictures. This September 11th business is really scary. Back in Guyana, we don't have problems like this. There are so many people of Indian origin in Guyana. They were brought over in big ships by the British, so many of our customs are the same as yours."

"Oh, so did you wear a sari for the wedding?" Sita asked.

"Uh huh." She pulled out a big white album. "Come see. The pictures came good," she said excitedly.

Sita looked at the photo of her friend. She was sitting demurely, and her head was bowed. She looked absolutely radiant. Her husband was not half bad looking. "You look beautiful," Sita said.

"A doctor," Roma said with pride. "You should hear about the patients he's been getting from the World Trade Center tragedy. The stories he tells me! He saves them you know. He's a good man."

Sita listened half-heartedly, as Roma told her about the woman from Cantor Fitzgerald. "You know this woman—I can't remember her name—she was caught in a ball of fire from the elevator shaft. The woman, her name is Lauren—I remember now, told people that she heard a noise as she was entering the Towers. Instead of waiting outside, she hurried in, and that's when she was attacked by the ball of fire. She felt herself being thrown. She grabbed on to the door, to stop being plunged into the street. Bad mistake! The door was so hot her fingers got burned to a crisp. Then she started to run, to get away from this ball of fire that was chasing her," Roma said. She gesticulated wildly and opened her eyes big, "but it followed wherever she went, attacking, burning, hurting." Roma frowned expressively, and tried to convey with her expressions, what words could not.

"She was on Oprah. There is a book about her. It's entitled, *With Love Greg and Lauren*. It is a collection of e-mails written by her husband. It is so good. It tells everything she went through, as though they were writing to let me know. Do you know she had burns on most of her body and had only a 10% chance of survival? But she did survive—all because of everyone's prayers, and the love of her family, especially her husband. She was one of the most difficult cases. My husband is a good doctor—a good man. He would have been a big help if they had asked him, but they already had enough doctors." She pointed to a picture of a handsome man who was leading her around the nuptial fire, "See that's him, right there."

"Very nice," Sita said absently. Her mind had drifted to another place, another wedding, and to another man. He had stood by her side, tantalizing her with the lingering scent of cologne, with his deep voice, and endearing patience with Rohit's questions.

Oh darn! She thought. *I never meant to be so rude the last time we met. I do not hate you.* "I wish I could tell you."

"Tell me what?" Roma asked.

Sita realized she had spoken out loud. "Uh huh," she stammered. "I meant I wish I could have seen you at the wedding, and told you how beautiful you looked," she lied.

Roma smiled back, and Sita went back to her desk to mull over Raja. "I do not hate you," she repeated softly. And a little voice inside her head said, *there is a fine line between love and hate. If you do not hate him, could it be that you're in love?*

The thought was pushed right out of her head by the never ending work. There was one particularly angry e-mail from the managing editor about a whole string of problems. She had no clue how to deal with this new crop of problems. She forwarded the email to her supervisor. She couldn't wait for the day to be over. When it was, she slapped on her headphones, put on her sneakers, and walked away.

The subways were beginning to get crowded again. People had decided that they couldn't hide in their houses forever. Life had to go on. A toy-seller made his way down the narrow aisle in the railway car. One arm curved around myriad colored boxes, he jerked his arm upward, pushing the boxes further up his armpits to keep them from slipping away. His other hand was bouncing a light-up yo-yo, up and down, then again up, and then down. A swirl of multi-colored lights preceded him as he walked down the aisle with the yo-yo, going up and down, over and over again.

A little boy's eyes lit up. "I want that," he said.

"How much?" the thin scrawny woman, with the bandanna on her head, asked.

The man released the yo-yo in a tumbling series of bright lights. "This is very good. See here. Only one dollar," he said.

Rohit would like that Sita thought. "I'll take one too." She handed him a dollar. The toy seller turned to her gratefully. The scrawny woman was still digging for change in her handbag to pay for the yo-yo.

"I have more things." The toy salesman shifted the boxes under his arms. "See this plane here—six dollars only. But for you, I'll give it for five dollars." He ran his short fat fingers over the plane again and again. "Such a beautiful plane, so nice," he said.

Sita's eyes scanned over the assortment of vehicles in his grasp. "What's that," she asked pointing to a robot.

"This one is expensive," the man said grudgingly. "This one costs ten dollars."

"What is it, though?" Sita asked.

"It is a convertible," he explained. The station came, and the woman who'd bought the yo-yo made for the exit without paying.

The toy man ran after her. "Madam, give me the money please."

She scowled and handed him the change. He poured it into his pocket and then turned to Sita again.

"Yes madam," he said. "This convertible goes from robot to car. See it is very good."

"That's neat," Sita said. "I'll take it." She handed him a crisp ten dollar bill. She was rewarded by a big smile, and a flash of teeth, startling white against his swarthy complexion. With a flourish, the man inserted the money into his pocket and patted it carefully to make sure it was safe.

The doors opened at the Jackson Heights station, and Sita was buffeted around by the surge of humanity trying to enter the train at the same time that she was trying to get out. Sita put her arm around her handbag protectively. She managed to get out just as the doors were about to close.

It took almost twenty minutes to walk home from the station. She rounded the corner to her house, and her steps quickened. She was anxious to find Rohit and see what he would enjoy more—the yo-yo, or the robot.

There were a couple of cars parked in the narrow driveway. *Whose were they?* She wondered. She side-stepped her way, and squeezed past them in the narrow driveway. She took the green linoleum stairs, and hoped to sneak upstairs without being seen.

The door opened, and she stopped in her tracks. It was Rohit. A milk moustache covered his upper lip. He had just drained his glass of strawberry milk. His eyes shone. "You'll never guess who is here!" he said.

"Who?" Sita asked. She hid the toys behind her back. She would give them to him another time when she had his undivided attention.

"Roz is here," Rohit announced.

"Visiting Aunt Priya?"

"And me."

"Of course," Sita said absently. "But I thought Roz said she was going to meet Tom."

Rohit grinned from ear to ear. "He's here too," he said. "And, there are some other people Mom knows. So are you coming down?"

"Sure let me go and change, and then I will be right down."

Good! Sita thought. *It was only Roz downstairs.* Now *she wouldn't have to worry about wearing the right clothes. Jeans would do just fine.* She kicked off her shoes, and stepped into a pair of stretch white jeans that followed every curve of her lithe figure diligently. She found a bright magenta blouse, and on a whim she knotted it just above the waistband of her jeans. She brightened her lipstick, and tinted the color with a bright magenta. Happy with the carefree image that stared back at her in the mirror, she decided she would take the toys down, after all. She put them in a plastic bag and went downstairs.

She knocked on the kitchen door gently. Nothing happened. Everyone was probably in the living room watching television. She pushed the door open quickly.

"Ouch!" someone exclaimed. There was a clatter as a plate and fork hit the floor.

"I'm so sorry," Sita began. "I didn't know anyone was behind the door." She hurried to pick up the overturned plate and the splatter of left over curry and rice, that had fallen all over Aunt Priya's immaculate kitchen floor. She crouched down to scoop up the mess, and felt the heat of someone's eyes boring into her. She got up, and found herself staring into Ms. Shah's piercing black eyes.

"Well, well, well!" she exclaimed. "We finally get to see you in your true colors." She stared at Sita's slim fitting jeans and bright blouse that had become separated from the waistband of her jeans during her cleaning spree.

Aunt Priya waddled into the kitchen to see what the commotion was all about. "My, my, so nice she looks in true bright colors, doesn't she?" Aunt Priya glared at Ms. Shah and dared her to elaborate on her snide comment about "true colors."

"There you are!" Rohit exclaimed. "I was wondering why you were taking so long. Roz was looking for you. Come."

"Sure, I'll come and say hi," Sita said, glad to be getting away from the dragon lady.

"You do that," Ms. Shah said to her retreating back. "I'm sure Mr. Shah would also like to see you in your true colors. I mean—bright colors," she added quickly when Aunt Priya glared at her.

"Hi, there!" Roz said as Sita walked in. She made no attempt to get up, or leave Tom's side. Today, Tom's unruly mop was brushed back, and his huge frame dwarfed Roz. She sat nestled close to him on the sofa.

"Come sit with us," Tom offered. "There's room for three."

"Two's company and three's a crowd," Sita retorted. She saw Tom's hand was covering Roz's knee protectively and, Roz in turn was stroking circular patterns on his thigh with her scarlet nails. It became clear they hadn't come to visit her, *so why were they here?*

She was still standing and Rohit came up to her and said, "You look different today. Sort of like Roz. Hey!" he exclaimed, "I can see your underwear." He traced the outline of her underwear that was visible in her skin tight white jeans. Mr. Shah who had not said a word to her when she entered, but had stayed glued to the television, finally averted his eyes to give her a long scathing look. Sita quickly subsided into the nearest chair to stop Rohit's exploring fingers.

"Come" she said, "see what I got for you." She reached into the plastic bag. He was easily distracted. He wrapped the yo-yo string around his little fingers and tried to get it to go up and down. "Going down is easier than coming up," he said. He tried to grab the yo-yo as it came up, but it rolled down, out of his grasp.

"Come, I'll show you how to work it," Roz disentangled herself from Tom. "See, you can do all sorts of tricks with it," she said, and proceeded to show him.

Mr. Shah kept watching television news updates, and flash backs of the same ball of fire devouring the World Trade Center.

"Such a pity!" he said over and over again. "So many lives lost. So many people hurt. Others crippled for life. Who would have thought in America this could happen? Those towers were a landmark. You could stand anywhere below 34th street and you would see the Empire state to the north and the Twin towers to the south. Yet, some people had the nerve to say there was nothing special about them, except that they were big, and there were two of them!" he said angrily.

Sita wondered if she should comment, but Mr. Shah did not seem particularly friendly today, and except for the scathing look he had given her, he had said nothing.

"It was the home of the top downtown financial firms, of Americas best and brightest. Government firms were also there." *How did he know?* Sita thought. *He was a foreigner.* "The New York State Department of taxation was there, and the cruise missile manufacturer Raytheon, Cantor Fitzgerald, to name a few. There were so many International firms. I remember going to the Bank of Tokyo," Mr Shah said.

Roz joined in the conversation. "There were people from Great Britain, people from Pakistan…from so many countries. It's good to know British prime minister, Tony Blair, and the Pakistan leader, Musharraf, are behind our president," she said.

"Yeah, but it might be too little, too late," Tom said. "Man you know, when they were built I remember not many people cared for them. They were not as nice looking as the Chrysler building, and they didn't have what people call, "cinematic tradition" of the Empire State Building. In fact they were just so many office buildings stacked up like a bunch of kids building blocks—one on top of the other."

"Well they were more than blocks," Mr. Shah said with unexpected indignation. "It was quite an engineering achievement. I read about the creator Minoru Yamasaki on Wikipedia. He had a difficult task of creating 12 million square feet of office space on a 16 acre site that included subway connections, and the Hudson River tunnel. The buildings used a sort of tube design so that the load was supported by a central core. The vertical lines on the outside that give it the lattice effect, were constructed to safeguard against wind and other environmental hazards. Everything about the building was innovative," He spoke quickly, and tapped on the couch to punctuate his words.

"What the heck is he talking about?" Sita muttered. "How does he know so much about the towers? He's from India. Even if he read everything on Wikipedia, how can he repeat it so easily?"

"He must have an engineering degree of some sort," Roz whispered back. "He's a very intelligent man. Besides he has a son who worked there."

"Mr. Shah had a son there? How do you know?"

"He's Tom's buddy."

"Who is Tom's buddy?"

"Mr. Shah's son."

Rohit interrupted the conversation. "I'm bored," he whined. "What are you guys talking about?" Then he saw the plastic bag lying on the floor. "What is in there?" Is it for me?" he squealed excitedly. "Can I see?" He ran toward Sita.

"Watch it!" Roz screamed. But it was too late.

The glass of cherry coke on the table was sent flying, and toppled straight into Sita's lap.

"I'm so sorry," Rohit said quickly. Then he found the package and forgot about her.

Sita looked at the large brown stain that was growing between her legs and was glad for the excuse to go back upstairs. Maybe she would catch up with Roz later.

"Sita wait," Aunt Priya called. She noticed the large brown patch on her pants. "You are going up to change? I wanted to say Ramu dada is coming in a little while. You know how he is? You think you can wear something more Indian?"

"I won't wear a *salwar kameeze*," Sita said quickly. "Besides what will the Shah's think....that I am changing to impress them?"

"I never thought you cared what the Shah's thought," Aunt Priya said.

"I don't," Sita snapped.

"I knew that." The two of them glared at each other. Then Sita left.

Chapter Twenty

In her room Sita wrestled with the wet jeans. The cola soaked fabric clung stubbornly to her thighs, and she struggled to be free of the sticky mess. She pried the jeans off, and kicked them out of the way. She toweled herself dry, put on a pair of shorts, grabbed an ice cream from the freezer and made herself comfortable in front of the television. *She was in no mood to deal with Ramu dada today.* She slid deeper into the recliner to enjoy her ice cream—a vanilla bar coated with chocolate. Like the time when she was a little girl, she licked off the chocolate first, and then tackled the vanilla, savoring its sweet coldness.

The Oprah show was on. Oprah was talking to a Bahraini princess Merriam Al-Khalifa and, to a US marine Jason Johnson. It was hard to imagine this unlikely duo as husband and wife, but they had been recently married in a Las Vegas chapel and, there they were on stage holding hands and acting very much in love. Dressed in a little black dress that fell just below her knees, and tie up shoes from the eighties, the princess had raven black hair that framed her chiseled features. She looked classy, though not like a typical storybook princess. Her husband had an overgrown crew cut that made a poky halo around his head.

Oprah asked all the right questions in her usual direct manner, and got appreciative *oohs* and *aahs* from the audience. "Did you live in a castle?" she asked. "Tell us what it was like being a princess."

The princess blushed and said how it really wasn't a castle, but more like a house big enough for the family, and had this really high wall around it.

"So how did you meet?" Oprah was asking.

There was a tap on the door, and Roz walked in.

"What are you doing?" she asked. She took in Sita's bare legs spread out on the recliner, wearing the shortest of shorts.

"Shhh, listen to this. This princess.... I can't say her name right, she met this marine when he was posted in Bahrain. Where's Bahrain anyway?"

"It's a tiny island in the Persian Gulf... I've seen this show before," Roz said. "This princess eloped with the marine. It was all over the news and in the papers. He forged some papers and smuggled her into the country. Then the princess got thrown in jail for entering illegally, and after 3 days got released into her husband Jason's custody."

"Shh let's listen. Don't tell me everything. I like to hear it the way Oprah tells it."

"You gave up everything to be with this man," Oprah said. The princess nodded.

"Didn't you have second thoughts?"

The princess described how she hesitated before climbing the rope ladder, she took a last look at her home, and at everything she had known, and then started climbing without looking back, until she had reached the other side.

When Oprah asked if she would feel differently after she had lived in the army barracks, done laundry, washed dishes, and had to do all the different chores she had never done as a princess, Merriam said she loved doing all the new chores. It was new and exciting. Persistent as usual, Oprah asked what would happen when the novelty wore off. The princess affirmed firmly, she would feel no different ten years from now.

"That was all a bunch of baloney," Roz said. "When the going got tough, she ran back to mommy and daddy, and left her husband alone."

"What do you mean?"

"I read news reports she was back in Bahrain and considering divorce. So much for love! But you don't believe in that anyway. Right Sita? I think you're too scared to ever fall in love."

"That's mean."

"Telling it like it is," Roz shrugged. "Your Ramu dada is here, and he's got some plastic surgeon lined up for you as a possible husband, so you'd better come downstairs."

"What plastic surgeon?"

"I don't know. Come down and find out."

"You make me sound like a sack of potatoes being readied to be hauled away by the next grocery truck."

"What? Where do you come up with these analogies," Roz shook her head. "Any way you had better hurry, because that Ramu dada is beginning to look impatient. And Aunt Priya looks pissed. If you don't want to go out with this doctor, I have a feeling Aunt Priya will support you."

"Aunt Priya wanted me to marry Mr. Shah's son so I guess she is mad." Sita said quietly.

"So how come you never told me? You never said a word about your trip to India."

"Mr. Shah's son was the guy I went to India to check out."

"But Mr. Shah has no sons in India. They all live here."

"What do you mean *live* here?"

"Ajay works in the same bank as Tom, and Raja used to work in the World Trade Center. He and Tom were good friends.

"What do you mean *were*?" Sita said with a catch in her voice.

"They still are. We're going over to his place. Raja was burned pretty badly at the World Trade Center, but he's pretty much out of the woods now. Tom helped him get out."

"How?"

"Duh! He's a firefighter. That's what he likes to do."

"Listen, get up and get dressed unless you want Ramu dada to come upstairs and see you wearing those short shorts. I've never seen you in anything so short before," Roz eyed her slender length. "You know some women would kill to have those legs, but you always have to keep them covered up."

"Can you imagine me going downstairs in this?" Sita said. "Where did Ramu dada find this doctor he wants me to see?"

"Apparently he is Raja's doctor."

"Oh!" Sita wondered how long she could conceal the turmoil in her heart. "What shall I wear?" She turned away so Roz could not see the pain in her eyes. *No one had thought to tell her Raja was hurt. She could understand why the Shahs did not say anything, but what about Aunt Priya. She could have said something. Did they think she had wished this on Raja? How was he now? What did Roz mean by 'out of the woods?' How badly was he burned?*

Roz interrupted her thoughts and said, "Don't you have any of those pretty embroidered *Kurtis*? Remember the one Aunt Priya bought me because she thought the blue matched the color of my eyes."

"She bought it for you because it covered the tattoo on your back." Sita said. "But that's a good idea—I could wear one of those with jeans."

"Yep. As long as your butt is covered in a top that's long enough, Aunt Priya should be okay."

"You do care a lot about what Aunt Priya thinks!"

"I do. She is a dear lady."

Both girls climbed the stairs at the side of the house to Aunt Priya's apartment. The worn linoleum with curled-up edges almost tripped Sita. She stamped it down out of the way, wishing she could stomp away the confusion in her mind just as easily.

They heard raised voices, and learned soon enough that Ramu dada was involved in a heated conversation with Aunt Priya.

"I have found her such a good match, and all you can do is make excuses."

"I have never met this plastic doctor and I don't know if he'll get along with Sita."

"He is a plastic surgeon. Surgeon, you understand. He makes good money. Our niece will be the queen of the house."

"Let's wait here," Sita said. She paused outside the kitchen door. "Let's not interrupt them."

"You just want to eavesdrop, don't you?" Roz said, but made no move to stop her.

"Money is not everything," Aunt Priya said.

"I don't know what's gotten into you," Ramu said. "At least you didn't force her to marry that Raja. He is not king anymore, and our Sita would have been the queen of misery if she had married him. He has no job, and his health is gone."

"Don't talk like that. He will be fine."

"You're not thinking of Sita and Raja again! Are you? Just because the Shahs are your friends, you wouldn't want to ruin your niece's life."

"The Shah's have been my friends, and they will remain my friends regardless of whom Sita decides to marry."

"What do you mean by saying, *decides to marry*? She won't decide. *We* will," Sita heard Ramu dada say.

"Ramu, I have told you before, and I will tell you again, you can take a horse to the water, but you cannot make it drink. If you haven't learned that yet, Sita will teach you."

Sita had heard enough, but it was easier to pretend that she had not heard a word. She walked in, hands folded in traditional Indian greeting, and said "Namaste." She looked around the room quickly. The Shah's were gone. *Thank goodness.*

"*Namaste beti*," Ramu dada said congenially. "That is a nice *kurti*," he said pointedly. Sita sensed he was holding himself in check, and not saying anything about her jeans.

"You re such a nice girl," he said. "Not only pretty, but smart too. You had the sense to turn down that Raja in India and look what has become of him." Sita felt Roz's eyes bore into her. She had never really discussed her feelings for Raja with anyone. In the old days she would have told Roz, but Roz and Tom were so wrapped up in each other, there was no time for girl talk.

"Raja is a very nice young man," Tom defended his friend. "He will make one lucky girl very happy someday."

"Oh I hope you are right. Say my hellos to him when you see him," Ramu dada said sheepishly. "I wish him well."

"I'll let him know," Tom said stiffly, "when I see him tonight."

"You're going to see him tonight?" Sita perked up. "Can you take some cookies—they are Glaxo biscuits I picked up from the Indian store on the weekend, and I have some other snacks he will enjoy."

"Sure," Tom said, "Give them to Roz. We usually go out together to hang out at his place."

"I didn't know you knew Raja," Roz commented, "or that he was the guy you went to India to see. How come you never told me?"

"She doesn't *know* Raja," Ramu dada said quickly. "She saw him at some family gatherings. She has a good heart. Our Sita does." He looked to Aunt Priya for support. "Am I right Priya?"

Aunt Priya frowned and said, "She never gave me those cookies when I asked for them—told me she didn't have enough."

"Because you are not sick," Ramu dada said.

Sita left to get the cookies and did not see Aunt Priya's brows all scrunched up on her lined forehead.

"Looks like she cares for Raja," she told Roz.

"The same way she cares for anyone who is sick," Ramu dada insisted. "Remember the stray kittens she adopted when she was little, and her ma was all upset?"

"That was me. Not Sita," Aunt Priya said. "This is interesting." Then quickly, she cleared up the frown on her face because she heard Sita's footsteps on the stairs. "Very interesting," she repeated.

"Well if she likes Raja, she can always come and hang out with us. We see Raja often."

"No," Ramu dada said. "That cannot happen. Her marriage is being arranged with Dr. Singh. Dr. Singh is a very busy man. He has cured Tom's friend Raja, and so many others from the September 11th crisis. So you see, she should be honored to see him."

Sita came up the stairs just in time to hear the last bit of the conversation.

"You want me to see Dr. Singh? Okay I'll go," Sita said. "When do I get to meet him?"

"See. What did I tell you? We have a very sensible niece."

Sita dutifully bowed her head as Ramu dada expected her to, and from the corner of her eye she saw Aunt Priya looked very confused.

"What's the matter Aunt Priya?" Sita asked.

"You were never so willing when I asked you to see anyone. You gave me such a hard time."

"I've learned my lesson."

"Something is fishy, what do you think Tom?"

"Ask Roz. I really don't know."

"Looks like I am the only one who knows." Ramu dada said pompously. "Sita understands that I know what's best for her."

Aunt Priya slapped the frying pan on the counter. "Well I am not sure of that. Until you can convince me that that you know what you're doing, I will give you a hard time."

"Isn't she a firebrand," Tom said with a big smile.

"With a heart of gold," Roz said.

"You're right about that." Tom had to bend almost double to give Aunt Priya a peck on the cheek. "We'll be going now, see you soon. Actually, my mom is having a sort of celebration party at her home in Long Island. It would be great if you can come. It's like a celebration of some of the heroes of *Nine Eleven*. Some of my friends, some of hers, and some of Roz's friends, will be there.

"That will be great," Aunt Priya grinned from ear to ear. "I love parties. And I would love to meet your mother. Such a wonderful boy she has raised."

"Yeah and isn't he gorgeous," Roz said, winding her slender arms around Tom's waist. She planted a kiss squarely on his lips. Aunt Priya turned away quickly, "Look at her Tom," Roz said, noticing how quickly Aunt Priya averted her gaze, "she blushes when I hug you. Isn't she a sweetheart?"

A red tinge swept over Aunt Priya's well-powdered face at this public display of affection. "You know you and Tom's mom will get along great. You're both so much alike—both wonderful people," Roz said.

Aunt Priya blushed some more, and was at a loss for words.

"See that!" she said after Tom and Roz left. "Such nice things they say about me."

"Too much praise from white people is making you swollen-headed," Ramu dada said.

"White people are good too," Aunt Priya said—almost as if she had just come to this conclusion. "You wouldn't understand. Good thing they never invited you."

"I wouldn't want to go. They will serve all boiled food with no spice. Only thing—keep Sita away from that Raja if he is there."

"She's not a dog I can keep on a leash. Who knows, maybe your Dr. Singh will be there, and they will hit it off. She did say it was a celebration of heroes. Your Dr. Singh according to you was quite a hero, helping so many people after the disaster."

"So why don't you like him?"

"We'll just have to wait and find out why."

Aunt Priya bustled around the kitchen banging pots and pans, pretending to tidy her kitchen. Ramu dada remained standing there. "I chose Raja for Sita, not just because he had money, but because I knew the family backgrounds were the same, and the personalities of both young people would click. They both love kids, see how good they're with Rohit. They both like to read, and talk about all those books all the time, they both like theater. They are so similar." She shook her head. "So stubborn—Sita has a mind of her own, and Raja will always stand on his own two feet. You just watch and see. He will do fine."

"Well, Dr. Singh is a very nice person," Ramu dada said.

"Doctor's families are the most neglected," Aunt Priya snapped. "Always busy with patients. Sometimes they even have to work on Christmas and New Year to take care of patients. It's about *patients, patients, patients,* all the time." Her voice got louder and louder when she spoke. "Many weekends they are on call. They don't get any, how you say—breaks? Then these days in America, people like to sue doctors. They will do anything to get big money for the tiniest excuse. It is so unfair. My friend's malpractice liability insurance went so high, she was thinking of leaving New York State, or taking early retirement."

"Doctors make a lot of money," Ramu dada said again.

"You won't understand. Let me pack some food for you to take home," she said in a last ditch effort to be rid of him. The ploy never failed. She was back in her expected role of cook and caregiver, and Ramu was soon on his way home, carrying a pyramid of utensils filled with his favorite leftovers.

"Thank goodness he's gone," Aunt Priya said, "I gave him all the leftover chicken and everything else." She looked sad. "Now I will have to cook again."

"I thought you like to cook."

"I do like to cook—but not because I have to, but when I want to." She sighed. "Sita we have shopping to do. Let's go to Macys. You buy yourself something, and help me pick out a dress."

"Dress for whom?" Sita said.

"For me—for the party," Aunt Priya said. "Matching shoes I want. You'll help me?"

Sita burst out laughing, "You're not serious. You've never worn anything other than a sari. You'll look comical in a dress."

Without a word Aunt Priya walked away. "You're no different from Ramu dada. Always want to put me down."

Sita was contrite. "Aunt Priya I'm sorry. I really am. I'll go with you, and maybe we should ask Roz to come along too."

"Don't worry about it. Just buy yourself something. I can take care of myself," Aunt Priya said biting her lower lip to keep more words from spilling out of her mouth. Sita looked on, and Aunt Priya waddled away with her head held high.

Chapter Twenty-one

"Hurry up!" Aunt Priya yelled. "We have a party to go to. What is taking so long?"

Aunt Priya was wearing a plain lavender silk sari, and a matching blouse. A string of pearls hung loosely around her neck.

"Nice?" she asked. She twirled around in a swirl of silky sari pleats. "Roz said a plain color would make me look slender. See the blouse? She picked out the matching fabric, and came with me to the tailor. She wanted me to wear the blouse longer. She said short blouses make me look fatter than I am. This one looks good?"

"Oh absolutely," Sita said. She remembered the rolls of flesh that invariably escaped the bright strawberry-pink number Aunt Priya usually wore, and smiled.

"You are laughing at me," Aunt Priya said.

"I am smiling because I think you look very pretty," Sita lied quickly.

"I can tell when you lie. This is the reason I ask Roz for help, not you."

"How did she talk you out of wearing a dress?" Sita asked.

"She said a dress made me look like an overstuffed dumpling."

"She told you that! You let her talk to you that way?"

"What's wrong? She said the dress was wrong. Not *me*. She said I should be myself, and wear the sari. She came with me to pick it out. I like your friend."

"Yeah—lately she is more your friend, than mine."

"Oh, that's not true," Aunt Priya said, but Sita could tell she was secretly happy.

Roz was waiting for them at the Long Island Rail Road station in Woodside.

"Hi guys!" She grinned in greeting, showing off her small pearly white teeth in a tanned face. She too, was wearing a dress in lavender—the same shade as Aunt Priya's sari. The sleeveless dress with a flared skirt fell just above her knees, fitted tightly in just the right places, and showed off her figure to perfection.

"Rohit you look great. Is that Scooby Doo on your shirt? That's cool. Hi Sita." She walked quickly past them toward Aunt Priya.

"You look so pretty, Aunt Priya," Roz gushed, clearly happy that the older woman had taken her suggestion about what to wear.

"You too dear," Aunt Priya said. "But what have you done to your makeup? Or did you go to that tanning salon again?"

"As a matter of fact I did," Roz said, smiling to show another flash of white teeth.

"You know, I spend all my time trying to get lighter, and have a nice fair complexion, and you spend way too much money to get darker. Do you know, I spent yesterday doing *uptum*?"

"What's that? But wait let's find the train, and you can tell me there."

"Okay." Aunt Priya walked faster. "Why didn't you say anything to Sita? She looks nice in her slacks and sweater?"

"She looks alright." Roz said. "Why?"

Sita heard them whispering her name and caught up with them. "You're not trying to hook me up with someone at this party are you?"

"Look at her," Aunt Priya said. "Every time I tell her to dress up, she says I am trying to marry her off. Do you know yesterday she wouldn't let me do *uptum* on her?"

"What is that? What is '*uptum*'?

"It's a paste of turmeric and gram flour moistened with cream. It is very good. It makes you fair."

Roz crinkled her nose the way she did when she was confused. "It comes in a jar?"

"No, I make it myself with fresh cream from cows' milk. It lightens the skin," Aunt Priya reiterated. Her breath came in gasps from the exertion of climbing so many stairs to get to the proper platform.

"Doesn't sound so nice," Roz said.

"Believe me it is nasty to sit around with goop on your face," Sita said.

Aunt Priya looked up at another seemingly endless flight of stairs to the train platform. "What happened to Tom?" she asked.

"He had to run some last minute errands for his mom, but he will bring us back. We won't have to take these stairs again," Roz said.

Aunt Priya picked up her sari pleats and hurried along.

They got to the double decker that would bring them to Port Jefferson, Long Island in approximately two hours.

"Oh this is nice." Aunt Priya's eyes widened at the cushioned chairs and light gray interior, so different from the subway.

"Do people sell toys here, like they do on the subway?" Rohit asked. He remembered the yo-yo and robot that Sita had bought him.

"I'm afraid not hon, but there are lots of things you can play with when you get to Tom's house."

Then in an aside to Aunt Priya she said, "Tom's mom always keeps a bunch of toys on hand for her youngest visitors. He'll have fun. It's really nice out there too. These trains should move faster though. Port Jefferson is not so far—only about 60 miles from here."

"Oh, you young people are always so impatient," Aunt Priya rubbed her legs, feeling very glad to be finally sitting down. "See we are moving now. We are going faster and faster." She watched the yellow line at the edge of the platform blur into a runaway stripe as the train picked up speed.

Rohit and his mother sat together, with Rohit claiming the window seat. Sita and Roz sat together. For a while, Sita stared out of the window taking in the changing landscape. Little by little, dilapidated houses and well-worn brownstones huddled together like cardboard boxes carelessly thrown together became harder to find. Then the two family brownstones disappeared, giving way to single family homes. The concrete jungle of the city, gave way to more greenery. All the houses in Nassau County had well-manicured lawns trimmed with landscaped shrubs. Some of the houses looked really large, but were shrouded from view by forest land dotted with an assortment of flowering shrubs.

Sita eyed the hydrangeas growing wild and bursting with bright pink blooms in the middle of nowhere. "Look how pretty! I wish I could uproot even one of these wild shrubs, and plant it in my garden," Sita said wistfully.

"It wouldn't fit in your garden," Roz said, remembering the tiny flower bed in front of Sita's house in Queens.

"It's peaceful here," Sita yawned. The train had begun moving faster, and the trees were beginning to blur. The automated system that announced the stations had been turned off. There were no sounds in the car, except for Aunt Priya's gentle snoring. Rohit too, was fast asleep.

"It's certainly relaxing out here," Roz said. "Did you notice there are no sidewalks here?"

"Oh yes," Sita said. "I just noticed that. No sidewalks. The lawns just roll out their welcome all the way to the street. No wonder, there isn't anyone walking around. No kids on the street."

"Well, everyone has a big backyard, maybe a pool. In fact the further east you go, you see more houses with pools. You can't walk anywhere. Everything is so spread out. You would get nowhere if you started to walk."

"So your mother in-law has a nice big house with a pool?" Sita asked.

"Did you just say "my mother-in-law"? I have to say "yes" to Tom before I get a mother in law!"

"So what's the problem?"

"Nothing—just scared I guess. So what's up with *you*? Did you go on your date with the plastic surgeon?"

"Yeah, I met him. He's a good doctor."

"And?"

"Nothing."

"What do you mean *nothing?* What did you talk about?"

"He told me about the different kinds of skin grafts for burn victims."

Roz raised her eyebrows.

"Well, I was the one asking the questions. I asked him what was easier to work with, homografts from a skin bank, or autografts that use a patient's own skin. Some of the autografts use a mesh 2 to 1.

Roz rolled her eyes and Sita continued. "They use a special machine that creates a mesh in the donor skin and allows it to be applied to a burn area 3 times as large."

"Since when did you know so much about skin grafts?" Roz asked.

"Well, there was an article on autografts that used the patient's own tissue in one of the medical journals we publish."

"Why would you talk about grafts?"

"Well, that's what he does for a living. Right? Graft skin among other things. Besides, I'd also been reading the book by Greg Manning."

"Who's that?"

"You know the guy who wrote *Love Greg & Lauren?* It was about his wife who had 80% burns and survived the World Trade Center disaster. His name was Greg Manning."

"Oh yea! I saw that story. It made first page of the *New York Times*. Well, at least you were talking about a news story not some obscure medical article in a journal that he's most definitely never read."

"Our journals are not obscure."

"I'm sure." Roz said abruptly. Then after a long pause, she said, "Why do I get the feeling you are not telling me everything. What's the real deal here? C'mon we've still got an hour on this train ride. Spill the beans."

"Well, I only agreed to meet with Dr. Singh because I heard he was Raja's doctor," Roz confessed.

"What?"

"Well no one had thought to tell me Raja had been hurt, so I figured this was my opportunity to find out for myself."

"No one thought you were interested, so no one told you anything. Why didn't you ask?"

"Well if I had no clue he was hurt, why would I ask?"

"Looks like you fell in love with Raja. Wait till I tell Tom!"

"Don't you dare! Promise you won't say a word to Tom or I'll just die of embarrassment."

"So you *do* like Raja," Roz said. "Okay I won't say anything. But there's something I can't figure out, so help me. Tell me what happened in India that made Aunt Priya decide not to tell you Raja was in America."

"Well, I was rude. I was more than rude. I was out of control. Now that I think of it I behaved like a bazaar woman."

"What's a bazaar woman?"

"She is someone with no breeding, and no home training. Like someone from a low class family."

"Amazing!"

"I know."

"No. I said 'amazing' because I was thinking how you all still talk about the class system even though it's been years since the British left, and quite some time since the caste system was abolished."

"Oh. Well we still have a social hierarchy and people from good families are supposed to act a certain way." Sita said.

"So what did you do?"

"I told him he was not what he seemed to be, I was not fooled by his charm, and I knew what he *really* wanted. I told him I knew he wanted to use me to get to America. That his family was made up of all conniving tricksters, looking to get a foothold in America so they could expand their export business. And I was not going to be anybody's ticket to the Promised Land."

"Is that what you thought?"

"No."

"What did you think?"

"That Raja was the most handsome guy alive. He has these gentle brown eyes, and was the perfect gentleman every time I saw him. He was great with Rohit…." Sita blushed.

"Then I don't understand. Why did you say what you did?"

"What do you want from me?" Sita said defensively. "I felt I had been carted like a sack of potatoes from America to marry a boy. I was supposed to be grateful because he was such a "good catch". Nobody said anything good about *me.* I felt no one was even paying any attention to me."

"So you had a temper tantrum. That's not like you though." Roz said thoughtfully.

"I thought Raja had wanted to hang out with me. I never knew Aunt Priya was trying to manipulate everything and going to extraordinary lengths to push us together. What would the family do next? I felt the water closing over my head, so I lashed out at him and it came out all wrong. Oh I hate his mother! She has the nastiest controlling black eyes!"

"You hate his mother, so you lashed out at him? Told him he was a user and a bum. Turns out he made it to America without your help—so much for that!"

"I know, I know. I knew he was intelligent and hardworking. But you know every girl, even one having an arranged marriage dreams that the guy will marry her because he likes her, and not only out of a sense of duty to his mother."

"What about the father?"

"The father was cool. At least, that was before I had this tirade with his son. Now of course he pretends I don't exist. I saw them at Aunt Priya's house. I said "hello," and he never answered."

"You're way too sensitive. You know they may all be there today, at Tom's place. You might see them all. In fact I am pretty sure you will, because Raja and Tom are best friends."

"So you see Raja a lot?" Sita asked. "You know, I did write him more than one apology letter. They were all returned to me." Sita showed the ones she still carried in her handbag.

Roz glanced quickly at the bundle of letters in her bag. "Yes we do see him quite a bit. So fire away, and I'll tell you anything I know about him."

"Well I found out from Dr. Singh that he was burnt on 25% of his body, and that he had multiple skin grafts. I also heard all about atrophied muscles, and how the joints have to be worked and the extensive physiotherapy that is required to make them work properly. I know all about his pain medications, and I know he had to wear some sort of pressurized clothing to minimize scarring."

"Hang on just a moment. Why would Dr. Singh tell you this? He would be violating doctor and patient confidentiality."

"I told him I was romantically involved with Raja, and Ramu dada did not know."

"Wow! I would never have expected that from you. You must really like Raja a lot! So shoot. What did you want to know?"

"Well I know all about his injuries. What I don't know is how he was rescued, or who rescued him."

"Okay" Roz said. "I can fill you in on that. Tom told me it was Raja's second day at work. He worked on the 78th floor of Tower 1. He was in the office, and he heard a loud boom and then the room shook hard enough to make him lose his balance and fall back into his chair." Roz paused, opened her eyes wide, and tried to remember everything Tom had told her. Sita waited eagerly.

"Tom tells this better," Roz said. "It's not going to be as dramatic as when I first heard him say it. Anyway, I'll do the best I can—Raja faltered past the doorway into the corridor to see what the heck was going on. He heard someone scream. He turned to see a child crying, "Mommy I'm stuck. Help me!" He turned to see her partially trapped under an overturned file cabinet. *What was she doing here?* Raja quickly reached and extricated her, "Come," he said, "come quickly. Hold your mommy's hand." He urged mother and child to the top of the stairwell, to make their way down," Roz said.

She took a deep breath then continued with her story. "He decided to run back to his office to grab his briefcase, and cell phone. That was a huge mistake. As Raja came out into the corridor again, a flaming inferno from the elevator shaft closed in on him. He tried to beat at it with his arms, and stamp it out to find a clear path out of there. His legs were burnt badly, and so were his arms. When Tom found him, his clothes were charred and melted into his flesh. He cried out in pain when Tom tried to touch him to try and move him along. They had met before briefly, but on that day with his face so burnt, he was barely recognizable. Tom told me he kept moaning and saying, *Leave me here. Just let me be.*"

Tears welled in Sita's eyes, as Roz continued her story.

"But Tom would not leave him. "Come down with me just a few flights," he urged. "Then I'll leave you alone." Then after a few flights, when Raja begged to stop, Tom told him, "You're almost all the way down. You're doing great. I'm going to be right here. Can you imagine how worried your family will be if you don't see them?" He never let him stop. They were only on the 30th floor when he told him they were almost all the way down. Little by little, others followed Tom's lead and encouraged everyone to keep moving. "You can't stop mid-way," they said. "You'll be obstructing everyone else. We're almost there, they lied," Roz said.

She paused and said, "Now Raja says it was Tom who saved him. If he had known he was still on the 30th floor when Tom said he was almost out, he would have given up. Tom did not leave till he made sure Raja was in good hands. Then he went off to help others."

By this time the tears Sita had been holding back, spilled over. Hurriedly she rubbed her eyes. There was no point in looking foolish. The train was pulling into the station. Aunt Priya had woken up just in time. "Wake up Rohit." She shook her son, gently.

"Oh we're here," Aunt Priya announced when she saw *Port Jefferson* written in big letters. The train came to a halt in front of a quaint looking station house. The parking lot was not full. Roz quickly hailed a taxi cab. "So much space here," Aunt Priya observed. "It must be easy to drive over here. I wish I knew how to drive."

"I could show you," Sita said. Aunt Priya turned to look at her to say "thank you."

"What's the matter Sita?" She narrowed her eyes. "You look like you've been crying."

"Her contacts are bothering her," Roz said quickly.

Sita looked at her gratefully.

"Then you must take them out and clean them. You spoiled your eyes by reading so much all the time." She shook her head. "Fix those lenses and do something to your makeup." Aunt Priya eyed the smear of runny mascara down her cheek. "I don't want Raja to see you with red eyes." Then, she realized what she had said and tried to change the subject.

"Come, let's go quickly and party." Aunt Priya led the way though she had never been there before. "It will be so nice to meet Tom's mom, and everybody else," she said. Sita wiped the smear of mascara, fixed her makeup and followed.

Chapter Twenty-two

Tom's mother stood at the doorway of their colonial home smiling broadly. The red cherry cone she was still holding in her hand, explained the splash of bright red that looked like it had been finger-painted across her lips. A mop of premature gray hair framed her rosy cheeks, and tickled the chin of the tall, thin gentleman who stood behind her, smiling tentatively at the group of visitors entering their home. At first glance, one could tell that the little lady was the sociable one. Her husband was always two steps behind her, and followed her lead.

"Hi there!" Tom's mother shouted out as soon as they were within earshot. The laugh lines along the corners of her mouth were creased in a welcoming smile.

"Tom has said so much about you," she told Aunt Priya, who was the first to get out of the car. "All of you," she added, as Sita and Rohit jumped out too. "It's wonderful to meet you all." Her husband stood behind, and nodded.

"Oh it is so nice to meet you too." Aunt Priya picked and pulled at Rohit's shirt to give her nervous fingers something to do.

"Your sari is so beautiful—so graceful," Tom's mom said disarmingly.

"Thank you," Aunt Priya patted herself and stopped picking and pulling Rohit's shirt. "What is your name?" she asked Tom's mom. "I don't know it...My name is Priya. Priya means most loved."

"Wonderful! My name is Sue. C'mon in." Tom's mom said. She welcomed them with a peck on the cheek as they filed past her.

"Next time you must come to my house," Aunt Priya prattled on. "Then you can sample my Indian cooking and you can try on the sari."

Sue smiled warmly, "You know, I'm going to take you up on that offer real soon. C'mon let's find something for this young man to do." She took Rohit by the hand. "That's a real neat shirt. Is that Scooby Doo you have there?" she asked. "Come, let me show you Ginger. She just had pups. Want to see?" Rohit grinned and his eyes lit up. "Be careful she doesn't get out of the backyard gate. So many people don't like dogs. They won't like it if she is wandering around, even though the poor gal is pretty harmless."

Aunt Priya asked Tom's dad where the kitchen was, and got busy. Roz had found Tom. The two were glued to one another, making up for lost time, quite oblivious to anybody else that was in the room. Sita shifted uncomfortably from one foot to the other, wondering whom to talk to. She had stared long enough at the picture frames, and the curios on the mantel and wondered when the twosome would separate so she could ask them where she could find everybody else.

Aunt Priya poked her head in and saw Roz and Tom entwined in each other's arms. "Children these days!" she said. Sita knew she was clearly biting back the words that sprang to her lips. She saw Sue and said, "Children these days are so honest, so open. Sometimes I think I can learn from them!" Then when Sue turned around quickly, she added, "Other times I think too much is no good. They should be a little shy. What do you think Sue?"

"Oh absolutely! I think those two should hurry up and get married."

"So why you don't say something?" Aunt Priya asked.

"Well, I can't *make* them get married. Arranged marriage like they have in India….I can't do that."

"Neither could I. I tried with Sita, you know. She gave me such a shock. She turned down the boy I thought would be so good for her. Even after she turned him down, I thought she would change her tune when she saw him again in America and saw how good he was. Now I don't know what to say. He is a nice boy but, now he has no job. He worked in the World Trade Center and, as you know everything got blown up. I feel he is a good boy. He is my friend's son. He will find another job, but what if he doesn't? I can't arrange a marriage to someone with no job, now can I? I am so confused."

"Well if Sita already said "no," you can't get too pushy. Just let things take their course," Sue advised.

Sita wandered out into the porch. She didn't want to be caught eavesdropping. *It was good Aunt Priya had made friends so quickly. Unbelievable! That she knew Raja was coming to America and hadn't told her. That explained why she hadn't argued with her too much in India about rejecting Raja. She knew she would get a second chance when he came to the US. Of course things had changed now, because he had no job. If only, the other guests would arrive quickly, maybe there would be someone she could talk to.*

She stood on the porch overlooking the large expanse of green on Tom's property that was just shy of one acre. A number of patio umbrellas dotted the grass where tables had been set up for the barbecue. Sita stood alone, overcome by the peacefulness of the place. The wind blew her long hair back, and pressed her clothes against her, outlining her hour glass shape.

A car was coming up the driveway. Sita turned to go in and tell someone that guests had begun arriving. Aunt Priya was pouring punch, and laying out the sandwiches, and offering Tom's father cookies. She was carrying on as though she were a part of the family.

"Aunt Priya, where is Roz? I think the guests have begun arriving," Sita said.

"Roz and Tom have....how you say....have some catching up to do. You go and open the door, and make everybody sit down. I will tell Sue her guests are here."

The car had already pulled up. Sita wished she could shake the uneasy feeling in the pit of her stomach, and went outside to welcome the guests. The first one out of the car was Ms. Shah.

"Well, well," she said. "You decided to come out after all. We didn't think you would. We saw you on the porch. And then you fled."

"Nice to meet you, Ms. Shah," Sita said. Ms. Shah gave her a piercing stare, and narrowed her eyes.

Mr. Shah walked past her with a curt nod.

Sita turned to follow them inside and a familiar voice behind her said, "Hello Sita, fancy meeting you here!"

Sita wheeled around to come face to face with Raja. She had not seen him in so long. He was thinner. There was a soulful look in his eyes that hadn't been there before.

"Hullo," she whispered. "How are you?" They looked at each other for a while. No one spoke.

He broke the silence and said, "You look well—as beautiful as ever. I saw you standing by yourself on the porch."

Sita blushed, and was at a complete loss for words.

"Oh there you are." Roz breezed into the porch. "Hi, Raja. Good you two have met. Sita was asking about you."

Raja raised his eyebrows.

"Yeah. She often does."

"Does she really? You never said so before."

"I guess it never came up," Roz shrugged.

Roz eyed the long white gloves Raja wore on his forearms. "How does the burn feel? Do the pressure gloves help?"

"I guess they will control the scarring," Raja said. He turned toward Sita, "But tell me about yourself, do you still work as editor in the same place?

"Yes," Sita said. She was glad that he had remembered. "Actually Roz and I work together."

"She never mentioned it!" he exclaimed.

"She didn't know I knew you."

"Do you really? *Know me*, I mean," he asked quizzically. When she didn't answer he said, "At our last meeting you gave me the idea you had no clue about me."

"C'mon Raja don't harp on that. She was upset," Roz said. Sita had forgotten Roz was there. She had been so quiet.

"How do you know? I thought you didn't know about Sita and me?"

"She told me on the way here."

"I see," Raja said skeptically.

"Listen," Roz said. "She didn't know you were in the World Trade Center. She didn't know you were hurt, and in fact, she didn't even know you were here in America. She was busy writing you apology letters in India."

"I never got any letters."

"Sita, why don't you give them to him, and then we can get on with it and enjoy this party."

Obediently, Sita opened her handbag and gave him the one Roz had read in the train.

"The address is wrong."

"I didn't know," Sita said quietly.

Raja read the letter quietly. But instead of saying "never mind," or "don't worry about it," as she had expected, there was a strange bitterness in his voice. "So I'm supposed to forgive and forget," he sneered. "Get on with my life just so you can go about yours? How was your date with Dr. Singh? Is he the rich and famous guy you always wanted to marry? Is that why you are here?"

"Raja come off it!" Roz snapped. "Sita is here because I invited her. Not to see Dr. Singh, or anyone else for that matter."

Raja quietened down as quickly as he had exploded. "Just letting off steam—I'm entitled to, aren't I?" he asked sarcastically, "or are there different rules for me and for Sita?"

"Stop it," Roz scolded. "If I didn't know better, I'd think you were jealous of Sita and Dr. Singh getting together."

"No need to be jealous about me," a gruff voice said. Sita wheeled around to see Dr. Singh.

"Your fiancé made it amply clear to me that the only guy she was interested in, was you. Sorry man, I had no idea you were engaged."

"How did you find out that I was?" Raja asked quickly.

"Sita told me over dinner," Dr. Singh replied.

Sita's heart beat fast, and the blood rushed to her face. She walked away quickly.

"What did I say wrong?" Dr Singh asked Roz. "She didn't want him to know I had dinner with her? I would never have asked her out for dinner if I had known she was involved with Raja. Her Ramu dada had no business setting us up," he said heatedly. "Anyway the only topic of conversation at the dinner was Raja's wellbeing. It was hardly a date! Not very flattering to me, is it?" he commented wryly. "You know what, I can have my pick of women because of the money I make, but the one woman I found interesting doesn't want me."

"I think I'll go and help Sue in the kitchen," Roz said.

"Running away again," Raja said. "You and Sita like to run away a lot, don't you." When Roz hesitated, he said, "See you later. I'll catch up with you. Tell Sita especially, she can count on that."

Sita could see Roz, but she dared not leave the safety of the kitchen. *There was no way she could face Raja again,* she thought. She picked and pulled at the paper napkins arranged in neat rows. The punch bowl was full, and the sandwiches were ready to be served. There was nothing more she could do in the kitchen. Still, she stayed. Her fingers tapped a restless beat on the table. She decided to check her makeup. She pulled out the mirrored compact from her handbag and gazed wide-eyed at her reflection. Her cheeks were flushed, her lips still stained an inviting pink were slightly parted, her mascara had smudged a bit, again, and enhanced her expression of a cornered deer.

"There you are." Roz breezed into the kitchen. "Have you seen Rohit? Sue can't find her dog and she is sure Rohit would know Ginger's whereabouts." She paused, "I have a message for you from Raja, but first we must find that dog. Drat that animal."

As if on cue, there was a yelp from Ginger, followed by the clatter of overgrown claws on the kitchen floor. Then there was a swoosh sound, and Ginger dived under the kitchen table, tilting the punch bowl and upsetting the neat rows of paper napkins. Rohit followed close behind, armed with a water gun.

"Not in the house, Rohit," Sita yelled. "Give me that water gun," but Rohit escaped through the screen door, out on the patio, and was out of ear shot. Ginger shot out from under the table, tilting the table again and spilling punch all over the paper napkins.

"Sita can you get the two of them?" Roz looked down at the punch drenched napkins. "I'll stay and clean up this mess."

Sita raced out. "Rohit come here," she yelled. Rohit was still with the water gun. He was trying to incite Ginger to rush around in circles, but Ginger had tired of the game. She shook off the last squirts of water to settle down comfortably in the sun. One minute the dog was sitting down, and Sita thought she would be able to grab her, but the next minute she was off like a dart. She had seen the neighbor's dog across the street, and was in hot pursuit. The yard was not fenced, and before Sita could stop them, Ginger was in the middle of the street and Rohit was close behind.

"Watch out," Sita yelled. A red minivan screeched to a halt. She saw Ginger's bushy tail appear from behind the van, and the dog was fine. She waited for Rohit to appear unscathed, but there was no sign of him. She hurried across the large expanse of green lawn to the curb, but Raja was there ahead of her.

"Is he okay?" she yelled.

"The van did not hit him," he yelled back.

"Why is he crying?" Sita rushed forward. Rohit was curled up on the side of the road bawling his lungs out. His forehead was bathed in blood that spilled over his Scooby Doo shirt. She averted her eyes. "Oh Lord!" she whispered.

Raja pointed to the splatter of blood on the stone border that encircled the rose bushes. "Looks like he tripped on this stone, and hit his head on the bricks here. He's going to need stitches. We have to get him to the hospital." Raja took charge. "Go find Aunt Priya and call 911 for an ambulance."

Grateful to have something constructive to do, Sita followed instructions. The ambulance arrived, sirens blasted on the quiet dead end street. All the guests gathered in the corner of the lawn.

"Was this an automobile accident?" the paramedics asked, looking at the red minivan nearby.

"No." Raja said, "Rohit was chasing the dog across the street. He tripped and hit his head."

The paramedics looked at Raja and Sita standing together. "You are the parents?"

Aunt Priya pushed her way forward through the crowd. "I am the mother." She pointed to Sita, "This is my niece, and that is her....her..."

"Her fiancé," Raja added softly. "Right Sita?"

Aunt Priya did not hear. With a sweep of her arm she told the paramedics, "All of us are going to ride in the ambulance. She waddled up to the ambulance. The driver told her Raja and Sita would have to come on their own, and she did not argue.

Aunt Priya was whisked away in a blare of sirens. The local hospital was less than a ten-minute ride, and soon Rohit was being hurried inside. Aunt Priya waddled about. She tugged at her purse and tried to extricate her insurance card while trying to push open the door. Raja and Sita had also reached. Aunt Priya yelled at them, "You both—you don't just stand there. Do something. Hold the door, or something. My poor boy bleeds to death, and you just stand there."

Rohit lay motionless on the stretcher. A gaping wound stared angrily up at her. Sita did not want Raja to know she was squeamish, and averted her eyes and focused on Scooby Doo on Rohit's T-shirt. "You're going to be fine," she said bravely. She involuntarily grabbed Raja to steady herself when she saw all that blood. Raja stared pointedly at the red talons curled around his wrist.

"Sorry," she said quickly.

"No problem," he smiled. "You are squeamish?"

She nodded, grateful not to have to pretend any more. Raja took charge the way she had always known him to. Soon he was standing by Rohit regaling him with the latest episodes of the Spiderman movie.

"Did you see him swing from building to building?" Rohit was asking.

"Sure did," Raja replied. "Pretty amazing, huh! That was a really neat movie."

"I want to be Spiderman for Halloween."

"Great! We'll go look for a costume as soon as we get outta here. What do you say?"

Aunt Priya turned her head quickly, "I heard that," she said. "He's not going to go anywhere today."

"Oh Mom!" Rohit wailed.

"He must be better," Aunt Priya muttered. "He is arguing already. It must be just a small cut. A few stitches perhaps, huh? What do you think Raja?"

"I think you are absolutely right." He flashed his most disarming smile at the Triage nurse. "Do you agree?" he asked her.

"Sure looks like it," she replied "We'll have it all patched up and ready to go, just as soon as we finish the x-rays and make sure there are no broken bones."

Aunt Priya clicked her tongue. "That nurse likes you. Why she has to smile at you so much?"

"She's just doing her job," Sita replied.

"Aha so you noticed too!" Aunt Priya said triumphantly. "Didn't it make you mad?"

"No, why should it?" Sita said. A tell-tale blush sprang to her cheeks. Raja turned to give her a piercing look.

"I think you two should stay together in the waiting room and I will go in with Rohit," Aunt Priya said.

"I want Raja to come," Rohit whined.

"He must stay with Sita," Aunt Priya replied.

"Aunt Priya if I didn't know better I would think you were match making again," Raja said.

"And why do you think you know better?" Aunt Priya said.

"Well, I'm hardly marriage material," Raja said depreciatingly. "I don't look the same, I've got no job, and I have nothing to offer anybody."

The nurse called Aunt Priya away. Sita had nothing to say to Raja. He guessed her thoughts and said, "I don't want anyone's pity—least of all yours. No one is going to arrange my marriage ever again."

"I understand," Sita said quietly, "Aunt Priya can be quite overbearing sometimes."

"She told you to introduce yourself as my fiancé, didn't she?" he asked.

"No," Sita said quietly.

Raja did not believe her. "Then it beats me why you did."

"Aunt Priya can be a pain but she does know where to butt out," Sita said.

"I love Aunt Priya," Raja said.

"Me too," Sita said.

"Probably the only thing we have in common."

"We don't know that for sure."

"And we'll never find out," Raja said dismally.

Sita did not know what to say to him, and was quiet.

Chapter Twenty-three

"Guess what?" Aunt Priya asked the following weekend.

"What?" Sita asked with some trepidation.

"I got my learner's permit. Now, you can teach me to drive. And I don't need to use your Papa's car. Ramu left me an old Volkswagen Beetle to practice on. He said a small car will be better for me, and I won't be scared about scratching it up."

"That's really nice of him," Sita exclaimed. "Let's go look at this car."

"No hurry, we can go later." Sita was already half way down the stairs. "I want to see it."

In the driveway, Sita saw a little orange car that had been through a lot. Almost twenty years old, the peeling paint and rusty exterior took Sita by surprise.

"It looks old," Aunt Priya said defensively, "but it runs well."

Sita took the keys from her Aunt's hand. "Let's try," she said. She looked inside and took a deep breath. An assortment of wires dangled from the dashboard. When she looked down, she could see a gaping hole in the floor from where the concrete driveway was visible. Her jaw dropped. "You want to drive this! Is it safe?"

"Everything in it works," Aunt Priya announced. "It looks like the Noddy car in Enid Blyton books."

"But it's stick shift," Sita said. She desperately wanted to get out of this driving lesson.

"Ramu dada said if I can drive a stick shift, then I can drive anything else," Aunt Priya said. "So it is a good thing that it is stick shift."

She got into the driver's seat. "Let's go," she said. "Tell me what to do."

As usual it was easier to obey, than to argue. Sita got into the bucket seat alongside Aunt Priya. "Put on your seat belt," she said.

"You think I will crash, don't you," Aunt Priya muttered.

"Check the mirror, and start the car."

Aunt Priya turned the key and the car spluttered, and then roared to let everyone know that the exhaust was broken. Patrick peeked out from under the blinds of his apartment building to look. Sita knew everyone in the building must be peeking to see what was going on, but were being more discreet than Patrick.

Aunt Priya put the car in first gear and came down on the accelerator. The car lurched forward. Then she hit the brake just as quickly, and the car stalled out. With a determined look on her face, Aunt Priya started the car again.

"You must keep your foot on the clutch when you are changing gears," Sita said gently. "Otherwise the car will stall out." They tried again, and this time they got as far as the gate of the driveway. "Stop!" Sita shouted above the noise of the exhaust, scared that Aunt Priya would run over the "Wa Wa" man or any other person on the sidewalk.

In the beginning, Aunt Priya would splutter along right up to the point she had to stop at a red light, and then, she came down hard on the brakes and the car stalled out. The light changed to green, and she would still be struggling to put it into gear. There was a pile up of cars behind her, all honking impatiently. But after the brief period of difficulty, they did better. Round and round the block they went, and Aunt Priya did a surprisingly decent job of changing gears and making her turns.

"I drive good," she announced.

Sita realized that she had been gripping the seat tightly. "Yes! You drive quite well," she said. "Perhaps now we should go home."

"I want to try and drive to Rohit's school," Aunt Priya said.

"We're almost at the school now," Sita said. "It's just five blocks from the house."

"But when it snows, those five blocks feel like fifty," Aunt Priya said. "I want to drive there. Take me."

So they went, crawling down the avenue at about 20 miles an hour. Aunt Priya checked the rear view mirror umpteen times to double check that there were no cars behind her that would hit her, or overtake her. Her face would push forward slightly, as though by extending it forward, she would get to her destination that much sooner. Her eyes stayed hypnotized on the empty street ahead, and she concentrated hard."

"I'm doing good," she said again. "Now we can drive to the Indian stores. I have to do my grocery shopping."

"Maybe in a couple of days," Sita said, "when you are more comfortable with the car."

"I'm comfortable. Let's go."

Sita was anxious not to prolong the lesson any further. "You can give me your list and I'll pick up the stuff for you later. The shopping area is crowded, and you don't know how to parallel park yet, so we will go there in a couple of days."

"Let's go now," Aunt Priya said again. "I will do what I can, and then you can park the car for me."

So they went. Sita found parking two avenues away from the Indian shops and felt relieved. Aunt Priya would not have to maneuver the car through the crowded area. Aunt Priya opened the trunk and found an old umbrella stroller. "This is good," she said taking it out and opening it up.

"For what?" Sita gasped.

"To carry the groceries—I put it there for just this purpose," she said. "It's Rohit's old stroller."

"Why don't we get a shopping cart?" Sita said.

"What's wrong with my cart?" Aunt Priya said with determination. She opened her bag to put back the car keys. A stray penny rolled out. Aunt Priya's gaze followed the get-away penny, and she scooped it up and put it back where it belonged. "A penny is money." she told Sita. "Let's go."

There were a string of small hole-in-the-wall establishments, really tiny stores but the prices were substantially cheaper than the supermarkets. The vegetables were fresh, still contained in the wooden crates, and they sold more of the ethnic varieties that Aunt Priya liked so much. She tested a couple of okra by flicking off the tops, and then took fistfuls and deposited them in the plastic bag. She looked for some bitter gourd, and then saw the squash, examined it by sinking her nails into it to test for ripeness, and decided the price was too much. She walked over to the shopkeeper to nickel and dime the poor man.

"Why you are charging two dollars and forty-nine cents for okra? The other shop sells it for two dollars and twenty-nine cents."

"Madam, my cost price was higher."

"That is not my fault." Aunt Priya said. "I will give you one dollar ninety-nine cents."

"Just pay what you can," the shopkeeper said anxious to end the argument.

She also bought some curry powder, coriander, lentils and some other spices. Everything was put in plastic bags, and deposited on the seat of the stroller, one bag piled on top of the other, until some squished eggs oozed out of the plastic and wet her hands. Aunt Priya then decided that she would hang some of the bags on the handle of the stroller.

"Careful it doesn't tip over," Sita watched as one bag after another was hung on the stroller, "and don't knock anything over." There were many little bottles of spice lined up precariously on dangerously low shelves. "Here let me get it." She pushed the top-heavy stroller out of the tiny store to the sidewalk. "Let's go and put this in the car quickly." She was afraid someone they knew would see her.

As luck would have it, Tom and Raja were walking down the sidewalk. Sita wished she could distance herself from the offending stroller and leave it outside the store. The wretched thing was so top-heavy it would certainly tip over, and empty its contents in the middle of sidewalk if she left it alone. She held on to it and smiled in embarrassment. Aunt Priya was completely unaware of Sita's discomfort and greeted both men effusively. "Oh my, so happy to see you both, I am," she said. And then she kept talking and talking nonstop. Sita looked down hoping they would not comment on the stroller laden with groceries.

Raja smiled politely at her. "Where is Rohit?" he asked. "Want to help me pick out a Spiderman costume for him?"

"How nice," Aunt Priya said. "Let us buy this costume and both of you come home with us in my car. I can drive you know."

"Sure we'll do that" Tom said.

"I'll wheel the stroller," Raja said, relieving her of her burden and acting like it was perfectly normal to be wheeling groceries in a stroller that squeaked and rattled as the little tires were separated from the wheel beneath the unusual weight.

"Let's just pick up the bags," he decided. Aunt Priya did not object and, between the two men the groceries were safely carried to the trunk of the Volkswagen Beetle. Tom's eyes widened when he saw the little car, but he kept quiet.

"Sita," Tom can help me now," Aunt Priya said. "You and Raja get in the back seat," she ordered. Once again Sita was confined in a small space with Raja. *He surely must hear the flip flop her heart was doing. Did he feel anything at all? She would never know.* She turned her head away to look out of the window, and they traveled the short distance back to the brownstone in silence.

Tom spoke in a low soft tone to Aunt Priya, reminding her to look in the mirror, to signal, put her foot on the clutch, change gears the right way, slow down before coming to a complete stop. It was quite a smooth ride, until all of a sudden the car lurched to the side. Aunt Priya's car was spluttering along and straddling two lanes, until Tom's gentle voice urged her back to safety. "What happened?" he asked. Both Sita and Raja turned away from the window to look at her.

"Look there," she said nodding toward the sidewalk. Sita followed her gaze, but all she saw were a young couple very much in love, wrapped in each other's arms.

"What?" she said.

"Did you see how they were spitting in each other's mouth?" Aunt Priya said. "Why they have to kiss like that in the middle of the street when I am driving."

"It happens when one is in love Aunty."

"What do you know about love?" Raja asked. Sita looked at him, didn't know what to say, and she was quiet again. Her eyes were glued to the sidewalk, taking in the street side vendors. They stopped at a traffic light that was by a palm reading place. "Readings by Crystal," the sign read, and Sita commented it might be fun to go get a reading for five bucks.

"Waste of money," Aunt Priya barked. "That's all bogus."

"I can do a free reading for you," Raja said. He took her hand in his. "Let's see," he said. Sita felt a warm glow as she looked at his big hand holding her little one.

"My you have a lot of scratches on your hand." He rubbed her palm as though he was trying to erase them all. "That means you worry too much. Is that right Sita?"

"What worries you have?" Aunt Priya enquired.

"Keep your eyes on the road," Tom said gently.

"Tell me, do you worry a lot," Raja asked in a way that made her feel he would take care of all her problems.

She nodded quietly, not trusting herself to speak.

"Well you have a nice long lifeline." He smoothed out her palm with his thumb. "But why is it so jagged? Have you been seriously sick?"

"No." Sita said.

"Let's see about your love line then," he said. She tried to snatch her hand away, but he held on tight. "Oh look," Raja pointed at a line on her palm, "it says you will marry a person of your choice and you will be very happy."

"You don't know anything about palm reading," Aunt Priya barked. "Stop trying to scare me."

Raja made no attempt to let go off her hand. "Okay, I won't read her palm anymore. Together they traveled in comfortable silence until they were already outside the brownstone. The little car roared up the slope of the driveway.

"I did great!" Aunt Priya congratulated herself. She took her foot off the accelerator too quickly, and the car started rolling down the slope just as Sita opened the door to get out.

"Hit the brake," Tom told Aunt Priya gently. She did, but she was visibly shaken. "I could have hit someone on the sidewalk," she said. "I'm no good," she moaned.

"You're just fishing for compliments. You just want us to say how well you did," Sita said. She rushed upstairs to make sure the house was neat enough for company. Trust Aunt Priya to invite people over with no warning! Sita knew everyone would come upstairs with the groceries because Aunt Priya did most of her cooking in Sita's house. She always said she didn't like being all alone on the first floor.

"Raja and Tom are here," Sita told Rohit, and he bounced off the chair and ran toward the door. Quickly she removed his sneakers from the middle of the room, and the bag of potato chips from the couch, cleared the dishes from the dining room and threw them in the sink. They would have to be washed later. It looked like Mom was out, and Papa was immersed in his newspaper and wouldn't know if Rohit had the place upside down. The two men were just coming up the stairs carrying the groceries. Tom put his bags down and scooped Rohit up in his arms. "Look what Raja bought you." He gave him the plastic bag with the Spiderman costume. Rohit squealed his "thank you," squirmed his way down, and ran to give Raja a hug. "I thought you would forget!"

Raja smiled and Sita noticed how tender his look was. He crouched down beside Rohit and said, "You didn't really think that, did you? Let's take a look at that hurt."

Rohit tugged at the Scooby Doo Band-Aid to show Raja. "It's all better now," he said.

"That's good," Raja said kindly. "Go try the costume on, and show me. I'll put away this stuff." Turning around he asked, "Sita where do you want to put the vegetables?" He was taking out the okra, the eggs, and the gourd, and arranging them on the counter top.

"I'll do it," Sita said quickly. "You go and make yourself comfortable in the living room."

"Let him help," Tom said. "That way he'll get used to it. Do you know when he first came to the US, he used to sit around waiting to be served. He's a lot better now. I remember the first time I asked him to throw the chicken in the oven, he put it in frozen—gizzards and all."

"I remember that," Raja said laughing. "It was burnt on the outside and raw on the inside because I did exactly what Tom told me to—threw the frozen bird in the oven. I've gotten better since then."

"Thank heavens," Tom said. "This is America. No servants around to fetch and carry for you."

"No wife either," Raja said. Sita looked at him quickly. "Just kidding. I know better than to ask my wife to do all the household chores. Come Sita, show me where these spices go, and where you want the stuff put away."

Sita felt a warm rush of blood to her face. She did not trust herself to speak and pointed to a drawer full of empty jam and sauce bottles that Aunt Priya saved to store her spices. "Why buy bottles when you get them for free," Aunt Priya told Sita's mom who complained about empty bottles taking up space. "I don't like to throw things away." she had said.

"Aunt Priya likes to empty the spice packets into the jars" Sita said, "but we can do that later." She was not comfortable in the intimacy of doing everyday tasks with him.

"I'll do them quickly," Raja said. He emptied the coriander seeds into the jar, and did the same with the cumin seeds, the paprika, the curry powder and the lentils. Soon everything was neatly lined on the counter top and then Raja who was so much taller, put everything away in the kitchen cabinets.

Sita heard the flip flop of Aunt Priya's slippers. She was coming up the stairs with more bags. "Why you have to put Raja to work like that?" Aunt Priya clicked her tongue. "You should have done that yourself."

There was no point in saying anything. Sita asked Raja to join her in the living room. Aunt Priya got busy in the kitchen whipping up some snacks for everybody to enjoy. Rohit had put on his Spiderman costume. "Look," he said, and took a giant leap from the couch to the loveseat. Papa finally emerged from behind the newspaper. "Hey, watch it," he yelled. He seemed surprised to see Raja and Tom and asked Sita why she hadn't offered them something to drink. "Where is Priya?" he asked. He knew his sister would provide the snacks and quieten Rohit. Rohit thought he had acquired special powers simply by wearing the Spiderman costume and continued with his antics.

Sita went to find Aunt Priya. She was frying *pakoras*, dipping finely sliced potato and spinach into a batter made of chick pea flour until they turned a crispy golden brown. "Sita come and do this so I can go check on Rohit."

"I'll do it," Raja said.

"Sita stay with him then," Aunt Priya ordered Sita. Raja and Sita stood together in companiable silence, cooking.

"I could make a habit of doing housework," Raja said.

"Your wife will be very lucky," Sita said in a small voice.

"I'm glad you think so." He brushed her forehead with his lips.

What now? Sita thought. *Did he think of her as his friend?* She wondered *what it would be like to be kissed by him on the lips.*

Aunt Priya was back in the kitchen complimenting Raja on the wonderful job he had done. "I never knew that you could cook," she exclaimed. "Come and rest now."

Rohit was calmer now. He handed out the plates and napkins. Everyone oohed and aahed over Raja's *pakoras* and said how good they were.

"We must get together more often," Tom said. "Maybe we can get together for Thanksgiving which is less than month away. I really must be going now." He got up, and bent over to give Aunt Priya a kiss. Raja did the same. Then he scooped up Rohit, gave him a kiss too, he shook hands with Papa. Then it was Sita's turn. She stood hesitant at the doorway. "Bye, bye" she said, and when everyone had gone, he brushed his lips on hers, and before Sita knew it, he was gone.

Chapter Twenty-four

Thanksgiving was fast approaching. There was a slight nip in the air, but it was still not warm enough for a heavy coat. Sita walked through Madison Square Park on her way to work. The trees had dropped their leaves which collected in little golden heaps around them. The branches were almost all bare, stretched heavenward preparing for the long winter nap. When winter came, the bare branches twisted and curled in the cold would wear a covering of snowflakes and ice that clung and shimmered like evening-wear all through the day. Soon, there would be no people in the park. But today was different.

It was still fall, and still warm enough to enjoy the park. People walked through the park, cutting through it like Sita did, to get to work; a couple of people walked their dogs. There was one person with a three-legged dog that hobbled along a push cart. When he did his business, the owner gently eased him into the cart and rolled him away. Homeless people still slept on benches, preferring nature's offering to the smelly confines of a homeless shelter. Sita saw one person waking up to reach for a cigarette tucked safely behind his ear, and a squirrel under the bench scurried away with a nut for safe keeping.

Soon it would be too cold to stay outside, and there would be fewer people in the park. There would be no lunch hour visitors, no children playing under the canopy of trees, and when it snowed, the snow would remain virginal white untouched by snow plows.

Sita's life too had been untouched and uncomplicated until now. She knew she would always work, that she would get married to a man the family chose, she would have two children, a girl and a boy, and she would live happily ever after. Now she was not so sure. Aunt Priya had really thrown a curve ball with Raja. She hurried to work. Today was "Cookie Day" at the office. In anticipation of Thanksgiving, each member of the staff had been encouraged to bake something—a special treat to be shared with co-workers. Sita never had a chance to bake, so she stopped at the local bakery and picked up some pastries.

Before she had even put her bag down, the phone was ringing off the hook. It was Aunt Priya. "What took so long?" she barked into the phone. Then without waiting for a response she said, "Sue called yesterday after Tom left. She wants us to go over there for Thanksgiving dinner. What shall I do?"

Sita kicked off her sneakers, wore her high heels, put her bag away, and tried to talk to Aunt Priya at the same time. "Why don't you want to go?"

"I went last time. I thought we would get together at my place. But I am not sure if my turkey will be good enough."

"Well then, why don't we just go there, let her do the turkey and offer to bring some Indian dessert or something else."

"Good idea," Aunt Priya said and hung up.

She went over to the conference room where the table was already covered with a wide variety of cookies and cakes, enough to give everyone a sugar high.

"We'll be hanging from the ceiling after eating all of this," Ms. Valentine said in her usual brusque manner, but that didn't stop her from taking a second helping of sugar treats. Sita and Roz connected, and both girls decided to travel together to Sue's house for Thanksgiving. "Tom will probably come and pick us all up," she said "and we won't have to take the train. It will be quicker."

"Okay good, I really should do some work now." Sita took another piece of cake in a paper napkin, and another cup of coffee, and went back to her desk.

The next time she saw Roz, was at the party. Aunt Priya brought an assortment of containers, of all shapes and sizes.

"I thought you were bringing dessert," Sita said.

"And few more things." Aunt Priya opened the lids to show rice pudding, carrot *halwa* and an assortment of homemade toffees. There was also some tandoori chicken, nan fresh from the oven, and some fish curry cooked in plenty of onions and tomatoes, with a dash of spice.

"This is a whole dinner," Sita protested.

"I want to do this." Aunt Priya closed the lids with determination and packed all the containers in a big cardboard box. "I don't want it to spill," she said. Sita looked on feeling very afraid that Aunt Priya would pull out her multi-colored tape to seal the box. But fortunately she decided to leave the box open. "That way I can add more things, and if anything is leaking I will know," she said.

"Tom should be here soon with Roz," Sita said. As if on cue, the doorbell rang. She went to answer it and stood speechless as Raja greeted her at the door.

"Aren't you going to let me in?" he asked smiling.

She stepped aside quickly and she heard Aunt Priya yell, "Raja, is that you, come and help me with this box."

She waited by the door for Tom and Roz, but they were too busy making the most of their time alone in the car. She saw that their car was parked near a hydrant so they would definitely get a ticket if they left it there. Sita turned around and went back upstairs. "Hi," she said again to Raja. Then to Aunt Priya she whispered, "You never told me Raja would also be coming."

"I forgot," Aunt Priya lied.

Rohit latched on to Raja the way he always did. "You didn't forget to tell *me,*" he said. Soon all three of them were walking down the stairs like one big happy family. Raja was carrying the cardboard box of food, and Sita was carrying several plastic bags. Aunt Priya took a last look round the house to make sure that she had not forgotten anything, shut off all the lights, and turned off the stove, and that Rohit had done pi before leaving.

Tom disentangled himself from Roz as they neared the car. He took the packages from Sita, gave them both his bear hug and sweet smile, and asked Aunt Priya if she would like to drive. "I'll sit with you in the front," he said, "just like last time. You'll get lots of practice."

"Oh yes," Aunt Priya brought her pudgy hands together in excitement. "Let's go." She slid into the driver's seat. Roz didn't look too happy with the arrangement, but she got in with Rohit who had already claimed the window seat at the back. Sita got in next to her, followed by Raja, so that the four of them were firmly squished together. Sita squirmed uncomfortably. *What was that tingle she felt to have Raja so close to her.*

"Okay?" he asked.

"Fine," she said quickly, afraid that he would find out how she felt.

"Good." He placed his hand on her knee. She looked at it, still patchy and red from all the grafts he had suffered through. Her eyes moistened and he was quick to notice.

"Do the scars repel you?" he asked quietly.

She shook her head. "No, they don't. It must have hurt so much."

He took his hand away from her knee, and put it on the top of the seat, barely brushing her shoulder.

"I'm okay," he said quickly. Sita noticed Aunt Priya's eyes in the rear view mirror starting to bulge. Fortunately, Tom was speaking to her, and she did not have time to dwell on their little exchange.

"Let's put on the seat belt and look in the rear view mirror." Tom was saying.

"This mirror shows me very interesting things," Aunt Priya said. She strapped on her seat belt. She had clearly seen Raja's hand on Roz's knee.

"Okay now, signal and pull out" Tom added, unaware of the meaning in Aunt Priya's tone. Sita knew, and color rushed up to her face. She sat up straighter and tried to inch away from Raja, very afraid of what Aunt Priya might say to embarrass her in front of everybody.

"Relax," Roz said. "Aunt Priya will do fine."

They were pulling out from their spot on 32nd Avenue. They made the left turn onto 80th street and then drove forward onto

Northern Boulevard from where they would take the Long Island Expressway that would take them to Port Jefferson. Aunt Priya was doing well on Northern Boulevard. She kept her eyes on the road, stayed within her lane, didn't try to pass anybody and kept her steady medium pace.

"I'm proud of you," Tom said.

"Thanks," Aunt Priya smiled. Sita noticed her eyes checked the rear view mirror repeatedly to see if she could see something interesting in the back seat.

Tom pointed to the ramp, "The expressway is coming up, start to signal, and get ready to enter."

Aunt Priya's hands on the steering wheel stiffened, and she sat up a little straighter. She must have been surprised by the sudden curve in the road, but managed to get on the ramp. She slowed down enough to cause the truck behind her to honk.

"You're on the shoulder," Sita observed.

"Always you have to say something bad," Aunt Priya snapped. "This ramp is very curvy. I don't like driving on the edge." She opened her eyes wide, and pushed her head even more forward, as if she was trying to use her neck to propel herself.

"You're doing fine," Tom said. "Let them honk. Now whenever you're comfortable, take a quick look over your shoulder, judge the space you have, and accelerate to merge with the flow."

"Okay," Aunt Priya said abruptly, but that was easier said than done. Instead of merging smoothly, she stopped dead in her tracks in an unusual attack of nerves. Tom kept his calm. "It's okay," he said. "I'll watch the traffic for you. You just drive." Now, there was pileup of cars behind them. The truck that had honked before was still behind them. When Aunt Priya moved a little bit ahead, he managed to slide out from behind her on to the highway.

"Why he did that?" Aunt Priya muttered.

"You can move now," Tom said.

Aunt Priya took a deep breath, looked over her shoulder, and then Tom said "Go." She shut her eyes briefly, and hit the accelerator.

"Very good" Tom said. Aunt Priya smiled broadly.

"What do you think Roz?" Aunt Priya asked.

"Very good," Roz said politely.

"Yes," Sita said exhaling. She hadn't realized she had been holding her breath since the time she noticed the pileup of cars behind them. Now she slumped back into the seat, and felt Raja's fingers brush the top of her arm. She looked up at him, and noticed for the first time, the long scar near the shirt collar, and the angry red skin that peeked from under the collar. He saw her looking at him, and pulled her closer. She stayed nestled to his side. Roz and Rohit were happily occupied reading the exit numbers and trying to read the names of the towns they passed.

"There's Huntington," Roz said, "now we have only forty-five minutes to go."

"Maybe less," Tom observed. Aunt Priya had been picking up speed the further east they went, because the traffic was less. The expressway seemed to widen, leaving behind the congestion of orange barricades that separated the construction work from the traffic. The only annoyance was the huge trucks that continued to bother Aunt Priya. After they had been driving for about fifteen minutes she announced, "I am not going to drive in the right lane. There are too many trucks, and all the cars that need to exit always want to cut me off and go in front of me." She looked over her shoulder, and deftly changed lanes.

She overtook the truck. "He ate my dust," she said. Just then, another truck in the right lane overtook her. She muttered to herself, and came down on the accelerator. Fortunately, Tom was there to hold her in check.

"Let's not get carried away," he said gently, and Aunt Priya fumbled for a bit, started to straddle two lanes the way she did when she was nervous, but then quickly recovered, found her bearings and started to drive straight again.

"Kings Park," Rohit announced. He was reading the name of the town they were passing through on the green highway signs. "What a funny name. Is there a Queens Park?" he asked.

"No, but there is good old Queens," Roz said. "It's where you live—Jackson Heights is in Queens," she explained.

Soon they were passing through Smithtown, St. James, and finally Stony Brook. This time Aunt Priya did a much better job of navigating the car through the merging traffic. Tom guided her down Nicholls Drive on to Route 347. Aunt Priya was the perfect driver now. "Look for big blue signs that say *Taxes*," Raja said. She turned to stare at him in the rear view mirror, and saw his arm around Sita. For an instant the car went crooked again, but Tom was quick to straighten the wheel.

"What's the matter?" he asked. "There's the blue sign." He pointed at the billboard for Soloway Agency that was more prominent than the street sign. "Make a right here. That's Greenhaven Drive. Go straight down the drive and you will come to our house." Aunt Priya kept her eyes on the street, and managed to drive safely with no further mishaps.

Sue was at the door to greet them. Rohit bounced out of the car glad to be able to stretch his legs. He saw the retriever behind the fence. "There's Ginger. Can I go and play with her?"

"Oh," Sue said, "last time you had a terrible accident."

"I'll only play in the backyard," Rohit pleaded. "There's a fence there, see. Just for a little while, please."

"Oh okay" Sue said.

Rohit found his way outside to an ecstatic Ginger. He picked up her ball, wiped the drool on the grass, and then flung it away. Ginger was off like a shot, but unlike Brandi did not know how to fetch. She grabbed the ball and sat down with it in the middle of a heap of autumn leaves. Rohit followed, and soon dog and boy were hunting down the ball, covered in dry red and yellow leaves.

"You come in right now," Aunt Priya yelled. She was still in the driveway holding the cardboard box, and the many plastic bags.

Tom quickly ran to the backyard to bring Rohit in.

"He never said hello," Sue complained. "He thinks he got too big to say hello to his mother." Roz gave her a quick hug and followed Tom outside. There they lingered long after Rohit came inside, and when Rohit asked Aunt Priya "What are Tom and Roz still doing outside?" She replied very quickly. "Making up for lost time." Sita smiled, amused at their exchange. When Rohit persisted she said they were taking care of grown-up business. Rohit paused for a while and then said, "Oh they are kissing." Aunt Priya looked embarrassed. "Bad boy," she said. She had set the cardboard box down on the kitchen table. She took out each container and carefully explained what was in each one of the little boxes. Sue was saying over and over again, "Oh you shouldn't have," until Aunt Priya asked "Are you offended I cooked? You can put this food away, and save it for after Thanksgiving. Today we will eat your turkey."

"Oh my," Sue said. "I did not mean that at all."

"Good because I like to cook," Aunt Priya said, "but I won't feel bad if you eat this tomorrow—as long as you eat it." Let's go to the living room and sit down." She made herself comfortable on the couch and held out the miscellaneous plastic bags. "Come, see what I brought you."

"We don't give presents on Thanksgiving Aunty," Tom said. He and Roz had finally come inside holding hands.

"I brought nothing for you. I brought your Mom a sari with matching blouse and petticoat."

"Oh how beautiful," Sue enthused, exclaiming over the embroidery of the tanchoi silk sari in a very pleasant aquamarine blue. "This is lovely," she said again. "Will you show me how to wear it?"

This was the invitation Aunt Priya had been waiting for. "Let's go now. I brought a petticoat and some safety pins. I'll put it on you. Then you and I can be twins," she said.

The two women had retreated to the bedroom. Rohit was busy watching the Spiderman movie in the other room. Roz again grabbed Tom for some more togetherness, and Raja and Sita were left standing in the middle of the living room.

"I want what they have," Raja said suddenly and then, without warning he reached for her and gave her his first long kiss. She staggered backward, and then forward again, like a pendulum with no resistance. They were joined in a lip lock when Aunt Priya walked in with Sue dressed in a sari. Both women stopped dead in their tracks—there was a mixture of surprise and consternation written large on Aunt Priya's face.

Sue recovered quicker. "My, my," she said. "There is some real progress here. As I recall the last time you both were together, you were barely speaking to each other."

"What is going on?" Aunt Priya asked bewildered.

"I thought you would be happy," Raja said to Aunt Priya. He turned quickly toward Sita. "That is not why I kissed you."

In answer Aunt Priya walked back into the kitchen. Without a word she got to work. She got the turkey out of the oven, arranged it nicely on the platter with all of the trimmings, poured out the gravy in the gravy boat, brought everything to the table, then went back to bring more stuff, going back and forth between kitchen and dining room, not speaking a word. Sita looked on helplessly.

Finally, Sue sat her down at the kitchen table. "I will change out of this sari if you don't talk to me."

"What have I done," Aunt Priya wailed. She buried her face in her hands. "Raja has no job. If something goes wrong everybody will blame me. Say I set her up with a hoodlum with no future. I never thought they would take it this far."

"They were only kissing," Sue said.

Aunt Priya's angry glare spoke louder than words.

"Let's not spoil Thanksgiving," Sue said. "You go out there and put on a happy face for everybody—for my sake, for Rohit's."

"I'll try," Sita heard Aunt Priya say.

Chapter Twenty-five

The Holiday Season arrived in full swing after Thanksgiving. Retailers looked forward to the days ahead to make some quick profits. The holiday decorations were up, and each store window looked like it was all set to out-do the one next to it. Tinsel and glitter were everywhere. Little red bows were invitingly attached to different items to urge customers to buy them as presents. Macy's was a large department store, and it was no surprise that its windows were the best. Santa and Mrs. Clause waved to the crowd from one of its numerous windows, and delicate glass balls in all colors, ranging from traditional red to iridescent pink and ivory hung from the holiday greens. They looked so delicate and fragile, just as fragile as Sita's emotions. She didn't know what to make of Raja, and was just as confused by Aunt Priya's icy disapproval. After all, Aunt Priya had tried so desperately to throw the two of them together, and that was what she had wished for, all these months.

Thanksgiving Dinner had ended pleasantly enough, with everyone minding their Ps and Qs. Raja had said he would call Sita the next day. Aunt Priya said that Sita had some thinking to do, and it was best that he did not call. Sita did not have the courage to contradict her. Raja had looked at her long and hard, and when she said nothing, he simply shrugged his shoulders and went about his business. Sita kept up the façade of enjoying the rest of the evening but she felt hollow inside, as though everything was show, and no substance, just like Macy's boxes wrapped in gold paper with red bows and hung all along the walls as

Christmas decorations in the mall—just like those fake presents, she too felt all empty and hollow inside.

Aunt Priya wanted to go out and pick up a Christmas tree. "You will come with me," she told Sita, "or maybe I should ask Tom." Sita's eyes lit up. *Where Tom is, Raja is close behind* she thought. "Don't even think it, missy," Aunt Priya said with uncanny perceptiveness. Then with a huge sigh she said "Why you have to do everything *topsy turvy.* You should have said "yes" to him in India, and everything would have gone smoothly. Now he has no job, no plans, and is not quite well." She sighed loudly. "Yesterday you looked like you liked him *too much!* Always you have to do the opposite of what I want."

"What if he lost his job after we were married?" Sita asked.

"That is a completely different matter," Aunt Priya said. "No need to argue just for the sake of argument. Let's go get that tree. We can manage with no men, you and I."

So the two of them went to the local supermarket where freshly cut evergreens were lined up against the wall. Aunt Priya picked one that was two feet taller than she was and said, "This will look nice in your living room."

"You're not going to put it in *yours*?"

"For what? Rohit is always upstairs, and so am I."

"But Mom likes the artificial trees," Sita protested. "These needles make a mess."

"I'll talk to her" she said with determination. "Once she smells this fresh pine tree she will know it is so much better. Then if she still gets mad, I'll take it down and give her my little plastic one that talks." Sita could imagine her mother cringing at a miserable looking two-foot tree that said 'Merry Christmas' over and over again, and knew that Aunt Priya would certainly get her way with the fresh evergreen. In India after all, they used fresh pine—a branch lopped off from the pine tree growing in the backyard. It was never quite straight and grandma always said "It looks fine. No harm if it tilts forward a little bit. It looks gracious and welcoming." Sita had looked at her oddly. Today too, she did not argue. They paid for the tree and it was safely tied to the roof of the car. They got it home, and then yelled for Papa to come help them bring it up the stairs.

"This is coming upstairs?" Mama asked. She had seen the the splatter of pine needles that had shed across the hallway. "Take it down to Priya's place." But they were already starting to climb upstairs, and she didn't say more. Then Aunt Priya brought up a bashed cardboard box of red and gold ornaments, most of them bent and warped-looking, and a tangled mess of multi-colored lights. Then Mom put her foot down. "I don't want multi colored lights on my tree," she said firmly.

"But these are chasing lights." Aunt Priya held out the jumbled pile of wires which no doubt had several broken bulbs because of the way they had been stored. "They give color and life to the Christmas tree."

"This fresh tree has all the life that's needed. It's *my* house I want clear lights and will use my ornaments," mother said firmly.

In the end, Papa took on the role of mediator and said maybe they could use some of Aunt Priya's ornaments, and that way she would have enough left over for her own apartment downstairs.

"I suppose I should also have a small tree downstairs," Aunt Priya said, "where I can use these wonderful red and green lights. She threw everything back in the box and cracked some more of the glass balls before she took the battered box downstairs. "Don't know why you don't like them. These are Christmas colors," she said.

When it was done, Mom's tree looked classy in mostly white and gold. It was not the traditional tree, but matched the living room perfectly. Pastel ornaments highlighted the colors of the living room and Sita noticed that once again, Mom's favorite ornament had been prominently placed close to the stop. Made of pink metal that was looped back like a ribbon, it was the traditional breast cancer symbol of hope. At the bottom of the ornament the name "Lata" was inscribed. This was Mom's way of remembering her sister who had fought and lost the battle against breast cancer more than three years ago, at the age of forty. Since then the ornament had come up year after year, and taken its prominent place. The clear lights showed off the name inscribed below. Since her sister's death Mom had participated in every breast cancer fund raising event and attended all sorts of rallies.

One such rally was being held by the local hospital, *and because she didn't want to be around Aunt Priya and think about Raja* Sita thought she *would spend time with Mom. Besides it might be a good idea to give Mom moral support at the rally.* So she went.

The rally was held outside in the parking lot, sheltered from the weather by a huge tent. She was surprised to see so many people. People had come from as far out as Long Island. The train station had been festooned with pink balloons, and that weekend the Long Island Railroad carried passengers free of charge from as far out as the eastern most tip of the island.

People came in all shapes and sizes. Young women sporting tank tops, older women who had battled cancer and won—some still engaged in battle, who wore wigs to hide their battle- scarred baldness. They came with husbands, boyfriends, and kids. They came to give thanks for those who had made it, and to remember those who had not. There were hundreds of survivors, each trying to cheer the other on, and finding comfort in their shared battle against the insidious disease.

Sita was glad she had accompanied Mom because her mother always got very teary eyed at such gatherings, and Papa felt uncomfortable going. There were too many testimonies from people who had fought and won, but knew of others who had not. There was seldom a dry eye in the audience. Papa just couldn't take it, and never went. Hospital spokesmen were there, local politicians had also come. One of the doctors got up and spoke about her personal battle with breast cancer and the importance of regular screening and early detection.

Just as the mood was becoming too somber, the place erupted with really loud music, and one of the survivors on stage started doing the Macarena. The crowd looked up puzzled, "Let's palpate ourselves and do the Macarena," she said. She bounced around the stage, raising her arms and running her fingers down her chest. The crowd started giggling.

From time to time she pointed to a woman and asked "How many years?" The woman instinctively knew what was being asked, "Survivor for eighteen" she yelled back, and everyone clapped. "C'mon," she said, "join me." She bounced off the stage, down the aisles, and was in the midst of the crowd, whipping them into a giggling, palpating frenzy that brought home in the most absurd way the importance of screening and early detection.

Others came off the stage and joined the crowd. Someone kept asking "How many years…how many years." "Who knows, who cares," someone yelled as they all joined in the ridiculous victory dance. Young and old alike, men and women both, were shaking their behinds unafraid to look ridiculous. Then the doctor went back to the stage, and the crowd settled down, out of breath, but a lot less tense.

The highlight of the event was Mrs. Clinton's arrival. Even though she was no longer the First lady, she had quite a fan club. Nurses and hospital workers all came out to take a peek at her and watched from the sidelines as she arrived in an innocuous blue Subaru with hardly any security detail. She was dressed in a peach pant suit, and looked quite lovely. Her hair was well-styled, and gold highlights framed her face. She smiled a lot, and gave a short speech. She said breast cancer was a topic dear to her because her mother-in-law, Bill's mother, had fought the good fight.

She spoke fondly about the senior Mrs. Clinton who had gone through the rigors of chemotherapy. "Mother put on her fake eyelashes, and said *world here I come.* She went about her business living each day to the full just like so many of you do." Mrs. Clinton saluted the brave women who, like her mother-in-law face their problems, the chemo, the tiredness, the nausea, and roll with the punches every day. She continued talking about the need for more breast cancer research, and couldn't resist a jibe at the Republicans saying that they did not allocate enough funds for this important cause. She said as senator, she would do everything to make it her priority. The crowd roared its approval. Sita watched as Mom's eyes again misted over, because she realized it would be too late for her sister.

Then just as suddenly as Mrs. Clinton had come, she was gone. The crowd dispersed and made their way to the tables where free lunch was served. They each got a box with a turkey sandwich and an apple. Co-sponsors of the event were also handing out vitamin water, and Sita and her mom grabbed some thirstily. Others were handing out t-shirts, pens, and picture frames—small consolations. The crowd took their goodies and made their exit beneath the arch of pink balloons. All of a sudden, those balloons took on the grotesque image of so many pink tumors tethered together, and Sita was so tempted to set them loose from the arch, to let the helium balloons fly away in the sky, taking with them all disease and worry.

"Let's go to the mall and cheer ourselves up," Sita told Mom. There too, Mom gravitated toward the fundraising event sponsored by the breast cancer coalition. For five dollars one could buy an ornament with their loved ones name and add it to the Christmas tree. And without fail, Mom put an ornament up in memory of her sister. A lot of people stopped by, and Mom told her the hospital collected almost 15,000 dollars every year to help toward the screening and treatment of uninsured women. The coalition workers were handing out some pamphlets about breast cancer and where to go for screening, and because Mom had already moved away, Sita took them politely and walked on.

"Let's go to the toy store first," Sita said because shopping for Rohit was always a lot of fun.

"Okay. Wonder how long we will be able to get away with the Santa Clause story," Mom said.

"Yes, he is already becoming suspicious because the last time we took him to the church pageant he kept asking where Santa's reindeer were, and how come he never saw them landing on the roof or flying back into the sky," Sita said. "Fortunately, there's still lot of Santa on television, so he is quite torn about knowing what to believe. But he is starting to question why Santa's wrapping paper matches Mom's paper, and why once he saw two Santas at the mall, and why Santa only comes when he is asleep to drink the milk, and eat the cookies."

Sita remembered how when she was a little girl she knew quite early that Santa was a fake. Although Dad took great pains to order the red Santa suit and wore the mask, his brown ears always stuck out from behind the pink mask giving the game away. Still, Christmas back then was a lot of fun. Sita remembered how she let her parents think she still believed in Santa for the longest time, just so she could get an extra present. But then, by the time she was ten, the game was up, and they knew she knew.

On Christmas day, they always went to the early morning mass. Mom would wear a new sari for the occasion, and Nani wore her finest white silk one. Papa would wear a suit and she always wore a new dress because she was not old enough to wear a sari. They would walk past the row of beggars lined up outside, rattling their tins hoping to catch parishioners in a generous mood on this festive day. People scurried past them, anxious that their fancy clothes did not touch these hapless humans who waited outside. At the end of the service though, some would be moved to share their happiness by dropping some change into the waiting cans.

The cathedral would be jam packed with people and extra folding chairs would be added to the pews to make space for people who never showed up the rest of the year. Mom and Nani always covered their heads with the sari *pallav* when they entered the church, and took off their shoes as a mark of respect when they went to the altar for communion. The altar was decorated with poinsettias, the traditional flower of Christmas, and the same Christmas carols that people sang in America, were sung in church. Everybody was all dressed up and stayed to show off their saris over coffee after church. The tepid liquid was served in chipped chinaware, and assorted sweets were served on plain white china. Cloth napkins were neatly arranged on the table. No one thought to use paper plates and paper napkins, because people just couldn't bring themselves to use something just once and throw it away.

After church, they all changed into everyday clothes and usually went out on a family picnic if the weather was warm enough. The servants packed a picnic basket with lunch and flasks of hot tea because Papa would be very unhappy without tea. The driver drove their little blue Fiat fifty miles out to the local zoo so Sita could enjoy the animals and the adults could relax. They took a huge blanket on which everybody lay down or sat up, except Nani. For her, they took a folding chair because Nani could not get down on the floor and did not want to be left out of all the fun. They gave the driver some money so he could go off on his own and buy himself whatever he wanted because there was no way that he would be comfortable in his master's presence.

Sita remembered how much fun these trips were. She loved seeing the birds, and all the animals. Monkeys were her favorite—their tricks always drew a chuckle from everyone. She loved feeding them bananas and had got quite startled the last time, because the little fellow had reached out of his cage, extended his arm, and shook her hand vigorously. She had felt thrilled to be picked from the crowd, but then embarrassed, because the monkey scratched his bottom vigorously and then came back toward her for another handshake. This time she fled.

Christmas in New York was a lot different. There was still so much shopping to do. For some reason she couldn't recall having to buy so many things back home in India. They got fewer presents, but they spent a lot more time with each other. Already they had bought Rohit Lego, a remote control train, a whole bunch of action figures from the list he had made by circling almost every item in the toy catalog. They tried to buy it before somebody else did, went from store to store to make sure the Yogi-o action figure of the Red Dragon was available, obsessed over all the details that were important to him so that he couldn't say, *Oh but Peter's Mom bought him that, or someone's else's parents bought him something better.* It was almost as if how much they loved him was measured by what they gave.

They did manage to accomplish a lot. Papa got a new sweater. They also bought him a digital camera mostly because Mom had wanted one for a long time and all her relatives in India asked her why she never e-mailed family pictures. Aunt Priya got some more pastel cardigans because Sita and her mother plotted to try and get her to wear pastels more often. Ramu dada and Vijay Uncle each got gift certificates to the local electronic store, because neither Mom nor Sita could fathom what they would possibly like. Aunt Rita got a gift certificate to the local spa.

There was still more to be done. Sita still had to buy for Mom. She would no longer have to buy for Raja. She looked longingly at the hand held palm notebook with e-mail capability costing two hundred dollars. She had been thinking of buying it for him so he could keep in touch whenever he felt like writing her. There was no need now.

"Should we buy something for Raja?" her Mom asked unaware of the highs and lows of her relationship with him—a relationship if there was one, Sita thought wryly.

"We might see him over Christmas, and if we get something for Tom and Roz, shouldn't we buy for Raja?" Mom asked. Then she changed her mind. "Oh well, another day perhaps," she said.

Laden with packages they paused to buy a cool drink and a cinnamon bun at the Food Court before heading out to the car. The Salvation Army man dressed in red, stood outside the mall opening doors for everyone and collecting donations. Mom took out a five dollar bill and dropped it in the red bucket. They were rewarded by a big smile and they made their way to the car. The man remained standing outside shivering in the cold and opened doors for everyone to go in to the shop.

Chapter Twenty-six

The Pennsylvania train station in Manhattan looked very festive today. Its doorways covered with holiday greens embedded with glass ornaments welcomed thousands of people who passed through it. Some were going to work, others coming into the city to do some holiday shopping, and getting in early, to take advantage of the early bird special sales. Others were simply trying to get away for holiday travel and were waiting for the AMTRAK trains that would take them cross country. Everyone seemed to walk a little taller, a little quicker, as though they all had something to look forward to. Most of them stopped at the local cafes in the station for coffee and donuts, before leaving the safety of the station and braving the cold.

There were still so many police at the station that it was probably the safest place to be, after the terror attacks. The nation was at a heightened terror alert during the holiday season but everyone went about their business of working and celebrating the season. Not to do that, would mean the terrorists had won, and nobody, black, white, or brown, who understood America's pain after the disaster would want that.

Outside the train station, two-person teams from the Salvation Army stood in the bitter cold singing Christmas carols along with some much energized, if somewhat off key accompaniment. Each day, the Salvation Army folk set a new goal to collect a certain amount of money by the morning rush hour. "Let's try and get $100 by 7:30AM," they yelled into the loudspeakers. Throngs of people passed by, and a few paused to drop a bill into their red bucket of want. Every little while they yelled out how much more they needed and how short they were. "Just 10 minutes left to reach our target." As the countdown began, their appeals got more urgent. "C'mon everyone," they shouted to urge people to reach deeper in their pockets and to lighten their load.

Sita paused to drop a dollar bill, then braced herself against the cold, and walked out into the street. The wind made her coat flap around her and split open in front, almost to the waist. She tried to stay warm by walking faster. She had forgotten her gloves and now she tucked her palms in her coat sleeves. She trudged forward with arms folded across her chest to keep warm against the wicked wind.

Finally, she was in the indoor warmth of her office. Downstairs, a huge Christmas tree in red and silver sat in the lobby. Later she discovered every floor in the building had the exact same tree, a little smaller perhaps, but very corporate looking and predecorated in red and silver like the one downstairs.

Every cubicle, and every office, had its own little Christmas decorations. Some had wreaths, others red bows, and cutouts of angels and snowmen. Silver tinsel scalloped its way around the top of cubicles daring management to object. The Christmas spirit was in big supply, and the little corporate looking tree did not satisfy it.

Ms. Valentine surprised everyone by being the most original. Her office door was sheathed in silver foil, and red tape crossed over it with a big red bow smack in the center. Her office door looked like a huge big present. *But her Christmas spirit stopped right at the door.* Sita thought. *Woe to anyone who should open the present and walk in because Ms. Valentine's beady eyes and thin lips would wipe the smile off those who dared to enter.* Then she felt bad for being so uncharitable at Christmas time, and went to her desk.

She sat down and tried to stuff her bag into the bottom drawer and kick the drawer shut. The bag would not fit. She saw it was bulging at the seams. She would have to empty it out a bit to make it fit. She pulled out old receipts—some from clothing stores and ATM machines, and others from supermarkets where she had stopped to do Aunt Priya a favor by picking up this, that, or the other. Then she noticed the stack of pamphlets she had picked up at the breast cancer table at the mall and hurriedly stuffed into her bag. If she took those out, her bag would be much thinner. She was about to throw them away, but curiosity got the better of her, and she decided to put them in her top drawer along with her office supplies. She would get rid of them later. She turned on her computer, and looked at the phone longingly. She wished she had the nerve to call Raja. She hesitated, and then it was too late because one project after another claimed her morning.

Although the holidays were right round the corner, there was plenty of work to be done—journals had to publish on time to make the year-end financial closings. Many of the freelancers were on vacation and the suppliers would be closed for the holidays. There were scheduling problems to be addressed, and contingency plans to make so that the work continued.

There was an assortment of problems. A client who advertised in one of the medical journals was enraged because the colors had not printed well. After she had calmed him down and asked the printer for an explanation, something else came up. She was on the phone constantly, making a list of all the things that needed immediate attention.

Every time she opened her top drawer, the pink breast cancer pamphlets stared back at her. She looked at them briefly. The statistics were alarming. It said one in eight women would get breast cancer, and once in every three seconds a woman was diagnosed with breast cancer. Almost 40,000 women die of the disease each year. *Oh boy!* She thought. *At least she was young. There would be time enough to worry about such problems*. She had her routine annual physical scheduled for her lunch hour. Her physician's office was in Manhattan and it seemed so much easier to go on her lunch hour instead of taking a day off to go to the doctor. Dr. Kapoor had been the family physician for years, and Mom, Papa, and Aunt Priya, all went to him.

It was a 10-minute train ride to the doctor's office but she would probably have to wait to see him. She took the pamphlets with her to read on the train. Because breast cancer was uppermost in her mind she mentioned it to Dr. Kapoor.

"Well Sita, you're a little young to be thinking about such things," he said. "Not yet thirty. Breast cancer usually attacks older women, mostly those who are in their fifties."

Sita felt relieved wondering why strange fears had been nagging at her. *Maybe going to the rally had touched her more than she cared to admit, and she had become a hypochondriac. She must throw the pamphlets away, because all they did was stir up doubts and fears.* But Dr. Kapoor's next words unsettled her. After doing his usual exam, he stopped and looked at her thoughtfully over the rim of his bifocal lenses and started writing something on the notepad. "I'm going to give you a slip for a mammogram," he said. Her jaw dropped. Dr. Kapoor said, "It is the only way to be absolutely sure you're healthy since you seem to be worrying about it. It is not unreasonable to want to make sure everything is fine. It is a very simple procedure, and contrary to what people say it really doesn't hurt." He then continued to describe the procedure and Sita said, "But everything is okay?"

"It should be," Dr. Kapoor said noncommittally. "You are very young."

She went back to work feeling more unsettled than ever. She xeroxed the same proofs twice, and forgot to include hard copy in the package to the proofreader so she had nothing to check against. She sent manuscript to the typesetters and was able to get some work done as the afternoon wore on, but there was an awful feeling in the pit of her stomach. She walked over to Roz's office, saw that she was hunched over a mound of papers, and decided not to say anything. It was just a test after all. *Much ado about nothing* she thought, and walked back to her desk. The rest of the day was a blur, as were the next several days.

She went for the mammogram and saw that she was the youngest one there. First, they asked for her insurance card and once they had reassured themselves that services would be paid for, she was given a form to fill. Besides the usual medical history, both hers and her family's, she was required to state if she had any problems, did the breast hurt, was there a discharge, was there any redness, and similar icky questions.

When she had filled out the form she was taken inside to change into a paper shirt with the front open. Then a kind older woman put tape to cover her nipples so they would not show up as tumors. She was maneuvered standing up to a machine. She had to raise her arms and position herself between two metal plates that came down on her and compressed her tightly before taking the picture. "You have very dense breasts" the woman said. "It is hard to see."

"Is that bad?" Sita asked feeling very afraid.

"No. Some people do, and others don't. It just makes it harder to see. We want to be sure there is nothing hiding there. I want to give the machine some more juice and take another picture," she said.

"Of both breasts?"

"No, just the right one."

"Why is there something wrong?"

"You will get a letter in the mail from the radiologist explaining your results. I am only the technician." The woman positioned her right breast again under the metal plates and concentrated so hard that Sita did not ask any more questions.

Finally it was over, and Sita was free to go. And though she had been so eager to run out of there before, now she lingered hoping the woman would loosen up and talk, but the woman gave her firm pat on the back that dismissed her to go and get changed. The mammogram too, had been scheduled on her lunch hour because she was sure everyone would laugh at her for being so paranoid. She didn't think anyone needed to know.

Christmas preparations were on in full swing. Aunt Priya had put up Santa Clause lights and candy canes in her window so when one approached the brownstone, Santa's mechanically operated arm reached out and waved. From time to time, the suction cups holding the lighted figure would give way, and Santa would fall face down on the window sill. Aunt Priya picked him right up, and stuck him back, this time with her orange duct tape for added security. Mom had put up Christmas lights on the two evergreen trees in front of the house, and had agreed to have colored lights outside, so everyone was happy. Neighborhood lighting ranged from modest to extravagant.

The house in front of them only had lights in the windows, whereas the one alongside it had gone all out—running lights spanned the roof turning it into a shimmering fairyland. All the shrubs and hedges were bedecked with flashing lights. And the fence too, was covered in lighted red bows hung on green moving lights. Statues of the Holy Mother were flood lit, and many houses had a small nativity scene up front. Everybody, including non-Christians, did not want to be outdone or left out, and put lights outside so they could share in the festivities of the holiday season.

Christmas Day was pretty quiet. They went to church in the morning and then lounged around the house. Roz was probably at Tom's house and hadn't called, and of course Raja did not call. Aunt Priya made no mention of him. It was as if he was still as far away as India.

Rohit was the only one all revved up and ready for Christmas. He constantly counted the presents under the tree. He picked them up, checked the name tags, and counted how many were his. Some of them he would pick up from time to time, and shake, to see if he could tell what he got. "Did I get the "Red Dragon?" he would ask, and everyone had to make sure he did not worm the answer out of them. So much for the innocent looking big black eyes! "How come I only got 5 presents?" he would ask counting and recounting the small heap below the Christmas tree.

"Maybe Santa will bring you some," Sita said. Rohit looked at her wide-eyed wondering if he could believe that Santa was real.

Sita took great pains to preserve Santa's legacy. "If you believe he is real," she told him "you will see that he is real," remembering a line from one of the Christmas movies she had seen as a child. Then when they all got in the car to go to church, she raced upstairs and put Santa's presents all wrapped in different wrapping paper under the tree. She also put a glass of milk on the coffee table, drank half of it, took a bite of a cookie, and left the uneaten half in the plate to make it look as though Santa had been there.

When they got back from church, it was time to open presents. Rohit exclaimed over the additional presents under the tree, and looked carefully at the half eaten cookie. "How come Santa comes only when I am not here?" he asked. He did not wait for an answer but continued to rip open his presents, one after the other. Everyone got the biggest kick from watching his exuberance. Little by little everyone opened their presents and exclaimed over them. Papa loved his digital camera. Aunt Priya's eyes lit up when she saw it and said she would have liked that as well. "The sweaters are nice," she said, "must be expensive too." What she really meant was that she knew the camera cost a lot more. In the final analysis everything boiled down to how much money was spent on her. Still, she was happy everyone had given Rohit good gifts. Sita collected the torn up gift wrapping paper and put it into a large brown bag to be disposed later. She was quiet—still nagged by the fear of her mammogram results which would come in a day or two.

When everyone was done, and Sita had put her modest pile of gifts away, there was still a small pile of presents under the tree. We will have to give these to Ramu and Vijay and the others some other day," Aunt Priya bent over to pick them up. "Hello," she said. "What's this? Sita you didn't open this present." She handed her something in a long slim box.

"Oh I forgot," Rohit said. "Raja Uncle stopped by some days ago and told me to put this under the tree on Christmas." *That explained why she hadn't noticed it before* Sita thought. With shaking fingers she opened the present. She could feel everyone's eyes staring at her. She opened the box, and inhaled sharply. Aunt Priya waddled over to her side so fast she almost dropped the pile of presents she was holding. Inside the box was the most beautiful chain with a diamond pendant.

"That's not cubic zirconia," Mom said eyeing the piece closely.

"It's expensive," Aunt Priya said in awe.

"What is he doing giving out expensive presents to women when he doesn't even have a job!" Papa roared.

"Papa please, it's Christmas."

"You're not going to take such an expensive thing from him," Papa exploded.

"I'm keeping it," Sita announced defiantly and was too agitated to note that Papa's eyebrows had risen.

"We can talk about this later."

"I'm going to call and thank him now." Sita announced, and knew that Mom was looking at her very strangely.

"Let her go," she told Papa gently. "We raised her to keep her manners."

"This is not about manners and you know it," Papa muttered, but he sat down.

This time Sita had no hesitation in calling Raja. She called Sue's house knowing he and Tom were probably there. She wished Sue a Merry Christmas, and asked if she could speak to Raja. There was a moment's hesitation and then she heard his deep voice at the other end.

"Hi," he said. "Merry Christmas."

"Same to you," she said breathlessly. "Thank you so much!"

"Do you like it?" he asked simply.

"I love it, it must be so expensive. You shouldn't have!"

"I love you," he said quietly.

She felt her heart turn in her chest. "You never said that before."

"I thought I would say it after we were married," he said.

"Oh." Sita was at a loss for words. Her mind was reeling at the enormous blunder that she had made in turning him down in India.

"When can I see you?" he asked.

"Call me," she said. "Maybe next week you can stop by at the office, and then we can get together," she said feeling very daring all of a sudden.

"With Tom and Roz," he said.

"With Tom and Roz," she echoed wondering why he was still being coy.

She went to work the next day and Raja called. She felt the familiar quickening of her pulse at the sound of his voice.

"Can we get together Friday night?" he asked.

"Sure," Sita said quickly wondering *how she would get through the next four days.*

When she got home, there was still a smile on her face, and a spring in her step. She stopped to pick up the mail and then raced upstairs.

"What's for dinner?" she asked happily while she sorted through the mail. Her eyes zeroed in on the letter from the mammogram clinic. She picked it up and went to her room to read quietly. The letter was non-committal. It didn't say anything was wrong, and she read it over to see if she had missed something. But it didn't say she was okay either. Instead in the last paragraph, there was a cryptic note that said that there was an area of her breast that needed further investigation, and they wanted to take another look at it with ultrasound. They asked her to call and make an appointment.

Sita felt the bottom drop out of her world. With unsteady fingers she dialed the clinic. They told her they had an opening on Friday, and that she should not delay. The voice at the other end was quiet and firm. They told her 70% of all bumps and lumps were non-cancerous, but they just wanted to be sure. They told her not to wear any powder, and to come in a bit early, and bring her insurance card. This time she could not keep the news to herself. Well, she never had a chance to. The tears were spilling out from her lids in a steady stream. She tried to stem their flow with her palm.

Mom came into her room. "What on earth is wrong?" She picked up the letter and Sita saw her get very perturbed. She tried to say all the right things, but they came out all wrong. She tried to say she was sure it was nothing, but the hesitation and bewilderment in her face showed she did not believe her own lies. Her past experience had taught her to believe the worst. "Why didn't Dr. Kapoor tell us anything?" she murmured.

"You cannot do this sonogram on your lunch hour," Mom said. "You will take the day off, and I will come with you." Then she went and told Aunt Priya, who then insisted that she would come too. Papa wanted to come too, but then backed out when he was told he would be the only man there.

Sita took Friday off, and went to the clinic early in the morning so she could get it out of the way. This time she was made to lie down on a stretcher. Some cold jelly was applied to her chest, and then an instrument was passed over it and the picture was visible on the monitor to the side. It was not painful. Only stressful to lie there, and wonder what the result would be. As the technician passed the equipment over her, she looked up at the poster of flowers pinned to the roof of the room that was easily visible lying down. She kept her gaze transfixed on one tulip, to keep from looking at the monitor. Every little while she heard bells and rings, and the technician told her whenever she took a picture the machine gave a ring. When it was over, the technician gave her a wad of tissue to wipe the jelly off, and told her to stay lying down until the radiologist had a chance to look at the printouts. Then she would be free to go.

In a little while, just when the suspense of lying and doing nothing was killing her, a long haired blonde woman walked in, and introduced herself as Dr. Smith. She said she had seen the printouts, and wanted to take a look at the monitor. Again, the cold jelly was applied and the instrument circulated round and round only on her right breast, until it came to rest at the same spot the mammogram technician had targeted.

"Could be a cyst," the long haired doctor said. She was young, but seemed to know what she was doing. "I will recommend a needle biopsy," she said. "If it is liquid we will aspirate it using a very fine needle. It looks like it might be a cyst." She spoke as though there was a minor aberration in the way her body worked, and caused cysts—commonplace and nothing to worry about. When would you like to schedule the biopsy?" she asked.

Sita stared back at the flower poster trying to draw strength from its serenity. Mom and Aunt Priya were outside waiting to pounce on this young doctor. Sita figured she was here now—may as well get it over with. She asked if Dr. Smith could do the biopsy now. Dr Smith hesitated a moment, asked Sita if she was taking any aspirin or blood thinners. When Sita said "no," she said, "this is unusual but I am less booked up today, so maybe we should get it over with today."

Sita bit her lip, *please God don't let me cry before this elegant looking doctor*. Her voice shook a little. "Could *you* tell my family please?"

"I will," she said kindly. "You know 70 percent of biopsies we do come back benign." She repeated the catch phrase everyone used at the Breast Center. "It's probably nothing. We are just trying to be sure."

As soon as Aunt Priya heard the news she barreled into the small room. "It is only a test," she said to Sita loudly. "I know so many people who have biopsies, and they are all okay. Not to worry."

"Where's Mom?"

"Outside," she said in clipped tones.

"Crying?"

"Your mother worries too much."

Dr. Smith came back to the room and told Aunt Priya that family was supposed to wait outside. Aunt Priya's eyebrows rose high and she was about to protest, but thought better of it and left. The doctor talked slowly, and was as reassuring as could be. An antiseptic was applied to her breast, and then the numbing medicine. She felt no pain. There was a clicking sound and she noticed some drops of blood. Then more clicking noises and the nurse told her that what they were seeing, was not a cyst. It was solid. There was a quick change of plans. They would do a core biopsy instead of a fine needle one. They would use a larger needle and take out tissue the size of about one-inch long spaghetti. The tissue would be sent to the lab and she would have the results in four business days. "Not to worry," Dr. Smith said again. "Seventy percent of biopsies come out benign."

Gradually the numbing medicine wore off and she felt pain. She was told not to exert herself that day, and an ice pack was fitted inside her bra. She was given phone numbers of who to contact in an emergency if there was too much bleeding.

She was fine. She knew it. But the pain was there. A dull nagging reminder that maybe, she really did have cancer. She went home, and remembered the plans she had made with Raja. He had probably gone to her office as planned. Roz must have told him she had taken the day off. *Did he just shrug his shoulders and walk away. He must have asked Roz some questions perhaps, but she had not confided in Roz, and she would not know what to tell him.*

Chapter Twenty-seven

"Good morning!" Roz popped her head into Sita's office on her way to the kitchen for her morning cup of coffee. "What's new? You look kind of sad sitting there."

"Nothing much," Sita snapped. "Go get your coffee."

"Not thinking of Raja are you?"

"No!"

"Methinks the lady doth protest too much," Roz smiled. "By the way Raja was looking just as sad. You two fight again? Is that why you took the day off yesterday? Let me get my coffee and then we'll talk."

"What do you want to talk about?"

"Anything you want." Roz eyed her friend curiously. Sita's hair was tousled because she had been running her fingers through it over and over again. She had still not changed out of her sneakers, or put away her handbag. She was not drinking her usual cup of tea. She had not even bothered to wear her contacts and now stared at Roz with tired red eyes behind round glasses. Roz's friendship radar picked up on something serious troubling her friend. "What's wrong?" she asked again.

Sita hadn't slept well last night. She tossed and turned, remembering how frightened she had been lying on the stretcher, having the uncomfortably cold jelly being applied, and feeling a chill, go down her spine that had nothing to do with the coldness of the jelly. As hard as she had tried to focus on the flower poster, her eyes repeatedly strayed to the monitor to her side. She thought she saw a shadow. It looked big. Actually, she was seeing two shadows joined to one another, and they looked like the number 8. They were both on her right breast. She searched for a similar pattern on the left breast, but did not see one. She should have been happy, but seeing it just on one breast made it feel like it was abnormal. She had agreed to do the biopsy because she did not want to feel afraid every day. She wanted it to be over. But it would not be over for the next three days until she got the results.

She did not hurt any more. She could use her shoulder with no pain. A couple of pain killers and an ice pack had served her well the last couple of days. The pain was gone, but her mind was still numb.

"Nothing is wrong," Sita lied.

"Raja stopped by yesterday. He was upset you weren't here."

"Oh, I forgot."

"Is that all you have to say? Where were you? I called, and no one picked up."

"There was no message on the answering machine," Sita replied.

"I didn't leave a message. So where were you?"

"At the hospital."

"Were you sick?" Roz asked looking worried now.

"I don't know."

"What do you mean you *don't know?*"

"Look," Sita snapped. "I had a breast biopsy yesterday to check for cancer."

Roz sat down. "We're friends. Can't you trust me enough to tell me?"

Then the tears flowed. In sobbing gasps Sita let out all her pent up fears and frustrations and told Roz everything. She told her how she had picked up the pamphlets on breast cancer screening, and how she had checked herself. She thought she was imagining a lump. It was there before her period, and vanished after it as though it had never been there at all. She had mentioned it during her annual physical, and Dr. Kapoor recommended a mammogram, "just to be sure."

"But you're not even thirty," Roz interjected.

"But my Aunt died of breast cancer. It runs in the family."

"They just want to be sure," Roz said repeating what the doctor had said, what everybody said.

"Why did they have to keep calling me back?" Sita whispered in a fresh outburst of tears. "I'm just so scared."

"How come you never told me?" Roz repeated. Then without waiting for an answer she started to reassure her friend. "It's probably nothing—maybe just a cyst that fills with water every month. You do know 70% percent of all lumps are benign. Also, sometimes mammograms are not clear because of the density of the tissue, and they just want to be sure. Hospitals can be sued for negligence if they miss stuff."

"How do you know?" Sita asked surprised that Roz repeated the same things the mammogram technician had told her before.

"Tom's mother found a lump once, she told me. She got the same sort of letter. Then they did a sonogram and a biopsy, but everything was okay. It was just much ado about nothing. I'm sure there's nothing wrong with you." Roz made a hurried exit because she saw Ms. Valentine looking at them.

"Sita are those reports ready?" Ms. Valentine asked. She looked particularly severe in her navy suit. The next few days were spent trying to send two books to press. This meant dealing with last minute corrections and changes, and making sure the typesetters had made all corrections accurately. Was the cover okay, how about the title page? Sita remembered once how a book on breast cancer had a typo and the title printed as "Beast Cancer." There was quite a storm over that. Was the book layout fine? Had authors been informed that after a certain point in the schedule additional corrections would not be possible? Was all the advertising in place, and had the films or digital files been received? There was too much to be done, and Sita decided to go home and just come in early the next day. She had not heard from the Radiology people. No news was good news she hoped. It was almost 5 o'clock and the office had started to empty out. She sighed in resignation. She should go home and get some sleep, instead of staying in the office to spend the evening with the likes of Ms. Valentine.

That evening they all ate together as they usually did. "Did you hear from the Radiology people?" Papa asked.

"No," she replied quickly. Sita did not want to talk about what she had been thinking about all day. "Pass me the chicken curry please," she said.

"Take some vegetable also." Mom spooned the spinach curry on to her plate.

"That's enough," Sita said tearing a piece of *roti* to mop up the curry.

"Vegetables are good for you." Aunt Priya passed her the salad.

They thought she was sick. They were already treating her as though she was. Hurriedly Sita ate her food, left the plate in the sink, and excused herself.

Early next morning she got up a little earlier to catch the 7:00 AM train.

"Going to work?" Mom asked.

"Why not?"

"You should find a job close to the house instead of tiring yourself working in the city every day."

"Okay," Sita said only because she didn't want to argue in the morning.

Off to work she went, thinking about all the things she had to do. She was the first one in the office. She unlocked the door, turned on the lights, took off her jacket. She freshened her makeup and tried to hide the dark circles under her eyes with some concealer. Then she went and made a cup of tea, turned on her computer and waited for it to boot up.

A moment later the phone rang. It was the Radiology Department. "Good morning, Dr. Smith here." Sita felt her stomach turn upside down. "Do you have a minute to talk?"

"Yes," Sita whispered. She was so glad that it was early and the office was empty. She had all the privacy she could have wanted.

"I received the pathology results." There was a short silence then Dr. Smith said, "I'm sorry. The tumor is malignant."

The room seemed to spin around her. Sita buried her face in her hands. "It's got to be a mistake," she whispered. "I don't have cancer. I can't possibly have cancer. I am not thirty yet. They mixed up the samples. It's been known to happen."

"I wish I had better news. But there is no mistake." Dr. Smith said. "When we did the biopsy we had a feeling the lump was malignant."

"What do I do now?" Sita wailed.

"We need to find a surgeon. Look on the bright side," Dr. Smith said. "You felt a lump, thought it was probably nothing, but you did the right thing. You came in to have it checked out. Early detection is the key to a cure."

Easy for her to say! All of a sudden she wanted to talk. She wished people would hurry up and come in. She took the cup of tea she had just poured herself and emptied it in the kitchen sink. Then she made herself another cup, just for the sake of giving her hands something to do while she waited. She couldn't work now. She just couldn't. She wanted to say it out loud, "I have cancer." Days and weeks of uncertainty were finally over. Her worst fears confirmed. And there was no one to talk to. A minute later, Roma walked in. She took of her hat in the warmth of the kitchen. "Boy! It's freezing outside."

"I have cancer."

"What?" Roma saw Sita's tear stained cheek and hugged her close. Sita just kept repeating "I have cancer" like a talkie doll that knew only one sentence. "I have cancer," she said to Melody, to Tom, and to Larry. They looked at her and did not know how to respond. People she did not talk to every day, or was particularly close to, she was telling them all she had cancer. Finally, someone asked, "Did you just find out?"

She said "yes," and more tears followed. *Where was Roz? She was never there when she needed her to be.*

She decided to call up Aunt Priya and burst into tears the moment she heard the familiar "hello" at the other end of the line. "I have cancer. The doctor just told me."

"Oh God! Come home" she said. "Come home. Why are you still in the office? I have said so many times to quit that job. Still you want to sit there even though you have cancer. You listen to me now. You and I we are going to get through this. Do you hear me? Come home now. I will call Sue. She will help me find a good surgeon. You worry about nothing. Come home now. Why you have to sit there. You don't eat properly. No vegetables I'm sure—always eating junk food. Indian people never get cancer. Have you thought about what your poor parents will feel? Never mind I will handle this. You don't worry. Just come home."

"I will Aunt Priya," Sita said smiling through her tears. She knew she could count on Aunt Priya to get her through this. Well first things first. She would need to tell Ms. Valentine—might as well get it over with now.

Ms. Valentine was sitting at her desk wearing the same navy suit, or maybe she just had five of the same color. This morning her navy suit was as crisp as ever, and her shirt had its bow firmly knotted at the neck. Not a hair was out of place, and the familiar horn-rimmed glasses were perched on her hawk like nose.

"What's the matter Sita?" Ms. Valentine peered over her horn-rimmed glassed to look at Sita who was standing in her doorway.

"I was just told I have cancer," Sita said. "I wanted to let you know I will probably be gone awhile. I don't know how long yet, but I understand treatments take a long time."

"Oh my dear girl!" Ms. Valentine got up and walked toward her. She hesitated for a moment and then wrapped her bony arms around Sita, pulling her into the angular confines of a bony embrace. Sita struggled to find a comfortable spot on her rock hard shoulder. "You are going to be fine," Ms. Valentine said. Then suddenly she pushed Sita away, as though regretting her momentary weakness. Going back to her brisk tone she said, "I have the names of some really good doctors here at Sloan Kettering. See if you want to use any of them. Mention my name if you decide to go there. They will remember. They treated me for breast cancer."

"Oh," Sita said, staring down at Ms. Valentine's chest. "I didn't know."

"I elected to have a mastectomy," Ms. Valentine said following Sita's gaze. "It was many years ago. There are new treatments and other options these days."

"We may decide to find a doctor closer to home rather than the city," Sita said, "but thank you for the cards."

"Well, as soon as you know how long you will be gone, let me know, and I will arrange for your disability payments. You have been with the company a long time and I am going to make sure you get everything due to you."

"Thank you. You are so kind," Sita said. She was quite taken aback by the help she was receiving from this stone cold woman.

"We must get back to business now," Ms. Valentine said, and the shuttered look was back in her eyes. "I want you to put your journals in good enough order for someone to take over. Finish what you can, and the rest of stuff must be labeled in order of priority, and accompanied with a checklist of things to be done. I want no hitch in the timely transfer of the workload. Is that understood?"

"Yes Ma'am," Sita answered.

By the time she got back to her desk, the phone was ringing off the hook. Aunt Priya, Mom, and Papa were all on the phone.

"What are you still doing there?" Aunt Priya asked. "You want me to come and get you?"

"I was just talking to my boss."

"What sort of boss keeps you there when you are so sick," Papa exploded. "I agree with your Aunt Priya for once. Enough is enough. Your Mom has been crying all afternoon."

"I'm coming. Did you get a chance to tell Roz?"

"Yes Roz, Tom, and Raja know. Sue has promised to help."

"Back up a bit. Did you say Raja knows? I hope not," Sita said. "There's no need for everyone to be involved in my business."

"Raja just happened to be there when I called Tom," Aunt Priya said.

"How convenient!" Sita muttered. "Well, he must be thanking his lucky stars we did not get involved further. No one wants a sick woman," Sita said bitterly.

"What nonsense you talk even when you are ill. Come home right now." Aunt Priya shouted on the phone.

The subways were deserted. It was well past rush hour. Sita was alone in the car with only her thoughts for company. How could this be happening? Maybe this was all a nightmare and in the morning it would go away. Maybe it was gone already. She looked around quickly. No one was looking. She stuck her hand inside her blouse looking for the lump. She was hoping against hope she would not find it. But it was there—hard and defiant. She pushed at it. It did not hurt. *How could this thing be so dangerous?* She started crying.

How long had she had this cancer? The radiologist had said it was ductal invasive carcinoma. Had it spread? Almost forty-thousand women died of cancer every year in the United States. Would she be one of them? No she would not. She would fight till she overcame. What if she could not? What if she was disfigured? She would rather die, than have a mastectomy. *Oh God! Please help me. What did I do* wrong *to deserve this?*

The train pulled in at the Jackson Heights station. It was a nice day to walk. But then she noticed Papa at the station. Mom was there too. Her eyes were red from crying. Sita hugged them both. "Where's Aunt Priya?"

"At home—cooking vegetable curry," Mom said. "You don't eat enough vegetables. You never liked vegetables. What was I to do?" Mom cried.

"Mom it's not your fault I have cancer," Sita said. "Look at me. It's not your fault. Okay?"

"Aunt Priya has made an appointment with a good surgeon tomorrow evening. I'll come with you," Mom said sniffling. "Aunt Priya wants to go. But I am your mother."

"Sure Mom. Is the doctor far?"

"Pretty far," Papa said. The doctor's office is out on the Island near Sue's house. He used to be her doctor."

The next day Sita found herself in Long Island once again. Aunt Priya was there because she had refused to stay behind. Dressed in a bright red sari she marched ahead into a big beige and green frame house that had a sign that said "Surgical Oncology" followed by the names of the doctors. Sita hung back sticking close to Mom and Papa.

Sita signed in, and all of a sudden her thoughts drifted to Raja. *He knew she was sick. Would he try and contact her?*

The waiting room was unlike any other she had seen. A dark green couch and two other chairs were the only seats in the room.

"He doesn't get many patients does he?" Sita commented remembering the crammed waiting room in Rohit's pediatrician's office.

"Surgeons don't need many patients to make a lot of money. This doctor makes good money. He is so rich." Aunt Priya said.

"I don't care if he is rich. Is he a good surgeon?" Papa asked.

"Nice office." Mom said taking in the big arrangement of flowers on the coffee table. She got up to look closely at the curios on the mantel above the fireplace.

"Is he a good surgeon?" Papa repeated.

"Yes. Would I bring my niece here if he were not? Sue tells me he is young but very good. Better to go with a younger surgeon. They are more in touch with new treatments, and like Sue said, with cutting edge technology."

"Aunt Priya, I hope I don't have to have a mastectomy."

"Don't worry about that," Aunt Priya said. "We must make sure all the cancer is taken out. Let us see what the doctor says. This is America. They can do such good breast reconstruction. They know how to take the stomach muscle and make a new breast. And do you know what Sue was telling me, they can even make the nipple. They take skin from the vagina because it is little darker and then they manufacture the nipple."

"Gross!" Sita said. "Can you imagine the stomach migrating to the chest. I hope to goodness it doesn't come to that."

The nurse called Sita's name and she was taken to the examination room. "I want to come too," Aunt Priya stood up.

"Madam the doctor will speak to you later," the nurse said firmly.

"Come Sita." the nurse ushered her into the hallway. There was a paper top lying on the table. "Put that on with the front open. The doctor will be in shortly," the nurse said and disappeared.

Sita put on the peach paper and looked around at the assortment of scissors, gauzes, and all kinds of shiny equipment. *How had it come to this? Who could have thought she would get cancer. Oh Lord please. Let them not take off the breast. She could not bear the thought of being mutilated like that.* The door opened, and a young man walked in and introduced himself as Dr. Melandino. His handshake was firm. His eyes were kind. She had thought all surgeons were old and wise looking, but this one was young.

"Must have a young doctor," Aunt Priya had insisted. "Those are the ones who know about the latest treatment and, how they call it....*cutting edge technology?"* Aunt Priya was obviously repeating something Sue had told her. Papa would have preferred an older doctor, someone with many more years of experience under his belt, but Sue had said the older ones were more set in their ways, and it was far better to go to Dr. Melandino. She went so far as to say, if Sita were her own daughter, she would not recommend anyone different.

The surgeon was quiet as he examined her. "This is not a chick pea, we're talking about here. It's surprising it was not caught earlier." When he saw Sita's eyes dilate in fear he said, "It is 6 cms long. It's not humongous, but it's not a chick pea."

"Hardly anyone gets cancer in India," Sita said, feeling somehow that she had been betrayed because she lived in America. "People in India wouldn't even think of getting a mammogram," she said. "Very few have access to that kind of technology."

"That's the beauty of this country," the doctor said. "So many people have access to the very best in health care. Ms. Rampal, you and I will fight this together. I want to see you live to see your children and grandchildren. I want to see you live to ninety."

She wasn't even married yet. Probably never would be. A stray tear escaped her eyes, followed by one, then another, and then another. She was wiping her face with the palm of her hand.

"I know it's a lot," Dr. Melandino said.

"When will I be cured?" she asked.

"This is serious business," he said. "We are not dealing with pneumonia here."

The tears fell harder, and came down quicker. This time she did not even try to wipe them away. The surgeon stepped out and came back in with a box of tissues. She took one, and then another, and then a third.... "Aunt Priya wants to meet you." Sita wanted someone responsible to be around to listen to the treatment regimen. There was no way she could comprehend what was being said. She had begged him not to do a mastectomy. All she could think of was the horror of being mutilated. She waited for him to reassure her.

The surgeon made no promises but said, "Ms. Rampal, we will try to conserve the breast." He looked at her red eyes and still wet face. "However, the first goal is to save life."

Chapter Twenty-eight

Papa sat in the rocking chair staring pensively. The newspaper lay forgotten at his feet. His little girl had cancer. *How could that have happened? How could his princess be so sick?* Papa ran his fingers through his hair. He looked up to see his sister. Aunt Priya had just waddled into the living room in a jumbled splash of color. Her fuchsia colored sari clashed violently with her orange blouse.

"Have no fear, Aunt Priya is here," Papa muttered with a tinge of sarcasm that was completely lost on Aunt Priya.

"Yes that's right," Aunt Priya responded brightly. "Don't worry about a thing. I have spoken to the doctors. Here's what they are going to do." She tucked away the loose end of her sari and got ready to explain.

"What do you mean *you* spoke to the doctors? I am the father. The doctors are supposed to speak to *me*."

"There you go yelling at me again," Aunt Priya snapped. "Since neither you, nor Raja, nor anybody else had the good sense to stay with me and find out about the type of treatment, I spoke to…."

"What do you mean Raja? Who is he to be involved?" Papa yelled before Aunt Priya could continue with her monologue.

"He keeps asking Tom about Sita, so I didn't think there was any harm in letting him know about Sita's treatment," Aunt Priya said. She looked a tiny bit awkward.

"Just because my daughter is sick, there is no need to be yoking her with a loser." Papa yelled. "Raja has no job and no plans. No future. He has nothing. I don't want him near my daughter. Every Tom, Dick, and Harry does not have to know about my daughter's predicament."

"Raja is not every Tom, Dick...."

"Least of all Raja," Papa bellowed. "I don't need him to be involved. What is he going to do for her? Cure her?"

Sita walked in to catch the last bit of the conversation. "Papa is right," she said. "I don't want everybody to know. I don't want their pity." She had not called Raja to explain why she had not been in the office that day. It was too difficult to talk to him now.

Aunt Priya pretended not to hear Sita, "As I was saying," she said, "they have decided on a treatment program. They are going to do neoadjuvant chemotherapy. That means," she said opening her eyes very wide, "they are trying to shrink the tumor before they operate. In that way they won't have to cut so much. The surgery will be much easier. Not so big you understand. They won't have to do mastectomy. They told me it is called breast conserving surgery."

"I know, the doctor told me. It's quite a relief!" Sita sighed loudly. *At least I am not going to be disfigured.* The thought of being mutilated for life had been a recurrent nightmare. She was glad that's all it was—just a bad dream. "Thank goodness," she said out loud.

"Yes. Your friends think so too."

"How many people have you told?" Papa asked quietly.

"Those who asked," Aunt Priya said curtly. "I told them they are not going to remove the breast, because in India you know, in my time, if you get breast cancer that's the first thing they do. I told them they would remove all the lymph nodes, and for a few days she would have a drain on her side to drain out all the lymph fluid so that it did not collect anywhere else."

"Good Lord," gasped Papa. "Why so much detail!"

"You know, you're too macho to think your sister can do anything right. That she could not find out anything," Aunt Priya said. Her hands were on her hips in her customary battle mode.

Sita tried to stop the two from starting a fight. "Who is going to take me for chemotherapy? I've heard treatments are pretty brutal."

"I will," they both said at the same time.

"What do you mean?" Mom said. "I will be the one to take her."

In the end all three of them went with her. There was complete silence in the car. Papa's face was inscrutable as he navigated the morning rush hour traffic.

They pulled into a packed parking lot. "Amazing how many people have cancer here," Sita said. "Let's go." She had cried all night and now the tears were dry. If she waited by Papa any longer, she knew she would cry again.

Bravely she walked into the waiting room, signed herself in, and waited. Expecting to find a room of sad and deathly sick people, she was surprised. The waiting room was like any other she had seen, just larger, and there was a lingering smell of medicine that she would later recognize as chemo.

First, they took her to the lab where the nurse took her pulse, blood pressure, and weight. Then they took blood. She winced at the finger prick, watched the nurse squeeze out a few drops on a slide that was labelled with her name. They gave her a piece of cotton to press down on the finger and told her to wait in the hallway. She sat down in one of the two chairs.

She saw that the waiting room was filling up. Many of the patients were wearing scarves to conceal their baldness, no doubt. Others wore scarves, and had hair that escaped from it to frame their faces. Later she found out, that the hair was actually stitched to the scarf to make it appear as though it was natural. Others had a full head of hair that was well-styled, and too perfect for a drawn, lined face of a middle aged, sick person. And when she looked closely, she could see they had no eyebrows or eyelashes, and that the hair was really a wig. The waiting room was full of more people with all too perfect hair, and all the hairstyles featured a fringe designed to conceal the absence of eyebrows. There were a handful of really old people in wheelchairs, or those using walkers. Most of the patients were middle aged, and all of them were older than she was.

"You do not belong here," Papa said, "with all these sick people."

"She is sick," Aunt Priya said quietly.

Everyone treated her as though she were suddenly fragile. They were extra solicitous, extra kind. She was the new patient, and therefore at the top of the line until another new one came along, perhaps more serious than she was. She wished everyone was not so kind, that they would not make way for her as she walked down the hallway, or smile their sad quiet smiles. She wished they would just treat her with the antiseptic indifference of most physician waiting rooms.

She waited in the hallway until her blood report was ready. She saw staff wearing their hospital greens, nurses wearing white pants with a pastel top that had their name tag prominently displayed. Doctors wearing shirt and tie stood out in the crowd. They were well-respected. Patients trusted them with their lives, and nurses trusted their direction. They stood in the hallways—some of them poring over patients' charts to brief themselves, others went about their business making phone calls, issuing prescriptions, dictating medical reports.

One doctor wore a pink shirt, the breast cancer color, and a tie with happy faces. Another reminded Sita of the Energizer bunny who never stops. He was always walking. Up and down the hallway he went, looking for his patients in chemo rooms, stopping by to jumpstart their hopes, and to encourage. Walking fast and talking faster, he went from room to room searching and consoling, but his patients could seldom get a word in. Many had learned to write down their questions before he arrived, so they did not get side-tracked with his well-meaning fast talk.

Chemo was different now, they told her. Sita remembered seeing *Love Story.* She remembered the way Jenny looked while undergoing chemo—pale and deathly ill, with an assortment of tubes running through her as she lay in bed. Chemo was no longer like that. She would not have to stay in a hospital for treatment. The doctor took her in the office and said, "It is not how it used to be." He took a small piece of paper and drew a U shaped graph. "In the past," he said "the cell counts would dip to near zero." He looked at her over his bifocals. He was a middle-aged man with graying hair, and was well respected in the oncology practice. "Today, there are many antidotes to reverse the toxic effects after the initial infusion." He paused to make sure Sita understood. "There are ways to bring the white and red cell blood counts up. The day after chemo, you will come here and get a shot of Neulasta. A week later, we will check the blood again," he explained, "and if you need a shot for the hemoglobin counts at the time, it will be given. You will be closely monitored but you will be able to move around all through treatment." He went on to say that she would have her good days, and her bad ones, but she would be fine, and that they were all rooting for her.

Still she was scared. It didn't help that Papa kept pacing up and down the hallway, and that mother was on the verge of tears all the time. The only one who stayed solid and calm was Aunt Priya. She had struck up a conversation with a thin woman with a scarf knotted around her head gangster-like. Lord knows what they were talking about, but the woman came up to her and said, "Hi, is this your first time?"

"Yes," Sita said staring at this patient hooked up to an IV holding three big bags of liquid.

"My name is 'Happy.'" She extended her free arm, and smiled broadly.

She's got to be joking, Sita thought. She extended her arm tentatively.

Ms. Happy gave her a firm handshake. "It's not so bad. Just think positive. You're going to be okay." She pushed her IV pole ahead of her and walked over to one of the rooms, "This room has windows," she said brightly. "Want to join me?" She spoke as though she was inviting her to a cozy chit chat rather than some ghastly experience with toxic substances. Ms. Happy held the remote in her hand, "Want to watch anything in particular?"

"Oh nice room," Aunt Priya pushed her way past Papa and Mom who hesitated in the doorway. "Look there is a nice big TV, and so many magazines."

"What's your point?" Papa muttered.

"She's trying to make the best of the situation" Mom whispered.

"I can't find anything good in this situation." Papa grumbled. "My little girl is going to get all sick and bald." He choked up and stared pointedly at the red bandana on Happy's head.

"It's only hair. It grows back" Happy said.

The nurse walked into the room with three big bags of Sita's chemo. "It comes back thicker and brighter." She eyed Sita's long braid that hung down almost to her hips. "You might want to cut it though."

"Why?" Mom asked.

"It comes out in clumps," the nurse said gently. "You don't want hair falling in the food, in your clothes, or all over the house. It's a lot easier if there is less to begin with. You know what you might want to do," she tapped Sita gently on the shoulder, "go to a wig store. We will give you a referral, and the insurance company should cover it. Go buy it now. It takes about ten days for the hair to start falling. That way you will be all prepared."

"Does it all fall out at once?" Sita asked. She had never seen herself bald.

The nurse nodded gently. "Most of the time it's all gone by the time you've had the second chemo. It's better that way. Why prolong the trauma."

"Just remember it grows back," Happy said. "I bought myself two wigs—one red and another blonde. That way my husband gets to go out with two different women every weekend." She smiled. "And there is another plus side. You never have to shave your legs or underarms because that hair falls out too."

Sita smiled. "Wow! How do you stay so happy?"

"I have wonderful support. My husband—he is the greatest," she said dreamily. "I can't let him down. I must get better—for him, for my family.

"Sita here has very nice support from her family," Aunt Priya said. "Everybody loves her. She knows that. Right Sita?" She thumped Sita on the back as though she could make her spit out her acquiescence.

"Yes," Sita said quietly, "I have a lot of help from the family. Then for some inexplicable reason her thoughts strayed to Raja. *What would it have been like to be married to him? Would he have stood by her as much as Happy's husband seemed to? Maybe she should ask Roz if she had seen him.* Then she pushed all thoughts of Raja out of her mind, and braced herself for the needle the nurse was getting ready to insert and start the chemo.

"It's not so bad," someone said. "I've been doing it for months." Sita turned around and saw another woman in the room. "It helps to talk about it. That is why they don't put us alone in a room."

"Sita would never be alone. Sita has her family." Papa said.

"You're all set," the nurse said starting the drip. Then turning to Papa she said, "She's going to be just fine. If you want to come back in four hours, she will be all done."

"I am staying right here."

"Me too," Aunt Priya said. "Her mother will stay too."

The nurse looked uncomfortable. There's no place to sit," she said feebly.

"It's their first time," the second lady with the bandanna said. "Leave them alone. Then with no hesitation she unbuttoned the top buttons of her blouse to reveal a bump in her chest. "This is a port-o-cath" she said when she saw Sita staring hard. "My veins are real thin so they had to put in this sort of shunt like thing to be able to make sure the chemo goes in to the main vein."

"Uh huh," Sita shifted uncomfortably because she had been caught staring. She couldn't help herself. There was this valley in the lady's chest and Sita's thoughts were drawn to the horror of a mastectomy. *Oh dear God* she thought. *How must this poor woman deal with that?*

"Wow those are some tattoos" the nurse said buttoning up her blouse once the drip was inserted.

Sita turned her head away sharply. "Aren't they?" the woman said. Turning to Sita, she said in a matter of fact tone, "You know when my breast was removed, I begged the surgeon to save my tattoos. I have dragons tattooed on both breasts. Of course when

I lost the breast, I wanted to be sure he preserved the skin. You know he was so good. My dragon looks just fine."

"You like dragons on your breasts!" Aunt Priya said voicing the thoughts everyone else was thinking.

"I think I'll go for a walk," Papa said. "It's getting hot in here."

"Mom you go with Papa."

"I will stay here," Aunt Priya said. "I want to talk to Sita."

Happy looked up and smiled politely. "No problem. Pretend I'm not here." She buried her nose in the *Ladies Home Journal.*

"It is so nice you have a good man," Aunt Priya said to Happy. "You know I tried to find a good man for Sita too."

"Excuse me?" Happy said.

"You know what," Aunt Priya said. "What?" Happy replied. Aunt Priya continued. "Sita said "no" to a perfectly good man I found for her even though I now know she likes him. More than likes him…." She still hesitated to say Sita was in love. "I just don't understand it." Aunt Priya knotted her eyebrows in bewilderment as though the incident had occurred today. "I can't get over it." Happy looked confused and Aunt Priya said, "She would have been married by now."

"Oh Aunt Priya!" Sita said rolling her eyes, astonished that her Aunt should bring this up to a total stranger. "I just can't stand to be told what to do. I want to have some say in what happens in my life."

"Did you have a say in who gets cancer? We do not always have a say in everything that happens to us. When will you stop this foolishness?" Aunt Priya was quite red in the face after scolding Sita.

"I know how you both feel," Happy said placating her new found friend. "I too want to have a say in what happens to me."

"See!" Sita said triumphantly.

"You know I found it incredibly hard to trust my doctors. When a cancer treatment was chosen for me, I questioned, and counter questioned the doctors so much, I drove them nuts," Happy said. "When they told me to have surgery, I said why can't I just do chemotherapy? When they said chemotherapy, I didn't want to take certain drugs. And when they recommended hormone therapy, I told them it caused endometrial cancer and I wanted nothing to do with it."

"Why you do that?" Aunt Priya said. "You are not a doctor. You don't know what is good for you."

"Maybe, but I need to agree to a particular treatment. The patient does have final say, you know. I can refuse treatment. That is my right." She smiled at Aunt Priya whose face was all scrunched up. "Let me give you an example. "The chemotherapy drug the doctors wanted me to take was Adriamycin and I didn't want to take it."

"What do you know about Adriamycin that the doctors don't?" Aunt Priya said quickly.

"Well, on the internet they said it caused cardiac toxicity. I really don't want to trade cancer for heart disease," Happy said.

"So you refused it?"

"Well, I told them what I knew, and asked them if I had any other options."

"So in the end did you take this Adriamycin or not," Aunt Priya said tapping her fingers on the table impatiently.

"I did."

"So what was the point of your argument?"

"I agreed only after they told me of the other treatment options and they had to convince me that the benefits outweigh the risks. I needed to feel that though I had let them have their wish, it was I, who had the final say." Happy said.

"So you are saying I should have given Sita so many different options."

"Maybe," Happy said looking at Sita quickly.

"Let me understand this. If I had given Sita many options, presented her with more than one suitor, then she would have picked Raja. But because I kept telling her Raja was so good, she said "no," to spite me?" Aunt Priya said beginning a frenzied finger tapping on the table to vent her frustration. "Well, it's too late now. Raja is not what he used to be."

"Oh my!" Happy said laughing. "Have you asked this Raja what *he* wants?"

"Not recently.... I know he likes her. He gave her a very big Christmas present," Aunt Priya said.

"You know Raja is never going to be interested in me now. I should give back that jewelry like Papa had told me to in the first place," Sita said under her breath. "Aunt Priya I wish you wouldn't keep talking about me as though I weren't here." Sita said loudly.

"Sh sh," Aunt Priya said. "Don't say Raja will never be interested. We'll talk later. Your Papa is back."

Sita kept quiet."

Chapter Twenty-nine

Sita had not seen Roz for a while. The days had rolled into weeks and she had already completed three cycles of chemotherapy. Her hair had almost all fallen out except for two stubborn long clumps on the top of her head that fell below her ears. They covered the sides of her head, shrouding the bald expanse with its dull lifeless texture. She had bought herself a wig. It was a short style in black hair, with bangs. The salesman startled her by asking, "Do you want your head shaved?" When she backed away, he said many of his clients asked to be shaved. "Heads are cute, why keep all that hair when it is going to fall out?"

"No," she said firmly, grabbing her purchase and making for the exit. She clung to the two remaining clumps, arranging them over her baldness so no one would see it. But her head often felt cold, and she often woke up in the middle of the night looking for a scarf, or a cap to wear at night. She stopped washing her hair as often, hoping to preserve it for as long as she could, and when she did wash it, she would pat it dry trying hard not to uproot the last few strands. She stopped brushing it, and there was so little that it looked okay just patted into place. She knew she was only delaying the inevitable. Everyone had told her she would be completely bald. That she would have no eyebrows or eyelashes either. But that hadn't happened yet. Maybe if she never got water on her brows, they would just sit there. That's what she told her doctor. "Maybe I will be the exception to the rule. Maybe my hair won't fall out," she said. The doctor looked at her sadly, and his silence spoke volumes.

For a little while, her hair stayed. It was dull and lifeless but it was there, frozen into place, matted in part, but it stayed. Then one day Rohit sniffed the top of her head and said, "Gosh Sita! your hair smells like Brandi's. What did you do? Let me see." He tried to bring the lumps up to his nose. He tugged gently and the whole bit came out in his hands. His eyes welled with tears, "I didn't pull hard, honest I didn't," he said staring in horror at the bald side of her head.

"Don't worry about it," Sita said. "Let's take care of the other side too. Maybe we can shave it off. Then I'll look like Mr. Clean" she said bravely—Mr. Clean was the bald muscular man seen on household cleaner containers. Then without further ado, both the pieces were off. Sita stared back at Rohit's bewildered face, taking in his shock through the veil of her own tears. She pulled out her compact and looked in the mirror. She had never seen herself bald, and when she saw her face staring back at her, she closed her eyes to shut out the nightmare.

Sita did not see the door open, or notice the people who had walked in. She was staring at the last lock of hair in her hand.

"Hi there!" Roz said softly, and Sita turned red-eyed to her friend. Then looking past her she realized with a shock that Tom and Raja were standing there too. Without a word she started to get up.

"Running away again Sita," Raja murmured. "Please stay."

She sank back into the chair only because her legs were too weak to carry her, and it was just easier to sit down. Roz sat beside her. Raja sat down opposite both of them, and Tom sat beside Raja.

"Please let me help," Raja said. "Don't shut me out."

"I'm okay," she said embarrassed that he had seen her bald. "I have surgery tomorrow, and after that's over I should be fine," she said more bravely than she felt.

"Can I do anything?" he asked again.

"No," she said more abruptly than she wanted to.

"Let's go and see if Aunt Priya needs something," Tom said. Raja said 'okay', and followed. Roz stayed.

"I'll come tomorrow morning," Roz said. "I took the day off."

"Thanks. I'm supposed to be there 7:30 in the morning. I'm not supposed to eat or drink anything after dinner tonight. Not even my morning cup of tea. That's going to be hard."

"You've already gone through so much, you can handle that. Try not to worry too much," Roz said. Then she too got up to go, gave her friend a hug, and said, "Let me go see Aunt Priya, and I'll see you tomorrow."

Early the next morning Roz called. She said she wouldn't be able to make it, that she was feeling sick to her stomach, and that it looked as though she had contracted some sort of stomach virus.

In the end Mom, Papa, and Aunt Priya, drove her to the surgical building in the hospital. The parking lot was largely crowded. She went to the reception. They asked her who her surgeon was, then verified her name and asked her to wait. They asked Papa if he had a cell phone and requested that he turn it off.

A few minutes later, she was taken upstairs and given two hospital gowns. "Wear one with the opening in the front and one with opening in the back." What they forgot to tell her was that the first one opened at the back and the second one was worn like a regular gown with the opening in the front so that she was decent from the front and the back. When she appeared in her gowns they told her she had worn them wrong and she had to go back inside to change.

They gave her a plastic bag to put her clothes and shoes. After she wore her gowns the right way, she put on the cotton socks and finally a pair of navy blue disposal pants with a drawstring. They also gave her a blue hat. She had refused to remove her wig even in the hospital so she put on the blue hat over her wig. Finally she was ready.

Papa had been pacing up and down the whole time. He asked how long they would have to wait for the surgery. The nurse said it would be a while, and it may be better for him to go home and come back later. Papa looked at her, and she nodded. Sita really did not want him around because he made her anxious. But she didn't expect Aunt Priya and Mom to decide to leave and come back later. Aunt Priya said she had to drop Rohit to school, and Mom said she had forgotten to do something, and would be right back.

The nurse told her the surgeon had requested needle localization. It was a minor procedure before surgery they said, and a wire and a clip would be inserted at the tumor site. They would do an ultrasound to determine the site of the tumor. The surgeon had already explained that this was necessary because the chemo had shrunk the tumor and they could no longer palpate it. He needed the wire and clip to guide him during surgery.

Once again she found herself in the same ultrasound room staring at the same picture of flowers on the ceiling. She looked sideways at the monitor and the shadows she had seen earlier were a lot smaller. The technician was having difficulty determining what was scar tissue, and what was tumor. But in the end, they gave her numbing medicine, and she saw in the monitor across from her, the shadow of a probe being inserted into her. Thankfully, she felt nothing. Then she was taken away to a waiting room. She felt cold and numb, and terribly alone. She wished she had insisted someone stay with her.

A nurse came into the room with her chart. She drew blood and then started the IV. They put her in a comfortable chair with a reclining back, and gave her all kinds of literature about breast cancer and also some magazines to read. Models, scantily dressed, with well-made up faces stared back at her from the pages of the magazine. She wanted no part of them. She wanted to pi. All that fluid in the IV made her want to go to the bathroom. Her mouth was dry. It was already 11 AM and she had not had a drop to drink since midnight. She told the nurse she was thirsty, and she gave her ice chips. She had eaten nothing, and she was so tired of sitting and waiting.

The nurse came to take her pulse and blood pressure, and commented on her galloping heart rate. Sita told her "No one likes going to OR. I want to pi real badly," she said, "Where is the bathroom?" The nurse pointed it out. Sita pushed the IV pole along and made her way down the hallway to the restroom.

When she was back, the anesthesiologist was looking for her. He asked her routine questions about her medical history, pored over her chart, asked her if she wanted valium. When she said 'no', he disappeared saying he would be back soon. After he was gone, another nurse came and put her in a wheelchair, and took her to another waiting area. This time she couldn't control herself, and she started crying.

Everyone stared at her as if she were crazy. They pulled the curtains around her and she heard one nurse talking to another, "She's very emotional right now." Then another nurse poked her head in and asked Sita where her family was. She said, "I don't know," and the tears came down quicker and harder. Finally, a kind nurse came and sat with her. She took away all the literature about cancer and instead started showing her pictures of different wigs with a whole assortment of hair styles. She started telling her about makeup ideas, and different kinds of creams and lotions, and kept assuring her that she had a wonderful surgeon and there was no reason to worry so much. She stayed her with her all through, until it was time for Sita to go up.

Aunt Priya, Papa, and Mom were finally all back. But there was no time to chat. The surgeon had arrived. He had been seeing patients in his office and was still dressed in a suit. He shook hands with everyone, asked for the mammograms, and took the folder from Sita. He looked at the wire and clip and commented that the dressing holding the wire in place was already coming off, and she shouldn't move around so much. She was about to say something, but decided to keep her thoughts to herself. She could walk. She wanted to walk to OR, and she did. A nurse walked with her.

The room was cold, and all kinds of equipment were around the narrow table she was made to lie down on. The anesthesiologist was there. He was in a talkative mode. He talked to her about India, where she had gone to school, what she did for a living, and so on. She felt something cold on her palm. She saw her surgeon, now in his scrubs standing and looking at her mammograms in the distance. She saw that she was hooked up to an ECG machine, turned around and saw the nurse hovering over her, and then she was out.

She awoke to the voice of someone calling her name. "Ms. Rampal," he said, "are you there?" She did not have the strength to respond. Everything hurt. She felt like puking, and strange sounds came from her as though her insides were fighting to spill out of her. Someone thrust a cup on her chest. She reached for it, but nothing came. Then she saw her wig was lying on her chest and her arm reached up to her bald head in dismay.

She was moved to a stretcher and readied to go into the hospital room. Aunt Priya, Mom, and Papa were all in the hallway looking worried. "Don't fight," the nurse said quietly when she clung desperately to the gurney unwilling to leave it for something new, and perhaps worse. They were gentle with her. They took her to a nice big room. Something was attached to her legs, to keep the circulation going and prevent the formation of clots. She was still hooked up to the IV, and her wrist was beginning to swell a bit at the point the needle was inserted. Everything hurt, and she asked for medication every few hours in the beginning. The right side of her chest was swathed in bandages and she was scared to take a peek just in case her breast was missing. There was a drain attached to the inside of her hospital gown that was stitched to a surgical opening on her right side. She looked down to see it was nearly full of red liquid. Her axillary lymph nodes had been removed as a precaution, and now the fluid had to be removed by this drain. Her right arm hurt badly, and she was scared to use it. When they brought her breakfast the next morning, she ate it with her left hand, treating her right hand as though it was broken.

Then the surgeon came to see her. He asked her to extend her arm forward. "See it works," he said. He told her she should try and use it a little more. "You might get frozen shoulder otherwise," he said. He checked her dressing, and she saw that she still had the right breast. She felt an overwhelming sense of relief. She told him she wanted to go home. And she got her wish.

At home she improved rapidly. The pain got less. The liquid in the drain changed from bright red to a straw color, and got less and less every day. She tried to use her arm more every day. The bad news was, the moment she felt stronger, it was time to continue with her chemotherapy treatments. Roz came to see her many times at home, and the last time she brought Raja again.

"Maybe Raja can drive you to your next treatment."

"Sure." Raja said looking at Roz gratefully.

"Then that's settled," Roz continued. "Sita when is your next treatment?"

"I'm not the best company when I have my treatments," Sita stammered. "Maybe I should just go by myself."

"You're never good company around me. I'm accustomed to it." Raja quipped hoping to get a rise out of her.

"Gee thanks!" Sita said falling right into the trap. "I can be wonderful when I want. You just don't see it."

"Show me then."

She glared at him.

"So when's the next chemo?" Raja asked.

"Tomorrow at 8:00 AM. I have three more to go," she said. "I should be fine. I managed well so far."

"Sita I know you can. You managed chemo, surgery, everything. I didn't think you would want my help so I didn't offer before."

Roz tried to change the subject. "Do you have everything you need? Your anti-nausea medicine and the steroids you have to take before treatment. What're they called"?

"Dexamethasone" Sita said sadly. "I have enough."

"What about Gatorade and the lemon lime soda. Have enough of that? We can go get some."

"Ok." Sita said quietly. She hated thinking about chemo. Hated how it made her so sick, burping and puking all day long. The nausea medicine just barely helped. And for 4 days she was a miserable shell of a person. But more than the nausea, it was the feeling of being so dependent on everybody that got to her. Nobody asked her to do anything anymore. It was as if she weren't there. She wanted to work, but couldn't commute into the city. She asked for work to be sent home, but the company wouldn't do that. "You're out on disability Ms. Valentine told her, and there are legal implications of sending you work." *As if she would sue,* Sita thought in exasperation. She would have worked for free if they had let her—just to make her feel she was not useless. That she was not dying.

"I'll do the laundry" Mom would say. "You rest."

"I'll do the dishes," Papa said, and the poor man would don an apron and try and do the dishes—something he had never done back home in India. Aunt Priya did all the cooking. All Sita was expected to do was to rest. Even after the first week after chemo was over, she was just so tired. Sometimes the phone would ring, and she had no energy to get up and pick it up though she was just a few feet away. She stayed on the couch, getting more and more frustrated. The soap operas on TV were all the same. There was nothing to do. She had to keep going to the cancer center for blood work, and had to keep getting shots to raise her blood counts. *She was no more than a pin cushion* she thought bitterly sighing out aloud. *She was thankful to everybody who helped, especially her doctors, and she knew she would remember them long after this was over.*

"It will be over soon," Raja said. "You and I are going to get through this."

Aunt Priya waddled in. She looked straight at Sita. "So nicely you are all getting along. It makes me very happy today."

"Then you'll be even happier to know Raja is taking me for chemo tomorrow."

"Very nice, very nice!" Aunt Priya's eyes lit up. "I always knew Raja was a good boy, but I could never get you to understand."

Sita stiffened. She better not is trying her matchmaking tricks now. Not when she was bald and helpless.

Quickly, Tom changed the subject. "So Aunty, how've you been? I haven't seen you since the four of us went to see the Broadway musical."

"Who went to see a Broadway musical?" Sita asked.

"All four of us here, except you." Aunt Priya said quickly. "It was so good," she said putting both pudgy palms together in glee. "I'm so glad I listened to Raja and went."

"We took Aunty to see 42nd street," Raja said. "Have you seen it?"

She shook her head and Raja explained, "The story is based on a 1933 movie and the action takes place in New York and Philadelphia. It's about a young actress named Peggy Sawyer who arrives to try out for the new Julian Marsh extravaganza *Pretty Lady*. There's a lot of tap dancing and singing. It's just a good old fashioned love story." Raja said. "It was good. Maybe you can come with us the next time."

"Yes," Aunt Priya said. "I want to see them all. I want to see *Rent*. I want to see *Mama Mia*. We can take Rohit to see *Lion King*. I want to see everything!"

"I don't think you'd like "Rent" that much though Aunty," Raja said. "It's based on New York city life with all of its problems. It's not such a happy ballyhoo type of show that 42nd street was. We'll find another one for you."

"Ok." Aunt Priya said quickly. "You find all the good ones. Then we'll take Sita. She loves the theater."

"Do you really?" Raja asked.

Sita nodded.

"You're awfully quiet," he commented.

Well, Sita thought all this was just too much to take in. It seemed like Raja had become best friends with Roz, Tom and Aunt Priya—going out to Broadway shows and so on. It was just too much to absorb. But aloud she said, "I was just thinking about chemo tomorrow, that's all."

"You know I told you I'd be there," Raja repeated.

"I don't want your pity," she said quietly.

"I don't pity you. You're a survivor—I know it, just like me."

The next morning true to his word, he was there. Aunt Priya insisted on coming. She always stayed for each infusion of chemo, and Sita had learnt to count on her presence. She didn't have to be strong when Aunt Priya was around. Aunt Priya had enough strength for the both of them. She didn't have to pretend the way she had to when Papa came. From then on, Papa had dropped them off at the infusion center, and Aunt Priya stayed with her.

Today she expected Raja would drop them off, and Aunt Priya would stay.

"May I stay?" Raja asked.

"It's not fun," she said her eyes tearing. "Just go home." Then try as hard as she could to stop the tears they fell, fast and furious. She hated herself for being weak. "Sorry," she said wiping them away roughly with the back of her hand. "I'm just being silly. I've done this so many times before. I should be accustomed to it by now."

"Don't be so hard on yourself," he said. "It's not easy what you're going through." He stayed. He also came each time she had to have chemo after that.

In a couple of months it was time for her last session. The nurse came in and started the drip. Soon she was getting drowsy. The TV was on, and someone was talking about a cancer survivor. Someone who had written a book called "Heaven can wait." The screen blurred, and she just shut her eyes, allowing herself to sink into a drug induced rest. Every now and again the nurse came to check the drip and put in a different chemical.

"Run it slow," Sita heard Raja say once. "I've heard it's easier to take when it runs slow."

"Well, don't you want to get her out of here to celebrate?" the nurse said thinking Raja was her relative. "We're almost there now. She seems fine. Another few minutes and then she'll be done."

"Thank God," Aunt Priya said. "No more coming here."

"Stop by at the reception desk on your way out," the nurse said.

Sita stood up. She felt unsteady. She looked for Aunt Priya but she was already making her way to the reception area. Raja was there. He offered his arm, and she hobbled along leaning on him. At the reception area all the nurses were there. Toni, Laura, Lauren, Lorraine. All of them had helped in her struggle. They had heard her complaints, seen her cry, listened when she talked, and sometimes had comforted her quietly. She looked at them fondly. God willing it was over. She would never have to come for treatment any more. She gave them a hug, one by one. They clapped and cheered. Then they gave her a little Purple Heart Award signed by all of them. Her oncologist had signed it too. He had written "Peace; Happiness; Health always." She cried and hugged again. Then still clinging to Raja's arm she walked to the car.

Chapter Thirty

The next stage was radiation therapy they told her. Radiation is not a systemic treatment, and only treats a small area. The patient feels quite normal, aside from skin irritations in the area being treated—also, a little more tired.

Radiation sounds like it will be a lot easier," Raja said. "Let me know if you need me to come along."

He was probably tired of her. She wouldn't ask him again, Sita thought.

"I've got some things to attend to," he said.

"Yeah. Right!"

"I've been out of work so long. I must start looking for work more consistently. It's not easy to find jobs these days in the technology sector. You know, after Nine Eleven, everything changed. The economy is not what it used to be."

"Sure," she said quietly. "I can manage. You go ahead and do whatever you have to."

"But you'll call if you need anything?"

"Yes," she said to make him go away.

She went alone for radiation. It wasn't hard. In fact it was a piece of cake in comparison to what she had gone through before. During the first session, the therapist etched miniature tattoos, more like freckles really, to identify the treatment area. Radiation was going to be given diagonally in a tangential field over her chest. They were also going to treat the nodes in the neck, collar bone, and axilla. It sounded worse than it was. It wasn't painful. There was no nausea. She felt fine.

"You sure you'll be okay?" Aunt Priya said. Sita nodded.

"Holler if you need anything" she said, and Sita smiled at how different Aunt Priya was beginning to sound—more American.

The radiation facility was smaller and did not smell of chemicals. What a relief! Technicians in long white coats walked around. Some of them looked so young, almost as if they were barely out of high school. Others were more seasoned workers. All of them had a gentle, kind, demeanor that was well learned. She went every morning at 8:00 o'clock. She signed herself in. When her name was called, she changed into a gown. The room was readied, and the therapist took her in. She had to lie down on a narrow table, her arm raised above her head, and wait while the machines were manipulated to the right angle. Usually two people at a time worked on her. One called out the angle measurements, and the other one moved her. She wasn't allowed to help.

"Don't move," they said, so she lay there like a sack of potatoes letting them push and pull the sheets under her to find the right position. Once the angles were okayed it was even more important that she didn't move. Once she felt her nose itch, and had to ask the therapist to scratch it for her. They giggled, but they would rather oblige with that, than rearrange her all over again.

The therapists said "We'll be right back," and disappeared to start the machines. There was a humming sound and she saw a red light. Other than that, she saw nothing. She had thought she might see laser beams coming at her, but there was no sign of anything.

"Where does the radiation come from?" she asked and they pointed to two circular slabs with holes in them. Some of the holes were covered up and the ones in the correct angles were designed to let the radiation through. It was all so technical—so many angles, so many measurements. Every other day, they took X-rays, and then more scans for the medical physics department. Nothing hurt. Just as well. The only thing that happened after a few sessions was a feeling of soreness in the treated area. Then gradually when she thought she would get away with no reaction, she felt the skin start to pull and hurt. But they gave her an ointment and it helped. The discomfort was mostly localized to the treated area, and was very manageable—nothing like what she had gone through before. She felt a little tired, and for some reason her mouth felt dry, but that wasn't so bad, and she had already been warned about those side effects.

She had to go for radiation every day for six weeks, ten minutes a day. The days turned to weeks. She had not seen Roz for a while, nor did any one mention Raja. Roz was probably busy with Tom. *What was Raja up to?* She was just curious, she told herself. *There was nothing more to it.* Treatments were almost over. The residual effects of the chemo were wearing off. She was beginning to feel stronger. She could see hair stubble coming back, and that always cheered her up. Soon she would be able to go back to work. How she longed to be back to normal, to be able to work.

On her last day of radiation, a little old lady gave her a yellow rose. "I hope I never see you here again," she said wrapping her floppy arms around Sita's neck. "God Bless." She brushed her cheeks in a gentle kiss.

"The same to you," Sita said warmly. "I hope you too never need treatment again."

The lady smiled sadly. "My cancer has spread," she said. "I'm going to be here a lot." Sita hugged her tightly, and they both cried. "Don't give up," Sita whispered. "Never give up." She took her phone number, promising to stay in touch.

"Life has no guarantees," the older lady said. "Live each day to the fullest, and let the future take care of itself."

"And you have faith that it will," Sita said stumbling out of the radiation office with a catch in her breath. *The poor dear,* Sita thought. *Having faith was easier said than done. And yet, dear God, she prayed, help me to have faith that I will be well, and forgive my unbelief in times when I am weak.*

What would life bring her now? Sita wondered. Her oncologist had said she would have to see him every 3 months, for 5 years.

"What on earth for?" she said sharply.

"Sita, we are trying to treat cancer here. Not pneumonia." He said firmly. "Don't you want to follow this disease to make sure you are rid of it?"

Sita sighed deeply. *Well at least one good thing had come of it— no one would try and arrange her marriage any more,* she thought wryly.

Tom and Roz had set a date for their wedding and asked her to be bridesmaid. Roz had asked Aunt Priya to be the maid of honor, and Raja was Tom's best man.

Aunt Priya was thrilled to bits. She was grinning like a cat that had got all the cream. "Imagine," she said, "I am going to be in all the pictures. I must look nice. What shall I wear?"

"Ask Roz," Sita said. "She will need to pick the color."

"I won't look nice in a dress," Aunt Priya worried. "I have never worn one. I wish I could wear a sari."

"Ask her then," Sita asked in irritation. Imagine Aunt Priya waddling around in a sari while everyone else was trying to look sleek in a dress. She had seen the pattern Roz had picked and there was no way Aunt Priya would look even half way decent in the strapless number.

But Aunt Priya called Roz and came back grinning even more. "Roz said I should wear a sari. She said she would help me pick it out."

"Gosh!" Sita put her hand to her mouth to muffle her shock.

"Roz said she thought a light pink embroidered silk sari would look very beautiful on me. Then, you know what else she said? She said she would buy four more saris of the same kind and have everybody's dresses made of the same fabric, but style it in the American way," she said. "What do you think of *that*! I won't stick out. I'll blend in with all of her young American bridesmaids," she said excitedly. "She is such a good, kind girl— your friend." She wrapped her arms around Sita in a quick hug, "So glad I found her through you."

Sita drew back feeling shamefaced. Aunt Priya would always just fit right in whether she had the right clothes or not. But even so, she was quite startled to see Aunt Priya on Roz's wedding day. Quietly elegant in a light pink self-embossed silk sari that cleverly concealed all unflattering undulations, Aunt Priya looked quite chic. Gone were the white powder and the bright red lipstick.

Instead, her face was radiant with a natural glow of pure elation, accented with some blush. Her eyes were lightly made up to show off their bright happiness. She stood up tall, in her 4'10 frame and took her place right behind Roz.

Sita and the other bridesmaids were dressed in replica designer gowns fashioned out of Aunt Priya's rich silk sari fabric. Cut tight at the waist, and low in the front to show a hint of bosom, it made the girls look quite elegant. She thought she saw Raja look at her with narrowed eyes, but it was probably because he had seen her after a long time. She looked different. She was wearing a wig to cover the stubble of hair that had begun to sprout, but was not long enough to do without cover. Cut in a short bob that caressed her neck lightly, the wig was flattering.

Aunt Priya looked at her twice, and though her eyes lingered at the low cut bodice, she never said a word. Sita was grateful that she had escaped a mastectomy and sighed aloud. God, please let this cancer be gone, she prayed. May it never come back she said pushing away the lingering thread of fear that kept gnawing at her insides. She would live each day in faith, and not think about this anymore. She looked good. She felt better, and she was just going to focus on Roz's wedding today.

Aunt Priya was hovering round Roz, arranging and rearranging her dress, tilting her head this way and that, to make sure Roz looked just perfect from all angles. She needn't have worried. Roz looked absolutely beautiful! There was an almost ethereal quality to the way she glided down the aisle, head slightly bent per Aunt Priya's instructions, her hand resting lightly on her father's arm. Sita had never met her dad before. He was a thin man, almost frail looking, with a sad look on his face. He walked his daughter down the aisle while the organ played *Here comes the bride.*

Sita saw Tom turn around to look for her. From the way his eyes lit up, Sita knew he was definitely in love.

Tom looked unusually handsome. The mop of unruly blond hair was brushed back sleekly to show his well chiseled features and the kindest eyes. But it was the man next to him, who Sita kept staring at. Dressed in a tuxedo, Raja looked incredibly handsome. He stood by his friend who had saved his life, at the World Trade Center. Tom had picked him above all others, to be his best man. Raja was a good man. But, the last time he and Sita had met, he had promised to stand by her in her time of crisis. She had not seen him since radiation.

The choir had stopped singing. The congregation sat down. Roz was standing alongside Tom.

"Who gives this woman away," the priest asked.

"I do," Roz's dad said, taking her hand and giving it to Tom. Then he lingered, and Sita thought she saw his eyes mist. He continued to stand there until Aunt Priya said, "You have to go now. Your job is done." Then he walked away sadly. Sita felt bad. *She could imagine Papa doing the same. He would have found it incredibly hard to give up his princess. Well, he need have no fear. She wasn't going anywhere.*

Roz and Tom had said their vows, and the priest had pronounced them man and wife. They stood there, lips locked, while the congregation cheered. People were beginning to move out now. Many of them would be going for the reception to the nearby Hilton Hotel.

At the reception, Sita found herself face to face with Raja.

"Care to dance?" he asked. "C'mon," he said when she hesitated. "Look Aunt Priya is dancing."

Sure enough Aunt Priya was gyrating to the Macarena looking thoroughly pleased. Rohit was running around with a couple of other kids his age. Everybody was having a ball.

Why not dance? Sita thought, and she and Raja got on the floor.

"You look lovely tonight," he said. She blushed crimson. It was the first personal comment he had made to her.

"How do you feel?" he asked and her mood changed. He had reminded her of her awful disease with that simple question.

"Okay, I guess," she said getting short of breath. The music changed to a slow waltz. She was surprised how well he knew the steps. She was content to follow his lead.

She started talking. She told him about the little old lady in radiation. "I told her to live life with faith," Sita said, "and I told her never to give up hope."

"Good advice," Raja said. "I almost gave up hope. Thought I would never survive.... that if I did survive, I would never be whole again. Never find a job, never have a family. Things have started to look up again."

"Good," she said.

"I finally found a good job with Morgan Stanley. Now I make even more money than the job I lost."

"Great," Sita said automatically.

"Now I can finally take care of the girl I love, and ask her to marry me."

"Good." Sita whispered.

The music stopped and she was free to leave the floor. She saw Aunt Priya staring at her. Then she saw her making her way toward her. Sita hurried away. She was feeling all emotional and didn't want to talk to Aunt Priya. She would go get some food, find someone to talk to, and make sure the topic did not automatically stray to cancer. Today she would push the wretched disease out of her mind and have fun. She would not think of Raja, or of the girl he said he loved.

Finally, it was time for Roz and Tom to leave. Roz was going to toss her garter belt and the bouquet. The crowd gathered around edging closer to the bridal couple. Aunt Priya pushed her way toward Sita. "What are you doing so far away?" she said. "Move up," she yelled.

"What for?" Sita asked, and stayed where she was. She saw the bridal bouquet being thrown, and instinctively reached for it because it looked to be coming directly toward her. She caught it easily. She looked up to see Roz and Tom smiling. Aunt Priya was grinning from ear to ear.

Roz and Tom were waving to her to come to them. They were surrounded by friends and well-wishers. Raja was standing by Tom.

Sita made her way through the crowd, and turned around to see Aunt Priya pushing her way through the crowd to keep up with her.

"Raja has something to say to you," Roz said. "Hear him out."

"Will you marry me?" Raja asked simply.

"I am a sick woman...." she stammered.

"You will be sick in the head, if you don't say 'yes'." Aunt Priya grumbled.

"Will you at least think about it?" he asked.

"You, young people think too much," Aunt Priya muttered. "Why so much thinking? I don't understand."

"Your parents won't like you to marry me," Sita said remembering Ms. Shah and her beady eyes, and the way Mr. Shah had ignored her in America.

"They want what's best for me," Raja said. "I'll convince them you're the right one for me."

Aunt Priya was nudging her to say something. "Hurry up," she said in a loud whisper. "Remember how your Papa was acting all crazy about Raja—well I fixed that. Now there is no problem. So what is taking you so long," she hissed.

"Give them a couple of meetings Aunty," Tom said.

"No more than a few," she said emphatically. "I don't like too much dating. Besides," she said, "why should it take them so long to decide what I always knew from the start? They are such a good match for each other—can't you see that?"

"Sita is not the daughter of your world Aunt Priya. She lives in a modern world in America."

"What you mean? Sita is the daughter of two worlds, just like me!" Aunt Priya said.

"You certainly are," Roz said. "Look at you!"

Sita smiled, and for the first time since her awful diagnosis there was hope in those eyes. Hope that she would beat this disease to live a normal life with the man she loved. Happiness, that Raja believed she could, faith that their future was bright. It had all worked out perfectly, and she was so happy to be the daughter of two worlds.